Praise for Jill Winters
Plum Girl

"Quirky, sexy, fun!"—Susan Andersen, author of *Head Over Heels*

"*Plum Girl* just about has it all: great characters, romance, suspense, and comedy . . . an intriguing and fun read." —Romance Reviews Today

"[An] amusing, lighthearted romp." —BookBrowser

"A fun, sexually charged yarn for those who like spicy romance mixed with mystery." —*Booklist*

"Fans of contemporary romance novels will enjoy Jill Winters's amusing lighthearted romp."
—*Midwest Book Review*

"[A] fun read . . . very sexy." —*Affaire de Coeur*

"A vivid debut from an author with a natural voice for humorous romance." —*The Romance Reader*

"A zany romantic comedy with healthy doses of passion and suspense . . . countless laugh-out-loud moments." —Escape to Romance Reviews

"I don't know what was more fun, reading about Lonnie's yummy love interest or keeping tabs on her life at work. . . . Fun . . . steamy . . . a great read."
—Curvy Novels

"Newcomer Jill Winters, with her refreshing knack of writing as people speak, has done a first-class job with her first book, *Plum Girl*. . . . Ms. Winters adroitly mixes comedy with mystery and this, together with vibrant characters, witty dialogue, and candid observations, makes *Plum Girl* a must-read."
—Curled Up with a Good Book Reviews

"Lighthearted and witty . . . an interesting blend of romance and suspense." —*Romantic Times*

Also by Jill Winters

Plum Girl

Blushing Pink

Jill Winters

AN ONYX BOOK

ONYX
Published by New American Library, a division of
Penguin Group (USA) Inc., 375 Hudson Street,
New York, New York 10014, U.S.A.
Penguin Books Ltd, 80 Strand,
London WC2R 0RL, England
Penguin Books Australia Ltd, 250 Camberwell Road,
Camberwell, Victoria 3124, Australia
Penguin Books Canada Ltd, 10 Alcorn Avenue,
Toronto, Ontario, Canada M4V 3B2
Penguin Books (N.Z.) Ltd, Cnr Rosedale and Airborne Roads,
Albany, Auckland 1310, New Zealand

Penguin Books Ltd, Registered Offices:
80 Strand, London WC2R 0RL, England

First published by Onyx, an imprint of New American Library,
a division of Penguin Group (USA) Inc.

First Printing, June 2003
10 9 8 7 6 5 4 3 2 1

This book is dedicated to Pepper—whose insight, patience, heart, and friendship made this story possible.

ACKNOWLEDGMENTS

I would like to thank my mom and dad for their constant support and kindness. Thanks to my sisters and brother-in-law, who keep me laughing, even through writer's block. Thanks to my BF, who makes things brighter, and a big thank-you to Jessica, who, every so often, fixes my life.

Chapter One

"I'm escaping a bubblegum-pink ball gown with a big bow on the butt, so everything else is gravy."

Angela laughed. "You're exaggerating."

"I believe it's called accentuating the positive," Reese replied, and gunned the gas a little more so she could pass the fifth fuel truck she'd seen in half an hour. She had a significant phobia of riding behind them . . . or beside them . . . well, *of* them.

"Speaking of our dresses," Angela said, "Mom was worried because Ally hasn't gotten money from Lane yet." As far as brides went, Reese and Angela's little sister, Ally, wasn't the most efficient. She'd bought the four bridesmaid dresses herself, on credit, and apparently had yet to be reimbursed from her friend Lane. On top of that, she hadn't even gotten her *own* dress yet.

With her wedding only a month away, that was bad enough, but the fact that she'd ordered her dress off the Internet was sending their mother into a frenzied tailspin of nagging and "This is why . . ." speeches, while their father doled out unsolicited lectures about the Web being predatory ground for deviants and "confidence artists."

Reese had the feeling she was in for an interesting vacation.

"Hey," Angela said, "are you still there?"

"Oh, yeah . . . sorry. I'm just trying to see if this prick is gonna let me go." Reese pressed her gas pedal down harder, and cut the wheel to slip in the far left lane of Route 80 while she still had a minuscule chance. But at the last second, the prick sped up and ruined her opportunity. "Damn!"

"What?"

"Oh . . . nothing. Sorry, I just hate these drives home; they're such a pain."

"Yeah, a whole forty-five minutes. How do you do it every three months?"

"Okay, okay," Reese said, and brushed some messy, honey-colored hair behind her ears so she could see.

Her older sister was right, of course; the trip from New York City to Goldwood, New Jersey, wasn't all that unbearable. She just felt like whining because her winter break had officially begun, she had five nonschool weeks ahead of her, five weeks to do nothing but vegetate at her parents' house, and instead of taking full advantage, she had to work her usual weekly hours at Roland & Fisk, a large bookstore in Midtown Manhattan.

But still, she was *extremely* grateful for the nonschool part. She couldn't wait to set her bookbag aside, and not pick it up again for a month. Currently enrolled in a history Ph.D. program at Crewlyn College, Reese was on fellowship, which meant that her tuition was waived, but for all intents and purposes the school *owned* her. Crewlyn provided her with a graduate apartment, in exchange for her service as a professor's assistant.

Of course, an assistantship meant different things depending on one's professor. In Reese's case, working for Professor Leopold Kimble merely entailed grading all his papers, enduring his passive-aggression, and ghostwriting massive sections of his latest book for no credit. She was also expected to attend faculty wine parties to "facilitate his evening," and attend his lectures to "get a buzz going." And somehow she was still supposed to find time to finish her own epically long dissertation.

Speaking of her dissertation, technically Reese should use the winter break to work on it. But considering that it had yet to exist, she doubted it would happen. The truth was, she'd always dreamed of writing a novel, and lately she'd been thinking about it much more seriously. She hadn't told her parents or her sisters yet, who still mistakenly viewed her as the "academic" of the family. Anyway, they'd probably think the whole idea was an excuse to procrastinate, and they'd probably be half right.

"Now what were you saying?" she asked Angela, and popped a Christmas compilation tape into the cassette player of her used, rose-colored sedan.

"I was just saying that Ally never got the dress money from Lane. Of course, that's not surprising, since Ally is so oblivious to money."

"And Lane's a mooch," Reese supplied.

"I was going to say annoying phony."

"Well, yeah."

"Anyway, if Ally had gone with her first choice—you know, that big bubblegum thing—it would've been cheaper than the ones we have now."

"Hey, dignity's priceless," Reese said, "or at least it should be." Sure, to an assistant fashion show coordinator like Ally, the original bridesmaid dress was "retro pink, nouveau poof." To Reese, it was merely an embarrassing exercise in gift-wrapping her butt.

"Mom's also freaking out about your toast," Angela said.

Reese sighed loudly, and slid her rosy sedan into the middle lane. "Would she get over it already? It's just a toast. Why do I have to prepare it twenty years in advance and submit it for copyediting?"

Angela laughed. "She just doesn't want us to embarrass her."

"What are we, savages?"

"Don't act all innocent. Last time you were home you told Mom that in lieu of a toast, you were doing an improvisational dance to 'I Like Big Butts.' "

She grinned, recalling the memory of her mother, Joanna, eyes bugged out, jaw dropped open, while Reese somehow sustained the willpower not to tell her she was only joking. But, hey, that wasn't all her fault—her mother was too easy. "So what was the big deal about that?" Reese asked.

"Nothing, nothing," Angela said, with a smile in her voice.

Making Joanna agonize over the toast for Ally's reception was really only fair, since, in Reese's absence, she'd elected Reese to give it. Her rationale, of course, was that toast giving was Reese's "thing." Suffice it to say, that was news.

"So what's the deal with that guy in your program?"

"Kenneth?" Reese said. "Um . . . he's good."

"Well, are you guys officially dating yet, or what?"

"Not . . . really."

"What does that mean? Translate for the maritally enhanced."

Reese shrugged to herself, and ignored the middle finger she was just given by a clown car full of octogenarians. She also gave up on her perpetually tousled hair, which had flopped forward again. Blowing it a fraction, she said, "I don't know; things are sort of cooling off."

"How come?"

"I'm . . . I guess I'm just not that interested anymore. I don't know, the spark's kind of died out." What she failed to add was that she was looking for more than just one single, solitary, isolated spark, anyway. What she wanted was all-consuming desire—she wanted *heat*.

But how could she explain to her older sister how passion-deprived her love life was and how much it had been bothering her lately? How could she simply blurt that she was feeling almost desperate to experience the kind of red-hot sex that other people did? Well, she supposed she could blurt it pretty easily, but not over the phone.

So instead of getting into it, she said lightly, "Hey, not every guy's as great as Drew."

Angela fell silent for a moment, then replied, "Yeah, I guess." *Hmm* . . . Considering that her sister had been married to Drew Emmett for the past three years, and in that time the two had existed as one of those blissful couples bitter people disliked being around, her hesitation about his greatness was odd. Although, ever since Drew's sudden heart attack six months ago, Reese had wondered if they were having problems, but since Angela hadn't specifically mentioned it, she hadn't pushed.

Maybe now a little push wouldn't hurt. "Is everything okay?"

"Yeah, fine," Angela replied immediately—and emphatically.

So Reese let it drop—for now. "By the way, have you tried on your dress yet?" she asked.

"Oh, yeah. Supertight. I'm putting myself on a crash diet before I go for my fitting."

"That's ridiculous. You're gonna lose weight so the seamstress won't think less of you?"

"Yes."

"You're weird."

"Valid," Angela said matter-of-factly, waiting for the larger point.

"Well, I can't wait to stuff this apple-pear body into my dress," Reese said dryly, and veered to the right toward her exit ramp. "Plus the fact that with a high neck, I can't even get any cleavage action going to distract attention away from my potbelly and balloon butt."

Angela laughed. "God, why do you exaggerate so much?"

She wished she were. The Brock girls were all fairly short, but Angela and Ally managed to stay slim and narrow, too. Reese, on the other hand, had no clue about that—her curves always felt big and bouncy, and just a few pounds away from being not so cute anymore.

"Anyway, at least you don't look like a soccer-mom yuppie, like me," Angela said.

"What are you talking about?"

"Well . . ."

"C'mon, what?"

"I sort of got this haircut," Angela said, distinctly unenthused, which was probably to be expected, since she hadn't gotten more than a trim since junior high. Both she and Ally had the same long, dark hair, and intensely dark eyes, while Reese had inherited their mother's golden-brown "waves" and light green eyes that frequently required reading glasses.

"You got a haircut? No way, what's it like?"

"Like a geeky, PTA-woman's bob, that's what."

Reese laughed. "So how come you decided to cut it?"

"I don't know; I just . . . needed a change." She sounded almost wistful, and Reese vowed to find out, face-to-face, what was wrong. "Anyway, you'll see it when you get home."

Angela and Drew lived in a condo fifteen minutes outside of Goldwood, while Ally still lived with their parents. Until the end of the month, anyway. After that, she'd be married to her longtime boyfriend, Ben Alderzon.

Reese, however, remained undeniably single, despite the fact that she was the second child, which meant she really *should've* been married before the third, and despite the fact that her mother had recently started lying about her second daughter's age to acquaintances.

The whole "single" thing was damn annoying, of course, but what could she do? She couldn't accelerate the Mr. Right process (not that she really believed in it, anyway), and hell, she was only twenty-seven (and a half). She still had plenty of time . . . right?

Up until recently, she'd had something going with Professor Kimble's other graduate assistant, Kenneth Peel. The problem was, she had no idea *what* they had going. Whatever it was, was lukewarm at best. It had started two months ago, when Kenneth had hinted that he wanted to go to the movies. After that, they had met for lunch almost every day, and done datelike things on the weekends. But Kenneth had a naturally formal demeanor that was hard to relax, and so far they'd only kissed a handful of times— each encounter consisting of barely-there things that had left Reese totally unsatisfied.

Actually, they left her feeling *cheated*. She'd been trying so hard to make things work with Kenneth, and for what? Just to have a boyfriend? Please—what good was a boyfriend if he didn't want to rip your clothes off (yet didn't, of course, because of his respect for you and all women)?

Really . . . was she being so unreasonable?

At first, Reese had been totally enamored of Kenneth's intellect, and had rationalized that it was *because* of his intellect that he wasn't very good at dating. The poor boy just lacked normal social skills, she had decided. And as long as Reese had been chalking up his weirdness to inhibition, she had remained sure that it would pass. But now she didn't care all that much if it did or not. She was tired of putting forth the effort to loosen Kenneth up—tired of trying to get blood from a stone.

It was only logical. Yet for some reason it seemed too complicated to explain to her older sister at the moment. "Listen, I'm gonna go; my battery's dying. But I'll call you tomorrow."

"Okay, no problem," Angela said.

After Reese hung up, she tossed her pink-and-silver cell into the backseat, and cranked the volume up on George Michael's "*Last Christmas*." Speeding down the highway was giving her the same nostalgic feeling it always did. The same stores, the same restaurants, the same construction projects that still weren't finished. It seemed like nothing changed in or around Goldwood and, as far as she was concerned, that was a good thing.

Thinking about what Angela had said about the dresses, Reese found herself squirming a little in the worn upholstery. She'd put on a few pounds during finals week, and even before that, she was a snug size eight. And not one of those streamlined, statuesque snug eights, but a five-foot-three snug eight, which was a whole different kind of thing.

Despite her worries about the upcoming fitting, she found herself, five minutes later, sliding into the parking lot of a familiar fast-food restaurant. As she wound her car into the drive-through line, she fast-forwarded her tape to the Sinead O'Connor track, and started chewing on her lower lip.

She couldn't believe Ally's wedding was only a few weeks away. It would be strange to see her baby sister married. Granted, she was only a year and a half younger than Reese, and granted, she was keeping her name. But still, it seemed like an enormous change.

The ceremony itself also promised to be fairly weird; their mother had invited half the town because she'd "felt bad," and now was freaking out because Ally and Ben were so disorganized. She'd made it clear that she expected Reese to mingle with all of the guests, so no one would feel uncomfortable (except Reese, of course—mingling with virtual strangers was apparently her thing, as well).

On top of that, Ben's best man was Brian Doren— someone Reese had shared a long, soulful, tongue-tangling kiss with two years ago, and had never seen since. (And speaking of red-hot passion, that kiss was probably the closest she'd ever come.) Seeing Brian again might be *very* uncomfortable, but Reese had already devised a plan: When she ran into him at the wedding, she was simply going to play it cool and act like they'd never met. How could she possibly go wrong?

Inching forward in her car, she smelled the heavenly aroma of fatty grease and fried, processed meat. She figured she might as well have one more really great meal before she got to her mother's house. That was when junk food would cease being fun. Not that her mother *meant* to be annoying—she just couldn't help herself—and she had this maddening habit of interrogating the family about their diet, always wanting to know what they were eating and *why*. Reese had already exhausted every conceivable answer, even: "Junk—because I'm using food for love." Still, her mother never got the hint.

Basically, Joanna Brock was a slave to her own

high culinary standards. She'd been a French chef for twenty years, and now that she was retired, she was running a French dessert business out of her home, and had French food on the brain twenty-four-seven, even though the entire family was Irish (with just a splash of Italian).

The last Reese had heard, though, Joanna had expanded her obsessions. According to Ally, their mom was now completely addicted to *The Wedding Story*, a TV show on the cable station TLC. What had apparently started as a reference for planning Ally's wedding had turned into an extensive, annotated VHS collection with back episodes. Their mother was sort of a strange little woman.

"W'ome to Bur'ing; can I ta'order," an annoyed-sounding voice grumbled through the call box.

"Oh, yes, hi!" Reese chirped eagerly—a habit she'd formed years ago because fast food servers always seemed just a little too misanthropic. Her hope, of course, was that if she laid on enough obsequious gratitude, no one would tamper with her food. "May I please, please have a double cheeseburger with extra pickles—"

"Val'ml!" the voice barked.

"No, no thank you. Not the value meal—but thanks for asking!"

"An'thng else?"

"Yes, please. May I also have a medium Diet Coke, not too much ice—but only if it's no trouble!"

The voice snarled the total price, but Reese couldn't make it out, so she grabbed a handful of bills from her glove compartment and steered around to the pickup window. When she got to it, a scowling pubescent boy with symmetrical acne on his cheeks and a fuzzy hint of a mustache snatched her money and shut the window wordlessly.

She waited. And waited. Made sure not to roll her eyes in case they had a hidden camera somewhere. And waited. Soon cars on line behind her starting beeping—long, dragged-out sounds that could only come from leaning on the horn like an ass. Still, it was flustering. What did they expect *her* to do?

Come on, come on.

Finally the maroon-clad preteen returned with her food and change. "Oh, thank you, thanks a lot," Reese said ingratiatingly. He didn't bother responding, or explaining what the delay had been. In fact, after he deposited her bag and soda, he slammed his screen shut and turned back to his mike. *Okay.* Reese's cup of soda felt like a brick, it had so much ice. And then she glanced down at the change in her lap, and realized it was wrong. She had handed him at least six bills, and gotten back only forty-two cents.

Another horn sounded. She thought quickly. Okay, she supposed she could deal with being short-changed, and diet soda really wasn't good for her anyway, but if there weren't extra pickles—

Beep! Beep! Beeeeeeeeeeeep!

As horns blasted, Reese threw her car into drive. She pounded her foot on the accelerator and blew out of the line. Soon she was on Route 46, having shamelessly bowed to peer pressure. But then, that was pretty fitting. There was something about coming home to Goldwood that always smacked of mental and emotional regression.

Hey, she could live with that.

Chapter Two

Reese turned her car into the comfortably familiar driveway of the stone-and-brick house she'd grown up in. It was set high up from the street, with lush evergreens enclosing it, as well as densely planted rhododendrons that would've been blooming a gorgeous deep pink if it weren't December.

After she set the car in park, she cut the engine and sighed. No matter where else she ever lived, she knew she would always love this place. It was cozy but secluded, like the other homes on the street but special. She hadn't lived there full-time since that teenage angst known as high school. She'd gone to college in Boston, stayed there for her master's degree, and then moved to New York after Crewlyn had offered her a fellowship that included city housing. Still, she'd always have a room in the Goldwood house; her mom wouldn't have it any other way.

As a matter of fact, her mother had recently remodeled Reese's old bedroom in expensive Victorian décor with the hopes that she'd move back after graduate school. Assuming, of course, that Reese was still single then, which wasn't too wild an assumption.

"Hello?" Reese called out, shutting the heavy oak

door behind her and immediately turning the dead bolt—a habit she'd formed after having five dead bolts installed in her New York apartment. The two duffel bags she'd taken out of her trunk were weighing her down, so she dropped them by the stairs. "Anyone home?" she said, walking down the front hall toward the kitchen.

"Oh, hi, sweetheart!" Joanna called. "In here!" Reese followed her mother's voice, and rounded the bend through the kitchen to the family room. She found Joanna curled up in a little ball on the sofa, covered by a patchwork quilt. There was a fire crackling in the fireplace, and some maudlin *Wedding Story* piano music resonating from the television.

"Hi, Mommy," Reese said, smiling, and leaned down to kiss her on the cheek.

Joanna angled the VCR remote and pressed stop. Reaching up, she hugged Reese tightly. "Oh, sweetheart, I'm so glad you're home. Have you finished your toast for Ally's wedding?"

"Mom, I don't even have my coat off."

"Oh, well, I was just interested," she said innocently, and gave her another squeeze. Reese kissed her cheek once more, and pulled back to shrug off her hooded fleece jacket. "Oh, no, is that all you wore for a coat?" Joanna asked, alarmed. "For goodness' sake, it's December! Don't you have a winter coat?"

"Yeah, but—"

"We're gonna buy you a winter coat while you're home."

"I have one—"

"Sit, sit. How was your ride? Let me hear all about it."

"There's really not much to tell. What's new around here?"

"Nothing, really. Just last-minute stuff for Ally's wedding."

"Oh, yeah, I heard about her dress."

Joanna put a soft, delicate hand to her forehead. "Please. Don't even get me started."

Reese grinned. "Right, okay. So where is everybody?"

"Ally's out with Ben, and your father's in his study. By the way, there's left over *poulet à la crème* in the fridge."

"No, thanks. I had something on the way over." *Stupid, stupid.*

Joanna's head shot up. "You did? What did you eat? What?"

"Um—"

"Not fast food, right? Please tell me it wasn't fast food." Reese hesitated, and Joanna groaned as if in pain. "Oh, *please*, not fast food."

"It was just a cheeseburger, jeez." Reese felt a little embarrassed now, which was silly because this was her mother, but somehow the woman always managed to make her feel like a complete fool.

"Oh, but *why*?" Joanna asked, and fell back against the sofa cushions in martyrdom.

"I don't *know*. . . ."

She sprang back up. "Look, honey, I'm not trying to be a pain. All I'm saying is, why on earth have a greasy burger when you can eat something healthy and well-balanced here? You know I have good food. At the very least, you can always pick on the foie gras and brioche."

"Okay, can we move on now?" Reese said, flopping down on the opposite couch.

Joanna shrugged in response, as if it were no big deal, but she was obviously still itching to preach more on the extremely overdone topic.

"What were you watching?" Reese asked, knowing full well, but she was determined to deflect the conversation.

"Oh, I was bored, so I took out a tape of *Wedding Story*."

"Oh."

"Tape fourteen, episode two-b. Rodney and Claire."

"Ah. Well, put it on; I'll watch, too."

"Okay, great." She settled back under her quilt. "Did your roommates go home, too?"

Reese shrugged. "I guess. Well, two of them graduated this semester, and the other wasn't there when I left." Graduate living was nothing like undergraduate; roommates came and went, and were usually too busy to stop and chat along the way.

Joanna nodded and pressed play.

Reese watched as Rodney and Claire's story unfolded. It was one of those nauseating "the minute I laid eyes on her, I knew" stories. *Yuck.* Not that Reese was cynical about love—she wasn't. In fact, deep down, she was a romantic. But she *hated* hearing people claim they "knew" the moment they looked at someone, because real life didn't work like that. If it did, she would still be with her ex-boyfriend, Pete, instead of getting an occasional postcard from him in South America, where he'd bolted three years ago to do volunteer work.

She had looked at him, and only *thought* she knew. That was the point.

"Isn't that so *sweet*?" Joanna crooned, clearly taken in by the televised emotions playing before her.

"Uh-huh."

"I love this episode," she gushed, "because Rodney is such a nice, quiet, intellectual type." Reese held back a gagging gesture. "Like Kenneth," she threw in. Reese said nothing. "So how *is* Kenneth?"

"Fine."

"Well, he's still coming to Ally's wedding, right?"

"Mmm-hmm."

"But have you made plans to see him over break? Besides the wedding, I mean. When do you think you'll see him? I want him to come to the house again so your father can meet him. What's he doing for Christmas?"

"Mom," Reese interrupted, holding up her hand. Her mother might be an adorable little bundle but she was also a force that must be stopped. "I don't know what's going on with Kenneth, okay?"

Joanna's eyebrows shot up with alarm; she popped upright on the couch again. "Well, what do you mean? Did you two have a fight? Oh, no, what happened? What did you do?"

"Me? I didn't do anything," Reese replied. "Look, I just . . . it's hard to explain. I don't really feel like getting into it right now."

"But—"

"Anyway, it's not like Kenneth and I were having an official relationship."

"Well, not *yet*, but I thought—"

"You thought I could get my 'hooks' into a nice, quiet intellectual, I know." Joanna didn't bother denying the charge. "Face it, Mom, the only reason you like Kenneth so much is because he reminds you of Remmi Collindyne's husband. You even said so."

"That's not true!"

"Uh-huh."

"Yes, he has a similar demeanor as Remmi's husband—who's a wonderful provider, by the way—but I like Kenneth for who he is."

"You met him once."

Joanna held up her hands. "Honey, if it doesn't work out with Kenneth, so be it. That's fine. But I don't want you to ruin an opportunity, that's all. You need a man who's sweet and smart, and one who'll put up with all your quirks."

"Mom, please—what quirks?" Suddenly Joanna got all wide-eyed and shrug-crazy. And Reese decided she didn't really want the answer anyway. Besides, it was futile to reason with her on the subject of men, because no matter what Joanna said, she *was* obsessed with Reese "hooking" Kenneth Peel, and she *was* obsessed with emulating the Goldwood Women's Club president, Remmi Collindyne, and her self-proclaimed picture-perfect life.

Reese said, "Fine, I'll keep my eye out. Now let's drop it."

"But you've got to be open-minded, honey." *Mom's version of dropping it.* "You're not gonna have a solid relationship unless you give people a chance." People meaning Kenneth. *Very subtle, my mother.*

"And, I mean, you've got to take some chances,

sweetheart," Joanna was saying. "You know, you've gotta be *in* it, to *win* it."

She's applying Lotto slogans to my love life—this is getting depressing. "Let's change the subject, okay?" Reese asked, stopping just short of begging.

"Okay, okay," Joanna said, holding up her hands even higher. "Fine, whatever you want. I'm only trying to help you."

Reese locked her jaw and fixed her eyes on the TV screen—or more specifically, on Rodney and Claire, who were now smashing wedding cake all over each other's faces, getting icing clogged up each other's noses, and laughing like it was hilarious.

"They're cute," Joanna remarked. "I predict that they'll make it, because he's so devoted to her. And if he's an architect, there's no way she'll let *him* go."

"Mmm-hmm."

"By the way, you brought your laptop home, right?"

"Yeah, why?"

Joanna shrugged. "Just so that way you'll be able to work on your dissertation while you're home. The sooner you finish, the sooner I'll be able to call you 'doctor.' " She followed up with a trying-too-hard smile that was intended as nagging compensation. Reese feebly smiled back (okay, *smirked*).

Then she thought about her nonexistent doctoral thesis, and felt the familiar coiling of stress in her abdomen. God, she had less than zero interest in working on it. Even worse, she had no discipline, which meant it was never going to happen. Plus, she was more determined than ever to start her novel.

And even if all she ever had to show for it was determination, that was still more than she had to show for her dissertation.

But of course she couldn't explain any of this to her mother. Joanna would never understand. She'd only wonder why Reese was wasting her time with a fantasy when she was already spread way too thin with classes, Kimble, and shifts at Roland & Fisk.

"Do you want some tea?" Joanna asked, motioning with her *World's Greatest Mère* mug. "I have leaves from Cannes that are supposed to cleanse the system of toxins." Reese cocked her head, and her mother qualified, "I'm making some for myself, too. I thought you'd like to join me, that's all."

Reese grinned. "Okay, actually that sounds good. I'll go say hi to Dad and meet you back here in five minutes." Joanna pushed off her quilt, and both of them headed up the three steps to the kitchen, which was separated only by a stone half wall and a hanging plant.

Joanna went to fill her kettle, while Reese continued around the bend and down the front hall. "Honey!" she heard her mother's voice call out.

"Yeah?" When she turned back, she saw her mother standing in the open archway of the kitchen, with her soft, round body and haphazard golden hair that looked vaguely familiar.

"I'm just so glad you're home," she said, smiling.

Reese found her dad at his large oak desk, paying bills, smoking a pipe that smelled of pinewood and dried cherries. "Hi!" he greeted enthusiastically when he saw her crossing the thick navy carpet.

"Hey, Dad, how are you?" She met him halfway for a hug.

"Oh, I'm fine. Just paying the bills." She'd been hearing that refrain for twenty-seven years, so she'd already guessed that. In fact, she was well aware that virtually all Michael Brock did was pay bills, and virtually all Joanna Brock did was "sacrifice and slave." It was all very much common knowledge in the household.

She did a double take when she spotted *Poor Richard's Almanac* on the corner of her father's desk. "Oh, no, Dad." She grimaced. "Not again."

"What?"

"You're not back on that Ben Franklin kick, are you?" She motioned to the book with her hand, and sank into an adjacent high-backed chair.

"Oh, that," he said calmly. "It's not a kick. I was just looking through some of my books, and I rediscovered this one. I think it has some timeless insights, that's all."

"Mmm-hmm." It was hard not to be skeptical; the last time her father had reread *Poor Richard's Almanac*, he'd gone around quoting truisms like there was no tomorrow. She could only hope he'd learned to internalize his love for the book this time around.

"So how is your doctoral work coming?" Michael asked with interest in his voice, and what Reese recognized immediately as pride. Her gut churned. Damn it, why did that Ph.D. have to mean so much to her parents? And why did it suddenly have to mean so little to *her*? "Is your thesis coming along?" he asked.

"Yep," she said cheerfully, lying through her gritted teeth.

He nodded. "I'm glad. You know, your mother and I are so proud of you."

She swallowed and forced a smile. "I know, Dad."

"I've always regretted not finishing my master's degree," he went on, stroking the bowl of his pipe and looking up at the ceiling. "But your mother was pregnant with Angela, and other things took precedence. I wouldn't have had it any other way, of course. But still, it means so much to her and I that you've accomplished what we never could, and more."

Reese shrank guiltily in her seat. Could her parents just rip her heart out and stick it in the waffle iron?

"But enough of my musing," Michael said. "Now tell me, how's that professor you work for?"

Hmm . . . "Stalinesque" might be too academic, but "fat and ugly" seemed like a low blow. "He's okay, I guess," Reese said on a sigh. Really, she wasn't looking to complain, but sometimes just *thinking* about Professor Kimble could give her anxiety. The man was such a textbook washed-up hack with a diva complex, it bordered on ridiculous. Apparently he'd peaked with his first (and only) book the year he'd gotten tenure, and now, twelve years later, he was still desperately trying to achieve another academic publication before he *officially* became the laughingstock of the elitist, backstabbing history department.

This was Reese's third semester working for him, and she'd probably have a couple more to go, so she was trying to make the best of it. Next year she'd be ABD—or All but Dissertation—which meant she'd have completed her own course work and could focus solely on her doctoral thesis. Or that was what it meant to the average student. Since she was on fellowship, however, it meant that she'd have even more free time to do Kimble's bidding.

At least she had this break. Over winter vacation she planned to avoid even thinking about school. No Kimble. No bidding. She wondered if she deserved that kind of pleasure, but even if she didn't, she was still going to snatch it up with abandon.

"What's he got you working on now?" her dad asked.

"Well, I'm sort of ghostwriting most of his next book," she said, trying to keep the dread out of her voice.

"Ghostwriting?" he echoed, a little annoyed. "What kind of job is that? Are you even going to get any credit?"

"Nope. None." Okay, so much for not complaining. Hey, she'd tried . . . sort of.

Michael shook his head and brought his lighter to his pipe. Through serene-smelling puffs he said, "I've got to tell you, sweetheart, I don't like this guy."

"Nobody does. We had a department party last week, and everyone was invited with a guest. The entire faculty brought their significant others, but you know who Professor Kimble brought? No one. He went alone, misquoting something from Emerson about the essence of the individual."

Reese's father tilted his head, as if considering it, and said, "Well, there's nothing wrong with that, I suppose."

"Please, Dad, who's *buying* it?" He chuckled. "In fact, the rumor was, Kimble just couldn't find anyone to take—not one single person who could *bear* to spend a whole evening in his company." Okay, so "rumor" might be stretching it. Actually, Reese had come up with that theory herself. But she'd told Angela, who'd told Ally, and they'd all talked about it, so as far as she was concerned, that qualified as a grapevine.

Anyway, there was no way she believed Kimble's explanation. Not that she'd heard it firsthand, of course. Kenneth had told her about the party, because Reese hadn't been able to go. Kimble had put her on some draconian deadline for the sixth chapter of his book, and she had had to work day and night to make it.

Funny how Kenneth didn't seem to have half as much work to do for their professor as Reese did, but it wasn't his fault that Kimble was a sexist. Sure, Kimble couldn't *act* on it within the hyper politically correct walls of academe, where exhibiting blatant social bias was a sign of lower intelligence. But Reese could tell, at the core, Kimble was a good ol' boy who resented women for infiltrating the university and then far surpassing his own achievements.

But really, how hard was that to do? The man had "written" one book about the history of the BB gun twelve years ago, and now was forcing a twenty-seven-year-old student to compose another uninspiring treatise in his name. Surprisingly, it gave Reese little pleasure to know that despite her efforts, Kimble's book was just so dull and pointless it would ultimately be publishable only by a masochist. And even that was a gamble.

"The guy is desperate," she muttered.

"I take your word on that," Michael said, nodding.

"So what's this book about? The one that *you're* writing?"

"Oh . . . it's . . . well, it's sort of tedious."

Amiably, her father said, "Don't worry; I'm resilient. Let's hear it."

"Well, let's see . . . the basic thesis of Kimble's book is that history teaches people what they can learn about the discovery of the past."

Michael furrowed his eyebrows, confused—as well he should've been—and said, "I don't think I follow."

"Yeah, it's probably best not to try."

"Isn't that sort of the *definition* of history?"

"Uh, pretty much."

He squinted, still perplexed, and Reese shook her head. "I know, Dad. Believe me, I know."

"So is that his whole 'argument'?" Michael snorted. "Well, what are you supposed to do with *that*?"

She shrugged. "I don't know, this and that. Whatever fills the page, usually. But it's not all me. Professor Kimble usually gives me some notes or tapes of dictation, stuff like that."

"But what notes? I mean, what *sources* is the man using?"

"Oh, you'd be surprised how many books there are to misappropriate passages from." A small laugh burst suddenly from her throat, and then her father cracked up, too. *When you really think about it, hell, it is ridiculous. Sort of like my life.*

Michael chuckled a little more. He shook his head, puffed his dried-cherry pipe twice, and stated, "As I said, sweetheart, I don't like this guy."

Chapter Three

Reese reached for a towel and screamed. "Jeez, you startled the hell out of me!" she said on a breath, and scrambled to cover up her dripping, naked body.

"I'm sorry," Ally said, propping herself cross-legged on the toilet lid. "I knocked, but there was no answer. I wanted to catch you before you put your pajamas on."

"How'd you know I was gonna do that?" Reese asked, stepping out onto the fuzzy, peach-colored bath rug.

"Because I know your style," Ally replied.

"I have a style?" Reese said sarcastically.

Ally hopped to her feet. "Come on."

"Come on where?"

"Come on out with me and Ben," she said, gently pushing Reese out of the bathroom and down the hall.

"But I thought you'd already been out with Ben," Reese said over her still-damp shoulder.

"Yeah, we were skating at the pond. He's downstairs now, waiting for me." She steered Reese to the right and over the threshold of her bedroom. "We're all supposed to meet Lane and her new boyfriend out."

Reese came to a dead halt. "Forget it," she said firmly. "There is no way I'm gonna be the fifth-wheel single loser when I could be home watching television. Uh-uh, no way."

Ally laughed. "Come on; it's gonna be fun." Briskly she moved past her and went to Reese's closet. "Anyway, you've gotta come; everyone's expecting you."

"You liar."

"Now, would I lie to you?" Ally called out disingenuously, while rooting loudly through hangers and garments. "Let's see what we've got here . . . hmm, what can you wear?"

Reese ambled across the room, while Ally continued mumbling from the closet. As Reese took out a clean pair of underwear she said casually, "Um, just so you know, I haven't worn anything in that closet since I was nineteen. I brought my clothes with me." Keeping her towel clutched to her breasts, she pulled a pair of flannel pajama pants from her duffel bag.

Ally let out a sharp whistle from the closet doorway. "Stop right there—what do you think you're doing?"

"Um—"

"Reese, it's your first night home. Aren't you even gonna hang out with me and Ben?"

"But—"

Abruptly Ally softened her tone—going from indignation to soulful lament in 0.5 seconds. "Reese, we're sisters, and we never even hang out anymore."

She lowered her eyes and shook her head. "It's sad, really."

Reese let out a laugh. "Oh, please. Does Ben know this manipulative side of you?"

Ally grinned up at her. "Uh-uh . . . I've manipulated him into blind submission. Now come *on*." Reese realized that she would have to relent, despite the fact that she was tired and did not want to go out with two couples, and *especially* did not want to go out with Lane McBride and her latest guido.

Still, Ally was right. Reese hadn't spent much time with her in the last couple of months because she had been so swamped with school. Anyway, her little sister might be maddeningly uncompromising, but it was fabulous to see her again.

Ally crossed the room, coming up beside Reese, and pulled out a pair of blue jeans and a soft green sweater from the duffel bag.

Reese frowned, but took them. "Fine," she said, "I'll go, but don't expect me to make a lot of mind-numbing conversation with Lane. You know she drives me crazy."

"No problem," Ally said brightly. "Even though she likes *you*." Reese shot her a sideways look, and Ally held up her hands. "Hey, she does. I'm just letting you know."

"Mmm-hmm, thanks." Ally had always had a blind spot where Lane was concerned because they'd been friends since they were kids. Although, to the best of Reese's recollection, Lane had been annoying as hell even then. She was gorgeous, with long blond hair that was curly enough to be distinct, but relaxed enough to be "cascading"—and she was stick skinny with a big chest. Yet these were not even her most annoying qualities. The real problem with Lane McBride was her god-awful personality: cooing, cutesy, and fake to the point of nauseating.

Plus, despite the fact that she came from money and had brand names draped off every appendage, she was a hopeless freeloader. With Ally, who was clueless about money, freeloading was a snap. The bridesmaid dress was just the latest case in point.

"Did you have fun at the pond?" Reese asked as she zipped up her jeans and started shimmying in place to loosen the fabric's hold on her ass.

"Yeah, sure," Ally replied, now sitting on the floor, rifling through Reese's bag.

"Now what are you looking for?"

She shrugged. "I'm just seeing if there's anything good I can borrow while you're home."

"By the way, have you seen Angela's haircut yet?"

"Oh, yeah, it's sooo cute." She looked up from her scavenging. "What's up with Angela, do you know?"

"What do you mean?" Reese asked, wondering that very thing.

Ally shrugged. "I don't know; she just seems depressed lately. I don't think she's getting along with Drew."

"How come you think that?" Reese pressed, bending down to tie her laces.

"I don't know; it's just a vibe I've been getting when they come over for dinner. Maybe I'm wrong. She hasn't said anything, so—"

"No, I think you're right. On the phone she didn't sound completely like herself, but she didn't say anything about Drew, so I didn't push it."

"Hmm. Well, don't worry; we'll get it out of her. Now that you're home, it's probably all gonna come out."

"Why?" Reese asked.

"I don't know; you have that effect," Ally said simply, then jumped to her feet. "Ready, cutie?" she asked, smiling.

"Uh-huh," Reese managed. She was still not too thrilled about going, but she knew she couldn't get out of it. They left her room and headed for the stairs. "By the way," Reese said, as they descended, "where are we meeting Lane and her boyfriend?"

"Oh, some diner in Clifton. Ben knows which one it is."

"Oh."

"Yeah, it's easiest for everyone because Lane's boyfriend lives around there. And it's not too far from the city, so Brian Doren can meet us there with no trouble."

Reese came to a jarring stop on the fourth step from the bottom. She turned her head slowly. "W-what do you mean?"

"What?"

"I thought . . . I mean . . ." She licked her lips. "Brian Doren's coming, too?"

"Oh, yeah. Ben asked if he could meet us."

"But why?" Reese asked, trying not to sound as panicky as she was. She was definitely not prepared to see Brian again. What would she say? Would he mention that night they'd met? And if he did, would he say anything about the kiss, just assuming that Reese had told Ally about it long ago. She hadn't told Ally. In fact, she hadn't told a soul, and she wasn't particularly hoping that it would come out tonight.

Her heart was beating irregularly fast now, and her palms were clamming up.

"Ben wants to give Brian the rings. He's gonna hold them for us 'cause he's the best man, but Ben's almost lost them four times already, so I told him he has to give them to Brian—like, now."

Reese swallowed and forced a casual "Oh."

Okay, she had to get a grip on her nerves—she was definitely making too much of this. So it was one very hot kiss, two long years ago. Brian probably didn't even remember it, much less plan to bring it up in front of everyone. Really, for all she knew, he might not even remember *her*.

"Reese, come on; snap out of it," Ally said, tugging on her arm. "Are you ready or what?"

I sincerely hope so.

As soon as they entered the Applegate Diner, Reese's senses were hit by the glare of mirrored walls and the synthetic lilting of Lane McBride's laugh. "There she is," Ally said, waving at her friend, who sat in a booth across from a hulking man with short dark hair. She gave a coy but enthusiastic wave back, while her companion merely spared an apathetic glance.

Ally took Ben's hand and started heading over when Reese said, "I'll meet you guys at the table. I'm gonna go to the bathroom first." Looking from side to side, she quickly spotted large wooden placards designating "ladies" and "gents."

Once she was inside, her nose burned with the

pungent smell of disinfectant. She stopped in front of the large rectangular mirror trimmed with an overlapping diamond pattern. She honestly didn't know why she was lingering on her reflection, because she looked the same as she always looked. But for some reason, at that moment, she felt particularly unenthralled about what she saw in front of her. She sighed. Why was it some days people just looked innately uglier than usual? And why did she even *care* at the moment?

She lingered a few more moments, used the facilities, washed her hands, and left the rest room. She made her way down the narrow corridor, around the bend, and into the dining area.

And that was when she came to a dead halt. *Oh, God.* She'd known Brian Doren was supposed to meet them there, but apparently she hadn't been prepared for the reality of it—the intense, unsettling anxiousness instantly brought on by the sight of him. He must have arrived while she was staring pathetically at her lackluster reflection.

He looked different than she'd recalled—*much* more vivid. She'd remembered that he was about six-one, with soft brown hair and a lightly tanned complexion. And that he had an *extremely* sexy smile, magnetically dark eyes, and a thick, masculine voice that had made her blood run hot. Still, seeing him now was a jolt to her system.

Shivers rolled down her spine, and hard pulsations thumped in her chest and between her legs. She couldn't hear his voice in her head now; she only remembered the effect it had had when she'd met him two years ago. Of course that begged the question: Would it have the same effect when she heard it again today?

He was sitting next to Lane in the booth, and as usual, Ally and Ben were "riding the bus," so the only seat open was the one at the end—right next to Brian.

As she slid into the booth, her heart raced fast and hard beneath her breasts. Suddenly she was catapulted into a flashback of the night she'd spent two years earlier, when Ally and Ben had dragged her to a New Year's party, and she'd met Brian.

The party itself was somewhat of a blur. She remembered that she'd been almost immediately attracted to Brian. Tall, dark, handsome—she couldn't figure out why he didn't have girls all over him. Oh, wait, *she*'d been all over him. But that didn't really count because he'd been so adorable and sweet, and also, she hadn't kissed a man since Pete. And as far as kissing went, Brian's was *incredible*. Especially compared to every other man Reese had kissed in her life, who all came from the same school of hard mouths, whipping tongues, and biting teeth. Not that she'd kissed all that many people, but still, it was what she'd come to expect. But Brian was different; he'd raised the bar. Well, briefly, anyway. The only person she'd kissed since was Kenneth, who'd dropped the bar. Hell, he'd *buried* the bar.

Absently, Reese ran her fingers across her mouth now, remembering that moment—and the way Brian had moved his lips softly on hers, just gently coaxing them open. When he'd slid his tongue inside her mouth, it was slow and scorching. It had felt so unbelievably good that she'd lost control. Much like the boys who'd kissed her too aggressively in the past, Reese had been too excited to slow down.

Feverishly, she'd grabbed Brian by his sweater and pulled him down, while she stood on tiptoes, crushed her open mouth against his, and crushed *him*—body to body—against the wall, wildly French-kissing in the deserted hallway of an uptown apartment, at an otherwise overrated New Year's Eve party. She remembered him sliding a palm up to her breast, another over her behind, and lightly squeezing both.

It was only after the ball dropping excitement quieted, that they pulled apart, lips wet, but still vaguely connected by lingering saliva and unspent longing. Okay, obviously the night wasn't such a blur.

Reese remembered hearing Ally's voice from the other room asking if anyone had seen her sister. She remembered moving off Brian's body, feeling his hard, enticing groin before they parted, and wishing he hadn't waited until the end of the party to make his move.

Later, she'd felt too stupid to tell her sister. And when Brian had never pursued her afterward, Reese had simply buried the night—remembering it as a hell of a kiss, and a moment of weakness on her part. End of story.

Or not. Otherwise, why would her memory be stronger and more visceral now than ever? And why couldn't she force her damn feet to move?

Finally she snapped to attention and traversed the speckled tile, feeling more nauseous with each step. She couldn't begin to explain the jolting reaction she was having to Brian, even to herself. All she could do was pray that no one noticed it.

"Ooh, Reese, there you are!" Lane cooed, flapping her fingers. Reese's smile hello wavered as she very deliberately kept her eyes off of Brian. But she could avoid acknowledging him for only so long. He was, after all, right beside her. And more to the point, he was in the middle of saying hello himself.

"Hi, Reese." He was smiling, but he sounded somewhere between friendly and cursory—which kicked up Reese's need to act only vaguely aware of him.

"Hi," she said quickly, and turned her attention to Lane—always an act of utter desperation. "So, Lane . . . I haven't seen you for a while," she said. "How have you been?"

Lane glowed with radiant, Cheshire insincerity. "Ooh, I know—it's been *way* too long! Reese, I want you to meet Tom," she said, motioning to her companion across the table. "Tom, this is Ally's big sister." She hung on the word "big" a little too long to have been an accident.

"Hi," Reese said.

Tom wasn't quite as eloquent. He graced Reese with a quick nod, and went back to sipping his Coke. In that tiny span of time, though, Reese gave him a brief once-over: sculpted upper body outlined by a black spandex T-shirt, hair cemented in place with gel, a quarter-sized gold medallion hanging around his neck. The skin just below his eyebrows was exceptionally shiny, indicating a very recent wax, and his default expression appeared to be cocky-as-hell.

Yes, this would be what Ally often referred to as "Lane's type."

Lord, the booth was a tight fit. Reese shifted a little because that was all she *could* shift. Brian's leg was brushing hers, yet they'd barely said hello. For some reason that struck her as ironic. At the moment, Brian was saying something to Ben, who was across from him, and Lane and Ally were having a conversation diagonally over that.

Reese, however, was sitting there feeling unbelievably self-conscious and awkward, not to mention ashamed of her rudeness.

For over a year, she had known that Brian Doren was Ben's best man—she had known that she would see him at the wedding, and she had figured it would be uncomfortable, but nothing she couldn't handle. Remember her brilliant plan? So there was absolutely no excuse for the tailspin she was in, for the nervousness, for the unbelievably strong stirrings of sexual attraction that were fogging her brain.

God, this was not like her. Her nerves were so frazzled, she was afraid at any second she might throw up in Brian's lap.

"Reese?"

"Oh . . . what?"

Lane squeal-giggled, and said, "You were a million miles away! I was just saying that your hair looks different than I remembered." Reese automatically touched the back of her head. It *felt* the same. "Are you growing out a perm?"

"No," Reese replied, feeling her face fill with heat. "It's just . . . like this."

Lane tilted her head, confused, and everyone

glanced over at Reese's hairdo. Reese smiled a little sheepishly, as Brian's eyes caught hers, and he smiled warmly back.

The table was quickly distracted—Ally and Ben by the menu they were sharing, Lane and Tom by some inane conversation. Brian was still looking at Reese— well, more in her direction. It suddenly occurred to her that *he* might be feeling a little skittish around her, too. The thought alone helped calm her nerves.

"So . . ." he began softly, "Ally mentioned that you're still in school."

"Oh, yeah, I am."

"Crewlyn, right?"

"Yes, I—"

"Ooh, 'scusey, you two," Lane interrupted, lurching forward as she spoke. "I've gotta use the little girls' room."

"Oh, of course," Brian said quickly and politely, poising himself to slide out. Once Reese shuffled out of the booth, followed by Brian, Lane brushed past both. Brian turned his head and gave Reese a small smile before sitting back down—but then his expression changed. It was as if he had just noticed something odd.

What could it be? Did she have something on her face? Was her fly open?

After Brian casually averted his eyes, Reese glanced down to discover that it was worse. Much worse. She had gotten her paper place mat caught on her belt loop when she'd stood up, and had cluelessly trailed the whole thing off with her. God, she'd been standing in the middle of the Applegate Diner with a paper place mat hanging from her pants!

She snatched it off and considered her options. She could try to make a joke about it, if her tongue weren't suddenly feeling thick and heavy. One thing she *couldn't* do was look to Ally and Ben for comfort, because they were in their own world, deliberating between French fries and gravy and mashed potatoes and gravy. So she just sat back down.

Lane returned, having donned a fresh coat of lipstick. "Ooh, I'm back; 'scusey, you guys."

Reese wanted to roll her eyes, but refrained. Instead she slid out of the booth again, and as soon as she stood, collided with someone behind her. Startled, Reese whipped around and saw their waitress fuming. "Whoa!" the woman yelled, annoyed. "You almost made me lose it *all*!" "All" being the six napkin-and-silverware rolls she was carrying in her arms.

"Honey, you better start looking where you're going," the waitress chastised loudly, "or one of these days, you're gonna knock over a tray of food!" Reese felt color flood her cheeks and neck. Brian was averting his eyes again, obviously trying to be nice and spare her embarrassment . . . something the waitress might want to try.

"I'm sorry," Reese said, stepping completely out of the woman's way.

"I could've lost it *all*." Yeah, she'd mentioned that. Fortunately, though, after getting that last nag in, she seemed satisfied. Reese, on the other hand, felt foolish and ridiculous and never more like her naked self.

Brian stood to let Lane back into the booth. After they were all seated, the waitress took their orders.

Ally and Ben settled on the French fries, Brian got a chicken sandwich, and Reese ordered a Greek salad.

The next hour passed quickly, and Brian and Reese never did pick up the minuscule thread of their conversation. There was no opportunity, because the table talk had been almost solely wedding centered, and after Brian had finished his sandwich, and left money for the tab, he took the rings from Ben and apologized because he had to go. He said good-bye, and Reese responded with a vacant stare, then shrank back into the booth.

That was nothing like the reunion she had planned! What happened to playing it cool? What happened to acting like she couldn't quite remember him? *Oh, hell.* There was something about Brian Doren that irrevocably undid her reasoning and fried her brain cells.

But then, she had always been a little over-dramatic.

Chapter Four

"I don't want you to worry about anything," Brian said gently but firmly into the telephone.

"But if I go to the doctor again, I'll have to pay half the visit," his sister, Danny, said. "I can't afford that right now. And what would I even say? It's not like I have anything specific wrong with me."

"That's bullshit," Brian argued, then softened his tone. "I mean, don't be ridiculous. You can go for a checkup whenever you want." He felt the familiar tightening in his chest. His sister was only twenty-five, seven-and-a-half months pregnant, and abandoned by her boyfriend, whom Brian had already made a mental note to tear apart if they ever came face-to-face. "Danny, if you even think that dizzy spell was something, you have to go. I told you, I'll pay for it."

"B-but . . . I can't keep letting you do that. . . ." Her voice trailed off miserably. Brian couldn't stand this. If only she wouldn't bother trying to resist his help, they could both save a lot of time.

Danny wasn't stubborn by nature; she was a sweet, helpless angel, who didn't deserve this kind of stress. At least, that was what Brian's overprotective, older-brother instincts told him. Anyway, it was pride that was making her so crazy, and the last luxury she could afford at the moment was pride. "Listen to me," he said gently. "Please listen—please stop crying." Upon hearing his plea, she seemed to collect herself. "Don't worry about anything else but your health right now," Brian went on. "I mean it. I just mailed you a check. Go to the doctor, do whatever he says, and get whatever prescriptions you need, okay? Okay?"

Danny sniffled lightly and mumbled, "Okay." Then she burst again. "Oh, I'm so sorry for all this trouble! It was probably nothing anyway."

"Well, let's let the doctor decide that," he said, then hastened to add, "but I'm sure it's nothing, too."

"Okay."

Brian sighed, knowing that her pregnancy was making his sister more emotional than normal, and that the suppressed grief from losing her shit of a boyfriend wasn't helping. "It's all right; don't worry," he assured her. "Listen, I don't want you to even think about money. I'm going to take care of everything. All right?"

"But what about after the baby's born?" she asked, her voice rising with renewed fervor. "Brian, you can't support us for the rest of your life!"

"That's why we agreed you're gonna move to Florida with the baby, and live with Mom and Dad for a while."

"Oh, yeah," she said softly. "I forgot."

"But I'm still gonna help. That's just the way it is, so you might as well face it."

"I know. I love you," she said, and bawled a little more before they hung up.

Setting down his phone, Brian leaned back in his chair and swiveled it around to look out his apartment window. The view of Manhattan was definitely better from his office.

He sighed, thinking about his family, and tried not to let too much anxiety creep into his chest. Danny was the only Doren left in Boston. Brian had moved to New York City five years ago, after helping his parents move to their retirement village in Florida. Danny had been doing fine on her own, working as an office assistant for a large personnel agency, until she'd found out that she was pregnant. Now Brian was trying to help her and his parents, and for some reason, things seemed like a mess.

He felt tension invading his head, despite his attempt to unwind. He could tell within minutes that his cranium would be pounding relentlessly, as it did most nights. It wasn't just his family situation. It was his job, too—which, ironically, was the only thing allowing him to cope with his family situation.

Several months ago, Manhattan C&S had landed an important account to build a giant corporate complex uptown. Even though Project Blue was in its early stages, it had already landed Brian one promotion, and if all went well, it would get him another by the following summer. The downside, of course, was that he was working his ass off day and night, and sometimes felt so overwhelmed by everything, he didn't know if he could handle it.

But in the end, he always did. Yet that didn't say much for the *quality* of his life. "Sucked" summed up that pretty well. It was to the point that the only real enjoyment he had anymore was his daily lunches at Roland & Fisk, a bookstore a few blocks from his office. For one hour each day, he could sit and clear his head. He always had the beef mushroom soup and a double espresso while he read the newspaper. It was so peaceful there. Not to mention inexpensive—he didn't even have to buy the paper!

Jesus, when had his existence become so *pathetic*?

He should probably consider it a good thing, then, that his ex-fiancée, Veronica, wanted to reconcile. It would be so easy to slip back into their relationship. So easy not to be alone anymore. It should make him happy, but instead it mostly just confused him.

Now he got up and walked to the foot of his bed, where he always kept his briefcase. He should really look over some of the latest development sketches before work tomorrow.

But as soon as he picked the briefcase up, he knew he couldn't face it.

Maybe in a few minutes.

Lying back on the bed, he shut his eyes. An image of Reese Brock suddenly popped into his mind. He held on to it, smiling to himself when he remembered the place mat sticking to her belt loop, and how flustered she'd become. Had it really been two years since he'd seen her? He'd forgotten how incredibly cute she was. Definitely, very, very cute . . .

Brian had meant only to rest his eyes for a moment but, still in his shirt and shoes, he fell into an exhausted sleep.

*   *   *

Reese was finishing up breakfast, while her mother was sitting across the table staring at her. "Can I help you?" she said finally.

Joanna shrugged haplessly. "No, no . . . I'm just worried about you, sweetheart. You don't seem like yourself."

"I don't?"

"Did something happen with Kenneth?"

"No, nothing happened." *In more ways than one— ever.*

"Well, you haven't mentioned him, and every time I do, you seem to avoid the subject." *Take the hint.* "Have you made plans to see him over break yet? Why don't you invite him here for dinner soon? I'll fix something special, and you two can work on your dissertations together. What's he doing for Christmas?"

"Actually," Reese said, quickly rising from her chair, "I'm running late. I gotta go."

"Okay, but what about Christmas? You know you can invite Kenneth here."

"I *know*. You've only told me fifty times." She set her plate in the dishwasher, and prepared to bolt. "I'm sorry, Mom, I've really gotta go," she said, hurrying out of the kitchen.

"All right, but remember what I said!"

"Uh-huh," Reese called over her shoulder, snatching her jacket from the hall closet. She jetted through the door. Just as soon as she'd closed it, she heard it swing back open.

"Bye-bye!" Joanna called. "And remember, Moms know best—have a great day!"

*   *   *

Reese pulled into the underground parking garage of Roland & Fisk, which had ten whole spots reserved for employees. It was first come, first served, unless you were a manager, in which case you got a wide outlined space, right by the elevator.

Figuring she had no prayer of getting a space, Reese was absolutely elated when she saw a car pulling out of one. She glanced at the clock below the dashboard: 11:52 A.M. It had to be someone cutting out on the morning shift. Perfect, she could park and still have time to steal the last few sips of her coffee.

Coffee was a particularly guilty pleasure at the moment because it was strictly prohibited at work. This was somewhat ironic considering that the café inside the store was a caffeine addict's wet bar, and an ode to every conceivable souped-up milk-and-coffee concoction that included an excuse for whipped cream. In truth, all refreshments were frowned upon, but since coffee was the one that people needed most to function, the store manager was especially strict about it. It clearly gave her a sick thrill. But then, with that god-awful personality, probably nothing and no one else would.

Reese reached for her cup and took a long sip. Setting it back in the drink holder, she hopped out of her rosy little sedan and locked the door behind her, then hurried across the garage, her clunky brown heels clicking on the cement floor as she went.

Once inside the elevator she tugged on some of her clothes to straighten herself out. Under her jacket, she wore boot-leg khakis that were too tight on her hips, and a chocolate-brown turtleneck sweater that barely concealed her rounded tummy. *Okay, the diet starts tomorrow.* (She'd already had a croissant for breakfast, with some fatty egg-cheese thing her mother made, inevitably containing a quart of heavy cream, so today was out.)

On the ride up, she steeled herself for the wrath of her boss, Darcy Chipkin, who took totalitarianism to a new level. Darcy was always on the warpath about something, but because she was only twenty-three, everything came off more as a temper tantrum. Of course, the baby tees and face glitter didn't help.

Darcy had been there since she was sixteen, and apparently had worked her way up. So bully for her. That didn't explain why, along the way, she'd developed no actual managerial skills, just a knowledge of the store and a bitter need to whip her subordinates into submission at every turn.

The ultimate irony of Reese's job was that before she had applied, Roland & Fisk had been one of her favorite stores. But as soon as she'd begun working there, the place had lost a lot of its appeal. Sure, she got a 25 percent employee discount on books, and 40 percent on cappuccinos, so at least there was that. And the décor still rated high—big, roomy, and clean, with shimmery green carpet, warm lighting, and long wooden shelves punctuated by thick, suede armchairs.

So it wasn't the actual physical place that had failed her. It was the spiritual place—the ambiance the place took on when it was put into an employee context, which inevitably included clock punching and disgruntlement.

The elevator doors opened and let Reese off in the

back of the store, right next to the dreaded break room, which always felt more like a sterile examining room than a place to unwind and luxuriate in the permitted fifteen minutes. She had a theory that the room was intended as a form of psychological torture—the only hole, of course, was that Darcy Chipkin wasn't that bright.

Now Reese opened the door and entered the fluorescently possessed chamber of despair. As usual, there were a couple of people sitting at the table, not speaking. She smiled hello and, as usual, people averted their eyes and continued pretending to read.

Nothing new. Most of the people at Roland & Fisk fell somewhere between unfriendly and mute. She'd never forget her first day there, when she'd learned that important lesson. She'd been excited about her new job, and had this corny vision that she'd arrive and see everyone ensconced in ice-breaker games and camaraderie.

Hah! More like, she'd walked in and the managers hadn't stopped to introduce themselves. When Reese had said hello, nobody had even looked up! Finally, after several long moments, someone had motioned for Reese to go to the back, where others were unloading stock. She'd gone, and nobody had acknowledged her there either, or given her further instructions. They were all too busy mechanically opening boxes like drones.

She'd asked what she could do to help, and a long silence had followed before a manager silently responded. He'd pointed to Reese, then to a box. A bizarre directive to say the least, but she got the point, and began unloading the box—hence joining the silent ranks of work mules who didn't believe in formal or *in*formal introductions.

That was the same day she'd met Elliot, who was also new. Her only impression of him had been that of a chubby little guy who didn't say much. But then out of the blue, when they were Windexing the front glass, he'd looked at her and whispered, "Bookstore or Gestapo headquarters? You decide." After that, she knew she'd like Elliot.

Now Reese punched in on the wall computer. Good, she still had two minutes left on the clock. She might have enough time to swing by the new fiction table and check out the December releases. It wasn't like it paid to start her shift early—not when she was working in an environment where a "long" duration in the bathroom was docked as a sick day.

On her way out of the break room, she stole a peek at the work schedule posted on the door, listing who would be working with her that day. Her eyes roved across the sheet until they landed on the names Rhoda Dobson and Clay Duckman. *Oh, jeez.*

Rhoda and Clay both worked full-time at the store, and had to be the most pretentious people she'd ever met. The most basic problem with them was their shared delusion that if they sold books, shelved them, or in any way handled them in a professional capacity, they were part of the literati. Strange but true. They both earned eight dollars an hour, yet were imbued with so much elitism, they would mock customers who bought "mindless trash," rather than what Rhoda and Clay supposedly read, "very obscure poetry."

Please.

In many ways, Rhoda and Clay reminded Reese of the graduate students and professors at Crewlyn. More strangers she couldn't relate to—another place where she'd never truly belonged. Which begged the question, of course: Where *did* she belong? And with *whom*?

Now she shuffled around the bend and cut a quick right toward fiction. One thing about working at Roland & Fisk: It kept Reese's desire to write fresh in her mind, surrounding her with so many gorgeous books. . . .

Just then, an unmistakable shrill voice shattered the moment. "This isn't your post, *Brock!*"

"Oh! I-I know; I was just on my way there."

"Ooh, congratu*la*tions," Darcy mocked, and crossed her arms over her chest, partially covering the embossed glitter cursive that read *Baby Girl with Attitude.* It seemed totally inconceivable that Reese hadn't noticed how immature Darcy was when she'd interviewed for the job. She'd just thought she was "quirky." (*Another hah!*) "Quirky" implied some uniqueness of style. No, that was definitely not Darcy . . . who was twisting her pale blond hair around her finger while squinting her shimmery eyelids at her subordinate. "Now, maybe you'd better get to your post before you're docked for an extra lunch hour," she threatened—meaning it.

"Right, okay." *Teenybopper wench.*

"*Now,*" she whined, snapping her fingers in rapid succession.

Reese scrambled away, thinking, *My life is definitely lacking something.* She darted over to her post— known in lay-speak as the register. "Hi, guys, what's up?" she said to Rhoda and Clay, who were apparently engrossed in a conversation about feng shui.

They both said hello, and continued their pseudointellectual exchange of half-witted pontifications. Meanwhile, Reese busied herself by straightening the little gift items that were sold behind the counter. Looking at her coworkers, she'd guess they were both around her age. Rhoda was tall and slim; she usually wore a turban around her hair, large hoop earrings, and a vintage *Straight but Not Narrow* pin on her collar.

Clay, on the other hand, was preppy. Well, sort of. On more than one occasion, Reese had noticed a butterfly collar creeping out from under his J.Crew sweater. He had bleached-blond hair that was combed forward—a style Reese still struggled to understand, several years after its inception. He also wore black-rimmed glasses that angled up at the corners, reminding her of her late Nana, Maggie, except Nana's had been cooler.

"So you switched your hours?" Rhoda asked casually.

"Oh, yeah," Reese replied. "I'm on break from school now, so my days are free."

"That's cool," Clay added blandly.

Then they fell quiet. Maybe they'd temporarily run out of "obscure poets" to talk about—or around. Just then, there was a page over the loudspeaker: "Brock to the break room. Brock to the break room. *Now.*"

The three of them exchanged a confused look before Reese turned and scurried from behind the counter, across the expanse of the store, and to the back. As soon as she entered the break room, she saw Darcy coming out of the private office that she kept dead-bolted at all times so the employees couldn't see what was in there. Now, true to form, she hurried to close and lock her office door, but Reese still managed to catch a glimpse of an Eden's Crush poster hanging on the wall, and a black light on the desk.

"Hi," Reese said to Darcy. "Is there something you need?" *Like a soul? A bottle of Prozac? Hot coals to walk on?*

"Brock, people are on vacation, so you're gonna sub in at the café for the next two weeks," she said.

"Oh . . . I am?"

"Yeah, you're *bright*, aren't you?" she said sarcastically.

"Well, it's just that I never work at the café."

"You were trained for café duty, like everyone else," she said without sympathy. "God, Brock, it's not rocket *science*."

"Believe me, I realize that."

"If you have questions, ask Tina."

Reese shrugged. "All right."

"Um, maybe I should have made myself more clear," Darcy said slowly. "You're subbing in the café *today*. As in, *now*!"

"Right, okay, okay," Reese said. Rolling her eyes, she turned away and thought, *I knew there was a reason I hated that damn break room.*

Chapter Five

Reese took a moment to swipe her brow of confectioner's sugar, and suck on the soft spot between her thumb and index finger where she'd spilled scalding hot coffee in her mad frenzy to serve the lunch crowd.

It had gotten off to an awkward start. As soon as she'd come to the café, she'd met Tina, the café manager. She was a somewhat burly girl, with short, purply-red, frizzled hair. She'd tossed Reese an apron with what had to be a pitching arm, and announced, "We're gonna get along fine—as long as you know I'm not one of those phony people who's gonna smile and be all fake. I'm honest. I *always* tell people the truth."

And this is one of your attributes? Reese had thought.

Tina added, "And if I don't like you, I tell you *right* to your face."

Can't wait.

Now, though, they had a decent rhythm going. Tina was taking care of the register, while Reese baked, and so far she hadn't had anything told to her face. The baking was hard, but luckily all the recipes were posted up on the wall.

The only real downside to making the food was having her back to the rest of the café, which was the cutest little place to be. Square wooden tables broke up the cozy space, and the milk bar in the center existed as a pristine black Formica island. Strings of white lights were woven through evergreen garland, and a Beatles CD was playing in the background—lifting up the day, which had gone from cloudy to pouring-down-rain in the last hour.

Tina's cell phone rang. It was a special Roland & Fisk phone, distributed so Darcy could keep in constant contact with her operatives. "'Lo!" Tina said with authority. "Right. Right, boss. I'm on it. Over!" She hung up, set it back in her holster-type belt, and said, "Brock, I'm gonna leave you for a few minutes. I have to pick up lunch for Darcy. By the way, do you know if BK still sells Hershey's Sundae Pie?"

"Uh . . . I have no idea."

"Shit, they'd better, or I'm *dead*," she muttered, definitely to herself. "Okay, it's slowed down, so you should be fine by yourself for a while."

"All right," Reese replied, and Tina turned and stomped off—not angrily, but in what Reese had come to recognize as her usual intense style.

A few moments passed before customers approached the counter. Reese set down a pitcher of milk she'd been pouring into a bowl of batter, and turned to help them. "Hi, how are you today?" she said to the elderly woman waiting there, and the disheveled man standing next to her. "Can I help you?"

"Yes, are the cinnamon rolls fresh?" the old woman asked—challenged, really, as though she were used to being bamboozled where cinnamon rolls were concerned.

Reese said, "Um, ordinarily yes, but we actually don't have any more right now—"

"What?"

"I was about to put some in to bake—"

"*What?*"

"Mother, open your ears!" the man snapped, and then smiled tremulously at Reese.

"Oh, no, no, it's okay," she said brightly to defuse the awkwardness.

"*What?*"

"They don't have the cinnamon rolls, Mother! Why are you so deaf?"

"They don't have 'em?" she groused. "Why not?"

"Mother, stop causing a scene! I hate it when you do this!" he yelled, but his mother didn't even notice. Still, Reese swallowed uncomfortably.

"Really, it's fine," she said. "Um, can I get you something else? A fresh-baked muffin, maybe? A croissant?"

"A muffin?" she repeated. "Well, do you have bran?"

"Mother!" the man yelped, embarrassed, and making it weird when it didn't have to be. Well, weirder than it already was. What, was he afraid the café server would think his mother was concerned about being "regular"? (She hadn't until now.) And more to the point, why would she *care*?

Reese gave him a quick closed-mouth smile that was meant to assure him it was fine. He gave a closed-mouth smile of his own, only not as quick, sort of slow and drawn out, and his meaning was unclear. "Uh, we have oat-bran muffins," Reese said.

"*What?*"

Okay, it was time for a little *show, don't tell*, so she went over to the display case and, from behind, pointed to the muffins in question.

"What, *that?*" the old woman said, disgusted. "That's bran? It looks like turd."

"*Mother!*" The man's face reddened fully now, and he turned to Reese, rolling his eyes with exasperation. "She is such an embarrassment. I'm really, really sorry."

Reese wanted to shake him and say, *She's not a cat who peed on the carpet; she's your mother.* But she just said, "Please, it's not a big deal at all. Like I said, I'm putting in a new batch of cinnamon rolls. They'll take about fifteen minutes." She lowered her voice so other customers in the café wouldn't hear, and added, "On the house."

"We'll wait!" he volunteered eagerly. Then he flashed one of those odd smiles that were starting to look plain demented now. "Come on, Mother, let's go."

"What?" she quacked, as he pulled her toward an empty table.

Less than a minute had passed before Reese's cell phone vibrated in her pocket. When she saw the number of the Goldwood house on the display screen, she immediately answered, in case it was an emergency.

"Hello?" she said quietly.

"Reese? It's Mom."

"Hi, what's up? Is everything okay?"

"Mmm-hmm, fine, I just wanted to see how you were. But I don't want to bother you."

"No, it's okay," she replied, "I can talk for a couple minutes. What's new at home?"

"Oh, nothing much. I've got some *pâte brisée* in the oven, and *gâteau aux pommes* cooling on the counter; you know how it is."

Reese grinned. "Actually, for once, in a weird way, I do know," she said, taking a pan of lemon-poppy muffins out of the oven and setting them down on the counter. She slid the pan of cinnamon rolls in, and nudged the door closed with her elbow.

"Have you given any thought to your toast for Ally's wedding?"

"Well, the store just got in a new biography of Marcel Marceau," Reese said dryly. "I think I've found my hook."

"What do you— Oh, no—"

"But I don't want to ruin the surprise, so I'd better not say any more. Let's move on."

Joanna mumbled something under her breath, and Reese could tell that moving on was just *killing* the woman. "Did you have fun last night with Ally and Ben?" she asked.

"Yeah, it was okay."

"Lane went too, right? Who else?"

"Brian Doren." Just saying the name out loud brought back vivid images from the night before. He looked even better than Reese had recalled. But unsurprisingly, he hadn't seemed too impressed by Miss Place Mat Pants.

"Oh, that's nice," Joanna said conversationally. "I'm glad it was fun. So have you made plans with Kenneth yet?"

Reese rolled her eyes as she wiped some scattered flour from the countertop. Classic Joanna Brock power play: Lull Reese into a false sense of security with small talk, then unleash the propaganda.

"No, I haven't."

"Well, why *not*?" Joanna nearly wailed. She abruptly cleared her throat and tried to sound casual. "Uh, I mean, when do you plan to see him?"

"Look, I'll see him at the wedding, but I really don't know about anything else."

"But, Reese—"

"I'm sorry if that disappoints you, but I don't know what else to say. He just . . . look, I just don't think he does it for me anymore." She opened the oven to check on the cinnamon rolls. They looked okay, so she elbowed the door shut, wiped her hand on her apron, and poised her thumb on "phone off." She truly loved her mother to pieces, but this conversation was running out of steam. And fast.

"Okay, Mom, I gotta go."

"Wait, what do you mean 'doesn't do it' for you? I thought Kenneth was pretty darn good-looking! And I'm not just saying that. I mean it, sweetheart— mmm-mmm, what a catch!" She was audibly rabid at this point. Yes, it was definitely time for a more drastic approach.

"Good-looking?" Reese echoed. "Are you *kidding*, Mom? I don't think he's good-looking at all!" Not exactly the truth, but Reese was a desperate woman.

If she didn't dispel some of her mother's infatuation with Kenneth, she was going to be nagging her about him the entire time Reese was home.

"What? Well, you used to like him. You can't tell me you didn't."

"Yeah, maybe I liked him for, like, a minute, but that was back when I was trying to look at the *inner* man," Reese said. Actually, in the beginning, she had found Kenneth appealing, and not just his intellect, but also his unassuming, albeit nerdy handsomeness. But honesty was always secondary in conversations with her mother. Survival was what counted.

"But the outer man?" Reese continued. She made a sound like *blech!* and finished, "Let's just say it leaves *a lot* to be desired."

"Oh, sweetheart, you're exaggerating," Joanna said, sounding more confused by the second. "I met Kenneth."

"But you've never gotten a real look at him, Mom."

"Oh . . . well . . . I thought I did. I remember he has dark hair—"

"Yeah, he has dark *greasy* hair," Reese said. "That is, if you can even call it hair."

"What do you mean?"

"It's a piece."

"Wha—wait a minute." Joanna sounded scandalized. "He *told* you that?"

Reese scoffed. "Don't you think I can tell a rug when I see it?" She almost laughed; her mother was just too easy. "Anyway, he's missing teeth," Reese added, still improvising. "And he has chronic halitosis."

Joanna blew out a heavy sigh. "Oh, my goodness, I had no idea."

"I tried to tell you, Mom. We're talking big-time uggo here," Reese added. "And that's who you want to get me together with? Thanks a lot."

"No, honey, I just didn't realize!"

"Yeah, that's great. You obviously think I can't get anyone better. You're ready to throw me at any deformed misfit who comes down the pike. Boy, my self-esteem's doing great."

"Honey, no!" she yelped. "I was just . . . Oh, I should really stop interfering in your love life." *You think?* "I know I only met him the one time, but I thought you two were so cute together." Reese heaved an impatient sigh. "Okay, okay, you're right. I should butt out."

"Okay," Reese said, "well, I've got to get back to work now."

"Wait! You're not angry with me, right?"

"I don't know. . . ." Reese grinned to herself. "I need to cool down and think it over."

"Okay, but just remember that I love you!"

"Uh-huh," Reese said, feeling pretty victorious.

"You know you're my precious angel," Joanna added supersweetly.

"All right, Mommy, I'll talk to you later."

"Okay, have a great day at work. And remember, if any nice men come into the store, don't act all sullen and unapproachable. Bye, honey, I love you!"

Then she hung up before Reese could respond.

Sighing, she snapped her phone shut. Here she'd been feeling triumphant, and her mother had managed to one-up her with the most infuriating last word possible. Reese would love to try that herself sometime, but knew she couldn't, due to a double standard that had revealed itself roughly at birth.

Oh, well, she thought, just as she heard a deep male voice behind her. "Well, I have to tell you, that's the first I've heard about my teeth."

Reese whipped her head around and found herself face-to-face with Brian Doren. Her breath caught. *Oh, wow*. It was like every time he was the same, only much more vivid. The handsome face, strong jaw, clenched cheek—wait, the clenched cheek was new. And it seemed to come from . . . anger?

"You'd better look away," he said flatly. "I wouldn't want you to turn to stone."

What? What on earth . . . ? Oh, no. Had Brian somehow overheard her conversation and thought she'd been talking about *him* instead of Kenneth?

It seemed impossible, but when she mentally replayed the one-sided conversation he'd been privy to, she realized how it could have happened.

Brian turned and walked off, shaking his head, but Reese found herself momentarily paralyzed. She supposed she was still too shocked to see him. She'd been working at Roland & Fisk for six months and had never once seen Brian Doren there—she definitely would have remembered. In a distant part of her mind, she knew it should be easy to clear this up. To catch up before he left and simply explain. But her heart was racing, her palms were sweating, and her feet were inexorably frozen.

Brian had made it to the steps of the café by the time Reese managed to spring into action. "Brian?"

she called out, feeling guilty as hell, even though she technically hadn't done anything. He kept walking. "Wait!" she cried, and hurried after him.

She could hear the desperation in her heels as they clicked furiously across the shiny wood floor, and down the steps, onto the soft carpet of the store. "Brian, *wait!*"

Finally he stopped, visibly let out a sigh, then turned around. He made just turning around itself seem a laborious effort. *Oh, he's really annoyed. What a mess!*

"What?" he asked, his dark brown eyes suddenly falling hard on her.

"Let me explain," Reese said quickly, brushing a careless wave of hair out of her eyes. "What you heard right now was all made up. I mean . . . I had no idea you were standing there."

"Well, that was obvious."

"No, really . . ." Her voice trailed off momentarily, as she struggled to compose an explanation that wouldn't make her look like a complete *desperado*. But it seemed futile. "What I mean to say is, um, I was talking to my mother and"—*she's of the opinion that I'm turning into a real spinster*—"she was . . ." *blathering on in her usual relentless style.* "We weren't even talking about y—"

"Brock!"

Reese jumped at Darcy's voice, and watched with doom as her boss stormed toward her, her charm necklace clanging and her finger pointing accusingly. "Is *this* your post?"

Instinctively, Reese's face reddened. "No, Darcy, but—"

"What *is* your post?"

"I—"

"I can't *heeeaar* you." Then she brought her hands up to cup her ears dramatically.

"Excuse me," Brian said to Darcy, an edge in his voice, "I was asking this woman for help. Is there a problem?"

For a shocking twist, Darcy fell silent. So did Reese, but then, what could *she* say? Anyway, there'd been something in Brian's tone that sounded reasonable but firm, and calm but *very* intimidating.

"Oh, sir, of course." Darcy began groveling, and fiddling with her hair. Then she seemed to really notice Brian for the first time, and switched to an almost flirtatious tone. "I didn't mean to . . . I just figured that *she* was bothering *you*."

Reese shot an insolent look that Darcy didn't catch. But then she was pretty busy—kissing up to Brian the customer, and batting her eyelashes at Brian the *man*. Reese could not believe what she was witnessing! Darcy was licking her lips and contorting her head into unnaturally coy poses, while Reese was standing there trying not to slap her.

She didn't even spare Reese a glance when she said, "Brock, when you're done with this customer, go back to the café." Then she giggled out of context, and trotted off.

Reese resisted an urge to stick her tongue out behind the bitch's back, and turned to face Brian again. She could feel the flaming heat on her cheeks, and wished more than anything that she could take back the last five minutes.

No, ten. She never should've answered her cell.

She twisted her hands as she met his eyes. "Brian, you've got this all wrong. . . ."

He scoffed, like he couldn't care less anymore. "Forget it," he said, and walked away.

This time she didn't follow him.

She just stood frozen, shell-shocked and tongue-tied, watching him go. He moved briskly through the store to the front entrance, and then he was gone. Disappearing into the rain, into the masses of people clogging Fifty-fourth Street, and out of her life once again.

Chapter Six

By the time Brian got back to his office, he was royally pissed. There went his one hour of relaxing—or trying to—at Roland & Fisk. After four meetings that morning alone, all he'd wanted was his soup and his double espresso and to read the paper in peace. The last thing he'd expected was to be slammed by the help.

He also hadn't expected the help to be the sister of his friend's fiancée, or the girl who'd sat beside him at the Applegate Diner just the night before—or the girl he'd devoured like a starving man at a party two years ago. Speaking of that, what the hell was that halitosis crack? He'd never heard complaints about his breath before, and he wasn't missing *teeth*, for chrissake!

Damn it all. He was trying to forget what'd happened, but in truth, he was still rattled. It shouldn't bother him so much, but he was going to see her again at Ben and Ally's wedding in a few weeks, and if that was how she remembered him . . . He shook his head at the thought. Fucking embarrassing.

Just then the phone on his desk rang. "Brian Doren. Oh, right, I'll bring the paperwork. No problem, I'll be there in five minutes." *Great.* He'd forgotten about the status meeting at two o'clock. He released a deep sigh and gathered up some folders he'd need.

He made a mental note to call Danny afterward and make sure she was taking it easy. He'd sent her enough money to cover her expenses for the next few weeks, and he wanted to make sure she didn't need more. He also had to call his mom to make sure his dad wasn't driving, and to double-check that she had gotten her new eyeglass prescription.

Oh, yeah, and he had to call Veronica back. She'd left him two messages that morning.

As he made his way down the hall, he straightened his tie and ignored the clawing in his gut that must have been leftover Reese Brock–related tension. The whole incident at the bookstore had really thrown him. When he'd gotten to the café, he'd noticed that the girl working behind the counter was on the phone, and he'd assumed she'd be with him soon. What he hadn't assumed was that she'd begin talking about *him—insulting* him. *Him!*

He hadn't counted on realizing in a matter of moments that that cute round ass belonged to Reese Brock, and he hadn't counted on Reese Brock regarding him as Quasimodo. Balding, Altoid-needing Quasimodo. *Jesus.*

And had he officially gone crazy or did her memory of him seem completely divorced from the reality of that night they'd spent? They had talked for most of the New Year's party, and ended up in the hallway, kissing and pawing at each other, right there with fifty other people around the corner. Sure, he hadn't gotten the vibe from her that she was interested in anything more, but he hadn't picked up on her being *nauseated*, either.

And why was she talking about him like he was dying to get together with her? Had he ever *said* that? But he supposed he knew the answer to that—obviously his attraction to her had been more obvious than he thought. She must've picked up on it at the diner.

Well, so what? He was a male; she was a female . . . since when did that make him a charity case? *To hell with it,* he thought irritably. She was clearly unstable. And he was just in a rotten mood because he hadn't gotten his double espresso, and now had to face a long afternoon of meetings ahead of him.

The pounding in his head started again. It turned into a relentless beating against his temple the moment he entered the conference room.

It was normal to be exhausted after working a shift at Roland & Fisk, but this was the first time Reese also felt like she'd ingested her body weight in guilt. The incident with Brian Doren at the café had happened four hours ago, but it kept echoing through her brain.

"Reese? Is that you, sweetheart?" Joanna's voice called from the kitchen, as Reese set her keys on top of the antique grandfather clock by the stairs and made her way down the hall. She followed the smell of heavy, rich food, and the sound of Ally insisting that silver streaks in her hair, if done well, would look terrific at her wedding.

"Hi," Reese said, ducking in, and seeing her family sitting around the long wooden kitchen table. Both Ben and Drew smiled when they saw her.

"Hey," Ben said, while forking in what Reese now recognized as her mother's famous *soufflé de fromage aux truffe noire.*

"Hey, there," Drew said, smiling.

"Hi, guys."

"Your mom tells me you've got a new boyfriend," Drew said amiably.

"Oh . . ." Reese floundered. "Well . . ." Was this the same mom who frequently took "denial" to new heights? No, Kenneth was *not* her boyfriend—he didn't even act like he *wanted* to be her boyfriend. He was so damn passive—he never articulated anything he was feeling, for Pete's sake.

But she couldn't get into all that now. She supposed she could use the old stall tactic of pointing out that, well, Kenneth was a "boy" and also a "friend," so technically, that made him a "boyfriend," but that ploy was usually transparent, and always lame.

"Oh, no, did I say something wrong?" Drew asked suddenly and apologetically.

"No, no, of course not. Don't be silly." Reese didn't want to make her brother-in-law feel bad, especially when Drew always tried so hard to be a part of the family, yet not overstep his bounds. It was sweet. And Reese suspected it had a lot to do with the fact that he was older than the others. Besides, was it Drew's fault that Joanna was certifiably delusional where Kenneth Peel was concerned?

"Honey, you have a plate warming in the oven,"

Joanna said cheerfully, and then hopped up to get it herself.

"It's okay, Mom; I got it—"

"Sit, sit," Joanna said.

So she did. "Where's Angela?"

Just then Angela ducked out of the deep, walk-in pantry. "Mom, is this it?" she asked, holding a ceramic canister of French roast—and looking cute as hell with her new haircut.

"Omigod!" Reese began, hopping out of her chair, "I *love* it!"

It took a second for Angela to realize what she meant, and then she began her usual self-effacing qualifications. "Oh, please, it's dorky and it's too short." She brought a hand up to the straight, layered cut that came about an inch above her shoulder and had wispy ends on the side that turned out around her face.

"It is not dorky," Reese said, reaching out to touch it herself. The dark silky wisps floated through her fingers airily, adorably, and Reese only wished Angela could see herself the same way that others did. Reese added simply, "I think you look terrific."

"Right, I look like I tried to get the *Friends* haircut about eight years too late."

"No way," Reese said emphatically. "You look great."

"Angela, I'm telling you, it looks *nothing* like that," Ally piped in. "You have a distorted perception of reality. Drew, tell your wife how hot she looks."

Drew hesitated for a second, then said, "She knows what I think." His tone implied that he liked the haircut, too, but since he wasn't even looking at Angela, it took some luster off the remark. Reese stole a glance at Angela, who set the canister of coffee on the counter, looking quietly depressed. *What is going on with them?*

"You're hardly one to talk about distorted reality," Michael said to Ally. "You're talking about putting silver streaks in your hair for your own wedding."

"Your father's right," Joanna said in that "I'm sorry but I've got to be honest" voice—with that "raw naked honesty is just a curse" inflection, "That's going to look ridiculous, honey."

Ally scoffed. "It will not. It's gonna match my dress."

"*What* dress?" Ben said through a mouthful of food, and somehow managing a smile.

Ally shot him a look, and said to everyone else, "My dress is coming, so don't all freak out now."

"Oh, Ally, how can you *know* that it's coming?" Joanna asked, wide-eyed and martyred. "Of course we're worried. You order your wedding dress off the Internet—who ever heard of such a thing? Now the wedding's less than a month away, and you don't even have it yet!"

"It's *coming*," Ally insisted, exasperated.

"Okay, enough of this topic, it's making me too stressed," Joanna said with a deliberately shaky voice. She got up and started clearing the table. "Reese, eat, eat."

"I'm not done yet," Michael protested when Joanna tugged on his plate absently.

"And about the silver streaks," she was saying, suddenly back on the topic, "that's just not going to look right. It's not very traditional."

"Mom, I don't think that's your best argument," Reese countered, as Ally twisted three of her braids around her fingers, the short nails of which were painted electric blue.

"I want cool hair at my wedding, and that's it."

Michael smiled crookedly and said, " 'He that falls in love with himself will have no rivals.' "

"What?" Ally said.

"Vanity can be a very destructive thing," he explained.

"Yeah," Ben mumbled midchewing.

As soon as he set his fork down across his plate, Joanna bustled over. "Sweetheart, do you want some more?"

"Oh, no, thanks, Mrs. Brock," Ben replied, smiling up at her. "Well . . . what's for dessert?"

"What are you saying?" Ally demanded. "That I'm *vain*?" She held her hands out, as her gaze circled the table, silently asking, *What's wrong with this picture?*

"*Me*," she declared, "*I'm* vain. *Me*."

Joanna tapped Ben affectionately on the shoulder, winked, and whispered, "How does *crème brulée* sound?"

"Uh, great, that sounds terrific, Mrs. Brock." He flashed that hundred-watt smile again.

"Eddie Haskell," Reese heard Ally whisper under her breath, while Ben took her hand in his and sat back in his chair as though he were full (which was only an illusion, of course).

"Reese, I want to include something in the wedding program about your Ph.D.," Joanna called over her shoulder as she rinsed a plate.

"What? Why?"

"Because I'm just so proud of you, honey!" She clapped her hands together. "My little achiever!" Inwardly Reese groaned and felt more guilt creep into her chest.

"By the way, Al," Angela said, "did Lane ever reimburse you for her dress?"

Before Ally could answer, Michael muttered, " 'A fool and his money are soon parted.' "

Ally sucked in a breath, and Reese said, "Dad, please. I don't think that's helping."

Angela got up to make coffee, and Drew rose to help her.

"But about Lane—" Joanna began.

"Look, I don't *know* what's going on with Lane," Ally protested. "Can we maybe put someone else under the hot lights for a few minutes? Hmm, *Ben*, have you called the travel agent about changing our hotel arrangements?"

"Changing your *arrangements*?" Joanna echoed dramatically, and then threw head into her hand. "What are you talking about, Ally? You can't do this! When are you going to learn that you can't always save everything until the last minute?"

"All right, just relax, Joanna," Michael said calmly. "I'm sure Ally can handle it."

"Don't you mean *Ben*?" Ally said, again trying to bring the focus on her fiancé, but again it wasn't working.

"Why do you need to change your hotel arrangements?" Joanna asked Ally anxiously. "Why, *why*?"

She sighed. "Because they put us on the thirteenth floor, that's why."

Angela rolled her eyes. "Oh, you're not serious,

are you?'' she said from the counter, while she filled the coffeepot with water and Drew handed her a clean filter.

"There is no *way* I'm staying on the thirteenth floor, and that's that."

After the table was cleared, Angela and Drew served the coffee, while Joanna dished out the dessert.

"How was your boss today?" Michael asked Reese pushing his fork into the soft crème brulée. "Darcy, isn't it?"

Reese rolled her eyes, while she tore open a Sweet'n Low wrapper. "Awful, miserable, satanic, the usual."

"What's wrong with her?" Drew asked.

"Ech, where do I begin?" Reese said. "The woman is irritable, berating, crotchety, and an all-around Crab-Apple-Annie bitch from hell."

Drew smiled. "A real old battle-ax, huh?"

"Yeah, totally. Well, she's twenty-three, but still."

"All right," Joanna said, taking a pad from the counter. "While we're all here, let's have a quick meeting about the wedding." Everyone groaned.

"Do we have to do it now?" Ally asked.

"Ally, I'm doing this for you," Joanna said, sounding mildly annoyed. "Besides, I told you I wanted to have a meeting about the wedding tonight."

"Oh, I thought you said we were gonna have a meeting about having a meeting."

"Yeah, I like that idea," Reese said, in no mood to sit through a wedding-meeting, either. They always went the same way: Nobody knew anything, and everyone was disorganized except Joanna.

And she was still feeling painfully uneasy about

her misunderstanding with Brian Doren earlier that afternoon . . . how much more could a girl take in one day?

Joanna sighed. "Fine, fine. But when are we going to go over Reese's toast?"

Reese buried her forehead in her palm. It always came back to the toast, which her mother was only freaking out about because she was afraid Reese would embarrass her in front of the entire Goldwood Women's Club, whom, of course, she'd invited.

Diplomatically, Angela said, "Mom, let's go over everything another night when we're all prepared."

"No, we don't have time to waste," Joanna pressed, unwilling to accept the family standard: vague attempts at procrastination and empty promises to reschedule. Reese sighed and thought, *She's on to us.*

"Sweetheart," Michael injected calmly, "let's go with the consensus and have a meeting about the details another night."

Joanna threw her hands up in the air. "But it just seems silly to wait! We're all here, sitting together—"

" 'Graft good fruit all, or graft not at all,' " he said.

"What?" she asked, frustrated.

"Well, 'an empty bag cannot stand upright,' " he explained with a brief shrug.

"Oh, *Christ*," Ally mumbled, and Joanna brought her hand up to her throat in panic.

"But *when*?" she cried. "Nobody's telling me when we're gonna finalize everything! Oh, this is going to be so disorganized!" She shook her head, undoubtedly trying to lose the mental image of Remmi Collindyne having a less than five-star evening.

"How about we meet the night after tomorrow—Wednesday," Angela suggested helpfully (depending on one's perspective). "Around seven, does that work?"

After some groaning, everyone finally agreed. Joanna said, "Oh, we need to have Lane and Deb here, too. The whole wedding party, really."

"That's true; I guess we should," Ally conceded. She turned to Ben, who was sitting relaxed with one leg crossed perpendicularly over the other, looking only three-fourths into the conversation. "About Brian—"

Reese froze at the mention of his name. Did her family have to keep rubbing it in? She did not want to keep thinking about Brian Doren. *Jeez!*

"Do you think he'll be able to come?" Ally asked.

Ben shrugged. "I don't know. I think he's really busy with work lately. I'll call him tomorrow and ask."

Oh, God! Brian Doren might be coming to their house? The day after tomorrow? Reese's stomach muscles clenched and locked in a tight, anxious crunch. She suddenly lost the desire to finish her dessert.

On the one hand, she was dreading seeing Brian. Yes, she knew that she needed to explain their misunderstanding, but she was so damn intimidated by his presence. On the other hand . . . the sooner she cleared things up, the sooner she could move on and stop obsessing about him. "Reese?"

"Oh . . . huh? Sorry, Mom, were you saying something?"

"Yes, I asked you to have a draft of your toast by

Wednesday evening, so we can go over it at the meeting."

"*Mom*," Reese and Angela said at the same time that Michael pleaded, "*Joanna . . .*"

Joanna blinked ultrainnocently. "What?" she said. "Am I allowed even to ask a question anymore?"

"Okay, let's just save all this for the meeting," Ally said.

Can't wait.

Chapter Seven

That night Reese couldn't sleep, so she started cleaning out her closet. It was really the only thing she *could* clean, because ever since her mother had redone the room, it remained meticulously neat and orderly. Reese's closet, on the other hand, *looked* orderly, but upon close inspection, she could see that the clutter was just arranged well. And she was searching for a good way to release some energy, or to exhaust herself out of insomnia, whichever came first.

Straining on tiptoe, she struggled to reach a big cardboard box that was on the shelf above her clothes. Every time her fingers grazed the box, she fell back on her heels and had to start all over again. Finally she began jumping and swatting the box closer with each bounce. "Damn this thing," she muttered, as she leaped up and achieved one very fierce swat. Too fierce—the box tipped over, spilling out its contents as it tumbled headfirst to the floor.

Letting out a startled yelp, Reese hopped out of the way before her feet were crushed by a violent storm of cassette tapes and yearbooks. She let out a laugh, dropped to her knees, and started rifling through the junk. Now it was junk—ten years ago, it was "life."

And speaking of life, it was probably an odd time to start thinking about what a mess hers had become. But she couldn't help it. She was trapped in a Ph.D. program she'd grown sick of, and she was stuck ghostwriting a book that sucked instead of *really* writing a book of her own. She was sort of seeing Kenneth, who seemed incapable of passion, and was now having passionate thoughts about Brian, whom she'd kissed once, two years ago, and who didn't seem too interested. Oh, yeah, and she'd also emasculated him in public earlier that afternoon.

Mostly, Reese felt like a fraud. She hated school, she had no dissertation, and she was too much of a coward to do anything about it. Plus, despite all her protests to her mother, she really did want to find someone who would make her life make sense.

Just then her cell phone rang.

Startled, she hopped to her feet and tried to remember where she'd left it. Following the ring, she darted across the room, lunged across her bed, and grabbed the phone from her windowsill just before the voice mail picked up. "Hello," she said, mildly out of breath, which, if she thought about it, was sort of pathetic.

"Hello, it's me," said a very calm, cool, controlled male voice. New twist. Kenneth was actually calling her on his own, not merely returning her call.

Hmm, that shows initiative. "Hi, Kenneth. What's up?"

"Oh, not very much," he said. "And how are things with you?"

Confusing as hell. Sleep-deprived, sex-deprived, fun-deprived. "Great!" she said. "Um, it's so nice to hear from you." She tucked the phone under her ear, rolled off her bed, and ambled back to her closet. Might as well work while they strained to talk.

Awkward beat of silence, followed by awkward throat clearing on the other end. Followed by, "So, how is work going?"

Dispassionate nonsequiturs, okay, so much for initiative. "It's okay. The people are pretty weird, but—"

"What do you mean? What people?"

"Oh . . . you know, the people I work with at the store."

"Oh, yes, I see. No, I meant, how's your work for Professor Kimble coming along?"

Hmm . . . Dispassionate nonsequiturs followed by a discussion of the ogre who was controlling her life. Boy, this phone call just kept getting better and better.

"Oh, fine," was all she said, hoping that Kenneth would take the hint and move on to topics unrelated to their graduate program.

"Well, have you finished the latest segment of his book?" he continued. "Have you encountered any difficulties, or . . . ?"

She crinkled her face in confusion, but kept her tone neutral. "Uh, no . . . why?"

"No reason. I was just making conversation."

Well, it needs work, buddy, she thought. Then she felt a pang of guilt. Kenneth meant well—he was just unpracticed. She had to keep reminding herself that that had originally been part of his allure. He had always sat so studiously in their Cold War class, with thin-rimmed glasses, taking notes diligently and appearing brilliant. She hadn't gotten to know him then, though; that was just when he'd caught her eye. They had occasion to break the ice only after they were both assigned to Professor Kimble.

In truth, she didn't know what Kimble had Kenneth working on, but knowing Kimble, it could be anything from preparing his lectures to taking some of his kitschy seventies suits to the dry cleaners. Who knew? And more to the point, who *cared*? But it was becoming clearer and clearer that she and Kenneth had little else in common to discuss.

"So is that book you're working on for him almost done, or . . . ?"

Okay, this was just getting annoying. "Actually Kenneth . . ." she said lightly as she chucked a dusty Pearl Jam tape back in the box. "Do you mind if we don't talk about school? I just don't want to think about it right now." When he fell silent, she added, "I mean, just because we're on winter break and everything, you know?"

After a moment he said, "Certainly, I understand."

"Thanks."

"Well, I really should get going," he said. "I just called to say hello."

"Oh . . . okay. Hello." *And good-bye. Story of my life*, she thought, referring to Pete. And then: *Who are you kidding? Kenneth is no Pete.*

"Uh, yes, all right," Kenneth said, bordering on a stammer. "Well, good night."

"Bye-bye," Reese said, folding her phone closed,

and tossing it over her shoulder. It didn't crash, so it had to have hit the hamper or the carpet—good enough.

As she carelessly hauled the junk back into its box, she heard the crunching and cracking of plastic and didn't much care. There was something nagging at her, besides her off-putting relationship with Kenneth, and besides—thanks to Kenneth's reminder— her ever-encroaching deadlines for Kimble. She knew it involved Brian, and she knew it was more than simply embarrassment over what had happened in the café that afternoon.

It was more biting than guilt even. It was something that conjured memories of that very special New Year's Eve—how they had clicked so well, how Brian had made her stomach drop. Today he'd made it drop again, but she supposed she hadn't fully processed it because she'd been busy making a complete fool of herself.

Now, though, she was thinking more clearly, and she had to admit that seeing Brian again had stirred a strange feeling in her . . . like maybe they had some unfinished business.

Right. Ridiculous. So much for thinking clearly. She barely knew the guy. Reese sighed, and surveyed her cluttered closet, no longer anxious to clean it. Like everything else, the idea now seemed like a diversion from other things.

But she knew she wasn't tired enough to sleep yet.

Five minutes later she found herself in the sunroom, on Ally's treadmill. Reese left all the lights off so no one would be able to see her from outside as she struggled to maintain a fifteen-minute mile. The more labored her breathing became, the more disgusted she felt. *I've got to lose some fucking weight.*

Fine, she'd just add that to her to-do list, which also included making a final decision about Kenneth. Should she hang on, or turn him loose once and for all? More to the point, if she turned him loose, would Mr. Stoic even *care*?

After a few moments, Reese gave up on her dream of the fifteen-minute mile, and reduced the treadmill setting to "remedial." *Ah . . . much better.* Now she could breathe while she walked. Oxygen was good; it helped her think.

She was probably too young to be so cynical about love. But was it her fault that her last serious boyfriend, Pete, had masqueraded as the One, only to announce out of the blue that he was moving to South America to teach underprivileged kids how to read? Sometimes she really couldn't get over Pete's nerve. Albeit, those were very shortsighted, selfish times, but still. Wasn't she a little entitled? Especially after the man she'd thought she'd marry had traded a life with her for a shack in Caracas.

When the treadmill flashed *1.5 miles* across its display screen, Reese hit "cooldown." *Good enough.* As her legs slowed with the machine, a throbbing kind of relief flooded them, making the muscles feel heavy and full. She vaguely recognized the feeling, and knew enough to know it was a good thing.

Soon the walking belt had slowed to a dead crawl, then finally to a full stop. Reese remained standing, leaning her elbows on the display screen, and staring out the windows into the blackness of the night.

Her mind was still swirling with thoughts of Brian

and Kenneth and Pete. *Men*, she thought futilely and unoriginally, as she stepped off the treadmill, left the sunroom, and climbed the stairs to bed.

If she kept listening to that song, she'd swear she'd cry. And since an emotional breakdown didn't scream *competent financial analyst*, crying wasn't an option at the moment.

So Angela reached over and pressed "stop" on her CD-ROM. She released a sigh that felt nothing like a release. Her chest only got tighter, and she felt even more bereft of hope—if that were possible.

Suddenly her intercom buzzed. "Yes, Cyn," she said, struggling to keep her voice neutral—and restraining herself from unloading all her sadness, unsolicited, on her assistant.

"Bryer's on line two."

"Oh—"

"Sorry, I was using line one."

"No problem. Um . . ." The thought of going over "the numbers" with Bryer right now made her physically ill. Or maybe it was the thirty-two-ounce black coffee she'd had for breakfast to keep her awake, because she'd been up all night, thinking, sulking, and—*surprise, surprise*—crying. "Could you tell him I went to a meeting?"

"Okay," Cyn said, "I'll tell him you'll call him this afternoon."

"Make it tomorrow. Actually, next week."

Cyn paused and said, "Okay. Is everything all right?"

"Yeah, fine," Angela lied, feeling fresh tears sting the backs of her eyes. No, she would not give in; she would not break down bawling to her assistant just because she was a friendly face, a pleasant person, and a fellow woman. No, she *couldn't*.

"Thanks, Cyn," she said quickly, before she could change her mind, and pressed "off."

She spun in her chair to face her monitor, and stared at it, loathing everything she saw. It was a good job—in a prestigious, money-making sort of way. But it also filled her with dread every morning.

She didn't know exactly when the dread had started. After she'd graduated from college she had been an enthusiastic, capitalistic hopeful, like every other finance major. And with every promotion she'd achieved over the years, she had become only more committed to her work—to *numbers*.

Oh, brother. She was thirty years old, her personal life had frozen to lifelessness, and at work, it was numbers. How pathetic. Hell, if she was already depressed, she might as well turn her music back on.

She hit "play," and as soon as Angela heard Tori sing, "You're right next to me, but I need an airplane," a tear rolled down her cheek, because it reminded her of the night before.

She and Drew had gotten home from dinner with the family and said about ten words to each other before they'd changed for bed. And then things *really* took a nosedive.

"Do you like this new lampshade?" Angela had asked, sliding under the comforter and into bed beside him. (A decadent king-size bed, the springs of which, she knew, wouldn't squeak all night. Talk about depressing.) "It was on sale . . . I just thought it would be cute."

"Yeah," he said, glancing at the lamp on the nightstand. "It's nice."

"Thanks, really? I just thought it would be a nice change. The yellow goes with the wallpaper well, I thought."

"Mmm-hmm," he mumbled, and switched on C-SPAN.

She kept smiling at him, beaming, really, as if this *weren't* a pathetic conversation, but he didn't seem to notice. A few moments passed before her smile evaporated, and her hand started itching to give him a good smack—an urge she'd gotten a lot lately. She was fairly certain she wouldn't act on it.

"So . . . did you like the dinner?" she asked. "Mom gave me the recipe. I could make it for us sometime."

"What? Oh, yeah, it was good," he said, still watching the TV. She looked up to see what was so damn enthralling. *So news coverage of a soccer game is more interesting than me. Thanks, jerk.* She plastered another smile on her face.

Trying to inch closer without being obvious, she shifted her shoulder and just barely brushed her knee against his side. In response, her sullen husband remained stationary and unaffected. This marriage was getting to be hell on her ego.

Sucking in a breath, she looked up at the ceiling, silently pleading, *God, please make this man normal again, that is, if you're not too busy.* Then she glanced back at Drew, and that was when she noticed him tugging at the collar of his T-shirt.

He tugged again. *Oh, no.* He looked hot, constricted. A mental and emotional flag went up. Could he be feeling strangled? Short of breath? Oh, God, was he in pain?

"Honey, do you feel okay?" she asked, suddenly concerned, and reaching for him.

He held up his hand to stop her, but she ignored it. "I'm fine," he said.

"Okay, it's just you look a little hot, or—"

"Angela, I'm just getting comfortable. Can we not call in the National Guard on that one?" Then he settled back in on his pillows, and turned the volume up on the television.

Frustrated, Angela sighed and slid out of bed.

"Where are you going?" he asked.

"I forgot to take out my contacts," she replied, not even looking back at him. She went into the bathroom and flipped on the switch. The room filled with bright white light that always made her look pale and cellulite-y. Well, it didn't exactly *make* her look that way, but it never created a flattering pretense she could live with, so that was just as bad.

She reached for her contact solution, and came across Drew's medication. She usually reminded him, but tonight she hadn't because she didn't want him to get annoyed with her. Now she was rethinking that concept. Could she really just take a chance that he'd forget? No, she loved him too much to take that chance—even if men were the most ungrateful creatures on the planet when it came to things like love.

Angela emerged from the bathroom to find her husband still watching C-SPAN in silence. "Honey . . ." she said gently. "It's time." She had her hand out, open-palmed, with his pill ready and waiting, and a paper cup filled with water.

She came closer in spite of his sigh. "Here," she said. "Do you want some more water? I can fill another cup—"

He shook his head, and took the pill and cup. "Don't worry about it; this is fine."

"Are you sure, honey? It's no trouble. . . ." She motioned toward the bathroom.

"I don't *need* more," he said curtly. Then he drank the contents of the minuscule paper cup, set it down on the nightstand, and hopped out of bed.

"Where are you going?" she asked.

He ignored the question, and headed toward the bathroom. He must have thought the sound of the door closing on her was answer enough.

She just watched him walk around the bed, past it, past her, while her insides twisted with anguish, and her blood boiled with unspent emotion. *Zoom and now he's gone.*

Pretty soon the only sound left in the room had been the deep voice of a C-SPAN anchor, broadcasting some thoroughly depressing news.

She sighed now, thinking about it, ignored the ringing of her fax machine, and sank her face into her hands. She'd first met Drew at a cocktail party. He'd been thirty-five then, and striking to her, with his rumpled handsomeness and reserved charm. It hadn't taken long for her to realize that he was her soul mate—despite their ten-year age difference, and despite the fact that he was divorced, which used to be synonymous with defective as far as Joanna was concerned.

They had gotten married on her twenty-seventh birthday, and since then, had had three fabulous years together. Until six months ago, when Drew had had a sudden heart attack, and everything had changed. No one could believe it; he was forty and not in bad shape. Dr. Stone had explained that Drew's heart attack really had to do with a genetic precondition, and now that he was aware of it, he could control it with medication. He'd even told Angela not to worry.

Hah! As if that were an option.

She always tried to help Drew however she could—or *couldn't*, if most of the time was any indication. He seemed to hate her hovering. In fact, he'd been moping around depressed and diminished for the past six months, and all her help seemed only to make it worse.

Honestly? It was damn frustrating! The man resisted every effort she made to help him no matter how small. Yet every time she felt on the verge of giving him that smack, she remembered waiting in the ICU, clutching at her stomach, at some imaginary ulcer, and shaking too much to hold the coffee Reese kept bringing her. The memory was still so viscerally painful, it never failed to renew her sense of protection. Whether that annoying, pigheaded jerk liked it or not.

Of course, she wished she could talk about it with her sisters, but it was just too hard. She couldn't help feeling that she'd be violating the sacred bond she shared with Drew if she blabbed his personal problems to other people. Okay, so her sisters weren't just people. And Angela had already told Reese a million personal things about Drew, not to mention a few sexual things. But then again, those hadn't been problems.

And speaking of sex . . . Angela couldn't help noticing (daily) that she and Drew hadn't been intimate for almost three months. Since he was the one who was so emotionally distant, she hoped *he* would initiate something. She needed some reassurance, after all. But no, apparently it was not going to work that way.

Sure, Drew gave her an obligatory quick kiss hello and good-bye every day, but that was pretty much it. Angela never brought it up—all part of the futile effort to keep things light. *Hmm . . .* That begged the question: If she was keeping things light, why did she have an aching heaviness in her chest, and a sagging in her heart?

She clicked her mouse on the solitaire icon. She had about ten portfolios to look over today, but she really didn't give a damn. Nothing was going to keep her from moping. And playing solitaire would be the perfect sealing touch.

Several minutes and two lost games later, she broke. Forcefully pushing back from her desk, she bounced up out of her seat. *I'm not gonna take this anymore,* she thought, fairly sure she meant it, but uncertain what "it" really meant. All she did know was that she needed a change—a major change. She needed to fix her life, with or without her husband's help.

Although that wasn't totally realistic, because she needed her husband back more than anything. But that seemed like a lot to figure out at the moment, so instead she picked up the phone and dialed. After three rings, Reese picked up her cell. "Hello?"

"Hey, what's up?"

"Hi!"

"What are you doing? Just hanging out at home?"

"No, I was power walking. Or my unpowerful version of it," Reese said brightly.

Only then did Angela register the sounds of traffic in the distance, and a horn honking. "Where are you?"

"Just a couple blocks from home."

"Oh. Wanna go out for lunch?"

"Yeah, sure. When?"

Angela looked at her watch. "I'll leave now; I'll pick you up in fifteen minutes. Afterward, maybe we can go to the movies, or something."

"Oh, okay. But wait, don't you have to get back to work?"

Angela held the phone between her ear and her shoulder, while she took a pair of Nikes out of her bottom desk drawer. Shucking off her heels, she said, "I'm blowing it off."

"*What?* Okay, if this is Ally, you're doing Angela's voice really well."

"Be quiet," Angela said, grinning. "So, fifteen minutes?" she asked, already feeling a little better.

"Sure, okay," Reese said. "This isn't like you."

"My thoughts exactly," Angela said and turned off her computer.

Chapter Eight

Reese snapped her phone closed, and started climbing the tall flight of steps up to the front door. Her latest epiphany, which had come to her in a dream: If she felt better about herself, she might have the confidence to fix the other problems in her life. (Well, she never said it was *groundbreaking*.)

She paused at the top step and inhaled deeply, feeling much healthier just by being outside in the crisp, clean air. Goldwood had always exuded a special aura—a perfect blend of modern suburbia and rustic northeast. The houses were contemporary, but the trees were thick, and the air was often sweet with the aroma of wood-burning stoves. That was how it had always been. Reese usually forgot how reassuring it was until she came back.

Just as she fit her house key in the lock, she heard a withery voice call out. She turned and saw their tiny, white-haired next-door neighbor. Reese waved. "Hi, Mrs. Rosenburrow. How are you today?"

"Oh, I'm so excited for your sister's wedding!" Mrs. Rosenburrow called from her porch. Both of her fragile hands were clutching at the doily collar of her cardigan, keeping it closed around her neck. "Your mother tells me that you're going to keep me company there!"

Reese kept her smile frozen in place. "Yeah, definitely," she said, though that was the first time she'd heard about it.

"Your mother said you'll introduce me to some new people! Ever since Harvey passed, I've been wanting to branch out!"

"Oh, mmm-hmm."

"I wouldn't mind meeting a man! Your mother said you'll find me one!"

Reese was beginning to feel dumb having this conversation outside and at shouting level. Also, she couldn't help being irritated, yet again, by her mother's promises. Where was Reese supposed to find an eligible eighty-year-old for Mrs. Rosenburrow?

"Okay, great!" Reese called. Mrs. Rosenburrow took one hand off her doily collar to wave again. "Bye-bye," Reese added, smiling, and turned the key. She'd just nudged the front door closed with her hip when her cell rang again. Figuring it was probably Angela, she snapped it open and said, "Yes?"

"Reese?"

"Uh . . . um . . . yes?" She was stalling. She knew exactly who it was (she recognized the deep, authoritative voice, and the undercurrent of impending doom).

"This is Professor Kimble," he stated majestically. "I trust you're working hard."

"Um, uh-huh, sure, yeah, of course." *Quit babbling.* She couldn't help it—Kimble was the last person she expected to talk to. In fact, she'd given him her cell phone number only in passing, when she'd slipped up and mentioned she was going home for break, and no, unfortunately, her family didn't have a phone. She'd prayed so many times that he wouldn't remember the number, and when she hadn't heard from him in a few days, she'd thought she was in the clear until spring semester.

But no, things were rarely so easy with Kimble. Talk about an egomaniac. For pete's sake, this was her break! She was keeping up with his work, but did they actually have to *converse*, too?

"How far have you gotten with chapter eight?" he asked. No *How's it going? Looking forward to the holidays? Sorry to disturb you on your VACATION?*

"I'm almost done with it actually." At least that was true. Before she'd gone home for break, she'd finished most of chapter eight, entitled "Historical Documents and Their Importance in Understanding Documented History." She just had to ramble on in circles for a few more pages, find a few more synonyms for "discover" and "forefathers."

"That's what I was counting on," he said. No: *Thank you. Wow, almost done, already?* Or, *How do you stand writing that crap?* "I'll need you to make some additions, however."

"Oh, really?" That seemed hard to imagine, because as it was, she was having trouble eking out enough BS for a whole chapter.

"Yes, I've compiled some closing thoughts that will flesh out the analysis a bit more." Jesus, was that possible? Kimble had pretty much reduced the "analysis" to its most basic state.

"All right," she said, "if you just want to e-mail

me the new material, I'll try to take a look at it this
week—"

"No, I'm afraid that simply won't do," he said im-
periously. "I want to convey these ideas to you while
they're still fresh." *Fresh?* Reese stifled a laugh.

Rolling her eyes, she scoured the bureau in the
front hall for a pen and paper. No luck. "Hold on
just a minute," she said, and Kimble merely grunted.
Taking the steps two at a time, Reese sprinted upstairs and into her bedroom. She pulled a spiral notebook and pink ballpoint out of her book bag, and
said on a breath, "Okay, I'm ready."

Promptly Kimble began his usual mode of dictation: speaking as if he were at a poetry slam, every
syllable imbued with affected pretense, while Reese
tried not to toss her cookies. "Historical documents
provide a discourse," he said slowly, dramatically.
"No, wait. They provide . . . a discursive *framework*.
Yes, a discursive framework. Full stop."

She rolled her eyes again, and shimmied out of her
track pants. "Uh-huh." She managed a half-assed,
shorthand version as she rooted around for some
jeans.

"New sentence. Historical documents teach us—
and *allow* us to be *taught*."

She tossed her pad on the bed; she could invent
better bullshit on her worst day. With the phone
tucked between her ear and shoulder, she jumped
into a pair of faded blue jeans. As she worked the
button-fly, she heard keys at the front door.

Kimble droned on, while Reese jogged down the
stairs and found Angela in the kitchen. "Hey!" she

said, looking bubbly and adorable in a suit skirt, with silver Nikes and the BC sweatshirt Reese had given her years ago. Her hair was flipped out and wild from the wind, and her face was rosy, which only made her eyes appear more intensely dark.

"Hey," Reese whispered, pushing the phone away from her mouth. "You're *very* sultry."

Angela glanced down at herself, then said, "Oh, whatever." Reese held up her finger, because she thought she heard Kimble say something like, "Now, read it back to me." *Shoot!*

"Um . . . what?" More stalling.

"Wait, actually I forgot something!" he said. "Final sentence. It is crucial for people to uncover historical documents, and was it not Foucault who once said, 'Nothing ventured, nothing gained'? Full stop."

Reese hesitated, then said, "I-I don't think Foucault said that." Okay, she didn't give a damn about Kimble's book, and she didn't pretend to understand all of what Foucault *did* say, but this was just too much. Jeez, wouldn't Kimble allow her *any* intellectual honesty?

"Pardon me?" he said.

She held her ground. "I don't believe Foucault said that."

"*Ever?*" he challenged.

"Well, not *originally*."

Kimble paused, and Reese made a face to Angela that cried *Save me*. Angela just smiled, perched up on the counter, and continued picking on some leftover mini-éclairs Joanna had left in the fridge. Finally Kimble said, "Care to make it interesting?"

Reese scrunched her face in confusion. "Uh—*what*?"

"Well, if Foucault didn't originate the expression, then please find out who did."

Oh, God, he was actually serious. Talk about taking delusional to a new level! "Professor," she said carefully, "exactly how do you expect me to find that out?"

Ignoring the question, Kimble bulldozed forward, "And I'll need a revised chapter eight on my desk by the day after tomorrow."

She shut her eyes and ground the heels of her hands into them. Releasing an inaudible sigh, she said, "But how can I have it on your desk? I'm home on break." She had a feeling she knew the answer.

"I realize that. That's why I'm allotting you two days, rather than insisting on seeing it today."

Reese looked around the room desperately, not really seeing anything, except red. The man was such an incurable ass! Now he expected her to come all the way back to school just to put something on his damn desk. What if she'd gone somewhere besides New Jersey? Would she have to come back then? And what about Kenneth? He was staying in New York over break, but was Kimble bothering him twenty-four-seven? Somehow she doubted it.

Of course, she knew she could simply refuse, but it wouldn't benefit her. As Kimble's graduate assistant, she'd need a glowing letter from him to the doctoral committee, when the time came. "Is all of this clear?" he asked, sounding a bit impatient.

"Mmm-hmm," she mumbled miserably.

"Good. I look forward to seeing my work." She would've laughed at that, but she was suddenly too blue to crack a smile. "Until then. Good-bye."

After he hung up, Reese had to remind herself that throwing her cell against the wall would be only a temporarily satisfying release of emotion. So she laid the phone on the kitchen table, sank into a chair, and buried her face in her hands.

Who was she kidding? She would never have time to start that novel she'd always dreamed of writing. Kimble would keep her way too busy.

"Reese, what is it?" Angela said, concerned. She set aside the plate of éclairs, and hopped off the counter to come closer. "What's wrong?" she asked, touching her sister's shoulder.

Reese looked up hopelessly. "Nothing. I'm just wondering at exactly what point my life took a turn for the absurd."

Angela grinned. "Sing it, sister." Reese grinned back, and realized she was probably being slightly melodramatic. Angela tugged on her hand. "Come on. We're gonna go eat. My treat."

"Where are we going?" Reese asked, coming to her feet.

"Somewhere with ambiance," Angela said. "Then we're gonna talk. You're gonna tell me more about your school problems." Reese groaned. "And I'm gonna tell you about how my husband has morphed into a complete pain in the ass."

"Oh." Reese stopped, suddenly concerned. "Why? What's going on?"

Angela shook her head, not even looking that upset. "Come on; let's eat first. I can't male-bash on an empty stomach."

Reese laughed. In a weird way, she felt better already.

*   *   *

They were sitting at the Laughing Frog, finishing their third round of banana daiquiris, and life didn't seem so grim anymore.

In fact, Reese was finding everything downright hilarious at the moment, while Angela was enjoying her brownie fudge cake too much to be depressed. "This is fun," Reese said, slurping up the icy remnants in the bottom of her glass.

"I know," Angela said, breaking off a big chunk of fudge brownie covered in mocha ice cream. "This is the most fun I've had in forever." She stuck the whole overflowing forkful in her mouth at once, and Reese cracked up again.

Reese had told Angela about the misunderstanding she'd had with Brian Doren at the café, and Angela had found it funny. She definitely agreed that Reese needed to clear it up as soon as possible, her argument being: "You have to clear it up—it's too dumb not to clear up."

Reese had also admitted that she and Brian had semi–made out two years ago. She apologized profusely for not saying anything sooner, but considering Ally's big mouth, Angela understood Reese's need for discretion.

The part that Reese left out, however, was her current and burgeoning attraction to Brian. She wasn't sure why, but she didn't feel ready to discuss it. She only casually remarked, "He's pretty good-looking, huh?" and Angela absently replied, "Yeah, he's sort of cute."

Then they'd talked about Drew. Angela had only covered the basic plot points when they'd gotten interrupted by the waiter bringing dessert.

"So finish what you were saying about Drew," Reese said now.

Angela shook her head while she finished swallowing. "That's pretty much it. It just seems like he gets mad at me all the time—not that we ever actually *address* anything. I guess I'm hovering, but I really don't mean to. Oh, I don't know; the whole thing's so frustrating."

"Yeah, I understand," Reese said sympathetically. "Well, maybe Drew's just projecting his own anger onto you. Like maybe it's not you he's mad at, just the situation—what happened and how his life is different?"

Angela crunched on a chunk of ice that she'd spooned out of her daiquiri (which was a virgin, like her second had been). "Well, that's why I signed him up for a support group last week. It's for heart attack recoverees."

"Oh, that was a good idea," Reese said encouragingly.

"Yeah, but then he got this ludicrous idea in his head that the group was for 'old' people. Just because the meetings are held at the Twilight Pastures Retirement Village." Reese reserved comment. "I mean, where does he *get* this stuff?"

"Hmm."

Angela pushed her plate and glass forward. "Ugh, I feel sick."

"Me, too," Reese said, feeling a headache coming on, too, which threatened to ruin her buzz. "So he didn't end up going to the support group, then?"

"Oh, no, he went. He just sulked before and after, and probably during, for all I know."

Reese held her tongue because she didn't like giving unsolicited advice, especially to her sisters, who would definitely ask for advice if they wanted it. But it was difficult not to take a firmer hand with Angela, and insist that she be more confrontational with Drew. If they were ever truly going to fix things, they'd have to talk about what had happened.

Just then the waiter came over. "Anything else, ladies?" He smiled down at them in that flirty way young waiters always did to enhance their tips. It didn't even matter if they were good-looking or not; they still did it. Apparently they assumed that most women wanted to be flirted with. "Just the check," Angela said.

"Nooo problem," he said, and ripped the check off his pad. Angela already had her gold card out, so he took it and, before sauntering off, reflashed his smile.

Reese felt a little too fuzzy to smile back. Not to mention all the alcohol was starting to go south and settle in a pool of heat between her legs. Great, she was sitting in the middle of the Laughing Frog—with her *sister*, for Pete's sake—and she was suddenly feeling horny. That figured. Too much alcohol. Not enough sex. As close as she and Angela were, there was no way she would confess *that* bit of trivia.

"Reese?"

"I wonder if I'll ever have sex again," she blurted.

"What?" Angela said, letting out a laugh. "Where did that come from?"

"I don't know," Reese said. "Not that I've ever had really unbelievable sex or anything, but . . ." She expelled a sigh. "It's just been so long since I touched a man, I guess it's starting to get to me."

"What do you mean? What about that guy from your program, Kenneth?"

Reese scoffed. "Not even close."

"Really?" Angela sounded surprised. "Why not? What's wrong with him?"

"I don't know, nothing. It's . . . *me*." She sighed, feeling a little of the blueness creeping back. "I'm starting to realize that men just don't think of me like that."

Angela snorted. "Puh-lease, of *course* they do. You just don't put yourself out there."

"What's that got to do with it?"

"Well, if you've only got a few guys to base your experiences on, then you're not getting a very accurate reading. I mean, do you know how many duds I went out with before I met Drew?"

"So what are you saying?" Reese asked, slumping lower in her chair. "That I've got to date a string of losers before I find the right person?" Actually, that sounded pretty reasonable, and definitely true. That must have been why she hated hearing it.

"No, I'm just saying that you're too picky."

"What do you mean? I'm not picky."

Angela tilted her head, and said, "Okay, you don't think you're picky. Fine. Most people don't think they are. But let's consider this: How many men have you given a chance since Pete?"

Reese paused to think, and within a couple of minutes managed to calculate the grand total of one. "I rest my case," Angela said.

"But that's not because I'm picky," Reese said defensively. "I just never like anyone." Saying it out loud made her realize that was pretty much the same thing. "Okay, you have a point." She started shredding her napkin. "Let's face it, the real problem is, I'll never find anyone who can measure up to Pete." Sighing wistfully, she mused, "Pete was *perfect*."

Angela let out a laugh. "What are you *talking* about?"

"What?"

"Pete was not perfect—he used to drive you crazy!"

Reese squinted, trying to remember (and also, the Laughing Frog's warm lighting suddenly seemed too bright). "He did? I don't remember that."

"What do you *mean*?" Angela asked, scrunching her eyebrows. "Don't you remember how he never had enough time for you?"

"Um . . ."

"You used to complain about it all the time."

"I did?"

"Yes," she said emphatically. "Remember, he used to volunteer nights campaigning for the environment?"

"Oh, yeah . . ."

"And organize those monthly church retreats?"

"Oh, *yeah* . . ."

"And what about how you barely saw him on the weekend because he was assistant conductor of the youth group chorale, and that was when they practiced?"

"Oh, yeah!"

"Reese, it drove you up a *wall* when you were dating, don't you remember?"

"Yes, yes!" Reese said excitedly, sitting upright, perversely thrilled by the revelation that Pete—for all his rites of sacrifice—hadn't been a spectacular boyfriend, after all.

Angela leaned forward with the same momentum. "And remember when he brought that homeless person with him to your anniversary dinner?"

Reese slapped her palm to her forehead. "Omigod, that was insanity. He shows up at the restaurant, and is like, 'Honey, meet Bo-Bo.' "

Angela laughed, and Reese said, "What was I thinking? I was dating a freaking saint!"

Smiling, Angela said, "See? It's not you—it's *them*."

Reese smiled back. "Yeah, maybe you're right."

"I am."

"Yeah . . . I feel better. Thanks."

"Good. No problem."

Reese sighed. "I still miss the sex, though," she said after a pause.

Now Angela sighed. "Me, too."

The waiter returned and set the receipt and credit card down. "Thaaanks, ladies," he said. He knocked twice on the table before winking, and adding, "Come again."

Angela rolled her eyes after he left, and Reese giggled. "So you're not gonna go back to work today?" Reese asked.

"I don't know. What are you doing?"

Reese made a gagging gesture, then converted her nausea into words. "More crap for Kimble."

"Oh, that's right." Expelling a breath she mumbled, "Well, I guess I will go back to the office. I've got nothing else going on."

Reese looked at her watch. "Hey, Mom should be

home from the market by now—you can always help her prepare an elaborate, fatty dinner that no one can pronounce."

She'd meant it only as a joke, of course, so she was surprised when Angela's face lit up. "Yeah, that sounds *fun*." She signed the receipt, and then they stood to go. As they headed through the cozy bar and grill, Angela asked, "So what are you gonna do about Brian? I mean if he comes to the house tomorrow night."

"Oh . . . I don't know. Explain, definitely. Try not to say anything stupid."

"Good plan."

"What are you gonna do about Drew?" Reese asked, as they approached the door.

"What else?" Angela said. "Ride it out till I explode."

The words hit Reese hard. God, she *really* missed the sex.

Later that night, her dreams demonstrated exactly that point. Over and over. They were hazy dreams— the kind she couldn't fully remember afterward, but that left their imprint all the same. Images that were incomplete but still tawdry. A tiny breakout of perspiration on the back of her neck. A hard throbbing between her legs.

And Brian Doren's name running through her mind.

Chapter Nine

Reese ran some glossy, red-raspberry Chap Stick along her lips one more time, before she slipped on strappy black heels and headed downstairs to join the rest of her family. In sleek, hip-hugging black pants and a lilac angora sweater that clung to her curves, she was dressed up enough to feel quasi-attractive, but not enough to invite questions from her family.

Yes, she was sort of working it. But if Brian Doren was coming to the house, she couldn't leave anything to chance. After the vivid dreams she'd had the night before, she'd started seriously considering the possibility of seducing Brian. Maybe it was far-fetched, but she couldn't help noticing that he didn't wear a wedding ring. Sure, he might hate her *now*, but . . . well, stranger things had happened.

Reese approached the family room, a little wobbly because she hadn't worn heels this high in a year. As she entered, she spotted her mother sitting in an armchair across from Ally, Ben, and Lane McBride. Lane seemed to be entrenched in a story about her harrowing ordeal at the MAC counter, when she'd learned her lipliner shade was discontinued, so Reese figured that she could slip in discreetly, without attracting any real attention.

Unfortunately, though, fate conspired against her.

"Whoa!" Ben said as soon as she entered, forcing all heads to turn. "Why are you so dressed up?" Reese stopped in her tracks, feeling vaguely like a fool. "You got a hot date after this?" he asked, smiling.

She swallowed, and held back from admitting that *this* was her hot date—with any luck, that is, and if Brian came, and oh, yeah, if she got a chance to apologize, and if he even *accepted* her apology—

"Yeah, you look *hot*, girl," Ally said approvingly.

"Ooh, Reese," Lane crooned with phony camaraderie, "you look so *pretty*!"

Okay, now she was starting to feel stupid. "What, you guys? What's the big deal?" She casually moved over to the love seat. "Just go on with what you were saying."

"Oh, honey, are you wearing *lipstick*?" Joanna asked, leaning forward and squinting. "Let me go get my glasses—"

"*No*—I mean . . . no, I'm not wearing—"

"Yeah, what color is that? It's cool," Ally said.

"Uh, it's just Chap Stick," Reese said. "So, anyway—"

"You should really wear lipstick every day," Joanna urged—with enthusiasm for the idea that bordered on desperation. Reese shot her a look that said *Can we move on?* And Joanna ignored it—*quele surprise*. "Why don't you wear makeup more often? You really should—"

"*Okay*," Reese interrupted, trying to keep her tone

relatively neutral, as she felt her face turning pink. She hadn't been looking for this kind of attention; she'd only wanted to look good in case Brian came to the meeting. Now she was starting to feel a little ridiculous with the way everyone was carrying on. "Um, so what were you guys talking about before?"

Just then Angela and Drew called from the front hall, "Hi, we're here!"

A moment later they entered the family room carrying a bottle of merlot. Everyone greeted them, and Reese just barely got out a hello, when Drew said, "Hey, you look great! What's the occasion?"

She sank lower in the love seat.

"I know, doesn't she?" Joanna said excitedly. "I told her she should wear makeup all the time—it really makes her look *pretty*!"

"Mom, I'm not even wearing makeup—I mean, not really." Well, technically she'd put on some dark-chocolate eye pencil. And a bit of dark-chocolate mascara, but it wasn't like she had a choice there—the two had come as a set. Anyway, it was *supposed* to be barely noticeable.

"Ooh, Reese, I never knew you had such long lashes!" Lane cooed. "And your hair . . . did you get a body wave?"

Reese's cheeks flamed. *I never should have tried to style it.* "No . . . it's always like this."

"No, it looks a little different, honey," Joanna said.

Reese abruptly cleared her throat. "Um, so we should probably start the meeting?"

"No, we can't," Ally said with a shake of her head. "We're still waiting for people to arrive." *Yay!* If

Brian was coming, then all this gratuitous embarrassment wouldn't be in vain.

"Oh, no," Lane said, "Deb said not to wait for her; she doesn't think she'll make it."

"Then I guess this is pretty much everybody," Ally said.

What? No, no, we're missing someone. . . .

"Where's Dad?" Angela asked.

Try again.

"Oh, he should be coming along any minute," Joanna said, hopping up, and bustling toward the kitchen. "That reminds me, I'm gonna set some food on the table buffet-style. You can all help yourselves."

"*Yes,*" Ben said, rubbing his hands together.

"And Brian isn't coming, right?" Ally asked him.

Reese tried not to salivate, as she pathetically turned on Ben's response. He shrugged absently. "I left him a message about it yesterday, but I never heard back, so I'd say no."

Reese's spirits plummeted. Damn her luck. She'd let herself hope that Brian would actually come, and she'd get a chance to explain. And, if that went well, maybe to flirt a little. But of course he wasn't coming. But then, who *would* in the same situation?

There went her femme fatale act. She sighed, feeling dumb in hip-asphyxiating black pants, strappy fuck-me heels, and so much red-raspberry Chap Stick, her lips were starting to stick together. She supposed that now all she'd really like was to get on with the meeting, and put any romantic ideas about Brian Doren out of her head.

But could her family let her do that? *Noooo*.

"So you're never told us why you're so dressed up," Ben said amiably.

"I'm really not," Reese insisted. "I mean . . . it's just a sweater and pants."

"Yeah, but for *you*," Lane said.

Joanna came back in the room, carrying a glass of Chablis. "By the way, honey, you never told us why you're so dressed up!" Reese bit her lip hard in frustration. "Oh, my God! Do you have a date with Kenneth? Is that it?"

"No."

"Oh," Joanna said, disappointed. "Then where are you going?"

"I'm . . . going to the library," Reese lied.

Joanna's eyebrows shot up. "Dressed like that?"

"I am *not* dressed up, okay?"

"Who's Kenneth again?" Ben asked.

"Can we *please* change the subject?" Reese said, exasperated.

Joanna held up her hand, as if taking an oath. "All right, sweetheart, just calm down."

"I am calm," Reese said.

"Shh, okay, okay, take it easy, honey."

"*Mother* . . ."

"Sweetheart, just take a breath. You're a little high-powered right now," Joanna said—as if she were only trying to help with her unabashed, selfless honesty—then took a seat in the green silk armchair in the corner of the room.

Meanwhile, Reese swallowed a scream.

*   *   *

She didn't know how long they'd been sitting there, because she'd pretty much zoned out after she'd filled a plate with hors d'oeuvres and resumed her spot on the love seat. It couldn't have been more than an hour, that much she knew, but her untouched plate was now undeniably cold. The last thing she recalled was everyone sampling Joanna's cuisine, complimenting her cooking, and listening to her insistences that it was truly no bother at all.

Michael and Drew had been offering to freshen people's drinks, and Lane was informing the room that alcohol made her "feel icky" because of the high caloric content. And Joanna had reiterated roughly five times what she'd learned from *Wedding Story* about round bouquets making bridesmaids look "hippy."

So far, not much of a meeting. And after two and a half glasses of merlot, Reese was getting sleepy. Not to mention, she was dying to change—to put her hair up with a durable scrunchy, apricot-scrub her face, and trade her hip-huggers for oversize flannel pajamas.

This night had obviously not gone the way she'd hoped when she'd showered and attempted to put "sculpting spritz" in her hair. Maybe she'd just excuse herself and go change. She'd tell her mom she was too tired to go to the library after all.

Ugh, thinking of the library reminded her of school, which reminded her of Kimble, and of how he expected to see chapter eight of his book on his desk tomorrow. The Crewlyn College history department was about the last place in the world she felt like going. In fact, the only thing keeping her from sulking was the fact that she had to drive into the city to work at Roland & Fisk that afternoon anyway.

"Reese?" She registered someone whispering her name. Looking up, she saw Ben motioning toward her plate. "Are you gonna eat that?"

"Oh . . . no. Go ahead," she said, handing him the plate over the coffee table.

Meanwhile she heard her mother scolding her father, "You know, Michael, I could really use your input here."

Her father adjusted the unlit pipe in his mouth, and said, " 'He that speaks much is much mistaken.' "

Ally rolled her eyes, Ben grinned while cramming canapés into his mouth, and Joanna started writhing in her seat with that stricken, panicked look that usually indicated she was about to go off the martyr deep end. "Michael, that is not helping me!"

Quickly, Drew spoke up. "Joanna, I think what you said was a great suggestion. I think you should go with it."

"Yeah, Mom," Angela agreed supportively.

"Really?" Joanna said, getting immediately cheerful again. "So then you really think I should tell the caterer to fold the napkins in a three-dimensional diamond, rather than an origami formation?"

"Definitely, uh-huh, yeah, sounds good," everyone said at the same time. By the look on Joanna's face, she was supremely relieved that that crucial detail was covered, and she could cross it off the meeting "agenda."

"Okay, so then let's review so far," Joanna said, looking down at her pad. "So we agreed that Reese should drive the van from the church to the reception—"

"Yep."

"Uh-huh."

"Right."

"Sounds good."

"*What?*"

That one was Reese. Okay, she'd obviously missed something while she was staring into space, trying not to think about Brian What's-His-Name. Now, snapping to attention, she tried to find out what she'd been roped into. "What are you talking about?" she asked.

"What's wrong, sweetheart?" Joanna asked, her voice lilting with unnatural innocence. "We mentioned that before . . . don't you remember?"

"We did?" No, Reese did not remember; in fact, she hoped her mother forgot about it real soon, because it was *not* going to happen.

"Well"—Joanna brushed some of her own wavy hair away from her face, and pushed her reading glasses higher on her nose—"we touched on it."

"Refresh my memory," Reese said. "Why am *I* doing it? And *what van?*"

"Lane's brother is loaning us his van to take out-of-towners from the church to the reception. You know, sweetheart, several people won't have cars."

Angela piped in, "Reese, nobody else knows how to drive stick."

"Ben does," Ally offered, and Ben nodded eagerly.

"Ally, no!" Joanna scolded. "It's Ben's wedding day—that's not his responsibility!"

"He doesn't care, do you?" Ally said, turning to him.

He started to shake his head, and Joanna spoke for him. "It's unheard-of, Ally." She went back to her pad. "Now, Reese, it shouldn't be too bad. With almost two hours between the ceremony and the reception, you should have plenty of time. Anyway, we don't have that many who'll need a ride. You should have to make only two trips." *You spoil me*, Reese thought. "Oh, wait," Joanna said, pulling a page back in her pad and rereading. "Actually . . . you know what? Make that three trips. Some of the gals from the Gardening Society are going to need a ride."

"What? Why?" Reese asked, feeling her annoyance rise. "They aren't from out of town!"

"Well, some of them really like to 'tie one on,' you might say. So I told them not to worry about transportation, and I'd take care of it." Joanna's version of taking care of it often meant delegating it. She added, "I had to; I felt bad." *Famous last words.* She'd invited them in the first place only because she'd felt bad. Now *this*?

Joanna painted on a smile that said; *I may be pushing it, but after what you put me through in the delivery room, you'll cooperate with deference.* Reese ignored it, though, and threw up her arms.

"That's just great, Mom. They're your friends, and I'm supposed to be their designated driver now?" Reese turned to the rest of the room. "Does anyone besides me see how absurd that is? Dad, do *you* approve of this?" she asked, knowing that her dad was so conservative he would probably balk at the idea of his daughter facilitating the liquored-up antics of the Gardening Society.

But he didn't balk—he quoted. " 'There's more old

drunkards than old doctors.'" He gave a knowing
look to Reese, which was, of course, completely one-
sided, and somewhere in the background, Ally muttered, "Christ."

"I can take them if it helps," Drew offered. "I can
drive stick."

"No, absolutely not," Angela said immediately,
shaking her head.

He looked over at her, and she held her ground,
albeit gently. "I'm sorry, but I don't want you chauf-
feuring a van back and forth. It's too much pressure."

"This meeting is getting so irritating," Ally muttered, and then Reese felt a pang of guilt. She realized that she was being selfish. After all, what was
she going to do—make a federal case out of this,
and cause problems for her sister's big day? No, she
couldn't do that.

"Fine, Mom, fine," she said curtly. "I'll drive the
van."

"Ooh, Reese, you're the woman!" Lane cheered
with saccharine sincerity. Then she added, "I'd offer
but I always have trouble driving stick shifts, and it
makes me feel yucky."

"Mmm-hmm," Reese mumbled, and forced a
smile. Lane beamed a real phony one back, and Joanna made an annoyingly loud screech with her pen
as she crossed yet another item off the agenda (*Un-
load Bus Driver Duty on Robust Single Daughter*).

Well, fine. Reese just hoped her mother didn't mind
if the toast at Ally's reception touched on some latent
wounds from childhood. Perhaps the Christmas
Reese was in sixth grade and her mother had refused
to get her a crimper would come up. . . .

"Now for our next order of business," Joanna said breezily. "I got the floral wreaths from Betty." (Whom she'd also invited out of a bizarre, misplaced sense of guilt.)

"Pardon me," Michael intercepted, pulling his lighter out of his tweed blazer. "Does anyone mind if I smoke?"

"*Yes*," everyone said at once, both bothered by smoke and irritable in general. So Michael nodded with understanding, and excused himself to his study.

Lucky bastard.

Meanwhile, Joanna left the room to fetch the wreaths, and everyone released a sigh. "I'm gonna get some more food," Ben said, suddenly rising from the couch. "Anyone want anything?" he asked, while lovingly toying with Ally's braids.

"I'll come too," Drew said.

Ally said, "Wait, me, too. I need more wine."

As soon as she was gone, Lane whispered (well, first she looked from Angela to Reese in a cutesy "I've got a secret" motion; then she whispered): "Listen, I wanna throw Ally a surprise shower! I was thinking we could do it right after the main shower."

The main bridal shower was a pretentious high-tea thing that in no way reflected the Brocks' real lives, but projected the image Joanna wanted for the benefit of the Women's Club. Plus, Remmi Collindyne had recommended it as the only way to go— case closed.

"It's gonna be great!" Lane went on, clapping her manicured hands together. "I've got something special lined up— Oh, shh, shh!" Ally descended the three steps from the kitchen balancing a plate of crackers and Brie, and two glasses of merlot. She brought one over to Reese.

She took it, surprised, and Ally winked. "I thought you could use a fresh one, cutie." Reese smiled. "Thanks."

"Here they aaaare!" Joanna sang, and reentered the room, carrying a big plastic bag labeled in loopy, purple script; *Betty's Decorations on Main Street*. She plopped down in the armchair again and fished through the bag with a big smile on her face, as though they were really going to *love* this. Then she pulled out one of the floral wreaths.

Lugged was more like it. In fact, her brow creased as she hurled it out and set it down on the coffee table with a *whap*.

The room fell silent.

After a few beats, Joanna clapped her hands and said, "Well?"

Angela, Ally, and Reese all just stared at the monstrosity before their eyes—obviously Betty's twisted version of a subdued headpiece—and it was Lane who finally broke the silence. (Well, why the hell not? *She* didn't have to wear it.) "Ooh!" she squealed. "How *different*!"

Different was right. Huge holly leaves were strung together with heavy wire, and after every third leaf was a big, spurting bunch of bright red berries. Angela was shaking her head with slow comprehension, and muttering, "Oh . . . my . . . Lord."

"Mother," Ally said finally, "what *are* those?"

"What?" Joanna looked confused. "I love them, don't you? I think they're so unique! And it's perfect for the season. Holly. For Christmas, get it? Holly at Christmastime?"

Ally said, "Yeah, we get it, Mom. Now how do we get *rid* of it?"

"And look!" Joanna went on, picking up the wreath again. "It's not real holly; it's only a simulation! That way none of the leaves will die or fall off." Reese couldn't help wondering how that was a good thing. "Remmi says faux foliage is very 'in' this season," Joanna added enthusiastically.

"Oh . . . that's . . . good," Angela mustered.

"But they're gonna have fruit coming out of their heads," Ally said. "It's weird."

"Well, it's not real fruit, sweetheart," Joanna said, sounding frustrated. "The berries are just decoration. See?" She tugged on one of the unnaturally red, unnaturally shiny bunches—the entirety of which filled her palm.

"Oh, *plastic* gargantuan fruit. Much better," Ally said.

"Very comforting," Reese said.

"Yeah, we wouldn't want to walk around with real fruit on our heads; that might be gauche," Angela said.

Then Joanna put a stop to all complaints, which were futile anyway. "Now, *look*. These will just have to do. Betty wanted to surprise you with something different, and you can't very well insult her by not wearing them." She splayed her hand over her heart dramatically. "I'd feel bad. Besides, I'm sure we just need to see what it looks like on. Reese, c'mere."

"Wha—why me?"

"Well, somebody's gotta try it on."

"I repeat the question," Reese muttered, setting her wineglass aside and getting up to fulfill her duty as simulated-foliage model (yet another one of her things).

Joanna motioned for her to get lower, so Reese bent at the knees, crouching lower and lower, until she finally gave up and knelt on the floor. And then the torture *really* began. The wreath refused to stay on her head, no matter how much Joanna tried to set it in place. "Wait . . . hold *still*, sweetheart," she said with frustration.

"Mom, I *am* holding still; it's just too heavy." She knew her mother wasn't really listening, though. She was too busy digging her fingers into Reese's scalp, while struggling to manipulate the thick, immutable wire of the wreath.

"Ow!" Reese yelped at her mother's obliviously barbarous touch.

"Wait, Mom, turn her head toward me," Ally said. "Maybe it's not so bad."

"Okay, great," Joanna said airily, and forcibly twisted Reese's head.

"*Ow*," Reese repeated to no avail, grimacing in discomfort.

"Well, what do you think?" Joanna asked the room.

"Ooh, I think that's just so *different*!" Lane cheered with such high-pitched enthusiasm Reese almost lurched for her. Her aim would've been off, though, because some of the berries were drooping down into her line of vision.

Just then Ben and Drew came back into the family room, and they stopped immediately in their tracks.

"What the—" Ben started to say before Ally shot him a look. "Uh, where's Mr. Brock?" he asked, inching backward, toward the kitchen again.

"He went to go smoke in his office," Ally said.

"Oh, well, maybe I'll go join him—"

"Forget it," she ordered. So he crossed the carpet and sat down next to her.

Under its own power the wreath slipped a little lower, until it was falling in Reese's face. Joanna snatched it back up. "Here, let me just fix this," she said, absently yanking on Reese's hair and jerking her head backward in the process. "Hold *still*," Joanna said.

"I *am*."

"Honey, do you have hair spray on?" she said suddenly, as if she'd just identified the root of the problem.

And Reese did the only thing she could: She scoffed and lied like crazy. "No, of *course* I don't. Why would I put hair spray in my hair?" Heat crept into her cheeks. Damn her futile attempts to be a seductress!

"Well, there's something in here," Joanna persisted loudly, fingering roughly through Reese's mass of waves.

"No, there isn't," Reese said forcefully. "I didn't put anything in my hair—not a thing." *All right, shut up before you just look crusty.*

Just then Michael reappeared in the archway between the kitchen and the family room. Reese dreaded whatever *Poor Richard's* truism was coming next. Whatever he was going to say, she was *not* in the mood. But her father must have sensed as much because all he said was, "Hmm, that's an unusual headpiece. Is that for the wedding? It's actually quite festive."

"Yes!" Joanna piped up, smiling at him, grateful for his endorsement. "That's what I've been trying to tell them!"

He said, "Yes, that looks good. I like it a lot." Okay, nobody saw that coming. In fact, Reese wondered if he really liked it, or if he was just helping Joanna out. It didn't really matter either way. She and Angela were wearing that wreath, and they both knew it.

Reese looked around for her wineglass, and then decided to opt instead for food. Might as well salvage something of this night. Not that she was really *sad*— just unfulfilled, disappointed, and bored. She could deal with that, but she'd like the aid of something fattening, as well.

So she shook the cumbersome wreath off her head and escaped into the kitchen.

She was definitely in the mood for something sweet. Opening the fridge, she thought, *Do I know my mother, or what?* Three trays of pastries were already chilling.

Just then the doorbell rang. Lane called out, "Ooh, that must be Deb; I'll get it!" She darted out of the family room through the kitchen and down the hall to answer the door.

Meanwhile, Reese resumed her position, hunched over, with her head halfway in the refrigerator, searching for the richest, creamiest, most chocolatey thing she could find. Finally she zeroed in on a particularly luscious-looking napoleon. She reached in and took it, careful not to get any frosting on her sleeve, and shut the refrigerator with her hip.

But as she opened her mouth wide, hoping to slide the pastry right in, she heard Lane's voice from the front door, "Ooh, *hi*. I remember you!"

"Hi, how are you?"

Reese froze.

"Am I too late for the meeting?" she heard Brian say, as the napoleon hit the floor.

Chapter Ten

She had about ten seconds to snap to attention and straighten herself out. Thank God she'd stopped just short of stuffing her face with a napoleon. Somehow she doubted that chocolate running around her lips and pastry flakes lodged in between her teeth would do much for her sex appeal.

She ducked down quickly to check her reflection in the oven. Okay, her hair was a wavy mass that haphazardly descended several inches past her shoulders. Good. That was how it normally looked, so the wreath's damage had been minimal. Then she jumped up, tugged on her tight pant legs, and hurriedly crossed the kitchen to pose herself ultracasually against the sink. Well, hell, it was the best she could do in a matter of seconds.

I can't believe he's here. Her heart fluttered wildly, and her stomach tightened with fear and exhilaration and something even better.

"Follow me . . ." Lane said, entering the kitchen with Brian following behind. The instant Reese saw him, her throat convulsed into a hard gulp. He seemed to get better every time she saw him. More handsome, more magnetically sexy . . .

Tonight he was wearing a trench coat, under which she could make out a dark red tie and a white shirt. Had he come straight from work? For *this*? Suddenly he seemed even more appealing. And so unbelievably sexy . . . had she already mentioned that?

He froze as their eyes met, but his face remained blank. "Hi, Reese, how are you?" His tone was amicable enough not to attract any suspicion, but flat enough to make Reese antsy for a chance to apologize so he would no longer hate her.

"Um, hi." That was all she could manage; no other words would come. How ironic. Here she had expected that she'd turn into a blithering idiot, trying to explain herself, but instead she was too shell-shocked and nervous to speak. So basically, she now aspired to be a blithering idiot.

Snap out of it, she willed herself, but it was too late. Brian had already left the kitchen and followed Lane into the family room.

Breathe, breathe. Get it together. She could hear rounds of introductions in the next room, along with Brian's apology for being late. Meanwhile, back in the kitchen, Reese couldn't make her feet move. She couldn't remember the last time she'd felt this nervous. Probably freshman year at BC, she thought, when she'd attended her first Comm. Ave. party. Like then, she would just have to will herself to act normal.

As she descended the three steps into the family room, her nonchalant expression faltered the moment her right heel caught on the carpet, then slipped sideways, pulling her ankle down and nearly spraining it as she all but stumbled over. Her cheeks flamed as she busied herself by checking the rug to see what had made her heel catch—a lame and trite diversion, but it was better than bursting into tears.

Then she plopped onto the couch and tried to disappear. For once, she got her wish. She stole glances at Brian, and was consistently disheartened by the fact that he wasn't glancing back. Not at all. He didn't even know she was alive. Dressing up was a complete bust.

And speaking of busts . . . she couldn't help but peek down at hers, wondering why it obviously didn't look as fetching as she'd hoped when she'd put on her formfitting sweater.

Damn it all!

She quickly crossed her arms to cover her chest, and swallowed a humiliated sigh. Exactly how long had she cluelessly been sporting tacky erect nipples? Just long enough for her entire *family* to see? Oh, that was just great. Meanwhile, if Brian had seen it, he probably thought she was a complete fool. She tightened her arms now, pretty much hugging herself for comfort.

"Reese?"

She jerked up slightly. "What?"

"I asked if you'd fix Brian a plate," Joanna said.

"Oh . . ." She looked over at Brian, who was sitting with his leg crossed perpendicularly over his other, his expression blank again.

"Do you like French food?" Joanna asked him.

He smiled. "I like everything."

"Oh, Mom, that reminds me!" Ally said. "Both of Ben's aunts are vegans. I forgot to tell you."

"Oh, *Ally*. How could you for*get*?" Joanna moaned, clutching her neck.

"Why? What's the big deal?"

Reese stood up and said, "Come on, Brian; I'll fix you something good." Her voice didn't sound quite normal. He nodded, rising to his feet, and followed her into the kitchen.

Once her family was out of earshot, Reese picked up a wineglass, tried not to hyperventilate, and blurted, "About the other day—"

"Don't worry about it," he said quickly—calmly—and she had the distinct feeling that he *literally* wanted to forget about it. But unfortunately, that wouldn't do much for her guilty conscience, so that was out.

"Please let me explain," she said, finally finding most of her voice. "The truth is, I was talking to my mom and . . ." She dared a glance up, and saw that Brian's eyes were falling right on hers. Her breath caught. A moment passed before she got it back. "Well, to be honest, she was hounding me about my love life. . . ."

His eyebrows pinched quizzically now, and Reese realized how it had sounded—as though she'd told her family about their brief encounter two years ago, and they considered him part of her "love life." Talk about embarrassing—for all she knew, Brian barely remembered the night they'd spent.

"Um, but, she always does that," Reese qualified, "even though the woman is completely clueless about it. . . . But that's another subject . . . um . . . The thing is, we weren't even talking about you."

She sucked in a breath, and resumed rattling. "See, she'd asked who'd gone to the diner the other night, and I said your name, and then she immediately started talking about this other guy I know—who she's pretty much living for—and that's who I was actually insulting." Fussing with her hair, Reese looked up at him sheepishly. "Is any of this making sense?"

The corner of Brian's mouth hitched up. "Oh . . . I see. I'm sorry; I feel like a complete idiot here. I totally jumped to the wrong conclusion."

Reese sighed with relief. "Oh, no, I totally understand!" She let out a laugh. "I'm so happy we cleared that up!"

Laughter died on her lips quickly. Was it her imagination or had Brian just a moved a little closer to her? Her heart kicked up when Brian smiled down at her—a full smile of white teeth and warmth and sex appeal. *Oh, boy.*

They remained there, just looking at each other. Reese was still holding a wineglass for him, and he was holding an empty plate, and it was the strangest moment—as though time were suspended, and neither could look away. Reese wondered if she was imagining the sudden intensity of Brian's expression. Maybe she was just projecting. . . .

Finally he broke the moment. Squaring his shoulders, he gazed down at the buffet, then back up at Reese. "So . . . friends?" he asked, holding out his hand.

Reese smiled. "Friends," she said, taking his hand and never intending to hold it as long as she did. In her defense, though, it was hot, big, a little rough, and he was making no move to pull away. Instead, his hand lingered on hers, too, as he applied just enough pressure to spear heat straight between her legs.

Oh, Lord, what is he doing to me? (And would he be interested in doing *more*?)

Ally's voice sounded from the other room. "I don't know; let's get Reese's opinion. Reese, c'mon, we need to ask you something!"

Now the spell was broken—well, sort of. They dropped hands, averted their eyes, and behaved as though the sizzling moment hadn't just happened. But it had. And it would be a long time before Reese forgot it.

Brian followed Reese into the family room, watching her luscious, curvy ass the whole time. He hadn't intended to stare, but his eyes had wandered down and fixed themselves on black fabric molded tightly around each cheek, making his mouth water with every step.

It was such a bizarre relief to find out she hadn't said all those things about him. In fact, now that she'd explained the whole misunderstanding, it seemed so stupid.

Now that that was out of the way, Brian was left with the intense physical attraction he'd had since he'd met Reese two years ago. It was hard to believe that they'd really only interacted a handful of times now, because there seemed to be a sort of hot, ricocheting chemistry between them. Ever since that first time, New Year's Eve two years ago.

Although he hadn't given it much thought over the years, he could still remember the night vividly.

Especially the part when Reese had grabbed him and deepened their kiss, forcing him to sink against the wall, while his blood thundered and his groin throbbed. He couldn't deny how attracted he'd been to her then any more than he could deny that he still was. But how could he not be? She was cute as hell—so damn pretty—and there was something more to it, but he didn't know exactly what it was.

When he'd gotten Ben's message about the meeting, his first thought was that he'd have way too much work, and no time to drive out to the suburbs tonight. But after he'd finished with his paperwork early, and double-checked on Danny, he'd realized that he could do it, and he should do it, for Ben's sake. Ben was a good friend—definitely the most undemanding Brian had ever met. He'd asked Brian to be his best man a year ago, and hadn't asked one more thing of him since, so it seemed that the least Brian could do was to come to the meeting.

Not that he'd particularly wanted to face Reese after what'd happened at Roland & Fisk, as dumb as he now realized that was. He smiled faintly, thinking of how she'd frantically apologized, as if the whole misunderstanding were just eating her guts out. She was really sweet, he realized.

"Brian?"

"Yes . . . I'm sorry, what?" He was now sitting on the love seat next to Reese.

"I was asking if you liked the food," Mrs. Brock said, "because I was just about to put out dessert." She hopped up, and Reese's older sister got up, too.

Reese's thigh was touching his—just barely, but it was enough. He could feel her body heat warming him, touching him, sinking beneath his skin. Beside him, she shifted a little, rubbing up against his forearm in the process. "Oh, sorry," he said, shifting slightly, but not enough to break their contact.

"No, I'm sorry," she said quickly and quietly. She crossed her legs, and somehow grazed his wrist with her fingertips. He almost jerked up in his seat because her touch had taken him off guard. Then her hand was back on her knee.

Unable to resist, Brian darted an eye over, but all he saw was Reese calmly looking straight ahead. So she *hadn't* meant anything by it. Jesus, he was just reading into every move she made. He rested a hand on his knee, too, but it felt unnatural and artificially placed.

Hers appeared relaxed. He found himself studying them. They were creamy white and soft-looking, just like the rest of her. From their handshake in the kitchen, he knew they were more than soft—they were smooth, gentle, and warm.

"So, Reese, have you come up with any ideas for your toast?" her mother called from the kitchen.

"No . . . not really," she replied, sounding almost absent. Abruptly, she began tapping her fingertips on her knee—it was almost as if she knew he'd been looking at her hands. In a strange mating dance that might have existed only in Brian's head, he lightly drummed his fingers, too.

"So, Brian, what area of New York City do you live in?" Mrs. Brock called from the kitchen.

"Midtown," he replied, praying Reese's mother wouldn't notice when she came back in the room that his pants were starting to tent.

"Oh, did Ben tell you that we wanna move to Soho?" Ally said.

"Since *when*?" her mother cried. She ducked her head over the stone half-wall and said, "You're *not* moving to Soho; now please, no more of this talk—it's getting me stressed." Ally rolled her eyes, and Ben just smiled.

Brian attempted a friendly smile himself, but he wasn't really into it. The girl next to him was emanating so much heat, it was unreal. He tried not to concentrate on all the blood he felt rushing south—in strong, hot waves that flooded his senses and stiffened his dick.

Out of the corner of his eye, he saw the outline of Reese's big breasts. He shut his eyes for a second just to clear the image, but he only succeeding in replacing it with a more graphic mental one. *Shit.* Now he was as hard as a spike, thinking of Reese topless and straddling him. . . . Letting him suck her and squeeze her ass . . . spread her wider and shove the crotch of her panties to the side so he could—

"So how long have you been an engineer?" Mrs. Brock asked, setting down two trays of pastries. Angela followed behind, carrying a pot of coffee.

The others in the room descended on the food, but neither he nor Reese moved from the love seat. Reese uncrossed her legs. Experimentally, Brian very slightly pressed the outside of his thigh against hers. She pressed back. He turned his head to read her expression, but she was looking straight ahead, none the wiser.

Brian was starting to question his sanity. Okay, "sanity" was too strong. But his faculties were in serious doubt. God knew he needed to get laid—it had been way too long and his body was starving. But was it possible that he was so goddamn horny that he was imagining that Reese felt the same intense attraction?

"Brian?" someone said.

Oh, wait. Mrs. Brock had asked him a question. Except he couldn't, for the life of him, remember what it was.

"Mommy, no offense," Ally interjected, "but we need to roll this meeting along. Ben and I are going to a concert tonight."

"A concert," Mrs. Brock repeated flatly, and shook her head. "Ally, you'd better get organized here." Ally looked as though she didn't follow.

Nevertheless, the meeting did roll along after that. Within a half hour, it was nearly done. Brian was still preoccupied with the possible foreplay between him and Reese. She was still thigh-to-thigh with him, but a few moments ago she'd shifted her upper body, angling herself slightly to the side. It had brought the curve of her breast up against his upper arm. He'd expelled a breath, and battled more images— Reese peeling down her bra, putting her breasts in her hands, rubbing her nipples, and offering them to him.

This was crazy. He hadn't seen her or even thought much about her in two years, and now he was burning.

"All right, I think we're finally done!" Reese's mom announced. Ally heaved a dramatic sigh and flopped back onto Ben's shoulder as if exhausted. Angela muttered, "Thank you, God," and her husband said nothing. Mr. Brock had fallen asleep on the recliner.

Everyone stood up and headed out of the family room. Brian and Reese slowly got to their feet as well, not making eye contact. Brian was too aroused to think straight, preoccupied with a fierce urge to take her right there, against the wall.

As people filed out the front door, bidding their good-byes, Brian said, "Bye, Reese. It was good seeing you again."

She smiled a little shyly as her face turned a rosy kind of color that brought out the light green of her eyes. "Yeah, um, thanks for understanding, you know, about the café." Brian watched her lick her lower lip. Then he watched her bite it, and hold it under her teeth too long to be anything but suggestive.

Chapter Eleven

Brian stripped down and stepped into the shower. Lathering the soap, he rubbed it up and down his body in quick movements, eager to get finished so he could fall into bed. He picked up the shampoo bottle, threw a glob on his head, and scrubbed roughly. Then, with his chin tipped down, he took the brunt of hot, beating spray, and thought about Reese.

The whole night had been so unexpected. The Brocks were really a charming family. Ally had been her usual free-spirited self, and the older sister, Angela, was also sweet. Her husband seemed like a good guy, too. And Reese . . . there was obviously something about her that excited him on his most basic gut level.

Closing his eyes, he replayed one of his fantasies until his nostrils were flaring and his chest was tight. Bracing one hand on the shower wall, he used the other to soap and squeeze the hard, swollen part of him that was aching.

After his shower, Brian carelessly towel-dried his hair, shoved on some clean boxers, and fell into bed in exhaustion. When he heard his phone ring, he almost groaned. There was no way he was getting up. No. Way.

But what if it was an emergency?

He cocked his ear as his answering machine picked up.

"Hi, Bri, it's me." *Veronica.* "Well . . . I just called to talk. I hope you're having a good night. Where are you? Well, just give me a call at work tomorrow, okay? Sweet dreams."

Now he did groan—and roll onto his back to stare at the ceiling and think things through. He and Veronica weren't back together yet, but it looked like they were heading in that direction. She'd made it very clear what she wanted, and that was to resurrect the eight-year relationship they had ended two years before.

He'd met Veronica when he was nineteen, and they were both undergraduates at Ithaca College. They'd dated through college and graduate school. Brian had moved back to Boston to get his master's degree in structural engineering, while Veronica had stayed in upstate New York and tried to pursue ballet dancing. She'd pursued it on a very small, local scale, but it was her passion, so Brian had always been supportive despite the pain she was constantly in, and all the obsessing she did about her weight during their long-distance phone calls.

When he'd finished graduate school, he'd gotten a job at a small engineering firm in New York City. Shortly after, he and Veronica got engaged and moved in together.

He never in a million years thought they wouldn't end up together—he never could've predicted that he'd be lying here alone at thirty, unmarried and lost. Not to mention overworked and sometimes nearly miserable. But the two years they'd spent engaged had been by far the worst in their relationship. Veronica, who'd gotten a job teaching ballet at a high-priced dancing school, had always complained that Brian worked too much.

Of course, looking back, he knew that he'd thrown himself into his work partly as an excuse not to face how their relationship was dying—how they'd drifted apart, both having changed so much since college—but since they hadn't lived in the same city for so long, they'd never stopped to notice.

Ultimately, their breakup was mutual. A little over two years ago, right after Brian had started working for Manhattan C&S, he and Veronica decided to call off their engagement.

Then a few months ago, she had e-mailed him, and suddenly they were communicating again. If Brian had had someone special in his life, it would've been another story; he never would have encouraged her. But he hadn't been involved with anyone at the time—in fact, he'd been so swamped with other things that he hadn't had a real date in months.

The e-mails had begun very casually, but they soon progressed to semidaily messages, and then to phone calls. Brian hadn't really analyzed it, until two weeks ago when Veronica had confessed to him that she wanted very much for them to get back together. In fact, she had told him flat-out that she hoped they would get married. Her argument involved being older and wiser and realizing what really matters in life.

Still . . . he had doubts. Veronica had always complained that he took on too much. It had been a source of considerable tension then; he failed to see why it wouldn't be now. Especially when he was taking on the financial responsibility of his entire family. He'd told her about Danny's predicament, but only briefly; she had no idea how invested he was. He honestly didn't know how supportive she would be. He hadn't made any promises to her, though—he'd said that he would need time to think and for them to get to know each other again. But he couldn't shake the feeling that it might not be that simple.

Now Brian sighed and tried to will his head to stop the pounding it'd just started. He had no idea what to do. Part of him was so tempted to fall back into a relationship with Veronica. It would be so nice to have someone to talk to again—to *really* talk to—to have someone to sleep next to, someone to be warm and soft and comforting.

And it would be really great if . . . hell, if life would just work itself out. *Hah.*

The next morning, Reese found herself suffocated by the all too familiar walls of the Crewlyn College history department. They were mustard yellow, which was set off by the dark tan carpet as luxurious as burlap.

She adjusted the left strap of her bookbag, wherein lay the famous chapter eight of Kimble's book. After eking out as much baloney as she could, she managed to come up with only twenty pages. Kimble wanted forty; oh, well, he was in for a reality check.

Making her way down to Kimble's office, she passed the claustrophobic conference room where all graduate classes were held; the kitchen station where you needed a key to use the microwave, and only tenured professors got keys; and the pseudo-homey lounge where students got together to sling their daily bull.

When she got to Kimble's door, she was flooded by the usual ambivalence—dread, yes, but also a sense of anticipated freedom, because after the meeting, Kimble might be pacified for a while. She knocked. There was no response but she knew he was in there because she could hear the clicking of keys from inside his office. "Professor?" she called quietly, "it's me, Reese."

The clicking continued. So Kimble was typing—undoubtedly deluding himself that he was on a roll and couldn't afford to stop. Realizing she had a little time to kill before she had to be at Roland & Fisk, she rounded the corner, and held her nose as she passed the perpetually smelly men's room that was next to her office.

As soon as she opened the door, it slammed into the corner of her desk. Professors' offices were small, but grad assistants' were microscopic, and windows were generally frowned upon. Of course, this office was a particularly tight fit because she was sharing it with Kenneth, and between them they had two desks, a hundred books, and a lot of paperwork.

Squeezing through the narrow space between the door and the jamb, Reese let out a strained groan and sucked in her tummy. Once she cleared, she plopped her bookbag on top of her desk, which was already a cluttered mess of folders and homework. Kenneth's desk was opposite hers, and literally, the *opposite* of hers. It was as pristinely neat as a battered, thirdhand desk could be, with only a tape dispenser, a blotter, and a dim lamp. He had books neatly lined along the windowsill.

But Reese liked her desk clutter. She'd rather look at that than petrified wood with termite holes.

She dropped into her creaky chair with torn cushions, and spun around to face out. As she cringed at the sharp screech of the hinges, she spotted something peeking out from behind Kenneth's tape dispenser. Hmm . . . she was just bored enough to investigate.

She wheeled the short distance from her desk to Kenneth's, and picked it up. How odd. It was a hair clip—one of those old-fashioned tortoiseshell barrettes. It definitely wasn't hers . . . had someone left it in their office?

Oh, well. She couldn't spare the time to analyze it, after all—the sooner she met with Kimble, the sooner she could scoot her butt to Roland & Fisk. She headed back down the hall.

If Kimble ignored her knock this time, she'd just slide the chapter under his door. Lord knew it was skinny enough to fit.

She knocked, and Kimble told her to come in. As soon as she entered, she spotted the minirecorder he had poised in his hand. "Yes, good morning," he said, "I'll be with you in a moment; I'm just dictating some new thoughts before they escape me."

She nodded, and took a seat in the weathered chair in front of his desk. She shrugged off her bookbag and brought it around to lie on the floor by her feet.

"Now, where was I?" Kimble said to himself. "Oh, yes." He depressed the record button, and spoke slowly into the device: "Revisionists will often try to suppress the discovery of historical documents, but we must not let them encumber our pursuit of history. And was it not Karl Marx who once said: 'Never let them see you sweat'? Full stop."

He stopped the recorder and swiveled to face Reese. "Now, I assume you have my chapter?"

"Yeah," she said, managing a friendly smile. She retrieved it from her bookbag. "Here you go."

He weighed it in his hand, not appearing too thrilled with its lightness. He said, "Well, once you incorporate the new ideas I just dictated, it will be more substantial." He rose to his feet. "Now, if you'll just stand over there . . ." He pointed toward the left-hand wall.

"Wha . . . ?" she said, confused, and rising slowly and moving over. "Over here?"

"Yes, yes." He came out from behind his desk to stand a few feet away, facing her. "Now when I say 'lift'—"

"Professor, I'm sorry . . . what are you talking about?"

He blinked. "My bookshelves. We're readjusting their height this morning. I mentioned that to you on the telephone yesterday."

She nearly snapped that no, he *hadn't* mentioned it, damn it! But, ultimately, what would be the point? He would still expect her to do it now, and she'd just end up looking like a complainer. "Um . . . okay," she said, "but shouldn't we take the books off first?"

"No. Then I'll have to put them all back. Unless . . ."

Unless *she* would put them all back—and today. No, that wasn't going to happen. "You're right," she said quickly. "This will be much faster. Plus, I have another job I'm supposed to be at soon."

He did not acknowledge what she'd said, but merely gripped his end of the shelf, and shouted, "Lift!"

She did, and tried not to pass out from the immense weight, as well as the fact that she was clearly doing all of the work. Kimble's end was dipped so low, in fact, that once she set hers on the runners, she had to skirt to the other side, sliding her hands under the roughened wood, and lift Kimble's end up before all the books slid off. Kimble merely stepped aside.

"Good," he stated unemotionally when she'd finished. Her triceps were aching, her fingers were throbbing, and her palms were raw. "Now let's do the other five."

Let's. Interesting choice of words.

By the time Reese got out of there, her entire upper body was aching. And she couldn't help noticing that Crewlyn College got more unappealing with each visit.

"Good tarts, Brock."

"Oh, thanks," Reese said, as she watched Tina polish off two deformed cranberry tarts that she'd otherwise have to throw out.

"Did you do something special to the recipe? The cinnamon's not as overpowering as usual," Tina said, as she stood barrel-stanced, gripping her cell holster.

Then Reese realized. "Um . . . no, I didn't do anything." *Except forget to put in cinnamon.*

"Listen, I'm gonna go back and finish the freezer inventory," Tina said, hitching up her utilitarian white pants. "You gonna be okay out here for a while?"

Reese nodded, "Sure, no problem."

"Thanks, Brock. You're one in a million." The compliment was oddly touching. After Tina descended into kitchen, Reese switched the breakfast blend to the house blend, and pressed "brew." She hummed along with the Sundays CD playing overhead, and started wiping the counter down, when she heard a familiar voice.

"Hi, Reese," Rhoda said with apathy. Clay, who was also on break, stood next to her, and added his own aloof greeting.

"Hey, guys, what's up?" Reese tossed the rag to the side, wiped her hands on her apron, and went to take their order. "What can I get you?" she asked.

"Hmm . . ." Rhoda began, fiddling with the edges of her turban and scrutinizing the menu, as she always did. As if she hadn't seen it a million times—as if she didn't take her break there every single day of her life. As if she didn't know it backward and forward, and as if she weren't going to order the veggie sandwich on a soy-nut pita, with extra hummus, and green tea with a twist of lime. Too bad they were out of lime the last Reese had looked.

After thoroughly surveying the menu, Rhoda finally settled on—*shock*—her usual order. Then Reese broke the news about the lime. Rhoda responded with an overblown sigh. "Then I guess I'll just have nothing to drink."

"Okay, sorry about that," Reese said, and turned to Clay to take his order.

"Hi, Reese," he said, donning an artificial smile that curved up toward his Nana glasses. "I'll have a honeydew scone with a filtered water. Thanks," he finished with a closemouthed smile, drawing attention to his lips, which were shiny and freshly balmed. As Reese got jumping on their order, Rhoda talked about the acting company she was putting together, and Clay insisted that she star in the play he was currently writing.

Right.

"By the way," Rhoda said to Reese, "you and I are training a new girl tomorrow."

"Oh, really?" Reese said, surprised. "Darcy didn't mention anything to me about it."

Rhoda shrugged, and Clay handed Reese an employee debit card. After she swiped it through and returned it to him, he and Rhoda brought their lunch to their usual table. Grabbing the rag she'd been using before, Reese turned to wipe down the sink.

Just as she was scrubbing in time to "Bright as Yellow," she heard a low, purringly sexy voice address her from behind.

"Uh, can I get a little help over here, or what?"

Her heart banged against the wall of her chest because she knew who it was. Clutching the rag, she swallowed and turned around.

This day was looking up already.

Chapter Twelve

"Hi, Brian," Reese said.

"Hey," he said, grinning. "How are you?"

For a second, she was tempted to tell him *exactly* how she was—infatuated, curious, and still reeling from the night before. She'd dreamed about him again. Although she couldn't remember the dream with any real clarity, she knew that she'd woken up hot and horny and twisted in the Victorian sheets.

"I'm okay," she said. "How about you? What are you up to?"

"I'm on my lunch hour. I work around the corner, actually. I usually come here."

"Oh," she said, and fixed her gaze on his mouth. It looked so soft, especially compared to the hard line of his jaw. How could Angela say that Brian was "sort of cute"? The man was so ruggedly sexy, Reese was barely containing an urge to dive over the counter right now.

She leaned against it instead, and grinned. "So I guess today you'll take lunch *without* the barrage of personal insults?"

"Please," he said. His eyes were gleaming. And just like that, a moment zapped between them. Reese *thought* so, anyway, but then Brian quickly looked away and up at the menu board.

She watched him as he surveyed his choices. His neck was arched, giving her no choice but to imagine what it would be like to run her tongue down his throat. To pull off his tie, pop the buttons off his shirt, and blaze a hot, wet trial down his chest and stomach.

But why stop there? She wasn't a quitter, after all.

"Reese?"

"Oh . . . what? I'm sorry," she said, pushing some hair back from her face.

He smiled. "No problem. I just asked for a bowl of beef mushroom soup."

"Sure." She turned around to the cabinet and reached up to grab him a bowl. For some reason, bowls were kept on the top shelf, but Reese would never presume to mess with Tina's system. As she went up on tiptoe, she braced herself with one hand on the counter and stretched. Yay, she got it—too bad she'd also been bent just enough to thrust out her bottom, undoubtedly drawing Brian's attention to her ample rear end.

"Would you like something to drink with that?" she called over her shoulder.

"Uh . . . what?"

When she turned to face him, he looked preoccupied, maybe borderline dazed, but he snapped out of it quickly. "Oh, right, a double espresso. Please."

She nodded and brought his soup over. "So you're one of those?" she said, grinning.

"One of what?"

"You know, people who have hot drinks with

soup." She set the bowl down on a tray. "I don't get that."

"Oh, yeah, I know. . . ." His voice trailed off as their gazes locked. Reese's smile faded and a nervous lump took shape in her throat. Then Brian looked down as he took his wallet from his pants and poised himself to pay.

"Hold on," she said lightly, "I've still gotta make your coffee." Skirting over to the espresso machine, she pleaded with her nerves to calm.

"So . . . I've never seen you in here before. Did you just get the job?"

"No, I've worked here about six months, but I usually work nights. Also, I don't usually work in the café." Simultaneously, she dumped two shots of espresso into a small mug.

"Oh, really?" Brian said conversationally. "How come you're working here now?"

She brought his mug over and set it down beside the soup. "I'm on winter break this month, so—"

"Excuse me," a middle-aged woman behind Brian said irritably. "I'm sort of in a hurry here." She smacked her hands haughtily against her thighs.

"I'm sorry; I'll be with you in just a second," Reese said. In response, the woman began making a production of checking her watch. Brian flashed Reese a sympathetic look—one that seemed to say, *No problem, we'll talk another time,* and *People are jerks.* Then he took some bills out of his wallet.

"No," Reese said immediately. "It's on the house."

"Oh, no," he began, shaking his head and sounding firm.

"Brian, please," Reese insisted.

He tried to hand her the bills anyway. "No, I can't let you do that."

She put her hand on his to stop him, and he stilled. She withdrew instantly in case it had been too intimate a gesture. (Not to mention, his hand was so warm and inviting, she was afraid she'd pull it to her and cup her own breast with it. That would be hard to live down, at best.) "Brian, really."

The woman behind him cleared her throat loudly and clapped her hands on her thighs again. In a low voice, Brian asked, "But won't you get in trouble?"

Reese made a face. "Believe me, I'll get in trouble regardless."

He chuckled. "Well, okay. Thanks, if you're sure—"

"Ahem, I'm *really* in a hurry here," the hag behind Brian said angrily.

Brian smiled one more time at Reese before giving a politely apologetic look to the woman behind him. Then he took his tray to a far-off table.

The last thing Reese registered was his broad, strong-looking back, before she was in the throes of a huge order for the woman, who was apparently out getting coffee for her entire office.

When she finally left, Reese expelled a breath and reviewed the day's events so far. Okay, so now things with Brian weren't awkward. In fact, they were damn friendly. This was good—very good. The only bad thing was that *friendly* was about all they were. She hadn't picked up any romantic vibes from him. There hadn't been a trace of flirtiness in his manner. Just warm camaraderie. In fact, she was now starting to wonder if she'd imagined the heat that had been mingling in the air between them the night before.

She had desperately wanted to kiss him last night. While her mother had been droning on (and on), Reese had been conjuring up numerous NC-17 scenarios featuring Brian Doren. Things she'd never done with anybody had been popping into her head as if they were the most natural thoughts in the world.

In fact, she'd been so hot and bothered that she'd thought—hoped—it couldn't be *all* her. She'd assumed that Brian had to be radiating at least a little of that suffocating heat.

But now he was calmly eating his soup and reading. She studied him for several more moments, in which time he did not once look up from his newspaper. So much for a mutual attraction. The man barely knew she was alive.

Reese sighed and leaned her elbow on the countertop. Sinking her chin into her palm, she couldn't help thinking that her instincts were rusty as hell, and when it came to this man-woman thing, she was some kind of walking disaster. So what else was new?

Would he stop to say good-bye before he went back to work? Reese couldn't help wondering. Not that he *should*—they were only acquaintances, not good friends.

She understood this. But that still didn't stop her from completely, insanely fixating on getting a good-bye.

The café traffic had slowed to a crawl. Only Brian, Rhoda, Clay, and two young women were sitting there now, and there was no one on line. Reese had finished baking for the day, putting away the glassware from the dishwasher and wiping down the espresso machine. She supposed, therefore, she had time to sponge off the empty tables in the seating area. Hey, if she happened to strike up a conversation with Brian Doren while she approached his section of the café, so be it. It wasn't as if she were planning anything. . . .

Once she was out in the seating area, she went, quite involuntarily, into ultracasual mode—traipsing herself about and twirling her rag, which she *never* did. Vaguely aware that she was acting differently for Brian's benefit, she mentally urged herself to stop. Instead she started to whistle. *Get it together; stop acting so weird.*

Not that it mattered all that much—Brian wasn't paying any attention to what she was doing. As she swiped her rag across one of the vacant tables, she could hear Rhoda and Clay talking about *Lord of the Dance*. Rhoda was pretending that she'd had an opportunity to dance with the company, and Clay was pretending he knew Michael Flatley.

Reese moved on to the next table, then the next, and by the time she got to Brian's immediate area, instead of her anxiousness having subsided, she was so acutely aware of his presence that she abandoned any idea of striking up a conversation.

"Cool overalls."

She looked up, startled. Then she looked down at

the gray corduroy overalls in question. "Oh . . .
thanks," she said, slowly returning Brian's warm,
open smile.

"So . . ." he said, absently folding his newspapers,
"you never finished telling me about school before."

She had to think for a second, and then memories
of the impatient customer who needed twenty-five
coffees came flooding back to her. "Oh, right. Well,
there's not much to tell," she said, not wanting to
bore him.

Only he didn't act bored. "Well, what's your
focus? I remember you're getting your Ph.D. in history, right?"

Her heart soared—as pathetic as that was. "Yeah,"
she replied. "Well, I don't know if I'm getting it, but
that's what I'm there for."

She smiled and toyed with her rag and told him
about her fellowship. Then the inevitable question
came: "So what's your dissertation about?"

Reese tried to respond with the suave aplomb of
a Ph.D. student who was actually working on a dissertation. "Um . . . I still haven't completely locked
anything down that I want to write about. I have a
few different angles I can take." Luckily, Brian didn't
seem to know how odd that was for a second-year
grad student, who was going to be ABD the following year.

Good. She'd pulled it off. Until, for no conceivable
reason, she blurted out, "Actually, I haven't even
started."

The corner of his mouth hitched up. "What do you
mean?" he asked.

"I haven't done a thing on my dissertation, and

the sad part is, I don't *want* to!" He looked a little amused that she'd told him that. She was surprised herself, but somehow she was unable to stop the flow of confession. She didn't know exactly what Brian was doing to her, and she didn't know if she liked it. (Well, she was fairly sure she liked it.) "So at this point, my dissertation is just a fantasy." *The kind that makes me wake up screaming.*

"What are you gonna do, then?" Brian asked, grinning a little. She noticed a small line at the corner of each eye that appeared only when he smiled. And those eyes . . . soft, smooth brown, and hypnotically gorgeous.

"Um, about what?" she asked stupidly.

"Your dissertation."

"Oh . . . right. Hmm, excellent point. I guess I really should do *something*." A graphic and dirty idea immediately came to mind. "So . . ." She toyed with the rag again. "How do you like being an engineer?"

He made an *enh* face and said, "It's all right. Right now, it's really busy. Actually"—he looked at his watch—"I guess I should get back to work."

"Oh, okay," she replied, struggling to conceal her disappointment. As he stood, he shucked on his coat, and the motion wafted a hint of aftershave Reese's way—*yum.*

"Reese," Rhoda said, "there's a line forming." She *tsk*ed mildly, and Clay gave Reese a closemouthed, pitying smile. Their break was over, so it was obviously time to ruin Reese's day, as well. She felt blushing heat drift up into her cheeks. Nothing was more embarrassing than getting scolded at work when you were trying to pretend you weren't at work.

"Oh, I guess I should get back to my job," she mustered, suddenly aware of her stained apron and the smelly rag she'd been holding while she'd been trying to work the room.

Brian grinned down at her. "Every time I come here, someone's giving you a hard time. What's up with this place?"

She laughed, and when she looked up, their eyes caught again, only this time—just like that—a *zing*. A sizzle. A *zap*. The air was scorchingly electric . . . at least to Reese.

The question was, did Brian feel it, too? "Well, I should get moving," he said quickly.

"Oh, yeah, okay," she said, inadvertently clutching some of her thick hair to channel the sudden tension.

"Brock!" Tina called. Reese whipped around guiltily, but Tina didn't appear annoyed. "Would you take in the sign? It's supposed to rain, and Darcy doesn't want it to get ruined."

"Sure, no problem," Reese said too brightly, and turned to Brian. "C'mon, I'll walk out with you."

Once they were on the sidewalk, Brian motioned to the oversize, clunky Roland & Fisk sidewalk sign. "*That*?" he said. "They want *you* to take that in?"

Grinning, Reese nodded. "I know, little ol' me."

Brian's eyes appeared lighter outside—almost like tiger eyes. He said, "Well, let me help you—Jesus." He moved to the left side of the sign, and Reese was about to tell him no, when he picked the entire thing up himself. Her mouth dropped open, and he asked, "Where do you want it?"

"Just right inside," she said quickly, and pulled the door open for him.

He set it down in the store entryway. "Is here okay?" She nodded dumbly. "Good," he said, not sounding the least bit winded.

"Brian, that was so nice of you," she said sincerely. "You didn't have to do that."

He made an incredulous sound like *psfft*, and she smiled. "Well, anyway . . . have a good one," he said, offering a short wave and turning to walk up the sidewalk.

"You, too," Reese called after him, "Bye!"

Just as she pivoted to go inside, Brian called to her. When she looked back, he was grinning. "I'll probably see you tomorrow."

Smiling and biting her lower lip at the same time, Reese offered a friendly expression that said, *Tomorrow, fine*, but inside, her mind was singing. The rest of the afternoon passed slowly, as she tried to put Brian Doren out of her mind and stay focused on her work—on coffee and customer service and tarts without cinnamon.

Suffice it to say, it was a hell of an effort.

The next morning, Reese flew down the stairs in a running-late frenzy. Oversleeping had left her barely enough time to get dressed, and hair brushing hadn't been an option, so she fastened a ponytail while she jogged into the kitchen.

Angela and Joanna were standing at the table, with their fists in dough and flour on their faces. They were cracking up about something that involved using twelve eggs instead of ten—obviously a private joke.

"Oh, hi!" Angela said cheerfully.

"H-hi, what's going on?"

"Angela's helping me with the DeMarco order. That is, if she can ever allow a batch to leave!!" Joanna said, nudging her in the arm. Angela giggled.

"But it's Friday," Reese said. "What about work?"

"Oh, um . . ." Angela shrugged guiltily. "I'm playing hooky."

"Okay, well, have fun," Reese said, grabbing a can of Diet Coke from the fridge. "I'll see you later."

"Wait, sweetheart, I packed you something to eat!" Joanna called, as Reese made her way down the front hall. Joanna caught up to her at the foot of the stairs and handed her a brown bag.

"Oh, you didn't have to do that."

"Listen, don't forget about tonight," her mother said breezily.

"Huh? What about tonight?" Reese asked.

Joanna blinked. "You're coming with me to the women's clubhouse to hang decorations for the annual Christmas party."

"I am? I didn't know that."

"Sweetheart, I told you that a while ago."

Usually her mother told her things a thousand times, so it made sense that Reese hadn't retained the information after being told merely once. "All right, but Ally's going too, right?"

"No, she has plans with Ben. You're not going outside like that, are you? You need to wear a coat; it's freezing out!"

"My coat's in the car—"

"You left your coat out in the freezing cold!"

"Mom, please, it's not even that cold out."

"It's *December*."

"Mom, I really don't have time for this. See ya later."

"Okay, okay."

Reese headed out the door. She turned back quickly to wave. Joanna waved back with one hand, and used the other to run up and down her arm in exaggerated shivering gestures.

"Bye!" Reese called brightly, still not cold, and hopped into her car.

Joanna had just gotten back to the kitchen when the phone rang. She picked it up, gushed her hellos, then handed the phone to Angela.

"Hello?"

"Hi." It was Drew.

"Hi, is everything all right?" she asked.

"Yeah, fine," he said through audible cell phone static. "Listen, sorry I forgot to tell you I had an early meeting this morning." That made her feel a little better. She'd woken up that morning to find him gone—no note, nothing. She'd almost burst into tears. Instead she'd called in sick and headed straight for her mother's. Yes, she really was thirty years old.

Drew was a business consultant who worked on different projects with varying companies, which was why he was able to take so much time off after his heart attack. He'd started working again only last month.

"That's okay," Angela said, walking into the pantry with the phone and closing the door behind her. "How did the meeting go?"

"It went fine. Remember that software company I told you about?" While he went on to give a brief description of his meeting, Angela took a seat on a large plastic barrel labeled *The Pretzel Keg*.

"How did you know I was here?" she asked after he finished.

"I called you at your office, and Cyn told me you weren't coming in. I tried our place, so I just assumed . . . Are you sick? I didn't know you weren't feeling well."

"No, I just didn't feel like going today," she said truthfully.

"Oh."

"Yeah."

Silence. She sighed and looked around the pantry and wondered if it would ever be normal between them again.

"Well, I guess I'll get going," he said. "I have another meeting in twenty minutes."

"Okay . . . Drew?"

"Yeah?"

"Um . . . nothing."

"I should go."

"Yeah, okay."

"Love you," he said quickly.

"Me, too," she managed, and after they hung up, she hugged the phone to her chest and whispered into the emptiness, "So much."

Chapter Thirteen

"Let's go over it one more time."

Reese and Rhoda had been training the new girl, Amy, for the past three hours. Amy remained eager to please, but Reese had to stifle her twelfth yawn in twenty minutes. It wasn't Amy's fault; the register *was* confusing. And Rhoda's cryptic, pompous directives didn't exactly expedite the comprehension process.

"Okay, so, lemme see if I have this right," Amy said hesitantly, holding a scanner in one hand, and a discounted hardcover in the other. "For sale books, I type in zero-zero-one."

"Right," Rhoda said, nodding. "Same code for the mass-market paperbacks. For trade paperbacks, type in zero-zero-two."

Amy scrunched her forehead. "I'm sorry—what's the difference between the mass-market and trade paperbacks?"

"Oh, well," Rhoda scoffed righteously, "trade paperbacks are just *way* better books. They're the higher-quality, more intelligent types of books." Amy nodded vacantly. "See, the mass markets are, let us say, not too stellar—you know, from a *literary* perspective." Amy looked more confused than before. So Rhoda continued to "clarify." "You know, think of all the incredibly vapid mystery novels we sell."

"Oh, I love mysteries!" Amy said, obviously not getting that "vapid" wasn't a good thing.

Rhoda recoiled as if she had fleas, and Reese finally interceded. Straightening up from her slouch, she said, "Amy, the mass markets are usually smaller, and their ISBN numbers are printed on the inside front cover. Trade paperbacks are bigger, with the ISBN on the back. Also, they feel more like this." She handed one over for Amy to touch.

"Oh, I get it now, that's easy!" Amy sounded very relieved that she didn't have to determine on the spot whether or not a customer's purchase was "high-quality."

At that moment, Reese was experiencing a particularly strong urge to tell Rhoda just how full of baloney she was. But she realized that most of her irritability stemmed from the fact that she hadn't had coffee before work. Not to mention that as soon as she had entered the break room that morning, Darcy had accosted her. Barging out of her office (closing and bolting the door immediately behind her), she'd adjusted one of the pastel butterfly clips that ran in grooves down her scalp, and barked, *"You!"*

Reese had barely gotten out, "Me, what?" when Darcy had rolled her eyes and started singing, "Hello, Brock! Wake *up*—you're on the *clock*." And after that, she'd ordered Reese to conduct register training with Rhoda, and return to café duty when they had finished.

Amy was the real victim in this, of course. The

poor sucker, she really had no idea what she was in for. She'd even made the comment that Darcy seemed "really cool." Reese knew that it wouldn't take Darcy long to show her true colors, and when she did, Amy was in for the disillusionment of a lifetime. In other words, standard Roland & Fisk initiation.

"Okay, I think we're done," Rhoda said, fiddling with one of her immense hoop earrings. "Do you have any more questions?" Her bored tone of voice must have deterred Amy, who shook her head no, but still had stressfully pinched eyebrows.

Reese said, "Well, if you're confused about anything, definitely ask me. I'll be over in the café." Amy smiled and gave thanks. Rhoda did not jump to offer the same accessibility. A few minutes later, Reese headed to the café.

As she took a shortcut through the New Age section, a man approached her. "Excuse me?" he said angrily, "I noticed that this store only has two books on hypnotherapy."

"Oh . . ."

"Well, here's what I think of your store!" he barked, and swept his hand along one shelf, sending eight hardcovers tumbling off and clattering onto the floor.

One slammed right onto Reese's foot. "Ow!" she yelped. As the man stormed off, Reese hopped in place and frowned in pain until her nerve endings numbed. Then she stooped to pick up the books, sighing in frustration with all of the crackpots in this city who insisted on doing their shopping at Roland & Fisk.

So much for a shortcut, Reese thought, and bustled limpingly on to the café.

She spotted Brian right away. He was reading the paper, but his mug and soup bowl were pushed out in front of him, indicating that he was finished with them. That made her look up at the clock. Damn, it was even later than she'd thought.

Fortunately, there wasn't much of a crowd in the café, so she stole a moment to go say hi. "Hey," she said as she approached Brian's table.

He looked up from his paper and smiled. "Hey. I wasn't sure if you were working today."

Her heart kicked up. *He was looking for me—wondering about me.* "Yeah, I had to work at the register for a while."

"How's it going?" he asked.

Better now, more nerve-racking, but definitely better.

"Want to sit down?" he asked her.

Yes, she would *love* to sit down, and preferably on his lap. But when she pictured that happening, and Brian screaming in pain, the fantasy quickly passed. "Well, I was gonna start my shift," she said, motioning toward the counter with a loose, *who cares* gesture. Then she realized that she had worked four hours already, and was eligible to take her break. "Hold on a sec," she said, as she shuffled over to the counter.

Tina was breaking rolls of quarters into the cash drawer—brutally slamming and shattering each one. She did it with such military precision and intensity that Reese truly hated to interrupt. "Hey, Brock! How ya doing?"

"Okay."

"We missed you this morning. I had Marnie fill in but it just wasn't the same." Tina shook her head and blasted another roll open against the side of the drawer. "The girl's helpless with a marble loaf, that's for sure." Then she slammed the drawer shut, unwittingly so hard that the whole cash register vibrated and the display case rattled.

"Um, Tina? Do you mind if I take my break now? I know I just got here, but I've been training with Rhoda for, like, four hours."

"Four hours working with Rhoda?" Tina said, sounding disgusted. "You deserve a break after that bullshit!" She punched Reese in the shoulder in a gesture of friendship.

Reese wobbled, and held back a wince of pain. "Thanks a lot; I really appreciate it."

"No problem," Tina said, and started stacking baking pans (the metal clinked and clanged and echoed). Meanwhile Reese poured herself a cup of coffee and headed back to the seating area, hoping Brian was still there.

He was. And he looked as handsome as ever, too, in his navy work shirt, gray tie, and charcoal pants. Reese made her way over to him, eyeing his legs and doing her ultra*cazh* act.

"Hi," she said, smiling, and sat down.

"Hey, how was the register?" he asked.

Instinctively, Reese stuck her tongue out. Then she sucked it right back in, realizing how immature that must look.

But he just chuckled. "This store doesn't seem to . . . what's the word I'm looking for? Fulfill you." He grinned, and a laugh slipped from Reese's throat.

"Hmm, I must not be as subtle as I thought," she said, grinning back at him. "So how do you feel about your job? Does it fulfill you?"

Shrugging, he said, "Yeah, I guess it's all right."

She pushed for more information because to her, it wasn't just small talk. She wanted to know every possible thing about him. "So what's it like to be a structural engineer?"

Brian leaned back in his chair. "Well, what would you like to know?"

"Hmm . . . What's a day in the life?"

"Well, let's see." He ran his hand along his jaw, as if trying to come up with an interesting way to sum up his job. "I don't know, right now I'm working on a pretty big development project."

"Really?" Reese leaned forward with interest, and clasped her coffee cup to give her idle hands something to do. "What's the project?" she asked.

"It's called Project Blue," he explained, "It's a plan to develop a corporate complex uptown."

"Ah . . . I see." She figured the world had enough corporate complexes, but hey, he had to make a living. "So how far along is it?"

"Oh, my team's still in the planning stages."

"Your team?"

"Yeah. I'm team leader on the project."

He said it very offhandedly, as if it were nothing special, but Reese heard an edge of pride in his voice. She grinned, toying with the idea that he might want to impress her—maybe he didn't, but she let herself think it was a possibility, and smiled into her next sip.

"What?" he said, letting his elbows rest flat on the table.

"Oh, nothing. I was just thinking. So, you mentioned the other night that you worked for Manhattan C and S. How long have you been working there?"

"A little over two years," he said. "Before that I worked for a small firm downtown."

"Oh, are you from New York originally?"

He shook his head. "Boston."

"No way!" she said, pushing her coffee to the side, because she no longer needed the crutch. She could talk about Boston till she was blue in the face.

"Yeah, you've been there?" he asked.

"I went to BC," she replied.

"BC, really? Did you like it?"

"Are you kidding? After I graduated, I lay around in my robe for six months, staring into space, saying, 'I can never go home again.' My mom was freaking out." Reese stopped just short of admitting how many Price Club sacks of Oreos had helped to weather the crisis.

"I was majorly disillusioned with life after college, I guess," she went on. "You know, like a *St. Elmo's Fire* kind of thing." Brian looked confused for a moment, then nodded. "So is your family still in Boston?" she asked.

"Well, my younger sister, Danny, is, but my parents moved to Florida a while ago." Abruptly his eyes darkened just a little, and his shoulders seemed to stiffen. He sighed. "Actually, Danny's sort of having a tough time lately—"

"Bro-ock!"

Not now, not now.

"So *here* you are!" Darcy wailed.

"Yeah, what do you need?" Reese asked, feeling annoyed.

Darcy looked at Brian, and started licking her frosty lips and trying to pout at the same time. She looked vaguely like a frog trying to loosen a poppy seed. Not a pretty picture.

"Darcy?"

"Huh? Oh, right. I wanted to know if you were the one who flooded the employee bathroom this morning."

WHAT! Of course she hadn't. And did Darcy have to put that image in Brian's head?

"Well?"

"No, I didn't," Reese replied with steely calm.

Darcy tilted her head to the side, squinting suspiciously. "Are you *sure*, because—"

"Darcy," Reese said sharply, "I don't even know what you're talking about. And to be honest, I think this is really out of line, especially since I still have ten minutes left on break."

Darcy seemed taken aback by that one. But then, most despots were clueless about little things like employee rights and labor laws. Tugging on the hem of her lavender baby tee, and bringing it even tighter across her breasts, Darcy screeched, "Reey-eer!" and made a clawing motion with her hand.

Reese shot a look at Brian, who was looking back at her, his eyes locking with hers, as if sharing a sense of the ridiculous, as if totally unimpressed with Darcy and her breast trick and her bitchiness.

Darcy turned on her platform heel and charged over to the counter. Good, if anyone could deal with her it was Tina.

"Oh, God," Reese said after she'd left, "she is so annoying." She shook her head and covered her eyes with her hand.

Brian chuckled. "That's an understatement. How do you stand it?"

Reese shrugged. "I guess I try to see the humor. Well, some of the time. Most of the time I wallow in self-pity."

"Hey, not to change the subject," he said quietly, "but do you know that guy over there?" Reese followed the direction of his eyes. *Oh, yuck!* It was that creepy customer from the other day! "He keeps looking over here," Brian said.

"Looking over" didn't begin to cover it. He was standing at the milk bar, stirring his coffee over and over, round and round, while he kept a fixed gaze on Reese and a closemouthed smirk on his dissipated face. *This, I need.*

"No," Reese said finally, "I don't *know* him, know him. I just served him the other day." After a beat, she whispered, "Is he still looking over here?"

"Uh . . . yeah."

As she stole another look, the man deepened the smirk—making him look somewhere between lovesick and mentally sick. A familiar old woman hobbled up to him from behind. "What's taking you so long?" she nagged. "My corns are hurting!"

"*Mother!*" He pressed his mouth into a tight, furious line before shouting, "Can't you ever be quiet! I *hate* when you do this!" He slammed his coffee down on the milk bar and stormed out of the café; his mother trailed behind, appearing unaffected and clueless.

"So, looks like you've got a new boyfriend," Brian teased.

Reese laughed and plunked her head down on the table. "Great," she mumbled, "just what I always wanted." Brian laughed.

"What do you think *you're* doing!" Darcy yelled. Reese shot up automatically, but for a twist, it wasn't her being scolded. It was Elliot, who was just sitting down at a vacant table. "What are *you* doing out here?" Darcy shrilled. "I *told* you to shelve the new dog-care books and I want it done *now*."

Brian muttered, "Jesus Christ. Tight ship."

"I've gotta go help Elliot," Reese said apologetically as she glanced up at the clock. "I still have a few minutes left of my break."

Brian looked surprised; then he smiled warmly at her like she was the sweetest person on earth. *Please.* If he knew half the raunchy things she'd dreamed about him, he wouldn't think she was so sweet. But for now, let him think that.

He stood up with her. "Actually, what am I doing still sitting here? I've gone on about my job, and now I'll probably get fired if I keep taking long lunches like this."

He shrugged on his coat, and Reese tried not to stare at the broadness of his shoulders as they were covered.

They walked a few feet together—from the shiny wood floor down the steps onto the shimmery green carpet of the store. Then Reese leaned in closer than she probably should have. "Well, thanks for hanging out with me on my break," she said, smiling up at Brian.

Abruptly, he seemed to pull back.

His voice was a little distant when he replied, "Yeah, um, it was good seeing you. Bye-bye." Giving her a quick smile, he walked briskly out of the store.

Strange. Reese couldn't put her finger on it—yes, she knew they were friendly with each other, and nothing more, but still . . . there was something different in Brian's demeanor just now. Something guarded, as though he were establishing the casualness of their relationship.

Of course! she realized, suddenly feeling like a fool. Brian must have picked up on Reese's strong attraction to him, despite her attempts to hide it. Now he was trying to make sure that she wouldn't get the wrong idea.

God, was there anything worse than being pitied? Reese sighed as she made her way to the pets section to find Elliot. *Wrong idea.* Yes, that pretty much summed up her love life. In fact, if it ever was the *right* idea, she'd probably die of shock.

Chapter Fourteen

Joanna was getting in a little *Wedding Story* before she and Reese headed to the Goldwood women's clubhouse. "Now look at him," she was saying, standing by the television and pointing to the frumpy man on the screen. "Yes, maybe he's not a 'stud,' as you two would say, but he's obviously a sweet guy who'll make a good husband."

"I guess," Ally hedged, buttoning her long velour coat. "But his voice . . ."

"What about it?"

"It's all nasally; you didn't notice? Besides, I question his preferences in life."

Reese laughed from her perch on the stone half-wall that separated the family room and the kitchen. Joanna sighed, exasperated. "Oh, there's no talking to you two. You're both so superficial. Here's a solid, nice guy—"

"How can you possibly know that?" Ally said, rolling her eyes. "What else is he gonna say on television? 'I like depravity and misogyny—as much as I can get.' I don't think so."

"Well, *she* certainly couldn't wait to get her hooks

in," Joanna argued, referring to the frumpy man's betrothed.

"Face it, Mom," Reese said, shifting to dangle her legs off the ledge, "the guys on this show just don't do it for us. It's nothing personal."

"Well, then, who does 'do it' for you?" Joanna asked pointedly, no longer lumping Ally and Reese together, but directly addressing Reese. The message was perfectly clear: It was okay for Ally to be superficial as long as she had Ben.

Just then the phone rang. "I'll get it," Ally said. "It might be about my dress." She darted into the kitchen and grabbed the receiver on the third ring. "Hello? Oh, yes, who's calling? Oh, *hi*. Hang on." She brought the phone over to Reese and whispered, *"It's Kenneth. When do I get to meet him?"*

Reese ignored the question and took the phone. "Hello?"

"Yes, hello." It was Kenneth, all right—no missing the effusive, downright lovey-dovey greeting. "Am I interrupting anything?"

"Oh, no, no," she replied, twining the phone cord around her finger as she walked into the pantry. "What's up?"

"Oh, nothing in particular," he said. "How is your work going? Your work for Professor Kimble, that is?"

"Um . . . okay. I don't know; I'm trying not to think about it too much over break."

Did she have to draw this guy a *picture*? One of Kimble, his book, and then a circle with a line through it?

"So, what have you been up to?" she asked, trying to shift the conversation to something less agonizing. After all, Kenneth was on break, too. Surely he must have been doing some fun things. Playing sports, catching a movie, reading some good books . . . *anything*.

"Not too much."

Reese sighed quietly, and racked her brain to come up with something else to say. It hadn't always been this strained between them; in the beginning they'd discussed a lot of getting-to-know-you things. But over the past few weeks . . . well, maybe she was being especially picky now that she'd spent two afternoons talking to Brian Doren.

"Well, I was calling to invite you to dinner tomorrow evening," Kenneth said, breaking her reverie. "Yes . . . I would really like to take you out for a nice dinner."

Reese blinked. It sounded like Kenneth was actually taking some initiative here. First he'd called her without her calling first, and now he was asking her out for Saturday night, which definitely implied "romantic evening."

Hmm . . . Reese couldn't help feeling mildly intrigued. Maybe Kenneth had noticed her significant dip in interest, and now was trying to make up for it. He was always so stoic and reserved, Reese couldn't help being curious whether he was really capable of pursuing someone.

"Tomorrow night?" she finally said. "Yeah, okay, that sounds great." She'd never been good at hard-to-get, so she wouldn't attempt it now. "Did you want me to come into the city?" *Please say no.* She didn't have to work at Roland & Fisk over the weekend, and she'd rather not make the drive.

"No, no, that won't be necessary," he said. "If you give me directions to your house, I will drive there. Perhaps we can have dinner at a restaurant near you."

"Okay, sure," Reese replied energetically, figuring that Kenneth needed his assertive behavior positively reinforced. "I know a great Italian place, if you want, or—"

"Yes, that will be fine. Well, I really should get going. If you could, please e-mail me directions from school."

"Oh, sure. Definitely."

"Thank you. Good-bye."

"Bye," Reese said, thinking, *Life just got a little less predictable.*

As she exited the pantry, she found Ally and Joanna in the kitchen waiting with bated breath. "Well?" Joanna said, her eyes huge and hopeful. "Come on, don't keep us in suspense! What, *what*?"

"Mom, beg *off*—you're panting," Ally said, and looked at Reese. "So what's the deal?"

Reese set the receiver in its cradle and shrugged. "It's no big deal. He just asked me out to dinner tomorrow night, and I said yes."

Joanna clapped her hands in rapid succession and exclaimed, "Oh! A date! This is so wonderful; you and he are back on track!" She threw her arms around Reese. "Whatever you're doing, honey, *keep doing it.*"

Reese managed a faint half smile. She could always count on her mother's encouragement to be deluded, sexist, and just plain warped.

"Will this torture ever *end*?"

"Sweetheart, we've only been here two hours," Joanna said breezily, handing her another bulbous, shiny ornament that weighed a ton.

"But we've been doing all the work," Reese said, setting the final gold ball on the durable string of garland she'd hung around the activities room of the Goldwood clubhouse. "Where's everyone else?" she asked as she climbed down the ladder.

"I guess they're still in the kitchen enjoying the coffee and doughnuts I brought."

"Way to go, Mom," Reese said, grinning, as her feet touched down on the hardwood floor. She wiped her hands on her jeans and looked around. Not bad at all. The Christmas decorations were done, and the immense tree in the corner, glittering with tinsel and lights, needed only one thing.

"Okay, I'll put the star on the tree; then I need a break."

"All right, that sounds fair," Joanna said. They hauled the ladder over to the tree and leaned it against the wall. Reese climbed it shakily with the heavy glass star tucked under her right arm. When she was finally on eye-level with the treetop, she leaned sideways to set the star in place.

"Oh, be careful, sweetheart!" Joanna called from below.

"I . . . will," she eked out, as she tilted dangerously over and set the star in place. Once she'd climbed back down the ladder, she and Joanna walked down the wooded hallway into the kitchen. It was a large, clean room with shiny stainless steel and white tile everywhere she looked. Several club members were parked around the long table in the center, going to town on the coffee and doughnuts.

"Joanna!" Mrs. Claflin called, and motioned with a cruller. "Come sit with us; you've been working so hard!"

"Yes, sit, sit," some of the others said.

Joanna smiled, demuring the compliment, and took a seat next to Mrs. McBride—Lane's mother—who said, "Ooh, Reese, be a hon and put a fresh pot on, will you? Since you're up."

"Um, sure," Reese said, even though she'd been eyeing a free chair next to Mrs. Colby.

"So, Reese, your mother tells us you're working toward your Ph.D.," Remmi Collindyne said casually.

"Mmm-hmm, yes, I am," Reese replied, as she put a fresh filter in the pot. When she glanced over her shoulder, she saw her mom positively beaming with pride.

"Ooh, how interesting!" Mrs. McBride chimed. "How much longer till you get it?"

"Um . . ."

"Well, it all depends on her dissertation," Joanna said enthusiastically. "If she gets that done soon, she'll be a 'doctor' in no time. As it is, she's been earning *straight* As."

She must have meant "straight" in terms of the grades she selectively remembered.

"Ooh, wo-ow," Mrs. McBride crooned, "aren't you just so *smart*!"

"Reese, your mother also tells us you're dating a man in your program," Remmi said, biting into a frosted doughnut.

"Well—"

"Yes, she is," Joanna gushed, "and he's quite a dreamboat!" Now Reese lost all desire to sit—she just wanted to retch—while her mother launched into a testimonial that rendered Kenneth eligible for canonization any day now.

Reese tuned out a lot of it, and focused solely on the rhythmic drip of the percolator.

"And after she earns her Ph.D.," Joanna was saying, as Reese carried the pot to the table, "she's going to teach college. But I've always said that would be a perfect career for her, because academics, like most other things, come so naturally to her."

"Although I'm still not sure if I want to teach college," Reese said casually to the table. "I might, but I'm still deciding what I want to do."

"But whatever she decides, she'll be a shoo-in with that Ph.D.," Joanna said briskly.

Sure, Reese would've liked to amend, "*If* I get that Ph.D.," but she wouldn't do that in front of her mother's friends. She just wished that damn degree didn't mean so much to her.

"So, Reese, is it really serious with this boy you're dating?" Mrs. Beacon asked.

"Well, to be honest . . . I don't really know." Joanna shot her a scandalized look. "I mean . . . I'm not sure exactly how I feel about him." Joanna paled. "I'm just at a confusing point in my life right now," Reese qualified but got the distinct feeling she was digging herself deeper. She darted an eye down at her mother, who looked somewhere between perplexed and in pain. Reese didn't want to make it any worse, so she said, "Um . . . I guess I don't know what I'm trying to say."

The women around the table chuckled. Soon they were saying patronizing things like, "Ah, to be that young again," and Joanna was back to beaming. Now her daughter was a hit.

Reese just stood there smiling feebly, because . . . hell, what else could she do?

Brian had been on the phone with Veronica no more than twenty minutes, but it felt like longer. Much longer. She was still telling him about her day, and he was guiltily not hearing most of it. He hadn't meant not to listen—his focus just kept drifting to thoughts of Reese Brock.

She was so sweet to give up the last minutes of her break to help her friend, Elliot. And it was so cute how Reese played off her doctoral fellowship at Crewlyn College like it was no big deal, when in fact it was damned impressive. He wasn't sure why he'd ended things so abruptly today, except that he'd been feeling guilty. Although he and Veronica weren't back together, they seemed to be heading toward a full reconciliation and . . .

He just didn't know.

Christ, what the hell is with me? Thirty fucking years old and he still hadn't figured out how to fill the hole inside him—the emptiness that crept into his consciousness at the most unlikely times. Like when he was in the middle of the most chaotic day at work, or running from meeting to meeting with a hardly a moment to think—it would just hit him.

But in the past few days, he'd felt different—elevated, invigorated. It was as if that night on the Brocks' love seat had stoked a fire in him that was still going strong. And he liked the feeling. He liked *Reese* . . . with an intensity he hadn't felt in a long time. She was so easy to talk to—so fun to talk to. So goddamn *sexy*.

A vivid picture of her came into his mind: adorable and bright with gorgeous green eyes, a full pink mouth, one very luscious ass. . . .

"Brian?"

"What?"

"Brian, you're not even listening to me!" Veronica cried. "I was telling you about the new student in my on-toe class."

"Oh . . . no, I heard you."

"Then what did I say?" God, he hated this game. "Uh-huh, that's what I thought," she added bitterly.

He sighed, because he knew she was right, and he didn't know what to say to make it better. Frankly, he *hadn't* been listening, and he couldn't say he was too curious about what he'd missed.

Veronica sulked for a moment, and then started saying something about the winter recital, using lots of technical terms, and, for some reason, it annoyed him. Had she once asked about *his* job?

Not that he wanted to talk about his job, but still . . . She could've at least asked about Danny.

"So when am I going to see you?"

"Uh—"

"How about this weekend?" she pressed. "Brian, I really want us to get together and talk about the relationship."

He held back a sigh. "Uh . . . lemme think . . . this weekend, this weekend . . ."

"Well, what about some night this coming week?" she persisted.

"This week's kind of busy, if you want to know the truth. Project Blue's sort of kicking my ass right now."

"That figures," she said testily. "You and your job—as always."

"No, Veronica, it's not like that—"

"So, then, when? I want us to *talk*."

Finally, they made a tentative date for the week after next and, after a little more bickersome conversation, said good-night. Brian had to face the fact that he was getting more annoyed with Veronica than was fair. She really hadn't said or done anything out of character, and he'd found her character fine enough to be with for eight long years.

It was as though he were *looking* to find fault. But why?

Ultimately, he didn't search very long for answers; he simply flopped into bed.

Within minutes, he fell into a deep sleep that featured rapid eye movement and Reese Brock naked. His dreams were carnal and dirty, and the things she did to him with that full mouth hardened his dick like a rock and made him *ache*.

The night didn't last nearly long enough.

Chapter Fifteen

While Brian was tossing in bed, Reese was typing like a maniac. She'd been hit with an amazing surge of energy after she'd gotten home from the clubhouse, so she'd booted up her laptop and actually started writing. So far, she had five pages down.

Ironically, trying to explain to her mom's friends what she wanted to do with her life had strengthened her resolve. But it wasn't just that. She had noticed a change in her outlook over the past week. Her spirits were brighter, more positive, more driven, and she felt younger. Like the whole world lay in front of her. Like her life was out there waiting to happen.

Her cell phone rang. Startled, she glanced at her clock: 1:45 A.M. Who on earth could be calling her now? She hopped up from her desk and took her phone off the nightstand. Angela's number lit up on the display screen.

Flipping her phone open, Reese said, "Hi, is everything okay?"

"Yeah, fine. Why?"

"Just because it's late. How come you're not asleep?"

"Oh, did I wake you?" Angela said obliviously. "What time is it, anyway?"

"Almost two. You didn't wake me, though. I was up working on something."

"What?"

Reese debated for a few seconds, not wanting to jinx her newfound industriousness, but then decided to come clean. "Actually," she said, taking a seat on her bed, "you know how I always used to talk about writing a novel?"

"Yeah. Back when you were in college, right?"

"Uh-huh. Well, I'm sort of doing it now. Or trying to. Well, I just started."

"Oh, cool! How much do you have? What's it about? When can I read it?"

"I don't know," Reese said. "I mean, I don't know if it's gonna go anywhere, or if I'll finish it. I only have five pages so far."

"Oh, okay," Angela said, backing off. "That's cool, though. You're so lucky—at least you know what you want to do with your life. Anyway, keep me posted."

"I will. What are you doing up, anyway?" Reese climbed under her comforter and curled into the always gratifying fetal position. "Can't sleep?"

"Nah. I'm watching Nick at Night. *Taxi*'s on next, I think."

"Oh. Where's Drew?" Reese asked casually.

"He's in bed. I'm in the living room."

"So how are things, by the way? You know, between you two?"

"Same," she replied. She definitely didn't sound

like she wanted to hash it out at the moment, so Reese let that subject go, and heard the *Taxi* theme music playing in the background. A moment later Angela grumbled, "Oh, great, I just saw this one."

Reese wished she knew how to advise her sister, who was clearly depressed about Drew and her job, but she knew Angela would want to ask herself.

Just then, the call waiting beeped. *What the hell?* Reese had virtually no life these days, and now two calls in the middle of the night?

"Hold on. Believe it or not, it's the other line." She clicked over. "Hello?"

"Reese? I'm glad I caught you at a good time." What? It couldn't *possibly* be. Kimble!

"Professor? It's sort of late." *You freak!*

"Yes, I realize that, but I was very alarmed when I saw you hadn't included something in the chapter you left for me to review."

"Oh . . . I didn't?" Gee, how could he tell? Reese was sure that all of Kimble's "arguments" mirrored each other, but apparently not—apparently he actually had a method to his pronounced madness. "What did I miss?"

"I specifically remember mentioning my new theory about historical documents and how they translate history into the written word. Where was that?"

Reese rolled over and threw the comforter over her head. "I guess I forgot," she said on a sigh. "You know, Professor, it is sort of late. Can you e-mail me tomorrow—"

"Well, I'd like to get a couple notes to you while I have you on the line," he stated boldly and, of course, unapologetically.

Reese mumbled a dejected, "Hold on," then clicked back over to Angela. "Hello?"

"Hi, who was it?"

"Actually, it's Professor Kimble."

"*What?*"

"I gotta go," she said miserably.

Sympathetically, Angela said, "I'm sorry. Men are such losers. Which reminds me—have fun on your date tomorrow night."

Reese almost laughed.

Angela crept through the blackened bedroom, using the single stream of moonlight peering through a crooked blind to find her bed. She climbed into it carefully, so she wouldn't wake Drew, who was rolled over on his side, with his face buried between their pillows.

Sliding under the covers, she shifted a little to get comfortable, and that was when she heard and felt Drew shifting, too. In fact, he wrapped his arm around her, snuggling up against her side and pulling her close. Lifting his head, he moved it to rest on her pillow, and now she could feel the light waft of his breath on her temple.

She figured he was dead asleep and had no clue what he was doing, so the affectionate gesture didn't really mean much. She tried to turn onto her side without rocking the bed, and that was when Drew moved them both into a deep spooning position and kissed her neck. Experimentally, she ran her fingers down the forearm that was hugging her—and he tightened his hold.

Then he whispered, "I love you."

She whispered back, "I love *you*," and lifted his hand up to kiss his knuckles. And then she heard the soft, even sound of his breathing as he slept.

"Maybe this wasn't such a good idea."

"What are you talking about? It's a fabulous idea."

Somehow Reese doubted it. She still didn't know how Ally had managed to talk her into coming with her to the Goldwood Fitness Center. Reese hadn't worked out at a gym for so long, and it had to be for a reason.

"Oh! Wanna try the Butt Blaster?" Ally said, excited. "It's new; it's really cool!"

"No," Reese said emphatically. "I told you, I'm just gonna stick with the treadmill."

Ally shrugged. "Okay. Hey, Cora," she said to the young woman behind the sign-in desk. "How's it going?"

"Oh, hi, Ally," she said, smiling, and then eyed Reese. Her brow arched quizzically. "Are you new?"

"This is my sister, Reese," Ally said. "She's coming as my guest." Cora ran her eyes up and down over Reese's body blatantly. By her expression, she didn't seem bowled over by the gray sweatpants and long-sleeved T-shirt with a crab decal and the caption *I'm a little crabby.*

"C'mon," Ally said, and tugged on Reese's hand. "Oh! I'll show you the Gravitron—"

"Hold it right there."

They turned and found a petite middle-aged man, with a grayish balding head and a neon-green parachute suit. He was holding a clipboard, gracing Reese with a bland smile, and not bothering to introduce himself. "We like to get some preliminary information before nonmembers use the equipment," he said, coming closer, studying Reese, and then jotting something down. "Now, what's your height and weight?"

"Um, actually, I'm just here for the day, so—"

"But you'll be using the equipment, right?" he asked a little petulantly as he jotted something else down on his clipboard.

"Well, just the treadmill," she replied, inching away from him. "I'm her guest," she said, looking to her side . . . and not finding Ally there. Reese spun her head, trying to see where her sister had gone, and then give her the evil eye for abandoning her. "Well, she was here a minute ago. . . ." Then she spotted her about fifteen feet away, standing next to a mammoth machine labeled, *The Sonic Bulkalizer.* She was talking to two well-built guys who appeared to be swooning. Meanwhile, Reese was still inching.

"I'd say you're about five-three; is that right?" the man with the clipboard asked.

"Yeah, I am, well, thanks for asking—"

"And your weight?" he pressed on, his bland expression changing to impatient. Jeez, couldn't he let it die already? She didn't *know* her exact weight, and she didn't want to. She came here to feel better about herself, not worse.

"I really don't know the exact figures. So, thanks," she said, turning away.

"Well, before you head to the machines, I need to get your weight."

"Why?" she nearly snapped. Sounding defensive

hadn't been part of her plan, but it usually came pretty naturally. Anyway, how would he like it if she asked his follicle count?

He sighed and gently nudged her toward the tall scale against the wall.

She shrank at his touch, and was just about to yell harassment, when he said, "Step up, please." What could she do? Make a huge scene and shout, "No means *no!*"? Ally would love that. They'd have to leave because Ally had driven them. Not to mention, the story would haunt Reese forever. And, if she wasn't mistaken, Cora from the front desk was coming to the wedding. But then, who *wasn't*?

"Step *up*, please," he repeated, annoyed.

Swallowing tremulously, Reese set one foot on the scale platform. "Wait," she said quickly, "shouldn't I take off my shoes?" He shook his head, and jotted. Bringing the other foot to join the first, she waited as the man tried to balance the scale and get a reading. *Relax*, she told herself, *what's the big deal?* She was being silly. It wasn't like these numbers were going to be a matter of public record. The man was a discreet professional, after all.

"One-thirty-six!" he yelled at the top of his lungs. Reese's face got embarrassingly hot, and she all but jumped off the scale. She supposed she could point out—loudly—that she still had her sneakers on, and that she questioned the authenticity of the calibration, but . . . really, the damage was already done. Not that having her weight broadcast was a tragedy; it was just the principle.

"Hmm . . ." the man was saying as he examined her "chart." Nodding, he elaborated. "Yeah, you're gonna wanna reduce that high end." Huh? If he meant lose some fucking weight, she knew *that* already.

"Okay, um, can I go find my sister now?" Reese asked uncomfortably.

"First we need to go over your short-term and long-term goals. At the Goldwood Fitness Center, we offer—"

"Look, I'm a hands-on kind of person, okay? If I'm gonna join this facility, I need to try it out for myself." Before she lost her nerve, Reese turned around and left the man standing there. She'd say he was extremely judgmental for a short, graying baldy with a paunch—not that she was still bitter about that whole scale thing. Really.

She met up with Ally just as she was saying goodbye to the two guys she'd been talking to. "Oh, Reese! There you are."

"Uh, yeah, here *I* am." Ally didn't catch Reese's snide tone, which was just as well. Reese was feeling every bit like her long-sleeved T-shirt right now, and it really wasn't her sister's fault.

"Tony and Bill asked if we needed spots," Ally said brightly.

"Spots for what?"

"For the machines. I'm gonna use the Turbo Toner first. What about you?"

"I told you, I'm just using the treadmill," Reese reminded her.

"Oh, that's right. Okay, well, I'll see you in a little bit," Ally headed off to the right, and Reese headed to the left, hearing in the background people calling to her sister, saying hello, and asking if she was excited about the wedding. They were mostly guys.

Her little sister was right; this place was a real pickup scene. *Ugh.* Reese just hoped she didn't have to deal with getting hit on while she labored to keep a twenty-minute mile.

Well, no fear there. Almost half an hour went by, and not one single man approached her. And the Goldwood Fitness Center was definitely crawling with men. Young men. Preying men. Ally had stopped over once to say hi, and a trainer named Donny had come up to her to chat. She'd introduced him to Reese, whom he'd given the most perfunctory glance since Lane's boyfriend, Tom. What was wrong with her? It wasn't like Reese was interested in any of the guys at the gym, either, but still . . . it would've been nice if *somebody* attempted to talk to her.

Spoke too soon.

"Hey, you new around here?"

Reese looked over at the young man who'd just stepped onto the treadmill next to her. "Hi," she said, smiling amiably. "I'm just a guest."

"Oh, I'm hep."

"Sorry?" she said, unsure what he'd just said.

"What's your name?" he asked, grinning hugely. Reese noticed that his hair was slicked, winged out, and twirled on top like Elvis, and his T-shirt had a varsity letter stitched on it. Okay, so she didn't attract the regular guys at the gym—she attracted the *dorks* at the gym.

"Reese," she replied, shaking his hand.

"I'm rockabilly."

"Wha—I'm sorry, what was your name?"

"No . . . I mean, my name's Jim, but I'm rockabilly. You know, as in, I *am* rockabilly."

"I . . . okay," she said politely. And cluelessly.

"Haven't you heard of rockabilly?" Her guilty expression must have told him no. "You know, it's when a person's really into the fifties, but with their own modern twist on it." He shrugged. "Well, it's big in California."

"Oh," she said for lack of anything else.

"So how do you like this gym?" he asked. "I only come here because it's close to my house, but I can't stand the music they play here. I like the golden oldies, you know? Elvis, Dion, Buddy Holly."

"Yeah, I like Buddy Holly," Reese said.

"No, but I *like* Buddy Holly," Jim said, sounding suggestive. "I mean, I've got every track ever recorded, and pictures of him on my walls. Buddy Holly was the *man*."

Okay, so she didn't just attract the dorks, she attracted the latent-gay dorks. The Goldwood Fitness Center was doing wonders for her self-esteem.

"Hey, what are you doing after this?" he asked. "Feel like going back to my place, maybe listening to some forty-fives? Or maybe going somewhere to get a malted?"

Reese tried not to grimace. "Oh, you know what? I'm doing something with my sister. Actually, that reminds me." She stopped the walking belt abruptly, opting to skip the "cooldown." "I'm supposed to spot her now on the"—looking around, she selected at random—"Triangulating Combinator."

Rockabilly looked disappointed, but nodded and smiled broadly. "Sure, I'm hep."

She'd had a feeling he would be. "Okay, well, nice meeting you," she said brightly. "See you later." She hoped not. Finally Reese caught up with her sister at the drink machine. Ally was buying a Fresh Samantha for herself, and offered Reese one, too. Shaking her head, Reese pressed the Diet Coke button. Maybe she shouldn't have caffeine after a workout, but she was taking baby steps to self-improvement. Anyway, when it came right down to it, some habits were just too hard to break.

Chapter Sixteen

Reese had just finished putting Ally's perfume on her pulse points when the doorbell rang. Before darting down the stairs to beat her mother to the door, she stole a look at her reflection in her full-length mirror. She had settled on a long wool skirt, and brown high-heeled boots, with a formfitting, cream-colored vee-neck sweater. All in all, pretty conservative, but that had to be the best way to go with Kenneth.

Even though she took the steps two at a time, she was still too late.

"Oh, Reese, there you are, honey!" Joanna said, grinning enormously. Kenneth was standing politely beside her with his hands clasped in front of him, dressed in a button-down shirt and slacks and a tan winter jacket. His medium-brown hair was, as always, combed cleanly over, with a 1950s side part running perfectly down his head. Well, for a nerd, he was definitely good-looking.

As always, he was well shaved. In fact, Reese had *never* seen an errant whisker on his face, and had started to wonder if Kenneth actually grew hair there.

"Hi," she said, smiling at him as she tugged on

her purple leather jacket. "Well, we should probably get go—"

"Kenneth, are you hungry?" Joanna asked eagerly. "I have some food in the kitchen—"

"Mom, we're going to dinner," Reese interrupted quickly. "Well, come on, Ken—"

"Michael!" Joanna called out, beaming from ear to ear and holding up a finger so they'd stay right there. "Michael, come out here and meet Reese's young man! You've never met Reese's father, right, Kenneth?"

"I'm coming!" Michael called from his study. Within seconds he was joining everyone at the foot of the stairs, in a tweed sports coat with an unlit pipe dangling from his mouth. Extending his hand, he said, "Michael Brock. Good to meet you."

Kenneth hesitated for a second, then shook his hand in return, and stammered something like, "Yes, uh, pleasure." Then he cleared his throat—the transparency of which was getting ridiculous. Jeez, did *every* human interaction make him feel awkward?

Stop it, stop it. You're trying to give this a chance.

And why not? Kenneth was finally showing more initiative, which was what she'd said she wanted. He was there, romantically pursuing her, which was more than she could say for Brian, who seemed to view her only as his buddy at the café.

"Michael, this is Kenneth," Joanna said, because Kenneth hadn't.

"Kenneth," Michael repeated approvingly. "Pleasure."

"Okay, well, we're just gonna get going—"

"Wait, wait," Joanna ordered, holding up her finger again and going to the small bureau next to the grandfather clock. What was she doing . . . what on earth . . .

WHAT!

"I need to use up this film," she said, removing the lens cap from her clunky black camera. "Smile!"

"Mom!" Reese yelled—then softened her tone for the sake of company. "Mother, *please*. We don't have time for that."

"Nonsense, it'll just take a second!" Joanna sang merrily, looking through her camera and turning the lens from side to side.

"Joanna, maybe you should save that for another time," Michael advised.

"Okay, get a little closer together," Joanna said excitedly, ignoring her husband.

Meanwhile Reese felt like she was going to explode. This looked like the setup of the century. It looked like she put her mother *up* to this, for Pete's sake!

She glanced over at Kenneth, who appeared to be caught in a pale, dead stare as he began fumbling with the zippers on his jacket pockets. "Mom, *please*," Reese begged as she heard a click, and a burst of light zapped her vision.

"Okay, that's all!" Joanna said, holding up her hand in surrender. "I won't take any more—I just couldn't resist; you two are so cute! And you have such a great smile, honey!"

What smile? She'd obviously caught her in the midst of saying "please" with teeth gritted widely in desperation, and rationalized that it was a smile. Reese thought, *I can't believe I'm twenty-seven (and a half, damn it), and this is my life.*

But what was done was done. Now it was time to get the hell out of there. "Come on; let's go," she said, taking Kenneth's arm and leading him out the door.

"Bye, you two!" Joanna shouted, waving maniacally.

"Sorry about the photo shoot," Reese said dryly once they reached the driveway. Kenneth just cleared his throat again. "By the way," she added, "I don't mind driving us to the restaurant, since you drove in from the city—"

"Yes, that sounds good," he said, and not even gratefully, as she'd hoped he would be. Not that she was some sort of a martyr, but she'd hoped he'd be a *little* grateful.

She unlocked the passenger-side door for him, and he got in while she went around to her side. Once she was buckled in, she turned the key in the ignition, and music *blasted*.

"Oh!" she started as Kenneth jerked his shoulders against the back of the seat. Smiling sheepishly, Reese turned the volume down as Kenneth continued looking rattled to the point of annoyance.

"Sorry about that," she said lightly, and pulled out of her parents' driveway.

At Corelli's, the conversation stopped and stalled— over and over. As Reese finished up her salad greens, she attempted again. "So . . . seen any good movies?"

Kenneth waited until he was done methodically

chewing and swallowing before he replied, "I don't really enjoy going to the movies."

"You don't?" Reese said, surprised. "But we've gone to the movies a bunch of times."

"Oh, uh, yes, that's true. We have." He took a slow, slurping sip of his drink, while Reese processed this latest revelation. So all this time, Kenneth didn't like going to the movies. Yet in the two months they'd been casually dating, he'd taken her to the movies several times. Then again, she'd often suggested it, since Kenneth was rarely good at taking the lead. Could she have been reading his hints all wrong?

"However, I did rent an interesting film the other night," he said. "It used the premise of a controversial archeological dig to construct a social allegory. It was quite fascinating."

Reese couldn't help but smile. This was the brainy side of Kenneth she'd once found so attractive. He offered more analysis of the movie he'd seen, and for the first time in weeks, she was genuinely enjoying his company.

Maybe there was hope for them yet.

Reese was feeling so comfortable, in fact, that when Kenneth asked several moments later how her dissertation was coming along, she admitted to him that, frankly, it wasn't exactly bowling her over. "What do you mean?" he asked, clearly perplexed.

She shrugged. "I don't know . . . I'm just not that motivated to work on it right now."

"I . . . see," Kenneth said tonelessly.

"To tell you the truth," Reese continued, "sometimes I wonder if I'll even finish the program."

Kenneth's eyes shot wide with alarm. Suddenly Reese felt terribly exposed. She'd said too much.

Secretly, she'd been hoping for Kenneth's approval . . . or maybe she'd been testing him, in which case, he'd failed. Big-time.

"What do you mean, never finish?" Kenneth persisted. "Surely you wouldn't invest all this time at Crewlyn and not finish? Not to mention wasting fellowship funding so irresponsibly?"

Swallowing hard, Reese backpedaled. "Oh, no, you're right. I was . . . just exaggerating." Well, he'd made her feel like a major slug. True, she had been awarded a fellowship to study for her Ph.D. at Crewlyn, but it wasn't some effortless free ride. Both years she'd been there, she'd worked her butt off, keeping her grades high while assisting Professor Kimble and putting in double the hours per week she was stipended for. Maybe it was selfish, but as far as Reese was concerned, she didn't *owe* Crewlyn a degree.

Nevertheless, one thing was clear: If Kenneth was offended by her idea of leaving their program, she could never confide her fiction-writing aspirations. No way.

"Don't you like our graduate program?" he asked, refusing to let the topic drop.

"Um, yeah, sure, I like it," she lied.

"Haven't you enjoyed the courses you've taken? The diversified selection?"

What, did he moonlight in the admissions office? What did *he* care?

"Well, yeah . . . I suppose," Reese replied hesitantly. "But to tell you the truth . . . I don't find the courses all that diversified, actually. I mean, if I want to take an American history course, my only option is Professor Shamus. That's not right—there should be more than one professor in the whole department who can teach American history. What if a student doesn't like Shamus, or vice versa? It just shouldn't be like that. Ancient history's the same way—all you get is Professor Metzger, and he's an offensive creep."

Suddenly Kenneth's lips tightened and his eyebrows pinched. He clutched his glass so tightly his knuckles turned white, and as he spoke, he ground out his words. "Professor Shamus is a brilliant scholar, and a student would be blessed by her tutelage."

O-kay.

Professor Shamus was also an ancient spinster who was known for doling out grades according to the wild swings of her senility, but that was clearly another topic they weren't going to agree on. Predictably, then, the conversation stalled. After several beats the silence was almost painful. Reese would have loved a stiff drink but she was driving that night.

Then again . . . that gave her an idea.

"What are you drinking again?" she asked as she spotted their waiter.

"Ginger ale," Kenneth replied.

"Yeah, that's right. Um, do you mind if I order you something else? I mean, for after the ginger ale." He appeared profoundly baffled, so Reese brushed some hair behind her ears and explained, "It's one of my favorites. I'd love it if you tried it. Do you mind?"

Before he had a chance to answer that, Reese accosted their waiter as he was setting down their eggplant parmigiana. "Excuse me, can we have a Long Island iced tea over here? When you get a chance."

"Oh, sure," he said, and then smiled as if he knew her plan to get Kenneth drunk. Luckily, Kenneth had no clue himself.

Besides, she didn't really want him *drunk*, because he'd have to drive home later, but loosening him up for the next hour could not possibly be a bad thing.

"Long Island iced tea?" he repeated, as he began to cut his eggplant into tiny squares. "What's in that?"

"Um . . . I'm not sure exactly . . ." she lied, "but it's really, really good." Reese watched Kenneth cut his tiny squares into even tinier squares, and waited anxiously for the booze. And somewhere deep inside, she had the distinct feeling that this was all very pathetic.

Okay, so apparently Kenneth didn't get intoxicated—by women or, as Reese learned tonight, by wine. The boy was some kind of fortress, and it was wearing her out.

The entire meal, he'd sipped at his drink, barely draining the glass of even an inch of it, while he'd asked her a barrage of annoying questions about Kimble's book. By the time he asked her, "So when does Professor Kimble anticipate contacting publishers?" Reese gave up. At that point she was pretty sure she'd given up on men in general.

"You know what?" she'd said. "My head is killing me. Mind if we call it a night?"

"Oh . . . of course not," he responded a little stiffly.

Then he threw in, "You might want to use a cold compress on your forehead later—uh, but of course that's your decision."

"Yeah, thanks," she managed.

And so it had ended there. They'd enjoyed a mute ride back to her house, and Kenneth had planted a big dry one on the corner of her mouth, catapulting her into rapturous apathy for two whole seconds. Then he was off in his own car, heading back to the city.

Reese unlocked the front door and entered her house, which was brightly lit. But then, why wouldn't it be? It was 8:45.

How lame.

Probably the only thing lamer than that would be getting drawn into a family meeting about the status of her date, so she tried to book it to her bedroom before she was accosted.

"Reese?" *Damn, damn, damn.* "Sweetheart, is that you?" Joanna called from upstairs.

Lucky for Joanna, Reese wasn't in the mood to lay into her for her earlier antics with the Konica, but she really shouldn't push it. In fact, her mother had just better take the hint, because there was no way Reese was discussing her dinner date with Kenneth. Either Joanna would offer unsolicited, delusionally optimistic advice, or she'd blame everything on Reese.

Either way, she'd pass, thank you.

"Uh, yeah, it's me, but I can't talk now," Reese said quickly as she jogged up the stairs. Her mother got to her as she was crossing the threshold of her bedroom.

"Well? How did it go?"

"Um, Mom, I have a headache, and I really don't feel like talking. And no, nothing's wrong. I'll talk to you tomorrow, if you don't mind. Please, I hope you'll respect that. Thank you for your cooperation."

She closed her bedroom door and sagged her weight against it. If her mother cared about her sanity at all, she'd leave it at that.

And, shockingly, she did.

Releasing a heavy sigh, Reese kicked off her boots, shoved down her skirt, and all but tore off the clingy vee-neck sweater that she had hoped would be subtly sexy tonight. *Hah!* Subtlety was wasted on Kenneth Peel, and "sexy" didn't seem to be programmed into his cold, computerlike brain.

She couldn't believe she actually used to be interested in him! Over the past couple of weeks, he had managed to lose all of his nerdy-but-nice appeal. Now he was just aloof and inept. *Please.* Who had the patience for that?

Hey, she'd tried. She'd given it all she had, but some people were just not meant to be together— end of story.

Climbing into her bed and slipping under the covers in just her bra and underwear, she suddenly felt a little better.

Fine, so she and Kenneth were a bust. Did that mean she had to give up on men altogether (as she'd vowed to herself the moment that Kenneth had set down *exactly* $23.18 for *exactly* half the bill)? Maybe she had been hasty—they weren't *all* boring duds.

There were men out there like Brian. Well, there was Brian, to be more precise. Thinking about him warmed her up and renewed a sense of excitement deep inside her. Could there possibly be anything there? She honestly didn't know.

But one thing was certain: if she was going to think about anyone right now—as she forced herself to sleep at 8:45 on a Saturday night—it was going to be Brian Doren.

He came out of nowhere, and his face was blurry for a second before it became clear. Then it was blank. Brian was sitting down next to her on a sofa in the middle of Roland & Fisk. But he was sitting calmly, while Reese's frustration was ready to boil over any second.

They were watching something in front of them—some sort of movie, but it didn't really make sense, and Reese forced herself to ignore how hard her heart was beating, how hot the air was, and how much she wanted to lean over and lick Brian's neck. I'm ridiculous, *she said to herself.* He's totally composed, and I'm ready to tear my clothes off.

Suddenly she felt him getting closer . . . and closer . . . until his arm spread across her back. She turned her head a little, and barely registered the pronounced bulge in his pants before she felt hot breath fan her ear. "Is this movie turning you on?" *he asked in a raspy voice that melted her insides.*

You're turning me on, *she almost whispered, but didn't—couldn't.* "No," *she said, her voice sounding strained, almost like a croak, because she felt embarrassed but so aroused it was hard to speak.*

"Yeah, me either," *Brian purred into her ear, and lapped his tongue over her lobe, then inside.*

She gasped, startled, but didn't push him away. Embar-

rassment turned into something much foggier, much more undefined. Much more raw and untamed, and as Brian licked behind her ear and trailed a hot, wet line down the side of her neck, Reese cried softly, "Oh, please . . ."

Brian ran his open, scalding mouth on her skin, and Reese's head fell back limply. Shamelessly. She felt weak and sweaty. She ached between her legs. And she was leaning into him as he seduced her with his hungry hands, and his tongue, and then . . . oh, God.

Suddenly he was on his knees before her, pushing her legs wide apart and laving his tongue over the most intimate place, turning it into sweltering, throbbing fire.

Abruptly he tore off his suit jacket, bunched it up, and shoved it under her hips. He went on doing what he was doing before, only even more effectively, and Reese shuddered violently, on the verge of what she knew would be the most amazing orgasm of her life. It was all she could think about; it was all she wanted. Nothing else seemed to exist, and then Brian's mouth was gone. He was no longer on his knees, but lying on top of her, with her legs spread wide around his hips and his fingers sliding into her.

Reese roughly gripped his hair, moaning and rocking her body, so desperate for those unbelievable, hot tremors to take over. She needed them.

Brian took one of her hands off his head and brought it down to touch him, rock-hard and straining against his pants. She made guttural, throaty sounds as Brian rubbed her open palm harder and harder against him. She could hear his heavy breathing now. He was really there, he existed, he wanted her, too.

Yes, yes . . . She jerked at his zipper and would've torn it apart if she had to.

"God, Reese . . ." he groaned, and she felt charged and electrified and alive because his voice was real.

"Reese," he breathed brokenly.

"Yes," she said, now no longer whispering. "Yes."

Reese rolled restlessly onto her side. Her eyes flew open. The clock glared red: 3:20. Mindlessly, she stared at the blocky numbers for several more seconds before she sat up.

What had she been dreaming about? She couldn't remember, but it was the middle of the night, and she was feeling wide-awake and antsy as hell.

Bounding out of bed, she went straight to her desk as if it were the most natural thing in the world. She climbed into her chair, positioned herself cross-legged, and waited for her laptop to boot up, feeling a strong, instantaneous compulsion to write. In fact, the push inside her was so hard, it seemed crazy to think it hadn't always been there.

Chapter Seventeen

The following week Brian came into Roland & Fisk every day. Reese managed to synchronize her breaks with his lunches. It seemed so strange to think that only a short time ago she had been almost too nervous to talk to him, and now they were becoming friends.

Okay, yes, she still thought about him naked (a lot). And maybe she still got excited whenever he entered the café, and maybe her stomach still dropped, and maybe her heart pulsed frantically beneath her breasts. Fine, fine, so *maybe* other places pulsed, too. And burned . . . and throbbed. But so what? Some friendships were just like that . . . right?

By Friday afternoon she and Brian had managed to avoid any Darcy Chipkin run-ins, but in the standard fashion of life, all good things had to end.

But first, Elliot came over to their table. "Hey," Reese said brightly.

"Hi," Elliot said, smiling shyly and straightening his sweater vest. "How's it going?"

"Pretty good," Reese said. "Elliot, this is Brian. Brian, Elliot."

"Hi, how're you doing?" Brian said, reaching his

hand out. When Reese asked Elliot to join them, he told her he could only sit for a moment or Darcy would sniff him out and start shrieking.

"I actually had to ask you a favor," he said.

"What?"

"Is there any way you could switch shifts with me tomorrow?"

"Oh, I'm not working tomorrow," Reese said apologetically.

"Well, I can switch with you for one of your shifts next week." Sighing, he added, "See, Darcy put me on the schedule for tomorrow night, but I have karate class that night. I told her that already, of course, but she scheduled me anyway."

"Oh . . . sure, I'll do it," Reese said, not exactly thrilled about having to drive into the city on a Saturday night.

Elliot straightened his glasses and perked up. "Really? I mean, I don't mean to put you on the spot, but I can't think of anyone else who might do it." Quite a testimonial to their antisocial crew.

"No problem," Reese said, smiling.

"Oh, thanks! By the way, which shift of yours do you want me to take next week? Whichever one you want works for me."

"Uh, I don't know; we can decide later." Honestly, she didn't know her hours for the following week because she had deliberately avoided checking the schedule. Every time she stepped foot inside the break room, Darcy would burst out of her private office and pounce. It was like she had an animalistic sixth sense, which stood to reason since the girl was a beast.

"Thanks again," Elliot said, and got up to go.

As his body cleared, another came into view. *Major ick.* The creepy customer who traveled everywhere with his embarrassing old mother was sitting only three feet away. He was staring right at her with his characteristic demented smile, while he stirred his coffee round and round. A shiver ran up Reese's spine, and her flesh began to crawl.

Although she quickly averted her eyes, Brian picked up on her discomfort and asked, "What's wrong? What are you thinking?"

She shook her head, then whispered, "It's that weird guy again." Brian angled his head back, but Reese said, "No, don't look!"

"Oh, sorry," he said, now dropping his voice to a whisper, too. "What weird guy?"

"So you're working tomorrow night, huh?"

She looked up, and Brian turned around. The creepy customer sat smugly waiting for an answer to his question. Great, he'd heard that she was working Elliot's shift tomorrow night. Maybe she was being paranoid, but she did not want this weirdo knowing her work schedule, especially any hours that were after dark.

"Uh . . . I'm not sure . . . I guess," she said feebly.

Just then a familiar old lady hobbled over to the man's table, waving a muffin in her hand. "Hey, look at this piece of dog turd!" she shouted.

"*Mother.*" He banged his fists hard on the table, and some coffee splashed out of the cup. "Let's go!"

"What?"

"We're *leaving*," he snapped petulantly, stalking off and leaving her to trail behind.

When they were gone, Reese let out a sigh and muttered, "Great, just great."

"What's that guy's fixation with you?" Brian asked, sounding a little edgy.

"Hmm . . . any chance you're coming into the store tomorrow night?" Reese said teasingly. "I think I could use some protection."

"Oh, really?" he asked, grinning.

What the hell was she saying? She was coming on way too strong. She had to remember that Brian came into Roland & Fisk because he worked around the corner and liked the soup—*not* to see her. Sure, they had a great rapport, but it wasn't like he was going to go out of his way to get together.

"Sure," he said, startling her. "I'll come."

Her heart kicked up, and her breath stalled in her throat for a second. Finally she said, "Really? I mean, don't feel pressured."

"I don't."

Oh, God. I want this man. I really, really want this man.

And it was at that moment that Darcy flitted over to ruin the moment. Or to try, but there was no way she possibly could. "Brock, isn't your break running a little *long* today?"

"Uh . . ." Reese checked the clock. *Damn!* She hated when Darcy was actually right (the semiannual occurrence was brutal). She turned to Brian and said, "I gotta get back to work."

"Yeah, that would be *nice*," Darcy jeered, twirling her hair, as usual. "By the way, I found a snotty tissue in romance. Is it yours? I know you're always trolling that section when you're supposed to be working." Darcy looked at Brian and rolled her eyes.

Brian kept his expression completely blank, and lowered his gaze to the inside of his espresso cup. Reese could tell that he was containing his annoyance for her benefit.

She grinned. Hell, it was so stupid it was funny and, at this point, not the least bit embarrassing. "No, sorry, that wasn't me. But thanks for your concern." She saw Brian's mouth twitch up. Reese stood and added, "Any other crucial issues before I get back to work?"

Darcy looked supremely pissed. "Yes, there *is*," she said in a huff. "I saw you fooling around with the new hardcover releases before."

"Wha—oh, I wasn't fooling with them; I was fixing them. Some were out of order."

"Ooh, how heroic. Medal or monument?" Reese held back a laugh. "Anyway, I hope you liked doing it for free, because you're getting docked for that!" Darcy stamped her foot and turned to exit the café in a massive snit. On her way out, she called, "Tina! I want a triple-caramel chocolate latte with extra whipped cream in my office *now*!"

Tina came front and center behind the counter, and declared, "Right, boss!" before hustling over to the espresso machine to get started.

"Reese," Brian said in a low, smooth voice, as he rose to gather his coat. "You're way too good for this place." She smiled at the words. A sewer rat was too good for this place, but it warmed her heart just the same.

*   *   *

The next night, Reese wiped down the tables with palpable disappointment. Brian had never shown. It was now 10:45. Roland & Fisk closed at eleven. That seemed to say it all.

"Hey, Brock," Tina said, as she ran a wet mop along the strip of tile behind the counter. "Can I get your advice on something?"

"Sure," Reese replied, as she stacked the chairs. "What about?"

"Well, it's sort of about guys," Tina said, shrugging as though it weren't important, yet not able to make eye contact. "How can you tell if a dude's into you?"

Brilliant question. Reese would *love* the answer to that. "God, Tina, I have no clue," she said. "I sort of have terrible luck with guys."

"See, there's this guy I know," Tina went on, "but I think he only sees me as a friend. How can I be sure, you know? I mean, without making a big jackass of myself?"

Reese laughed. Maybe in the past, she would have offered some general advice. In Tina's case, maybe she would have even suggested—extremely tactfully, of course—that Tina "soften the edges" a little bit. As in, drop some of the military intensity, call people by their first names, things like that. Maybe lose the holster . . .

But not now. Now Reese had no reason whatsoever to hope her opinion held a shred of validity. She obviously could not read men at all—even the ones who were supposed to be her friends. And softening her own edges with dark chocolate eye pencil and red-raspberry Chap Stick hadn't gotten Reese anywhere.

Tina wrung out her mop and continued, "It's like when we're together, I'm feeling all romantic, but I don't know if he is."

"Hmm . . . well, what do you two like to do together?"

"You know, the usual, bowling, flag football, lifting, chugging contests."

"I . . . see," Reese said neutrally.

"I don't know," Tina said, and hurled a big ball of spit into the sink behind her. "I wouldn't mind going out for an elegant evening sometime, ya know?"

"Uh-huh, definitely. So why don't you suggest it?"

She scoffed as she coasted the mop along the floor. "I wouldn't even know what to suggest."

"Hmm . . . well, why don't we look in one of those city guides for something really cool? You could plan the whole thing—he won't even know what hits him," Reese said, smiling and putting up the last chair. She moved to sponge down the counter. "I'll help you if you want."

"Really, Brock? You'd help me?"

"Sure, why not?" Actually the prospect sounded fun. Why shouldn't one of them have an exciting, romantic adventure? Reese stopped wiping for a second. "Hey, maybe you guys could do a Broadway play."

"Yeah, that'd be cool! But not one with lots of singing and dancing. I hate that shit."

"Hmm, maybe Broadway's not for you. But don't worry; we'll think of something."

"Aw, Brock, you're the best!"

Reese took those very words with her several minutes later, as she headed out the back door and onto the street. She was *not* going to be depressed about Brian. He obviously blew hot and cold. That was his problem, not hers. Who needed the aggravation?

She folded her arms across her chest to keep some of the chilly night air at bay, and she walked carefully because the street was still slick with sleet.

She'd left her car at her apartment building so she wouldn't have to deal with parking. Normally it was easier to catch a cab on the back street than in front of the store, but at the moment it appeared deserted. And . . . creepy. Her imagination must have been in overdrive, because a sudden, sharp uneasiness hit her, and she turned around to go back inside the store.

She yanked and got nothing but resistance. *Damn it all!* The door had locked behind her. Her pulse skittered as she forced her feet to scurry down the street as quickly as possible. It was probably silly, but for some reason Reese had the disturbing feeling that the street *seemed* deserted but wasn't. That something ominous was around her . . . or behind her.

She walked faster. She heard the clicking of her shoes become rapid little taps on the cement. Quickly she looked over her shoulder. Her breath caught.

Nothing.

Maybe she was losing it. But then she remembered the creepy customer, who had suspiciously never shown tonight. Her heart beat faster. God, he was just weird enough to be a psychotic stalker. For all she knew, he was lurking in the shadows for her to get out of work.

Now she started to run. She should've felt ridiculous, but her blood was thundering and her heart was pounding too loudly in her ears for her to feel anything but fear. The corner was only a few yards away.

Come on, come on . . .

As she cut right around the corner, she shot a final look over her shoulder and slammed hard into someone. "Oh, I'm sorry!" she said, before she even realized who it was.

"Reese," he said. She was breathing embarrassingly hard now. Brian cupped her arms gently with his hands and looked into her eyes. "Are you okay?" he asked with concern.

"Um . . . yeah," she said almost absently, because her mind was still buzzing. Not to mention, her brain hadn't caught up to the shock of seeing Brian, after she had completely given up on seeing him tonight.

Glancing down, she spotted the watch on his left wrist. Eleven-fifteen. No, she definitely did not understand men.

He gave her arms an affectionate squeeze. "You sure?" he asked.

"Yeah," she said, and smiled. "I'm sorry. I just thought someone was following me. Forget it; it's dumb."

"Oh, no, that guy from the other day? Where is he?" he asked anxiously, looking over her shoulder, as though ready for a confrontation.

"No, no," she said, shaking her head and waving off the idea. "There wasn't anyone; I was just imagining it. Really. It was something about the streetlights and the moon, maybe, but the street just looked creepy." She let out a laugh. "And now I look really weird."

He grinned, and slid his hands off her arms. "I don't mind." *Meaning what?* she thought. "All right, come on," he said, lightly nudging her back until she fell in step with him.

"Where are we going?" she asked.

"I'll walk you to your car."

"But I thought . . . I mean, I didn't think you were gonna come tonight." She could smell a hint of aftershave or cologne or something very clean, athletic, and seductive.

"I'm sorry I was so late," he said. "I had some things to take care of. But I figured the least I could do was get you to your car safely. You know, in case your boyfriend's still lurking."

For the next few seconds Reese couldn't formulate any words because she was still so struck that Brian had come. And to walk her to her car—who *did* that? Or more specifically, who looked like Brian, wasn't getting paid for his time, and did that?

"So where is your car parked?" he asked.

"Oh, I forgot!" Reese replied. "I left my car at my apartment. I didn't want to drive back to Goldwood tonight. Anyway, I was just gonna take a cab from here."

"Okay. Then you can take a cab with me in it," he said. He was looking down the street casually, and not explaining further.

"But . . . what . . . why . . ."

"Here comes one." After he flagged it, the taxi

swerved over and skidded to a stop in front of them. Reese hustled in first, followed by Brian, who said, "Where's your apartment?"

She had to think before she remembered her address, which probably should have told her that she was in deep.

"Do you want to go straight home, by the way?" Brian asked. "Have you eaten yet?"

"Yeah, I had something on my break earlier," she said.

"We could go for a drink or something," he offered. "But if you're too tired after working, I totally understand."

"Oh . . ."

"Where do you go?" the cabby demanded impatiently.

"Um . . ."

"We could get a drink," Reese said quickly before Brian rescinded the offer.

"Great," he said, smiling, and told the driver where to go.

Reese sat back against the cracked, duct-taped upholstery, trying to make sense of the last ten minutes. Just when she'd been dismally disappointed in men, she found herself giddy and excited and lustful all over again. She should really be writing some of this down.

Chapter Eighteen

They'd been talking and nursing their drinks for the past forty minutes, and Reese was now in full flirt mode, which she'd never really considered one of her gears. She didn't even mean to do it, but it seemed to be happening under its own power. Right now, her life felt like hers, only better. Brighter. Bigger.

Brian had just asked her what she was going to do about her nonexistent dissertation, and in response, she felt her chin tilting down, her lashes fluttering up, and her mouth curving into a small smile. "I'd rather not talk about school, if that's okay," she said sweetly.

"Uh, yeah," he said, watching her intently, "that's fine."

She didn't know which undid her more—his eyes or his smile. Or was her vodka martini at all responsible for the dazed, heated, swirly kind of feeling she was getting in her stomach and head? She wasn't drunk, of course . . . she just felt good.

"To tell you the truth," she said suddenly, "I'm working on something else right now."

"Really, what?" he asked, leaning forward with interest. Brian's interest seemed far different from

Kenneth's, which always smacked of social stalemate and inept prying.

Reese sat forward, too, bringing their faces only inches apart. "I'm writing a novel," she said a little bashfully, "or trying to, but I've only written one chapter so far."

"No kidding," Brian said, smiling, and sounding impressed. "Wow, how'd you get interested in doing that?"

She shrugged. "I don't know; it's something I've been wanting to try for a long time." *All talk, that's me.* "And I've always loved reading novels." *Especially after my last boyfriend dumped me.* "So recently, I decided to take the plunge." *If one unrevised chapter constitutes a "plunge."*

"I can't even imagine doing something like that," he said. "You must be pretty creative. You're incredible; I know *that*." Blushing hotly, she looked to her martini for clarity. "You definitely have to let me read it sometime," Brian added in a low voice. "I mean, if you want."

"Okay," she said, biting her lower lip and braving a glance into his gorgeous eyes. As they burned through hers, she struggled to sound normal. "But enough about me. How's Project Blue going?"

"No way," he said, shaking his head. "If you don't have to talk about school, I don't have to talk about work."

"Oh . . . okay. What do you want to talk about?"

"You," he said huskily. She gulped. No hesitation, he'd just said it. Hot-blooded sensations that had been fluttering on the periphery of her body and mind now intensified. And thrummed and pulsed and roared. Did Brian have any idea how much she wanted to take an ice cube out of his scotch glass and rub it across the tips of her breasts? Or how much at this moment she wanted—*needed*—to contract the muscles between her legs?

She darted her eyes downward to break the powerful gaze between her and Brian, and that was when she noticed . . .

Oh, not again!

To her absolute horror, she spotted her nipples stabbing at the surface of her yellow angora sweater. *These damn things* (the sweaters, not the nipples).

Shooting forward, she tried to conceal herself with the table, but when she shot her eyes up to Brian's, she realized that if he hadn't noticed her aroused breasts before, he sure as hell did now.

He was dissolving her with his smoky stare, and she squeezed her thighs together, acting purely on animal instinct, as well as some distant memories of lust and heat and sex.

Finally she managed a weak, broken echo. "Me?"

"You," he said again.

"What about me?"

"Well, whatever happened to you?" he asked, leaning back, and cooling off some of the space between them. "I mean, two years ago I met you at a New Year's party, and then I never saw you again. I wanna know where you've been since then."

Not once in the time he'd been coming to the café had either of them spoken of that fateful night. Of course, until now, it hadn't seemed particularly fateful. Truthfully, Reese hadn't had the guts to ask Brian about that night. And if she did ask, she would feel

the need to add in a million disclaimers about how
she was "just curious" and "no big deal"—maybe
even, "I swear I'm not stalking you!" But Brian had
simply asked, openly and undefensively. He was admitting that he'd wondered about her, and that kind
of confidence was a turn-on, even if it was also a
come-on.

He took a drink of his scotch, but never let his
eyes leave hers.

She took a drink herself, feeling that warm haze
intensify and turn into a hot rush between her legs.
"Well, I don't know. I enrolled at Crewlyn soon
after . . . and that brings us around to talking about
school, so I'll shut up now," she said, grinning.

A long, loaded moment passed before Brian
grinned back. . . .

He was transfixed by her eyes. They were like lu-
minous green lights, smoldering green flames, even,
and they had been flickering in their own sexy, flustered way for the past half hour. Her face was
stained with a deep blush that could have been at-
tributed to the heat of the bar, but he strongly hoped
there was more to it.

"So . . ." Brian said absently, while his gaze
tracked Reese's finger as it played with her bottom
lip, which was slightly wet from her last sip of
vodka. At last, he mentally shook himself back to the
conversation at hand. "Remember that misunderstanding we had—when I thought you were slamming me, but you were actually slamming some
other poor guy?"

She laughed at that. "Yeah, mmm-hmm."

"Well, now I'm wondering . . ." His voice trailed off as he tapped his knuckles on his near-empty glass of scotch. "Forget it," he said suddenly, waving his hand. "Never mind."

"What?" she pressed.

"No, it's silly. Never mind."

"What? Come on; tell me." She was curious now, just like he'd hoped she would be.

"Well, I'm just wondering, if you *had* been talking about me to your mother, how would you have described me?"

A tiny wrinkle formed on Reese's forehead, and her blush got a little pinker.

"And not based on that night at the diner," Brian qualified. "Based on the *other* night."

"Um . . . well . . . I don't know, exactly. . . ." A beat of silence passed, before abstraction gave way to warmth, and she smiled up at him. His chest constricted. Instantly he realized that he'd been wrong: Her eyes weren't flickering lights, but wide pools of scalding green liquid.

Then her smile turned coy, as she rested her chin in her hand and said sweetly, "I really couldn't say. The whole night's sort of a blur."

"The kiss, too?"

She paused, then licked her bottom lip and said softly, "The kiss, I definitely remember."

He swallowed. "Well, how do you remember it?" he asked in a low, smooth voice. Then he waited patiently for her answer. . . .

Reese knew that Brian was being deliberately provocative, and that spurred a thrilling sort of curiosity as to what *exactly* he hoped to provoke. The possibilities alone fired her up. Brian naked, aroused, on top of her . . . sweating, grunting . . . with her ankles on his shoulders—

"Reese?"

"Oh . . ." She snapped back into focus, and tried a turn-the-tables stalling tactic. "What do *you* remember?" She hoped to buy time to formulate a good answer herself, and to figure out what she was going to do about all this suffocating desire.

"I remember that it was pretty damn terrific."

"Yeah . . . those were the days," she joked stupidly.

Brian grinned. "Yeah."

So much for formulating a good answer—she'd winged it with a stupid one-liner. But Brian didn't seem dissuaded in the least, and what really mattered was that he remembered the kiss, and seemed to be hinting strongly for another one. That was what she wanted, too. And more.

In fact, her body was fully on fire—some of the sensations were familiar, and some felt new in their intensity. She had a pit in her stomach a tightness in her chest, and a quivering in her inner thighs.

Involuntarily, she shivered.

"Are you cold?" he asked, concerned.

"Oh . . . yeah," she fibbed, and hoped she wouldn't have to sit there with her coat on to support the lie.

"Here," he said, pulling his sweater over his head, rumpling his hair in the process, and revealing his faded Ithaca T-shirt underneath. He handed it across the table, and Reese felt compelled to take it. She would have also loved to smell it and rub her face all over it, but she refrained.

"Thanks," she said with a soft smile, and slipped it over her own sweater.

Just then the cocktail waitress appeared and asked them if there would be anything else. Brian deferred the question to Reese. She shook her head, still feeling dazed. She was a little tipsy, burning up inside, and not wanting the night to end. Vaguely, she heard him say "Just the check," and when he signed the charge slip, she found herself staring longingly at the subtle curve of biceps under his T-shirt.

Soon they were outside on the busy sidewalk, and Brian was gently resting his hand on the small of Reese's back. "We can probably walk from here, if you want."

"Okay. Wait, don't you want your sweater?" Reese asked, starting to pull it off.

He stilled her with his hand. "No, I don't need it; you wear it."

On the walk to her apartment, neither said much. But it wasn't the awkward, empty silence that she shared with Kenneth. It was different. It was a charged, loaded kind of silence . . . it crackled with an undercurrent of sexual tension, and it sizzled with the kind of raging heat that made her gasp and sweat. Well, if she weren't in the middle of a busy street.

She wanted him so much, she spent the entire walk wondering if he would make a move on her when they got to her apartment. And if he didn't, would she'd have the guts to do it herself?

*   *   *

They got to her door, and some of the fog in her brain had cleared. Brian hadn't done anything like grope her or make suggestive comments during the walk, which was, of course, to his credit. The only downside was that Reese was once again totally unsure how to read him. Really, did Brian *like* torturing her?

"You didn't have to walk me all the way up. I'm sure that creepy customer is nowhere near me right now," she said, smiling over her shoulder as she turned the fifth lock and opened her apartment door.

"No, don't be silly," he said. "That guy's not the only weirdo in this city—in case you haven't noticed."

She grinned at him again, and led the way inside. Brian followed, shutting the door behind him and keeping a slight distance. "Well, thanks for coming out for a drink," he said. "I really had a lot of fun with you."

The fun doesn't have to end, Reese almost said. Instead, she went with, "No, thank you—for coming to the store tonight. I know you were busy earlier and everything."

"Oh . . . right," he said.

There they were standing in her front hall, looking around, grinning like idiots, and neither one making a move.

Brian said, "So . . . this is your place, huh?"

"Yeah . . . yeah," Reese said, nodding, and looking around as if she didn't remember what it looked like. "It's not much, but that's graduate housing." The apartment was dimly lit by the street lamps outside, but the front hall where they stood was almost pitch dark. Reese didn't want to turn on the overhead light, though, because she was afraid it might make her lose her nerve.

"Actually, two of my roommates graduated this past semester," she threw in for no reason.

"Ah," he said, nodding now, too.

"Yeah, so . . . this is where I live."

"Nice."

"It's all right."

"Hmm."

They both casually surveyed the place for the tenth time.

Then Reese broke. *To hell with this*, she thought boldly. She would never forgive herself if she let this night end without at least *trying*.

Mustering up her confidence, she inched closer to Brian. He inched then, too. Sucking in a small breath, she ran her palm lightly over his chest. "Well . . ." she began, lowering her voice, and praying Brian didn't share the same compulsion to recoil at her touch that Kenneth did.

"Well . . ." he said back, and moved closer—pressing his chest against her hand.

Ecstatically, she slid her palm up to cup the back of his neck, and things moved fluidly from there. Her other hand fell onto his chest and stroked it as Brian slipped his arms around her and lowered his head to hers.

"So . . ." she murmured.

"Yeah . . ." he mumbled, touching his lips to hers.

"Anyway . . ." she whispered against his mouth.

The last thing she heard before other senses took

over was Brian's low groan as he opened his mouth over hers. Then she was captured in a soft, slow kiss. It was almost sweet because it was so gentle, but it was too wet and too sexual to be sweet.

Brian's tongue was teasing hers, gliding and slicking enough to unbelievably turn her on, but not nearly enough to satisfy her.

She moaned and tugged on his neck. She needed him deeper—she needed *more*. Brian must have understood, because suddenly his lips pushed hard on hers, opening their mouths wider, and tangling their tongues in a wild, hungry frenzy.

Reese's neck tilted back as she tried to keep up and struggled to contain the ecstasy of this moment—of the exhilaration zinging through her, of the sweat breaking out, of her panties burning up.

Soon Reese was clawing at Brian's T-shirt. He hugged her tightly to him, then pressed her up against the wall. He was licking into her, sliding in and out, sucking on her tongue, nipping at her lower lip. . . . It was almost all too much, and certainly nothing like the halfhearted lip locks she'd shared with Kenneth. *Oh, God.* Brian's kiss was raw, hot passion. The kind of passion that shocked her body to the brink of orgasm.

"Jesus," he whispered gruffly, and buried his head in the crook of her neck.

She forgot that she was awkwardly and almost painfully perched on the very tips of her toes; she thought only of the heat and the contact. Of licking and fucking and writhing and climaxing. A shrieking moan burst from her as all the dirty thoughts filled her brain, and Brian growled—almost as if he could read her dirty mind. With barely restrained aggression, Reese cupped his jaw and folded her mouth into his hungrily, desperately.

Several moments passed before her fingers slinked up and furrowed into his hair. She gripped it for balance as he slid his hand up and down her back almost roughly. She vaguely heard knuckles dragging along the wall, and then Brian's fingers were kneading the back of her neck, weakening it until her knees buckled, and she almost slid to the floor.

Keep going. It had been so long since she'd kissed a man like this. Well, she was hard-pressed to remember anything quite like *this*. She moaned as he tugged gently on her hair, arching her neck, and trailed strong, suctioning kisses down her throat.

When he got to the curve, he sucked hard—the wet heat of his mouth and the light rasp of his teeth on her skin created an electric sensation that seared her nerve endings.

More, please . . . much, much more . . .

Brian worked his way back up to her mouth, which was open and ready. "Brian . . ." Reese murmured after the kiss broke. She hadn't thought about it, but his name had slipped out naturally and breathlessly. Brian pulled back enough to press his forehead to hers, and she could hear the ragged quickness of his breath. Coiling her arms tightly around his neck, she blurted on a whisper, "I like being with you."

He lifted his forehead off hers to look into her eyes. As his breathing slowed, a faint grin appeared on his face. He brushed some of her hair away from her face and said, "I like being with *you*." She smiled into the darkness, and then his mouth was on hers again, doing the same things as before, only harder. Deeper. Wetter.

She slid her tongue inside his mouth and he groaned.

Her back scraped up and down against the wall, as Brian's erection pressed and pushed into the soft, aching place between her legs. She rocked her hips and squeezed her eyes shut as she took his sudden, fierce thrusts. A few pumps of his hips, and she was panting and gripping his shoulders while her head rested against the wall, and she thought about *really* making love to him. It would be like this, only better . . . *so* much better.

He touched her breasts, she grabbed his butt, and then his cell phone rang.

At first he ignored it, but then he pulled back enough to mutter, "Damn it, it might be an emergency," and retrieve it from his pocket. "Hello," he barked. Then his voice softened. "Danny, what's wrong? Is everything okay?"

Now he disentangled himself from Reese to stand upright, pressing the phone close to his ear. "I can barely hear you . . . you're where? Hello, Danny?"

Reese felt beyond awkward standing there. And also a little embarrassed by how far one kiss had gone. Echoes of her moaning still ran through her head, and she blushed at the thought. Meanwhile it appeared that Brian had gotten cut off from his sister.

"I'm sorry," he said now, snapping his phone shut. "I've gotta go. It's my sister. She's . . . She's having some problems."

"Oh, no, is everything all right?"

He nodded. "Yeah, she's just freaking out about something with the insurance."

"Oh."

"Yeah."

She brushed some hair behind her shoulders, and he lifted a few strands and brushed them away himself. "I'm sorry," he said.

"No, no, I understand," Reese said. Meanwhile, her heart was sinking—sure, she was embarrassed, but that didn't mean she wanted to *stop.*

But the spell was broken, at least for the moment. They managed to say good-night without tearing each other's clothes off, and Brian kissed her just once more—sweetly, deeply, passionately—before he reminded her to lock up. And then he said good-bye.

Chapter Nineteen

Reese decided to stay in the city the following day, and do some work at the New York Public Library. She'd remembered a term paper that was due at the end of January, and figured she would get it done and out of the way. It was the new her. Okay, not really. It was the temporary awesome-mood-might-as-well-be-productive her. After last night she was floating in a happy delirium, and nothing as mundane as home-work could destroy her high.

She had her laptop set up in one of the cubicles, and notebooks, pens, a water bottle, and an "emergency" PowerBar strewn along the desktop so she would feel fortified. She kind of doubted that she'd ever be hungry enough to eat the PowerBar—it was the same one her mother had placed in her bookbag on her very first day at Crewlyn.

Now, staring at her blinking cursor, she was a million miles away. Thinking about Brian. Remembering the night before. Remembering how it felt to kiss him and hold him—remembering how wonderful his skin smelled, and how sexy his voice had sounded when it had turned low and raspy with desire. . . .

Okay, this study approach was not going to get

her work done. She had to stop reliving the previous night, as exhilarated as it still made her feel. She had to focus. Focus . . . On what, again? Oh, right, the term paper.

She opened a yellow spiral notebook to her left, and skimmed over her class notes.

Snore . . . Why had she ever enrolled in a class called The Structuralization and Politicization of the Global Economy? Oh, right, it was because she'd missed her registration time after Kimble had insisted that she stay in his office and take dictation while his ideas were "pouring out." By the time she'd gotten to the registrar, this was one of the few open courses left.

Okay, time to work.

Fantasizing about better classes, and Brian's incredibly sexy mouth and gentle touch would have to wait. Even though her mind was pumping with lust and adrenaline, she'd have to buckle down.

Just as she was about to write "The" her mind wandered.

It wasn't easy, but finally, over the next few hours, she eked out a seven-page paper, and made it to level forty-two of *Chip's Challenge*. Definitely a full day. Afterward she caught a bus back to her apartment, picked up her car, and drove home to Goldwood.

She was dizzily happy when she walked in the front door. She'd found a man she liked so much, who liked her back—desired her as much as she desired him—and for the first time in so long, her luck with the opposite sex was turning around.

"Hi, honey!" Joanna called, as Reese set her keys

on the clock and made her way down the hall and into the kitchen.

"Hey!" she said to Joanna and Ben, who were sitting around the table, going through photographs. They had three albums opened, and random photos scattered all around. "Where's Ally?" Reese asked.

"In here!" Ally called from the pantry, and then emerged, carrying a bag of Chex Mix, and wearing a big-skirted silver gown.

"Oh, my God! That dress is so cool!" Reese said enthusiastically, and came closer to touch the material. Then she screwed up her face in sudden concern. "But is it okay for you to wear it now?"

"Don't even get me *started*," Joanna said. "I've asked her a thousand times to take it off before she sweats in it."

"Mom, I'm not a pig."

"It's got nothing to do with that! I just think—"

"Okay, okay, I'll take it off. But let's just finish this first."

"What is all this?" Reese asked.

Ally said, "Oh, we were gonna put together an album of me and Ben—you know, like showing our whole relationship."

"That's a cool idea," Reese said, and suddenly spotted the large Christmas tree in the family room, glowing with multicolored lights. "Hey, you got the tree. I love it."

"Oh, yes, Ben and your father got it this afternoon," Joanna said. "I figured you could take over the decorating, since that's your thing."

"Okay," Reese said, and took a seat at the table.

"Oh, sweetheart!" Joanna exclaimed. "I can't believe I forgot! Kenneth called earlier. Twice. I said I'd have you call him back."

"Yeah, I can't believe you forgot, either," Reese said, grinning.

"Well?"

"Well, what?"

"Aren't you going to call him back?" Joanna asked, sounding close to desperate.

"Yeah . . . I will." *If I'm feeling masochistic.* "So where are all these pictures from?"

"A bunch of different albums I had," Ally answered. "Hey, hon, look at this." She handed the snapshot over to Ben, who chuckled in response, and passed it to Reese. It was a picture of Ally and Ben at a Halloween party. They had dressed as "Captain and Coke," with Ben in a sea captain costume, and Ally in a red dress with *Coca-Cola* scribbled in white across her chest, and bottle-cap earrings dangling down low.

"By the way, there's fresh pastry on the cooling rack," Joanna said. "Help yourself, sweetheart."

"Oh, no, thanks," Reese said, not even sparing the pastry a glance. For some reason, she had zero desire to stuff her face with sweets. She figured the feeling would pass quickly.

"What's this one from, Ally?" Joanna asked, passing another photo to her.

Ally leaned over to look at it. After a pause, she said, "Oh, yeah, that was that big Valentine's party we went to a few years ago. Remember, hon?" She leaned over and rested her head on Ben's shoulder.

"You look so handsome," she said. He smiled down at her and kissed the top of her head. "Oh, hey, there's Brian in the background."

At the mention of his name, Reese's heartbeat leaped to attention. Should she come clean with her family about Brian? Before there hadn't been much to tell, but now . . .

She looked at the photo, and her eyes zeroed in on Brian immediately. He was way in the background, and appeared to be frozen in a laughing moment beside a tall, skinny blonde. Reese swallowed an irrational lump of jealousy. Of course it was ridiculous to feel jealous, but she couldn't seem to help herself. She was strangely possessive of him now— he was *hers*.

Well, almost.

Maybe.

"Oh, yes, I see," Joanna observed. "Who's that he's with? She looks pretty darn interested in getting her hooks in."

"That was his ex-fiancée," Ally said. *Ex-fiancée!* Brian had been engaged? Reese had no particular reason to be shocked, but she was anyway. And even more irrationally jealous. "What was her name again?" Ally asked.

"Veronica," Ben replied absently, thumbing through another stack of pictures. "But I don't think they're exes anymore."

"What do you mean?"

"I think they're back together."

Reese's stomach dropped, and her throat clogged up. Ben couldn't be right—he just *couldn't*.

"Oh, really?" Ally said.

"Yeah, I thought I told you that. Brian said they were talking again, but I don't remember all the details."

No, there was no way Brian was back together with his ex-fiancée. It was not possible. If Brian were engaged, he would never have spent last night in her arms. He never would have kissed her so passionately. He never would have come to protect her from the creepy customer.

Not unless he was the biggest asshole on the planet, that is.

Reese's gut was churning, and her hands nearly trembling. What a fool she'd been to dream up a relationship with Brian—and not just a relationship, but a *perfect* relationship. One with friendship and companionship and white-hot passion.

Now it just seemed like a pathetically sad joke. Brian already had a relationship—with a slim, sleek blonde. Reese was just the chubby shrimp he'd made out with twice. Just fucking *wonderful*. "What does she do?" Ally asked Ben.

"She's a dancer, I think."

This just kept getting worse. Reese's eyes stung, and she knew she had to get out of that kitchen before she burst into tears. Holding her stomach as she rose from the table, she said as nonchalantly as possible, "Um, I'm gonna go take a shower."

Joanna said, "Do you feel all right, honey? You look a little pale."

"And your eyes are glassy," Ally added. "Maybe you're getting winter allergies."

"No, I'm fine—I mean, yeah, I'm getting allergies, I think." She turned to bolt.

"Oh, wait!" Joanna said, "don't forget to call Kenneth!"

"Uh-huh. See you all later."

She hopped the steps two at a time, flying right to her bedroom and locking the door behind her, which was sort of absurd because her family was not her enemy. But who *was*? Brian Doren, or herself? After all, she should have guessed that Brian was too good to be true—that she was merely a diversion from his *real* life—just like it had been with Pete, and just like it was with Kenneth.

Only with Pete and Kenneth, it had been much more obvious. With Brian she'd been completely snowed. Not once in all their talks about their jobs, their interests, their backgrounds, their lives, had he mentioned being engaged or even involved.

Sinking onto the floor, Reese sighed and buried her face in her knees and thought, *I knew those soft brown eyes were trouble the minute I saw them, and I should've just run away.*

Two minutes went by before the knocking began. Could Ally have sensed through their sister connection all of Reese's pain and torment? Did she simply know intuitively how hard Reese had been falling for Brian, and now had she come to offer her a shoulder to cry on? An ear, a support system—

"Sweetheart, we need you to come downstairs and try on your dress."

Not even *close*! It was just her mother, imposing on her for yet another tedious, prewedding spectacle. Well, that was it—Reese would not do it; she'd had it with this. Rising up, she opened her door only a crack. "Mom, no. I don't want to try on my dress right now."

"Come on, honey, we don't have time for you to be difficult. Everyone's waiting downstairs for you."

"What—why are they *waiting*?"

"Have you been crying? Your eyes look all red."

"No, I have not been crying," Reese lied, feeling the tears start again. "And I *don't* want to try on my dress now."

"It won't take long; I just want to make sure the dress fits so we know if we need to make another appointment with the seamstress before the wedding, since you and Angela completely neglected your last appointment. Now come on; don't give me a hard time."

"Mom, *please* . . ."

"Oh, fine, I give up!" Joanna shouted, looking to the ceiling for some commiseration. "I try *so hard*, and nobody *ever* helps me out!"

"Reese, please," Ally called from the foot of the stairs. "Just so Mom will let it die."

"See? Your sister is excited to see the dress on you, too!" Joanna chirped, suddenly happy again.

"Come on," Ally encouraged. "Let's see you work it."

Reese ground out the word "Fine," and Joanna skipped down the stairs, humming merrily—as in, *My work is done here*, and, *Hmm-hmm, I'm a great mother*.

Balling her hands into fists, Reese dragged herself over to her walk-in closet, where her bridesmaid dress hung beneath untouched cellophane. She had had her measurements taken when Ally had first picked it out, but she still hadn't tried it on. She figured it would be okay, since bridal dresses tended to run big. But all her beliefs were called into serious question when she put it on. Or crammed it on. Or stuffed the dress like a turkey. In fact, by the time she got the side zipper up, she was holding her breath, absolutely terrified of letting it out.

Lord, it was *tight*. How could this have happened? She couldn't have gained *that* much weight since they'd placed the order seven months ago . . . could she?

"Reese!" Joanna called from downstairs. "Do you need help?"

"No!" She stood dumbly for a few seconds, and then waddled frantically to her door. Cracking it less than an inch, she yelled down, "I'm not coming down in this!"

"What?" Joanna yelled back. Then Reese heard her moan, "Why is she doing this to me? Why won't anyone ever *help* me?"

"Fine, fine," Reese snapped, "I'll be right down." She shut the door and began panicking. God, Ally's wedding was two weeks away and her dress was turning her lips blue—this was *not* going to work. If she couldn't bear to show her mother and sister, how on earth could she parade the damn dress for half of Goldwood, not to mention Brian Doren?

"Reese, we're *waiting*!" Joanna called. Her mother sounded as though she'd reached the end of her rope—again.

"Don't worry," Ally said reassuringly. "I sent Ben and Dad to get Gummi Savers."

Her sister thought Ben and Michael were the prob-

lem? *Please*. They were the *least* of Reese's problems.
Try a zipper branding her flesh, and breasts oozing
out of the sides of the dress—she hadn't realized that
"high neck" also meant narrow neck.

"Come on; I'm sure you look great," Ally said.

Finally Reese quit stalling, because she had no
other choice. Steeling herself for their reactions, she
quickly rationalized that technically the dress was
supposed to be formfitting. Also, she always tended
to be too self-conscious, and who wasn't her own
worst critic, anyway?

She descended the stairs warily. "Looks good to
me," Ally said, smiling at her—relieving her. Next
she looked to Joanna, who chewed on her lip and
squinted.

Then she put on her glasses. They were reading
glasses, so this was not a good sign.

"Well, honestly . . ." Joanna said, "it seems rather
snug, sweetheart. You might want to lose a few
pounds before the wedding." Raising her hands up,
she added, "Just a suggestion."

Reese knew the dress was snug—beyond snug—
and she knew her misery was about more than simply the dress, but still—just like that—she exploded.
"No *kidding* it wouldn't hurt, Mom!" she snapped.
"You don't think I know that? You think you need
to fucking *tell* me that?" Joanna blinked, appalled.
"Maybe if you wouldn't make it so freaking impossible around here! Maybe if you wouldn't serve breakfast sandwiches on croissants with truffles and eggs
in hollandaise sauce every single day!"

"Well, I just want to start your day with a well-
balanced meal—"

"And what about all the café au laits with heavy cream?"

"Only because I know you don't like decaf—"

Reese rolled her eyes and shuffled down the hall—feeling vaguely like a hunter-green penguin along the way—and stormed into the kitchen. Joanna and Ally followed, watching Reese whip open the refrigerator door. "Just look at this, Mom!"

"What?" Joanna said, confused.

"Mom, please, look at the food you keep here. Pastries, quiche, goose-liver pâté, and about fifty cartons of heavy cream. And—what's this?" she asked, holding up a large Tupperware bowl.

"*Crème a l'Anglaise.*"

"Mother . . ."

"Oh, sorry, sorry," Joanna said, holding up her hands, and amended, "It's custard cream."

"Exactly my point. Ever hear of *yogurt*?" She shoved the bowl back in the refrigerator and buried her face in her hands as the tears began to fall.

"Oh, sweetheart," Joanna crooned, coming up to put her arms around her. "What's wrong?" she asked gently, while Reese hugged her back and cried a little on her shoulder. "What's wrong, honey?"

"Yeah, what is it, Reese?" Ally asked, and ran her hand down her sister's hair.

"It's just . . . *everything.*"

"All right, all right, shh, just relax," Joanna said soothingly. "It's okay."

Reese sniffled with abandon, and soon felt better. Joanna pulled back and brushed some of Reese's hair aside. "You know, *I* wouldn't mind losing a few pounds, myself."

Reese sniffled. "Really?" she mumbled, swiping her cheeks with the back of her hand, while Ally handed her a paper towel for her nose.

"Really," Joanna said, smiling warmly. "Maybe it wouldn't hurt to make some lower-calorie meals around here. I mean, for myself, too. And Angela mentioned that she wanted to cut down a little herself lately."

"I'll do it, too," Ally offered.

"And, you know, there are some wonderful Parisian fish dishes that I am *dying* to try out," Joanna said.

After a pause, Reese cracked a tiny smile. "Okay," she said, and kissed her mom's cheek. "Thanks."

So it was decided. For the next two weeks, the Brock women would have fish for dinner, and skim café au laits at breakfast, and with any luck they'd be in good shape for Ally's wedding.

To celebrate their resolve, Joanna took Ally and Reese out to dinner at The Wharf. Ben and Michael were a very crabby when they got home with the Gummi Savers because the Brock women had temporarily forgotten all about them.

Chapter Twenty

"So, is Scott treating you all right?" Brian asked.

"Uh-huh," Danny said, sounding more cheerful than she had in a while. "Scott's a *sweetheart*." He could tell by the effusive way she'd said it that his friend was standing right next to her. "He's even treating me to dinner. Oh, hold on. A number four, Biggie sized."

"You're at *Wendy's*?"

"Yeah, why?"

Brian looked at his watch and saw that it was nearly nine-thirty. "First of all, you should've eaten dinner already. Second, why are you eating that crap? Danny, you're supposed to be taking care of yourself."

"I didn't want to eat before my appointment," she argued.

"Well, what kind of doctor sees patients at eight o'clock on a Sunday night, for chrissake? Maybe we should find you another doctor."

"Brian, I *like* my doctor. He's one of those old-fashioned, grandfatherly types. It's nice. Anyway, you eat Wendy's all the time."

"Don't start; you know it's not the same thing."

"Okay, but still, Dr. Fisher said I could have fast food. Really, he said it's fine once in a while."

Brian heard a brief rustling in the background, and then a man's voice. "It's true," Scott said. "And fries too, if she wants," he added, using that not-for-Brian's-benefit tone of voice.

"Listen, thanks for helping me out," Brian said.

"No problem," Scott replied amiably.

"Is everything really okay?"

"Yeah, don't worry."

"Okay, thanks. Listen, put Danny back on, will ya?"

"Hello?"

"Do you want me to come home? I can drive to Boston at the end of the week."

"No!" she yelped. "Don't you dare. I don't want you revolving your entire life around me. Besides, I told you, Dr. Fisher says I'm fine, and he's gonna rush the lab results just to be a hundred percent positive. Don't worry, okay?"

"All right, but—"

"If anything comes up, Scott will help me."

Brian paused and considered it. Then he said, "Fine, okay. But I want to know the results of the ultrasound when you get them."

Danny agreed, and immediately after Brian hung up with her he heard a chime, which indicated that he had messages on his voice mail. God, he hoped it wasn't work-related. He'd already planned to spend tonight kicking back with pizza and HBO.

He dialed the number to retrieve his messages—good, only one; that was encouraging. He pressed "one" and listened.

"Hi, Bri," Veronica said, sounding sniffly and miserable. "It's me. I really need to talk to you. I just found out that Uncle Martin is having a relapse with the cancer, and I-I really need you right now." She stopped because she was crying, and then said, "Bri, I love you. I want us to be together again. Please don't keep shutting me out. I don't know what's going on with us . . . I don't even know if you're still taking me to Ben's wedding or— Please call me back. I love you."

Brian felt like he'd been kicked in the gut. Repeatedly.

Absently shutting his phone, he tossed it somewhere, and mentally replayed what Veronica had said. Christ, she'd sounded awful. His heart squeezed inside his chest, because he knew he should do something; he knew she needed him. How could he just turn his back on her at a time like this? They'd known each other for ten years—together for eight of them—and it completely undid him to hear her sounding so desolate and so alone.

Although Veronica wasn't exactly alone. She came from a big family, and had at least a dozen good friends. Still, he knew it wasn't the same as the kind of closeness they had once shared. And Uncle Martin . . . that undid him, too. He was a great guy, and he'd always been Veronica's favorite uncle. His cancer had been in remission for a few years . . . and now this.

Brian started pacing. What could he do? Reese popped into his head for the about the millionth time that day. God, what was he going to do about her?

He liked her so damn much; she exhilarated him more than anyone or anything had in so long.

But he was thirty years old, and he knew the time had passed for him to have it both ways. He couldn't be partway into this thing with Veronica forever, and certainly not now. She expected him to commit to her again, and if he committed to Veronica, then he would have to stop seeing Reese. Exploring any potential between them would no longer be an option. It was only right, and anything else wasn't his style, anyway.

Brian finally ceased pacing, and locked his gaze on his telephone. He thought about Reese again, and felt his chest tighten so much it was almost hard to breathe.

Then he thought about Veronica. He thought about what was right, and what was less scary, and what was the only thing he could do. Then he picked up the phone.

By Monday morning, Reese had worked up a superchilly attitude that she was almost excited to use when Brian came into the café. She had spent the past night slipping in and out of disappointment and sadness, until finally anger had taken hold, and she'd discovered that anger was much easier.

And if anyone had a right to be angry as hell . . . Brian had lied to her by omission and then led her on. He'd made her feel used and stupid. Now Reese couldn't wait for the smooth-talking jerk to show his face at Roland & Fisk, so she could give him a taste of her own kind of poison.

So it was just her luck when Brian never showed. Not for lunch, and not all day.

Reese had steeled herself to tell Mr. Suave what he could do with his double espresso—and then he'd never even come! She hadn't been able to try out her chilly attitude, and she hadn't gotten the chance to berate him until he gave her the answers she so desperately needed. Talk about a gyp!

Later, after the anger had subsided, Reese was back to sadness. She didn't *get* this. She was the one who was upset; Brian didn't even know that she knew about his not-so-ex fiancée. She missed him—the lying bastard. Where *was* he?

Brian did not come into the café for the rest of the week. Not once. In fact, the highlight of Reese's week had been helping Tina plan a romantic evening for "her boy, Freddy." By Friday afternoon, she had become somewhat numb to the Brian Doren situation. She still couldn't figure out how he'd managed to preempt her blow-off, but after a week of trying, she'd pretty much given up.

Now, as she swept up some spilled grounds, Tina came out of the kitchen and said, "Brock, I just realized! Today's your last day here."

"Oh, yeah," Reese replied, surprised. She'd forgotten that her sub assignment at the café was over. Tomorrow was Christmas Eve, and after the holidays she'd be back at her usual bookstore posts: the register and the customer service desk. She suddenly felt deflated. She had gotten into a comfortable groove there with Tina. She actually liked the baking, and sneaking sips of coffee was a hell of a lot easier in this part of the store. She'd even gotten used to the

lurking creepy customer and his "turd"-obsessed
mother.

Sighing wistfully, she set her broom aside and
emptied the dustpan into the trash bin. Soon it was
back to Rhoda and Clay . . . and Amy, if she hadn't
quit out of intimidation by now.

"I'm gonna miss you, Brock," Tina declared suddenly. She was tugging on her cell holster, and
avoiding direct eye contact.

"I'll miss you, too," Reese said, smiling. "But
you're still gonna keep me posted on what happens
with Freddy, right? I want details." The romantic
evening they'd planned included an out-of-the-way
restaurant, a romantic walk through a well-lit area of
Central Park, and a pricey dessert-and-coffee place
nearby. Reese was vicariously excited for her, and
was keeping her fingers crossed for total seduction.

It was only on the ride back to Goldwood that
evening that Reese really thought about Christmas.
It had sneaked up on her again this year when she
hadn't yet mustered up any true Christmas spirit.
Luckily, she'd bought her family's presents before
she'd come home for winter break, but still, for some
reason the holiday seemed to loom over her in a way
that was surreal and vaguely depressing.

Even though she'd told herself she was over Brian,
when she heard a sappy song on the radio, it all
came back. Not with tears, though—she was past
that. Now there was just a numb, gauzy awareness
that true love was never going to happen for her.
She would never admit that she believed that, because people would just try to predict how wrong
she'd be and try to deluge her with pat optimism.

And she would humor them, and pretend she believed they were right because they'd be trying to help.

But inside, she'd still feel alone. Inside, she'd know that her fate as kooky Aunt Reese the perennial spinster was sealed. *Ugh*—the mere idea made her feel sick. No, nothing even remotely resembling Christmas spirit.

Too bad she couldn't talk to her sisters about Brian, but Angela was bogged down with her own problems right now, and Ally . . . well, frankly, Ally had a big mouth. She meant well, of course, but she was impatient. Definitely a big believer in instant gratification. Even if she swore to secrecy, she would end up not only telling Ben, but hounding him to find out Brian's intentions. And if Ben couldn't produce results fast enough, Ally would confront Brian herself with something subtle like, "So, what's up with you and my sister?"

No, thank you.

As Reese pulled into her parents' driveway, she forcibly shook off her self-pity, which was starting to annoy *her*. She had a wonderful family, and it was Christmas, and she didn't want to waste her time and energy obsessing over a guy who had played her for a fool. It wasn't as though she had ever been able to read him anyway; it was really just as well.

That settled it then. She was going to enjoy Christmas if it killed her.

So she did. More or less. Holding true to their fish diet, Joanna and Angela made a Christmas dinner of *sole aux cèpes* that was actually good. TLC aired a

Wedding Story marathon, but Joanna relented and let Michael play a CD of colonial Christmas music instead.

While Ally arranged presents under the tree, Ben polished off the last of the jingle-bell cookies, and Angela and Drew seemed content, sitting quietly next to each other on the sofa.

Meanwhile Reese sat cross-legged on the thick, soft carpet with her biscotti. Kenneth had called her twice that day, and sent her a card. It seemed that ever since their dinner date, he'd shifted into *pursue* mode. Reese didn't understand it, and if this had happened a month ago, she would have been thrilled. But now, it didn't do that much for her.

Well, it was *flattering* . . . but she couldn't seem to stir up any real enthusiasm. This was, of course, not what her mother had hoped to hear. She had been bugging her relentlessly about inviting Kenneth to the house for the holidays. Although Reese had firmly refused, she couldn't completely blow the guy off because he was still coming to Ally's wedding, and she didn't want that to be awkward for either of them.

Professor Kimble had also sent a card, only his was thicker, and when she opened it she was less than startled to find an audiotape enclosed. The card read, *Best wishes for a Happy Holiday* (Hallmark not Kimble), and then, *Please transcribe this tape at your leisure. I'll need it by the beginning of next week.*

Hey, it wasn't like she had anything else going on. She hadn't worked on her novel in a while, and could not seem to get up any motivation.

By eight o'clock that night, Reese needed some air.

She'd snapped photos of Ally and Ben under the mistletoe, Angela and Drew under the mistletoe, and her parents under the mistletoe, and now she was beyond drained.

Grabbing her thick winter coat from the hall closet, she picked up her keys and wound a scarf around her neck. "Bye, you guys," she said.

"Where are you going?" Joanna said, pressing her head against Michael's chest, as they remained standing under the mistletoe.

"I'm going out for a little while. I just need to clear my head."

"Reese, I don't like that idea," Michael said with concern. "It's dark out now and—"

"Don't worry. I'll go somewhere well lit . . . um, the pond. How's that?"

"All right, sweetheart," Joanna said, "if you're sure."

With that, Reese headed out, hopped into her car, and headed to the frozen pond in the center of town that was usually mobbed with ice-skaters. There was a hot cocoa stand, and a skate rental booth, too. She'd spent a lot of time there when she was young—back when she still got the kids' rate on her skates, and had no clue that cocoa was fattening.

After she parked, Reese walked across the white, powdery ground, which had not yet been squashed into slush. She took a seat on one of the mahogany benches near the pond, situated under an old-fashioned-looking street lamp with colored lights twirling around it that were blinking slightly out of time. The skaters looked happy and serene, and bundled to the hilt, with foggy breath seeping out from under their scarves, as holiday music played over-head.

At this time of night, the Goldwood pond was crowded with couples instead of children, which proved to be depressing. Men and women were prac-tically hugging as they skated together, and Reese wanted to loathe all of the PDA, but instead she was just jealous.

"Reese, is that you?" a syrupy voice said.

Reese turned to see Lane McBride approaching, with muscle-neck Tom on her arm. "Oh, hey, Lane," she said, forcing a smile. "What's up?"

"Ooh, I'm glad I'm not the only one who ducked out on Christmas!" she cheered, and flashed big grin. Reese, you remember Tom, right?" They exchanged brief, pointless pleasantries. "Well, we were just leav-ing, anyway. Tell Ally I said hi, okay?"

When Reese agreed, Lane cooed, "Thanks, you're the best. By the way, don't forget about the surprise shower on Friday—you bring Ally and it'll be just us girls!"

"Oh, right. Don't worry; I haven't forgotten," Reese lied.

"Well, toodles," she sang, and dragged her boy-toy away with her.

A few long, solitary moments passed before Reese glanced over at the hot cocoa stand. A line was wrap-ping around it, with people chatting and laughing and shivering, and it hit her.

It was so damn obvious. There was a whole world out there full of people and laughter and hot choco-late, and she was wasting it feeling sorry for herself. How stupid!

She was suddenly filled with disgust. But it was a good kind of disgust—the proactive kind—the kind that made her get off her butt and do something about it.

Hopping up from the bench, she blew on her hands, and smiled into the night. Things were going to be different. No, really, she meant it this time. She was going to get back to her novel, and Kimble would just have to wait. Her dissertation would have to wait.

Chocolate would wait, too, she thought, as she deliberately avoided the cocoa stand; she was determined to lose a few pounds before Ally's wedding, and she couldn't afford to sabotage herself now.

After she laced up a scuffed pair of size sevens with obviously dulled blades, she said hi to Mr. Sapperstein, who mentioned that he and his poker club were looking forward to Ally's wedding. Then Reese headed onto the pond. "Break a leg!" Mr. Sapperstein called from behind, making her feel extremely jinxed.

And then she was out on the ice—floating around and around, letting the night wind tangle her hair, burn her cheeks, sting her nose . . . and breathe new life into her heart.

Chapter Twenty-one

The week after the holidays, Reese was back at Roland & Fisk and not minding it so much, because her mind was usually somewhere else. She was tired all the time, but in that eye-strained, stayed-up-half-the-night-writing, excellent kind of way that she would not trade for any amount of sleep.

The family had also been very busy finalizing the details for Ally's wedding, like arranging vegan meals for Ben's aunts, and revamping the head wreaths so they were not quite so mortifying.

On Thursday afternoon, Reese finished with a customer, and glanced up at the clock: 1:30. Good, her shift was already half over. She had taken the next three days off—Friday for Ally's shower, Saturday for the rehearsal, and Sunday for the ceremony and reception. Out-of-town guests would be staying at the Goldwood Villa Hotel, which gave Reese the idea to treat herself to a room, too. She figured the hotel would be a terrific place to get away from all the other distractions and chaos in her parents' house; it would be the perfect place to work on her novel. It was really coming along, but she definitely had to keep plugging.

For a Thursday afternoon, the customer service desk was pretty deserted. Reese still took her breaks in the café, and talked with Tina all the time. Her big, romantic evening with Freddy was only a day away.

Reese hadn't seen the creepy customer or his mother in a while, but she was definitely not complaining.

Just then a woman approached the desk. "Hi," Reese said brightly, actually glad to have a customer to assist. "How can I help you?"

"Yes, hello. I'm looking for a *New York Times* best-seller by either a man or woman. Um, it's about a guy, and something with a war . . . I think."

"Okay, do you know if it's been on the best-seller list for a long time?" Reese asked, figuring out exactly how she was going to track it down. At Roland & Fisk, the policy was simple: "Put the book in the customer's hand." The days of pointing them in a vague direction and letting them wander off into cluelessness were gone.

Normally Reese didn't mind walking with a customer to get a book. The only thing that boggled her mind was the overwhelming compulsion people had to make small talk with her on the way, desperate to fill the thirty seconds of silence. She'd never understand that.

"I don't know how long it's been on the list," the woman was saying, "and it might have been the *USA Today* list. I can't remember." Shrugging, she threw in a halfhearted "sorry."

Reese attempted to locate the book in the computer database, but after less than ten seconds, the woman grew impatient. "Maybe there's someone else who can help me?"

"Oh . . ."

"What do you need?" Rhoda asked, suddenly right behind Reese, because for the next four hours they would be sharing this tiny customer service cell, and Reese would be enduring Rhoda's endless condescension about all of the books people wanted to read, as opposed to the obscure ones Rhoda pretended to have read. What *fun.*

Then again . . . Rhoda's arrogance might come in handy. Really, if she wanted to take this woman off Reese's hands, more power to her. Stepping aside, Reese let Rhoda embark on what she knew would be a wild-goose chase.

Just then, she heard the creaks and squeals of a rolling cart. Poor Amy was wheeling an overflowing dolly of books that looked like they were about to cave and topple any second. "Do you need some help?" Reese asked, starting come out from behind the desk.

Sharply, Darcy yelled, "Do it and get docked, *Brock.*"

"Wha—?"

"She needs to *learn,*" Darcy said, and blew an obscenely huge bubble with her bright blue gum. "Come on, keep moving, Amy; the books won't shelve themselves!"

Of course, Reese felt bad for Amy, who had taken over Reese's place in the Darcy-torture department. Not that Darcy didn't still hound, harass, and haunt Reese all day, every day. She did—but not with nearly the same gusto. It seemed that she saved her zeal up for Amy. Claiming she was "breaking her in."

The poor girl still tried so hard, but what she failed to grasp was the most basic Roland & Fisk principle: There was little point in trying, because you were screwed either way.

Amy looked at Reese with a miserable, beast-of-burden expression of agony, while Darcy trailed behind her snapping her fingers and taunting her with threats.

Then the cart screeched into the distance, and Reese shook her head and let out a laugh. She couldn't help it; sometimes life just seemed so ridiculous.

As she straightened some papers on her side of the desk, she heard Rhoda ask someone if he needed help, and she heard that someone say no, thank you, he was there to speak with Reese. She kept her eyes glued downward as her heart raced and her pulse exploded in her veins. The voice was achingly familiar—low, smooth, and sexy—she'd know it anywhere, and it ripped her heart in two.

After steeling himself up to talk to Reese, Brian had gone to Roland & Fisk with the rationalization that they needed to clear the air before Ally and Ben's wedding.

Of course, he hadn't realized how much bullshit that was until he saw her. One look from across the store, and his chest had constricted, the breath joltingly knocked out of him. Immediately, he felt that inexorable pull—that helpless attraction. Christ, he was still totally intrigued, infatuated, and charmed. And everything else he had no right to be anymore.

He'd been about to approach when Reese had darted out from behind the desk to help some bedraggled cart girl. That was so Reese—so energetic, so damn sweet—and he'd known that about her, even as he'd picked up the phone to call Veronica two weeks before. He had made his choice to try to move forward with Veronica, and he couldn't very well go back on it now . . . could he?

Now that they were face-to-face again, he just wanted to reach across the desk, grab Reese, and pull her to him. To feel her softness against him, to hear her whisper his name, to hear her whisper so shyly, "I like being with you."

Every time he remembered the words, they pierced right through him. Reese had been so honest, so trusting, and he had disappeared on her afterward—using all his willpower to avoid the café altogether. And she still had no idea why.

She probably hated him. She had to hate him.

Judging by the cold, withering look she was giving him now, and the iciness in her pale green eyes, he'd say his instincts were dead-on.

"Hi, Reese," he said.

"Hello," she said crisply, averting her eyes abruptly to look at her computer screen. Busily, she dragged and clicked her mouse. After a moment she demanded, "Can I help you with something, *sir*?"

So they were back to square one. "No," he replied, coming closer and resting a hand on the desk. She eyed it for less than a second, then focused back on her monitor. "I just wanted to stop in and say hi," he supplied lamely.

Who had he been kidding? He thought they could simply go back to being friendly acquaintances now? After the raw passion that had exploded between them? *Psfft.* He could barely even look at her without his gut hollowing out, and his dick throbbing.

"Okay," she said curtly. "Hi." Then she began fooling with the same papers he'd seen her straightening before he approached.

He scrambled to think of something else to say.

She whipped her head around, no longer avoiding his eyes, but burning a hole right through him. Angry and impatient, but so goddamn beautiful. He struggled to slow his heart and get his brain back.

Meanwhile she snapped, "What do you *want*?"

"Nothing . . . I mean—"

"Well, I'm working here, sir, so, if you don't mind—"

"I'm looking for a book," Brian said quickly.

Squinting at him suspiciously, she challenged him with a sassy tilt of her head.

"It's true, I am," he insisted.

Finally she shrugged, and asked coolly, "Fine, what book?" as she poised those soft, kind hands on her keyboard. Time to improvise, and fast.

"Um . . . it's . . . a book . . . about . . . engineering," he said brilliantly. "It's, uh, one of those idiot's guides, or imbecile's guides, whatever." God, he was becoming a pathetic bastard, doing anything he could to drag out this encounter. And to what purpose? Hell if he knew.

"Okay, I see a listing," she said sharply. "Come on."

With that, she exited the customer service area and started charging down the nearest aisle, not even making a pretense of waiting for him. He followed, jogging behind to keep up.

He was too depressed to even enjoy seeing that curvy butt move. Looking at it only made him ache worse, and feel emptier. He looked anyway, of course.

When they got to the business reference section, Reese hooked a quick right, and Brian almost collided with her because she stopped so abruptly to look at the shelves.

"Oh, sorry," he said, stepping back.

She ignored him, and focused ahead. Then she squinted—which was cuter than anything—and took a pair of glasses out of her front pocket. Setting them on her face, she started scanning the shelves.

"Reese . . ." he started, inching closer to her because he couldn't help it. Instantly she inched away, still not looking at him, but manically reading the shelves from left to right. "Reese, I know you're mad that I just sort of disappeared after what happened. . . ."

She scoffed, and continued looking on the shelves, muttering something that sounded like, "Right, *that's* why—creep."

He opened his mouth to speak again, but she cut him off before he had the chance. "Fine, here it is," she said, reaching for a fat orange book on the top shelf. But she struggled because she was too short; Brian pulled it down for her, because he knew she wouldn't ask him for help. Haughtily pushing her glasses up on her nose, Reese said, "Well, that's it, then."

"Reese, wait," Brian said softly, and reached out to touch her arm.

She violently jerked it back. "What do you think you're doing?"

"Nothing, I'm sorry—"

"You should be," she said under her breath.

He sighed with frustration. "Well, I am. Reese, I'm trying to explain myself here."

"Well, that's very nice, but I'm on the clock." Great, she sounded like she was possessed by her boss now. "Maybe you'd like me to find you something else, though? Maybe something in the *bridal* section?"

"Huh?" he said, confused.

Reese scoffed and rolled her eyes, which appeared to be almost glowing from the way the light reflected off her glasses. Then, lowering her voice to an angry whisper, she said, "Please, Brian, I'm not a fool. I heard all about your engagement."

"Wha—you mean you know about Veronica?"

"Yes, I know! Did you think I wouldn't find out? How could you do that to me?"

"Wait, I don't get it—"

"What don't you get? The fact that I think you're a complete jerk? Good-bye, Brian," she said, pushing past him. "Have a nice marriage—"

"Whoa," he said, catching her arm. "I think you have your facts wrong. I'm not engaged."

"Stop *lying*," she hissed, whipping back around. "Just stop lying to me, you prick!" Then she kicked him in the shin—*hard*.

"Ow! Wait, Reese . . ." He brought one hand to his shin, and kept the other on her arm, gently holding her in place. "Veronica and I are *not* engaged. We were once, but we're not now."

"Oh, please, I heard Ben tell Ally you guys are back together, so don't even bother—"

"Wait, just wait, please," he pleaded, letting her go, and holding his hands up Joanna-style. Reese crossed her arms across her breasts and waited. On a heavy sigh, Brian explained. "Look, the truth is, Veronica and I *were* engaged once, but we broke off the engagement a couple of years ago—*before* you and I ever met." She still stood there, which was a good thing, but she had a grimace on her face as though he were a slug that had just had salt poured on it, which meant he'd better keep talking. "Reese, it's the truth. I swear."

"Right, I'm sure," she said dismissively. "That must be why you haven't stepped foot in the café for weeks."

"Well . . ." Christ, how did he explain *that*?

Reese must have taken his hesitation for an admission of guilt, because she plowed on. "Now it all makes sense, why you never told Ben about what was going on between us. You probably figured he'd say something to me about Veronica."

"That's not true!"

"Uh-huh."

"Wait a minute, what about you? You never said anything to Ben, either. How come?"

"I . . . because . . . wait, don't turn this around on me."

"That's not an answer," he pressed.

She paused and looked over at the shelves. "Maybe I just wanted to figure out what was going on between us before I told anyone." Letting out a humorless laugh, she said, "What an idiot I was."

"*No* . . . you weren't an idiot, or anything else," he said, moving closer. "Look, a few months ago, Veronica and I started talking again. But we haven't gotten back together . . . not *exactly*."

Reese squinted at that, as though mulling it over, then nodded. "Meaning that she wants to, and now you've decided you want to, too. Is that it?" He knew she was a smart little cookie. "Well?" she demanded.

He didn't know what to say, because that was exactly what had happened. At least, he'd thought so until now. Now he had the feeling that what'd really happened was that he'd made the biggest goddamn mistake of his life.

Swallowing, Reese murmured, "I guess you just gave me the answer. Good-bye, Brian." She turned and walked out into the aisle.

"Wait," Brian said, following and nudging her into the finance and fortune section.

"Hey!" she said, pushing at his chest, which reminded him of how she'd pushed at his chest before—rubbed it, stroked it, clawed at it.

"Look, it's hard to explain. Veronica is going through a really tough time lately, and I told her I'd think about everything. I told her we'd decide about getting back together after Ben's wedding."

Reese's jaw dropped. "You're bringing her to the *wedding*?" Then she shook her head and covered her face with her hands. "Of course you are," she mumbled, definitely more to herself, and Brian moved in a little closer.

"Reese, the reason I haven't come into the store lately is because I didn't think it would be right. I promised Veronica that I would give the idea of her and me a real chance, and I knew there was no way in hell I could do that if I were around you."

He set his hands on her upper arms, barely making contact, and finally she lifted her head to meet his gaze. She looked wounded and miserable and tired, and he couldn't believe a selfish asshole like him had done that to her.

"Why?" she asked softly.

"Why, what?" he said huskily, and gently rubbed her arms with his hands.

"Why couldn't you be around me?"

She knew the answer—she *had* to know the answer. To him, it was painfully obvious, and one look at his engorged crotch would show her just how painful it was. Sliding his hands down her arms, he lightly cupped her wrists, and bent to brush her temple with his forehead. He inhaled some of her scent, and spoke raggedly. "Because you drive me crazy. When I see you . . . when I'm with you . . . it's so good."

They were so close to each other now that heat was emanating off their bodies. It mingled in the space between them, and made Brian's breath catch. Reese was all soft warmth in his hands. He nuzzled her ear, and whispered into it, "I can't seem to resist you."

She started to say something, but then he opened his mouth on her ear and tugged her lobe with his lips. She let out a low, throaty sigh. Then he sucked, and her head fell limply forward. His erection was pulsing in his pants. He slid his palm down over hers, locking their hands, while his other palm moved to her waist. Unwittingly, he dug his fingers into the angel-soft material of her sweater, clutching it hard as he licked the spot behind her ear and heard her moan. It was a tiny, strangled little moan, but he'd heard it, and hot blood began coursing through him, flooding his groin, thundering through his veins, and without any rational thought, he cupped her breast. Right there in the middle of Roland & Fisk. And, as if that wasn't bad enough, he squeezed.

Reese pulled back. She was breathing almost as rapidly as he was, and Brian could *feel* the starry, aroused glaze in his eyes. Still, he immediately apologized. "I'm so sorry—I didn't mean to do that." Not exactly the truth, but it was the best he could do.

Reese bit her lip and looked down at the carpet for a moment. She probably wanted to hide her face from him, which was hot pink with . . . embarrassment? Desire? Or was it ferocious anger, more than anything?

Stepping back, she lifted her head and adjusted her glasses, which had started sliding down her nose. Then she said, "Brian, stop. I can't do this; I just can't."

"I know," he said almost hoarsely. "You're at work—I can't believe I totally lost control like that, and your boss could have walked by at any moment."

Shaking her head, she said, "No, I didn't mean that. I meant this, us. Look, if you picked Veronica once, then you'll pick her again. Being with her is obviously what you're most comfortable with, and that's fine. But please . . . just keep me out of it."

She turned on her heel and stormed away—or at least she *started* to. . . .

Chapter Twenty-two

She'd only covered about a foot of carpet before she smacked right into someone—a tall, lean man, whom she all but ricocheted off, and when she looked up, she was startled to see the one person she'd never expected at Roland & Fisk.

What on earth is Kenneth doing here?

Even though he lived in New York City, he'd never, to Reese's knowledge, come into the store. And frankly, this wasn't the best time for him to try something new.

Suddenly Reese experienced one of those surreal, jolting moments when life truly felt like a dream, and for a split second she wondered if it was.

But here she was, sandwiched between Brian and Kenneth, and all she wanted was to get the hell away from both of them. Even dreams weren't that strange. "Kenneth, hi. What are you doing here?" she asked, confused.

"I came to, uh, see you," he replied awkwardly. Then, in a stiff motion, he raised an unbent arm and set it across her shoulders.

"Wha—?"

"Who's this?" Brian asked, sounding annoyed.

Reese turned to face him again—not an easy feat, considering Kenneth's straight arm had all but locked her into position. With a cricked neck, she managed to reply coolly, "None of your business."

Brian narrowed his eyes at Kenneth, and then nodded. "You're right," he said quietly, "I guess it isn't my business." Yet he didn't make any move to leave.

Meanwhile Reese tried to jerk her shoulders free from Kenneth's perverse attempt at demonstrativeness. Unsurprisingly, he missed the nonverbal cues, and tightened his hold. Maybe the boy should stick to what he knew best—namely, aloofness, nosy questions, and throat clearing. "Hello," he said to Brian. "I'm Kenneth Peel. Reese's boyfriend."

WHAT!

What the hell was he talking about? Had he gone completely *loco?*

He most certainly was not her boyfriend! Although, admittedly, her protests were ironic, since only a few months ago she had wanted him to be just that. She had also wanted him to show more initiative, and now he was *oozing* with it. So why was she so creeped out?

Still, she didn't want to embarrass him in front of Brian. Okay, fine, so maybe she *also* didn't mind having Brian think she had a little more game going on than sitting and pining for him all day long.

"What, did you two just meet recently?" Brian asked.

"No, Reese and I have been an item for quite a while now," Kenneth replied, and bent his lead-weight arm just enough to draw Reese closer. Abruptly, he planted one of his trademark dry smackers on her cheek, and Brian jerked his head back a little. His eyes bore into hers, giving Reese a dry throat and a thick, clogging tongue. Yet she couldn't tear her eyes away for a second. She gulped almost painfully.

Of course, a big part of her wanted to shove Kenneth off—to ask him if he was on medication, and if so, it was certainly about time—but she just couldn't do it. She had to be tough, she had to be strong, she had to be a "woman of the millennium" and all that. Anyway, didn't Brian *deserve* to feel as misled and disillusioned and hurt as *she* had?

Well, she didn't know if he felt all that, but she did see his eyes darken, and his expression change from annoyed to jealous. And he was starting that pissed-as-hell, slow nodding again. "Well, I won't keep you any longer, Reese," he said.

She had the distinct feeling that Brian meant the words literally, and that twisted her stomach into a painful knot.

"Take care," he finished curtly, and turned and walked away.

As soon as he was gone, a gigantic lump of sadness and loss rose to the top of Reese's throat. It stayed lodged there, making it hard to swallow, hard to breathe, until she finally gulped it down, and immediately felt the burning sting of tears in the backs of her eyes.

More than anything, she needed to go somewhere to be alone, but she couldn't because she was still on the clock, and Darcy would sniff her out in no time.

Plus the fact that she had Kenneth weighing down

her shoulders, which would need a little more lee-
way if she were going to cry.

"Um . . . Kenneth?" she said, trying to tug herself
out from under his arm.

Kenneth was slow to get the point, so Reese
yanked away harder. As soon as she broke free, she
moved a few feet back as a preventive measure. Kenneth left his arm hanging stupidly in the air for two
or three seconds before he cleared his throat and set
it back at his side.

"You still haven't told me what you're doing
here," she said. "And how did you know where to
find me in the store?"

"Oh. A woman at the customer service desk
pointed in the northwest direction, so I came searching for you."

"Okay . . . but . . ." Jeez, there was just no tactful
way to say this, but she absolutely had to clarify
something. "How come you said you were my boyfriend? I mean, we're not really dating exclusively,
are we? Um, or at all?"

Kenneth began fiddling with the zippers on his
jacket pockets, and Reese forced herself not to back-
pedal to try to save him. They had never discussed
being boyfriend/girlfriend. And, not that she was
trying to be a stickler, but weren't boyfriends and
girlfriends supposed to touch each other—like,
frequently?

"Well, I was hoping we could spend more time
together," he said unemotionally. "You're right, I
spoke too soon about us having a, uh, relationship.
However, I'd like, uh, you to—*ahem, ahem*—stay open

to said possibilities. Let's begin with lunch today.
My treat."

Okay, a gold star for taking some major initiative;
a demerit for doing it way too late, after Reese had
lost interest and fallen for another man. Couldn't
Kenneth see the writing on the wall? They were not
couple material. Reese really couldn't believe it had
taken *her* so long to realize it.

"Oh . . . well . . ." she stammered lamely, "I'm
just not looking for a relationship right now . . . and
unfortunately I can't do lunch, either, because I already took a break earlier."

Expressionless, Kenneth nodded. "Well, I should
get going," he said tonelessly.

"Okay . . . um, thanks for coming by," she said,
overly cheerful.

"Yes, certainly," he said. Before he left, he looked
back and asked, "But I will still be escorting you to
your sister's wedding, won't I?"

"Oh, sure, yeah, uh-huh, great!" When she felt
guilty, she babbled—and loudly.

Kenneth disappeared around the bend, and Reese
just stood there, taking in all that had happened in
a matter of minutes. The last thing she had expected
was a confrontation with Brian today. She was sure
the lying pig would never set foot in the store again.
Or maybe that he would wait awhile, and then come
in acting like he couldn't quite remember her.

Wait, hadn't that been her plan before all this
had started?

What she really couldn't believe was that she had
kicked him. Thinking about it, it made her smile. Hell,
it almost made her laugh. She truly hadn't planned

to do it, but she supposed like all great poetry, it had been pure inspiration.

She didn't let herself think about how Kenneth was starting to weird her out; she only knew that he seemed to be there to stay. But since she wasn't interested in him anymore, that could not possibly be a good thing. Basically, when she put it all together, her romantic horizon was looking bleak once again.

At least that was the little epiphany she had standing in the finance and fortune section, pretty much out of luck.

"Hey, nice digs; can I crash here?"

"No way," Reese said, smiling, and hauled her overnight bag over the threshold of room 816. "This is my minivacation, and I want to be able to walk around naked."

"Okay, okay," Ally said, trailing behind with Reese's laptop. They set both down on the full-sized bed; then Ally plopped down into an armchair by the window. "This room *rocks*. How did you afford it?"

"How else? On credit," Reese said.

"So what are you gonna do here? Just work on your book?"

"Uh-huh, I hope so." She'd told Ally about her novel the day after Christmas, which was the same day that Reese had thrown herself back into the project. Since then, she had been more enthusiastic than ever. She had six chapters written, and she was starting to hear her characters talking in her head—which had to be a good, albeit disturbing, sign.

She had yet to tell her mother about her writing. Right now, there would be no point. It was all too hypothetical for Joanna to appreciate. Joanna liked concrete: a degree, a man. Actually, when Reese thought about it, her mother was a remarkably simple woman to please.

"But won't you get lonely?" Ally asked.

Reese grinned. "I doubt it. But if I do, I'll definitely call you."

" 'Kay."

"Anyway, with the bridal shower today, the rehearsal tomorrow, and the wedding on Sunday, I'm not exactly ensconced in isolation," she added dryly.

"Oh, I forgot!" Ally reached inside her over-the-shoulder bag and pulled out a small box of condoms. "Here, I'll get them from you on the wedding night," she said, and did some exaggerated winking.

"Okay," Reese said, tossing the box to the side. "But I still think it's ridiculous to hide them from Mom. I think she kind of knows you'll be sleeping with your husband on your wedding night."

Ally rolled her eyes. "You know how Mom is. She's helping me pack my stuff for the honeymoon, and if she sees condoms before Ben and I are officially married, she'll get all weird. I know she knows that we sleep together, but she doesn't *know* know."

"Can't Ben bring them?"

"He is, but this box is just extra," Ally said. "But I'm sure we'll need 'em." *Wink, wink.*

Reese grinned; then she realized the time. "Oh, we've gotta get going! The shower starts in ten minutes."

After Ally shut the door behind them, she said, "By the way, Lane's been acting all secretive. She keeps asking me if I'm gonna stick around for a while after the shower. Is anything going on?"

Reese shrugged. "No."

Ally grabbed her arm. "Is Lane planning some sort of surprise?" Reese hesitated for literally a millisecond, and Ally yelped, "I knew it! C'mon, what is it? Just tell me."

Reese threw up her hands. "I swear, I know nothing."

Ally smiled. "Hey, can we get a stamp made?"

Reese rolled her eyes and laughed. "You are so corny."

As soon as Ally's bridal shower ended, Lane gathered all of Ally's friends in the Gallery Room of the Goldwood Villa for her "special surprise." Right now, Ally was grilling Deb about the surprise, and Reese was accosting Angela, who had just come in late.

"I was hoping Lane would get food for this," Reese said.

Angela smiled faintly. "What, she didn't?"

"No. I mean, I know I'm technically on a diet and everything, but still." Angela smiled again but Reese could see that it was forced. "Hey, is anything wrong?" she asked.

Angela mumbled, "I think I've really had it with Drew."

"What happened? I thought things were better—I mean, at Christmas you guys seemed fine."

"Well, sometimes they are, but then he's distant again. I wish we could just talk about what's happened—I mean, we never really have."

"Still?"

"Well, we've 'talked,' but we haven't *talked* talked." Sighing, she said, "I mean, if he's angry with me, or whatever, I wish he'd just *tell* me."

Obviously Drew wasn't from the Tina school of saying things right to a person's face.

"Yeah, of course," Reese said, nodding supportively.

"But it's not just that," Angela went on miserably. "It's . . . well . . ." Her eyes pooled with tears, and her voice broke off.

"Angela, what?" Reese pressed.

Shaking her head, Angela said, "It's just that we haven't been intimate in a really long time"—Reese had pretty much inferred that after her conversation with Angela at the Laughing Frog—"and last night I tried to initiate something, and he blew it off cold." Swallowing deeply, she finished, "I'm starting to wonder if there's someone else."

"All right, girls," Lane announced, "we're ready to start!"

"Oh, never mind," Angela said quickly. "Forget I said anything. It's not a big deal."

Okay, this was *it*. Reese absolutely hated giving unsolicited advice, but her sister needed a shove on this issue, plain and simple. And it was long overdue. "No, it *is* a big deal, Angela," she said firmly. "In fact, it is such a big deal that I cannot believe you haven't confronted Drew yet."

Angela blinked. "What, you mean . . . ?"

"I mean that you've been handling this all wrong. Look, I'm sorry, but it's true. I'm not saying it's all your fault, but you're miserable, and you're just letting Drew control all of your emotions—all the time. If he's happy, you're happy; if he sulks, you can't even face going to work because you're so depressed. For Pete's sake, Angela, you're so obsessed with *his* moods, you can't even sleep!"

Angela looked stunned. "So what am I *supposed* to do?"

"How about acting instead of just *re*acting? He's manipulating you, and you're totally letting him. Look, you want to confront Drew, you want to talk to him about everything, including the heart attack, so do it. Especially the heart attack."

Angela swallowed, and looked down. A pregnant pause followed and stretched blaringly between them. Oh, no, Reese had said too much—she'd gone too far, and now her sister would be angry.

Finally Angela looked up, and said, "Okay, I will, thanks."

Then Reese said sheepishly, "Sorry about the tough love," and Angela let out a laugh.

"Hey, cuties," Ally said, coming over and sitting next to Reese. "So what's the deal, seriously? Did Lane get me a stripper?"

Sudden loud, twangy, B-movie music sounded through the room, answering Ally's question. "Oh, man!" she said. "This is gonna be funny."

"A real live naked man," Angela muttered. "This should be a refresher for me."

Reese grinned. "Please, it's like primer one for me."

"What are you guys talking about?" Ally asked.

"Oh, he's starting!" The women in the room broke into giggles as the "dancer" shook and wiggled into the room.

"So Lane set this all up?" Angela whispered to Reese.

"I guess."

"Who's paying for it?"

"Take a guess," Reese said, knowing full well that the Brocks would be getting an invoice in the mail after all the wedding smoke had cleared. That was Lane.

Introducing himself as Gino, the stripper donned a pizza delivery man's outfit that lacked, well, authenticity. But maybe it was just Reese who had never seen a delivery man in red satin shorts that rode up his butt, and a muscle-tee with a wide V cut down the front to allow his chest hair breathing room.

"Sooo," Gino drawled with blatant cockiness and a sickeningly feral smile. "Who ordered the *deluxe*?" He tossed the prop pizza box to the side and threw down his red cap.

Within moments his muscle-tee was gone, and he'd unzipped what there was of his fly. The shorty shorts dropped to the floor. As Gino stepped out of them, he did a high kick that sent them flying into the crowd.

Everyone shrieked wildly, clapped, and yelled, "Take it off!" even though he pretty much had. Well, everyone except Reese, who just couldn't muster up any cheers or whistles.

Maybe she was slightly afraid that if she opened her mouth, she'd end up asking Gino why his hairstyle of choice was a kinky-curly mullet that appeared to be sopping wet. And she didn't want to be rude, after all, or give him some sort of complex. Then he might start questioning some of his other life decisions, too—like setting the tanning machine on burnt orange and putting gold glitter on his nipples.

Okay, so she would never really say any of that to Gino. But still . . . she wasn't exactly drooling over the guy. In fact, all he made her think about—*quite* ironically—was Brian.

Damn it all. Why couldn't she just forget about him? Part of her was still livid over the situation with his ex, but another part of her just . . . missed him.

Gino danced around the room, and then back to the center, wearing nothing but the requisite G-string. As he did a mini–lap dance over Ally, she laughed and averted her eyes a little. That was when Gino made eye contact with Reese.

Shoot! How had *that* happened? *Please don't come over to me, please don't come over. . . .*

But he was coming over anyway. And even worse, he was pulling her up. Reese shook her head, keeping a smile plastered on, and trying as graciously as she could to refuse his offer to "dance." It didn't work, though, because Ally's friends were cheering them on, and Gino looked so turned on by *himself*, he was oblivious to Reese's discomfort.

Reese's face darkened as she became the unenthused recipient of Gino's bumping and grinding. She'd definitely need a shower after this. Her moves were awkward and out-of-time, and luckily it didn't take long for Gino to realize that Reese was cramping his style. So finally he winked at her and spun away—gyrating solo back to the center of the room.

Reese jumped back into her seat and warned her sisters, "Don't. Say. A word."

When the music kicked up, Gino's pelvic thrusts showed even more feeling, until, all of a sudden, something happened.

Just as he was doing something that looked like a cross between the Running Man and the Roger Rabbit, the music cut out. A blip and it was gone. It just *stopped*.

Gino froze, his bug eyes betraying how unprepared he was for the technical glitch, as he searched Lane's face for some explanation. Lane shrugged, and hopped out of her chair to go see what happened.

She was gone only about two minutes, but they were *long* minutes. Especially to Gino, who stood in the center of the room awkwardly, not knowing quite how to posture himself, and pretending to fiddle with tassels that hung above his balls. Not exactly a moment that oozed dignity. Apparently, without the music, his bravado and confidence were completely shot. Finally he looked up and laughed nervously. "Wonder what happened," he said.

Reese turned to Angela and whispered, "This is brutal."

She nodded emphatically.

Beats of silence followed; then women began whispering among themselves. Some were making small talk about the hotel, while others were saying ungroundbreaking things like, "I guess something's wrong with the sound system."

Not that Reese could come up with anything better. She was just sitting there like a dolt, resisting the urge to point out to Gino that he was actually living that famous dream of standing in a room full of people, wearing only underwear. Hmm—something told her he wouldn't appreciate the profoundly Freudian moment.

Finally Lane shuffled back into the room and announced, "I can't figure out what's wrong with the sound system." Bad news for Gino.

"But there's no reason why we can't still continue the fun!" Even worse news for Gino.

"Come on, everyone, let's keep the action going!" she added on a rallying tone that harked back to her cheerleading days.

Beaming, she added with grating peppiness, "We don't need music to enjoy a good old-fashioned hunk, right, ladies?" *Sure, just bring in the hunk.* "Go on, shake it, shake it!"

Reese didn't know whether to laugh or cry—either option would be at Gino's expense, of course. "Huh?" he croaked, still standing front and center and nearly buck, with one set of toes crossing over the other.

"Keep it coming stud!" Lane sang.

"W-what do you mean?" he asked, appearing frightfully concerned. "You actually want me to keep dancing . . . without music?"

"Sure, we don't need music!" The horrified look on Gino's face that said, *Maybe* you *don't but* I *do* seemed to go unnoticed.

Ally spoke up encouragingly; "Yeah, you're doing great!"

Finally he muttered feebly, "All right," and began

rocking his pelvis. Back and forth. Back and forth. In utter, blackening silence. He jiggled his hips, repeating the motion sporadically, and making the move look more like a spasm. Then he halfheartedly stroked his oiled torso. His face was deep red-orange. The women shifted uncomfortably in their seats as Gino turned around and clenched his butt.

"Oh, my Lord," Angela managed, while Reese brought her palm to her forehead, thinking, *My sentiments exactly*.

After a few more protracted moments, as Gino awkwardly caressed and flexed his body, while the room couldn't muster even the most benevolent catcall, Reese decided she couldn't take any more. Strippers had labor laws, too, right?

But just as she was about to demand some mercy for him, Lane ended his torture. "Okay, thank you!" she said, clapping her manicured hands. "Ooh, we'd better get some ice water in here, right, ladies?"

Gino smiled brittlely—hell, *everyone* smiled brittlely.

After one bow, he gathered up his strewn costume and bolted from the room.

No one said anything at first. Then the room broke into muted chatter, while Reese turned to her sisters and they all exchanged knowing looks. Words would only be redundant.

Finally Angela slapped her knees and said, "Okay, show's over." That was the best news Reese had heard that day.

Chapter Twenty-three

Drew was in the bedroom, sitting at his desk, going over bills, from what Angela could see, but his back was turned away from her—which it always was these days.

Balling her hands up, she steadied them against her thighs and sucked in a calming breath. Then she said the words she knew he didn't want to hear: "Drew, we need to talk."

"About what?" he asked with perceptible uninterest.

"I . . . um . . . I want to know if . . ." *Just blurt it, you wimp.* "Is there someone else?" Tears stung as she said it, because it felt like such an idiotic cliché. Asking if there was someone else usually meant, *I know there's someone else, but give me a rationalized denial I can live with.*

Drew just snorted, his shoulders jerking up. "Yeah, right. One of the blue-haired ladies in that support group you sent me to."

"That's not an answer."

"Oh, Christ," he grumbled. "What, did you find out one of your clients is lying again?"

"I wanna know if there's someone else," she said, feeling her temper rise. "I want to know *now*."

Drew spun his chair around. "Oh, so I'm not only an ineffectual invalid, I'm also a philanderer, is that it?"

"Who said anything about your being an invalid?" she cried. "What the hell are you talking about?"

He scoffed. "I see you didn't disagree."

"Oh, quit feeling sorry for yourself, and answer the stupid question!"

"Are you *kidding*?" he nearly yelled, and smacked the arm of his chair with his hand. "You think there's someone else? I can't even satisfy my own wife!" He rose and stormed toward the door, but she wouldn't let him get away that easily.

"You don't even try," she said pleadingly, as she grabbed his arm to stop him. He yanked away, still turned and refusing to look at her. "Drew, you . . . it's like you're not even interested."

"Christ, don't you *get* it?" he yelled. "I'm not the same man I used to be—I can't just throw you down and fuck you anymore!"

That was *it*.

She took one of her balled fists and socked him right on the back.

"Ow!" he said, startled, and bringing a hand up to rub his shoulder blade.

"You miserable ingrate! How dare you treat me like this? You think you can keep taking out all your self-pity on me? I've always supported you; I've given you all of myself. And now you're gonna try to turn it around like *I'm* the one who's not satisfied?"

She swept her knuckles across her cheek to wipe

the tears that had fallen. "You know what I think? I think that *you're* the one who's not happy. You're the one who wants out, and you just don't have the guts to say it!" She bolted for the door, because if she stayed in his presence one more second, she seriously might kill him.

Now he grabbed *her*. Before she could yank her arm free, he pulled her roughly against his chest. Instinctively she struggled against his grasp.

"What do you want from me?" he demanded, boring his gaze into hers until she turned her head, stubbornly averting her glassy eyes. "That's not an answer," he mimicked, and she whacked his shoulder with the flat of her hand.

"Christ, stop hitting me!" he said, frustrated, as she wrestled to get free of him. For an invalid he was remarkably strong. Before she knew what was happening, he'd hitched her up and was walking them backward.

"Hey!" she cried. "What are you doing—put me down, you jerk! I hate you! I want a divorce!"

"Like hell," he growled, and dropped her down on the bed. Then he fell on top of her. She tried to shove him off, knowing it was futile. Pinning her flailing arms down, he said, "What? What do you want from me?"

"Get off of me."

"Then *what*? See, you don't really want this."

"You're right," she said brokenly, "I want all of you."

He didn't say anything to that. Keeping her face turned, she stared at the window, and moments passed before she felt Drew's weight relax on top

of her. No longer pinning her down, he was almost
cradling her, as his hands softened and his body
curled into hers.

It felt so familiar, like the most wonderful feeling
she had forgotten even existed. The aggression had
melted . . . but now what would take its place?

Wordlessly, Drew dropped his head, burying it in
the crook of Angela's neck. Neither broke the silence
for countless minutes. This was what would come
next—physical affection, body heat, making love.

Drew still didn't stir, but there was no denying
what Angela felt probing at her. Her husband's groin
was nestling into hers, and he was fully, breathtak-
ingly hard.

Yes.

A shock of pleasure ran through her—a powerful
surge of white-hot excitement. Still afraid he might
push her away, but unable to resist, Angela snaked
her legs up Drew's hips and slowly coiled them
around his waist. She tightened them, locking his
body to hers, and waited for his reaction.

He didn't push her away, but he remained still
and silent . . . so she kept going.

Sliding her hand up his side and over his shoulder,
she sank her fingers into his hair. She brushed
through it gently as she caressed his scalp, then raked
her nails lightly down the back of his neck. She felt
chills rise on his skin.

Soon he was pressing his hips down on hers. Letting out a breathy, aroused sigh, Angela lifted her
hips to nudge his erection deeper.

Drew's face stirred in her hair, and she felt the
heat of his breath on her neck. A thrill ran through

her as he brushed his lips back and forth over her hair, and then whispered hotly in her ear, "I want *you* . . . only you." Trailing kisses down her neck, he chanted, "You, you . . ."

"Oh, Drew . . ." She moaned, bringing both hands to his head and angling him so she could lick deep inside his ear. "Then take me," she whispered. "Please . . . it's been so long." He turned his face and kissed her hungrily.

Their mouths were open and wet and devouring, and soon they were grabbing at each other's clothes. Angela yanked his shirttail from his pants, and Drew tore open the buttons of her blouse. He shoved the bra down until it hung below her rib cage. Feverishly he pressed Angela's breasts together and buried his face between them. She moaned and rocked her lower body against his, as she reached down to take his erection out of his pants.

He licked up her chest to her neck and challenged huskily, "Aren't you going to tell me to 'take it easy'?"

Ignoring the question, she curled her fingers around his engorged penis and squeezed. A harsh sound burst from his throat, and he took a nipple in his mouth. Using his hand, he kept her other breast pressed to his cheek while he sucked on her.

She cried out, and he sucked harder and rocked his hips, forcing her hand to stroke him. Usually he liked her to run her hand over him slowly and tightly, but there was no time for that now, she realized. Tonight it was fast and tight. She was hot and wet with need, so fast and tight worked fine.

Sliding her index finger over the head of him, she

realized that she wasn't the only one who was wet. Her breath quickened and caught—they needed to do this—*now*. He bunched up her skirt with one hand, and clutched the silk of her underwear with the other. Then he yanked her panties down to her knees. "Yes," she whispered, and he plunged into her.

She shuddered and groaned, and Drew said hoarsely, "Don't you dare fake it."

"Don't be an ass," she said breathlessly, and begged, "Oh, baby, *please* don't stop."

Her eyes drifted shut in ecstasy as sensations overtook her. He was thrusting hard and deep, and she was biting her lip and digging her nails into his butt.

"God, you're so beautiful." He groaned, and pounded her harder.

With little warning, her muscles began clenching and contracting, and her breath exploded from her lungs in choppy, harsh gasps. Desperately, she fused her mouth to his in a wet, furious kiss, and Drew pumped his hips even faster.

"I love you, I love you," she whispered frantically as she climaxed.

Drew grunted loudly, and pumped two more times before his whole body convulsed, racked by what sounded like anguished sobs, as hot semen jetted out.

"Oh . . . *God* . . ." she cried, feeling the heat and wetness—feeling *him*.

After it was done, Angela kept Drew cradled in her arms, and his groin still nestled warmly inside her body.

"I love you," she whispered one more time.

He made no move to push her away; he only snuggled closer. And Angela vowed to herself that she'd never let him go. No way. She would never lose Drew again.

"What are you doing, babydoll?"

"Giving you a medical exam," Angela said softly, as she coasted her hand lightly over Drew's abdomen, then through his chest hair, and lovingly across his heart. Pressing an ear to his chest, she said, "Hmm, still breathing a little fast . . ." She smiled up at him. "But nothing we can't handle."

He grinned. "Have I ever told you"—he slid his hand under her hair, and drew her on top of him—"how *crazy* I am about this haircut?"

A giggle slipped from her lips, and Drew kissed it away. Afterward, she murmured, "I'm sorry," against his mouth. She stroked his jaw and said, "Drew, I'm sorry that I've been smothering you ever since . . . I mean, I just get so worried, and—"

"I know," he said quietly, "It's not that."

"Then what . . . what is it?"

"Nothing, I don't know."

"Drew, *talk* to me," she said, looking soulfully into his eyes, and for the first time in so long, feeling that she was actually reaching him. "Tell me."

He tightened his arms around her, snuggling her against his chest. "I just . . . it's . . ." Then he looked away and said, "Shit, I'm tired. Can we just go to sleep for now?"

She gave him a long, assessing look, then said, "If

that's what you want, babydoll. We'll talk later." She laid her head against his shoulder and rested her hand on his stomach.

"Thanks," he murmured, kissing her hair and resting his chin on her head. A few beats of silence passed before Drew whispered, "You're so beautiful." Smoothing his hands over her back, he sighed. "Young and beautiful . . . Angela . . . you could have anyone."

She lifted her head up, confused. "What?"

Drew brought a hand down to brush some of her flyaways aside; he opened his mouth to speak, then shut it quickly.

"I'd never want anyone else," Angela whispered, holding his jaw in place, forcing his eyes to hers. "You know that . . . don't you?"

He smiled faintly, and then, in spite of her hand, turned his head to the side. She climbed up higher on the bed, bracing her weight with her elbow, and whispered, "Babydoll . . ."

He turned to face her, and she saw that his eyes were watery, making them a glassy hazel that painfully gripped her heart. Her husband had never cried before—at least not in her presence. But he blinked back the tears, not letting them fall, and said thickly, "You're so young, and I . . . I don't want you to wake up one day and realize . . . Angela, I'm just not the same man I used to be."

She clutched his shoulders, levered herself over him, and stared hard into his eyes. "What on earth are you talking about? Drew, you're only forty, for Pete's sake."

"But—"

"Dr. Stone said your heart attack was mild and had nothing to do with being an old man." He sort of grinned at that. "Well, I can't remember his *exact* words," she qualified. "But still."

"I'm just . . . I don't know."

"What?"

"I feel . . . Oh, forget it; it's so fucking clichéd." She waited anyway. He sighed. "I just feel useless."

"Oh, baby, no," she said, and hugged him fiercely. "That's all in your *head*. But nothing has really changed. Can't you see that? Nothing has changed."

"How can you say that? *Everything*'s changed, and now I'll never even be a father."

Angela blinked and pushed up on her hands. "*What?*"

"I mean, I knew that I'd be older than most parents when we decided to have children, but now . . . oh, forget it."

"I don't want to forget it," she said anxiously. "Drew, did you want to start trying? Is that what you're telling me?"

"No, I mean, yes, but what's the point? I won't even be able to play with them, or to coach soccer, or . . ." Running a hand over his eyes, he laughed humorlessly and muttered, "See? I told you it was all fucking clichéd."

Angela let out a laugh, even though the subject was serious, and even though she had tears welling up in her eyes.

"What's so funny?" he asked.

Shaking her head, she smiled as two tears streaked

her cheeks. "Nothing," she said, "It's just that we're gonna have a family and . . . Oh, Drew!" She flung herself on top of him. "I'm so excited!"

He hugged her back, but couldn't help rolling his eyes. "Hello? What about everything I just said? Too old, heart condition, any of this ringing a bell?"

She laughed into his bare, warm skin, and said, "Forget it. We're having a family, end of discussion. Case closed, period. Thank you."

"What, you've been thinking about it, too?"

"I guess it's been in the back of my mind for a little while," she said, making a breezy sound of total contentment. "But now I'm sure that it's time."

"But everything's changed," Drew pressed, not sounding half as convicted about that point as he had a moment ago.

"No, it hasn't," Angela said briskly. "Life took a slight turn, and we're handling it. I still love you more than anyone or anything in the whole world—that hasn't changed."

When he didn't say anything, she said coyly, "Well? Do you still love *me*?"

"You know I do," he said huskily.

"So then?" she asked, kissing his shoulder.

"I just don't ever want to lose you."

Angela sucked in a breath, and thought, *He didn't want to lose me so he's been acting like a jerk—men are so weird.* "What, are you crazy? Have you missed how devoted I am to you?"

"But—"

"Or how I love being with you . . . ?"

"But I—"

"Or how I think you're the smartest, most wonderful man in the world? And *no*, that doesn't mean I think you're a wise sage who's a hundred and four. I just love you, period. You're never gonna lose me. Not ever." Drew didn't say anything; he averted his gaze, and when he looked up at her again, his eyes were clear. "And we're gonna have a baby some-day," she whispered happily.

His face broke into a wide smile, and he simply said, "Okay, then."

"Okay. But remember, if you start getting upset about any of this—or anything—we have to *talk* about it."

"Okay."

"You can't just be all distant and weird."

"Sounds fair."

"Well, you're suddenly being agreeable," she said, smiling.

"Yep."

She laughed. "So why are we even lying here hav-ing this discussion like idiots, when we could be celebrating?"

"I— Wait, celebrating what?"

"My new career," she said, moving her lips to his chest. His hands locked on her back as she brushed her lips over his heart.

"What career?" he asked.

"Um . . . I'm going into the entrepreneurial game." She slid her mouth up his neck, over his ear, and then just behind it. He turned his head, giving her better access, and glided his hands lower, much lower.

"Meaning what?" he said on a hard breath.

"Meaning . . ." she murmured, feathering her lips

across his cheek, "I'm thinking about the French-
dessert business."

"Really?" Drew said, sounding surprised. "With
your mom?"

"Uh-huh."

"Hey, that's terrific—really, that's great."

He was trying to be extra sweet, which touched
her heart so much. That was the Drew she'd missed;
that was the Drew she adored. But on the other
hand . . .

There was a time to be sweet, and there was a time
for other things.

"I knew you liked helping her cook, but I didn't
realize," he continued, rubbing her back supportively. "The French-dessert business sounds perfect
for you—"

"Mmm-hmm," she said, cutting him off. She kissed
him on the mouth, sliding her tongue inside to move
against his as she tightened her thighs around his
hips. With her left hand she reached for his now-
erect penis.

Breaking the kiss, she smiled almost shyly and
said, "I'm glad you support my decision. And if
you're a good boy . . ." Then she whispered something in his ear.

His eyes darkened. "I'll be good—I promise."

"Mmm, I *know* you will," she said, and slipped
him inside her. He squeezed his eyes shut as she
started to ride him. "Don't ever leave me again."

He groaned and said, "I promise."

Chapter Twenty-four

Late the next afternoon the wedding party was rehearsing at St. Catherine's Church. Father Gregg provided a steady onslaught of corny jokes. Meanwhile Reese's gut churned with such a ferocious jealousy she thought she might explode.

She couldn't believe Brian had brought Veronica! How *dared* he bring another woman to the church where Reese was confirmed? Couldn't he see the indecency of that? The *anathema*?

When he'd introduced Veronica to everyone, he'd referred to her as his "friend"—please, what a crock. *Don't think about it. Forget him.*

But what was the alternative? Devoting rapt attention to the stale matrimonial humor that Father Gregg undoubtedly used at every ceremony he performed? Anyway, it wasn't Reese's fault that she was so fixated. It wasn't like she *wanted* to obsess on every single thing Brian was doing only a few feet away from her.

"Okay, let's run through it again," Joanna declared. Was there ever any doubt? They'd been "running through" everything for almost two hours; Reese was beginning to wonder if the abuse would ever end. "All right, bridesmaids come down here," Joanna said. "We're going to walk up the aisle." Dutifully, Angela, Reese, Lane, and Deb retraced their steps back to the front of the church. "Good, now, Brian, you come to my right." Joanna motioned to Ben's cousins. "And Chris and James, you get behind Brian."

"Hey, who's *running* this show?" Father Gregg cracked rhetorically. Out of the corner of her eye, Reese saw Veronica waving to Brian from her pew, and barely stifled a scream.

"Reese, you've got to pay attention!" Joanna said.

"I-I am paying attention," Reese lied. "Why, what did you say?"

Joanna heaved a great sigh. "I said, commence with the processional."

"Oh, right." She led the bridesmaids up the center aisle as the groomsmen began walking along the side.

"Actually—you know what?—wait," Joanna said abruptly, as she rubbed her neck. "I changed my mind. I think we should go back to the original idea of having the groomsmen and bridesmaids walk together in pairs. Here, come back to the front, everyone."

She motioned for the men to stand beside the women, and by the time everyone was sorted, Lane was paired with Chris, Deb was paired with James, Angela was paired with Drew, and Reese ended up right next to Brian. Could her luck get any worse today?

"This is perfect!" Joanna said cheerily. "I don't know why I couldn't see it before."

As the processional got under way, Brian's elbow accidentally brushed Reese's. "*Ow,*" she whispered, glad for an excuse to be a bitch. Well, not so much as an excuse as an opportunity. Brian muttered, "Sorry," but he didn't sound all that sincere.

When they got to the altar, the men veered to the right, the women to the left. Joanna motioned frantically for Ally to get off the pew she was lounging on, and to stand between her and Michael. Then she waved over Aunt Jacy and Aunt Aileen, who had raised Ben after his parents had died in an accident when he was seven. Both ladies were barely five feet tall, round as teapots, and clad in housedresses and wool cardigans. They scurried toward Ben, who stepped in between them, towering over both.

"All right, *team*work!" Father Gregg cheered.

Reese forced herself not to look at Brian, who was directly to her right, so close she could almost smell that sexy, masculine aftershave, and she could almost feel his heat.

She hoped her rage over Veronica's presence wasn't as obvious as it felt. True, she did have a scowl that wouldn't quit, but she figured her family would think she was just being a generic bitch today, and leave it at that.

Joanna, Ally, and Michael started up the aisle.

"No, Michael, you're not doing it right," Joanna scolded. "You're straying from the rhythm."

"I am?" he said, surprised.

"Yes, can't you tell? One foot, then wait. See? You're off."

He shrugged. " 'If your head is wax, don't walk in the sun.' "

"What's that one mean, Dad?" Angela said, angling her head back.

Michael smiled broadly. "It means I have no rhythm, and she knew that when she married me."

"Oh, Michael . . ."

"I *thought* you two looked familiar!" Father Gregg cracked.

Reese rolled her eyes, and spared a glance back at her parents. Accidentally, her gaze locked on Veronica sitting in the third-to-last pew, with her hair up in a perfect chignon and her delicate shoulders in perfect posture. Compared to her, Reese felt like a compact car: squat and clunky.

Sighing, she turned to face front again, and caught Brian's eyes on her. He was watching her—studying her. She swallowed hard, while her pulse pounded in her ears, and she willed herself to look away . . . but *herself* never did listen too well. And something was sparking between them right there in the middle of St. Catherine's Church.

Finally she tore her gaze away. Maybe Brian had brought Veronica to the rehearsal just to hurt Reese. Or maybe he hadn't given any thought to Reese's feelings at all. Or maybe he was so crazy in love with Veronica, he couldn't bear to spend even one moment apart from her. Well, none of those scenarios was too comforting.

Just thinking about the rehearsal dinner tonight, and sitting across from the lovebirds, made her fume. Then pout . . . until finally her anger was replaced with total sadness. A lump formed in her throat, and her eyes watered. *No, you can't cry. He's a creep; don't cry.*

"Reese!"

"Huh?"

"*Sweetheart*. You're supposed to collect all the flowers from the other girls and set them down on the altar."

"We don't have any flowers now."

"You still have to *rehearse* it." Joanna turned to Michael, and in a strategically unsteady voice, said, "This is getting too stressful for me."

"Can we just get this done? *God*." Ally said.

"Hey, I thought *I* was the only one on a first-name basis with Him!" Father Gregg said, laughing and holding his belly.

After that, Ally and Ben went through the drill of saying their vows.

Twenty minutes later the rehearsal finally wound down. Then, on their way out the door, Joanna suggested that everyone run through it again. "Just once more."

Reese wouldn't have expected anything less.

Reese went down to the hotel lobby at 6:15 to meet Kenneth. She'd told him he didn't have to come to the rehearsal dinner (hint, hint), but he'd insisted. She supposed she was a little relieved to bring a date, since she knew damn well Brian was taking Miss Prima Ballerina.

To boost her confidence, Reese was wearing a low-cut, black wraparound dress and silver high heels. She'd also put on a silver heart necklace that had never particularly brought her luck, but she liked to pretend it was her good-luck charm. She'd done the whole red-raspberry Chap Stick thing again, but this time it was just for her.

Kenneth came through the rotating glass doors and approached efficiently. "Hello, Reese. How are you?" he said, and handed her a red rose.

"Hi. Oh, thank you," she said, smiling, and feeling pretty uncomfortable. "How was the drive?"

"It was very good, thank you. Not too much traffic."

"Oh, great," she supplied lamely. "Well . . . do you wanna get going? We're meeting everyone in the dining room."

"Yes. That sounds good."

Everyone was already seated at the table when Kenneth and Reese arrived, and everyone said hi except Brian.

"I'd like you all to meet Kenneth—my date," Reese said brightly.

Brian locked his jaw, and opened his menu.

"Oh, I'm so glad you could make it!" Joanna gushed.

"Kenneth," Michael stated, "good to see you again. Glad you could join us." Kenneth cleared his throat and mumbled something quasi-gracious.

At that moment, Reese decided to play up this Kenneth thing for all it was worth.

"Brian, you remember Kenneth, don't you?" she said, forcing him to acknowledge them.

"Yeah, hi," he said curtly.

"Oh, you've met Kenneth?" Joanna asked Brian conversationally.

"Yes," Reese said, "they met at the bookstore last week. Kenneth stopped in to say hi, and I introduced them."

"Oh, you and Reese know each other?" Veronica asked, sounding surprised.

Brian started to answer when Reese cut him off. "No, we don't—believe me." She and Kenneth took their seats at the table, and Reese stole another look over. Brian was staring at his menu with his cheek clenched, and she felt a perverse sense of satisfaction.

When she looked down at her own menu, all the words blurred together.

"What's that flower, sweetheart?" Joanna asked.

"Oh, this?" Reese said, holding up the rose for everyone to see. "Kenneth gave it to me—wasn't that sweet?" She leaned into him a little, beaming.

Lane said, "Well, aren't you two *cute.*"

Brian still wasn't looking at her. He was busy studying his damn menu like it was a physics textbook.

"Baby, what do you think you'll get?" Angela said, leaning over to share Drew's menu.

He leaned over and pressed a quick kiss on her temple. "I don't know, babydoll; what will you get?"

Huh? Had Reese missed something crucial here? Angela and Drew were holding hands on top of the table, and appearing more blissful than ever. Reese would definitely have to grill her sister for details as soon as she got a chance.

Drew smiled amiably at Reese. "Hey, Angela told me you got a room at the hotel for yourself. You wanted a taste of the good life, huh?"

She grinned with self-deprecation. "Oh, yeah. I'm a real hedonist."

"You've got a room?" Aunt Aileen asked, wiggling her eyebrows suggestively. "What do you need one of those for?

Joanna said, "Oh, she's in room eight-sixteen, so if anyone needs anything before the ceremony, or anytime, just ask Reese." She smiled brightly at her daughter, thanking her for volunteering, which of course she hadn't.

"By the way, sweetheart," Joanna went on, pushing her luck as always, "without you biting my head off, have you prepared your toast for tomorrow?"

"What toast?" Aunt Jacy asked.

"Oh, we're having Reese, as the maid of honor, say a few words at the reception," Joanna explained.

"But aren't you the maid of honor, too?" Aunt Aileen asked Angela.

"Yeah, but—"

"Public speaking is Reese's thing," Joanna explained matter-of-factly.

Right. If public speaking were Reese's thing, why couldn't she think of a damn thing to say to Brian right now? All she could manage was to shoot him daggers with her eyes (and he wasn't even looking, of course).

"You know what would be a good idea?" Jacy said. "For the best man and the maid of honor to say something together. I saw that at a wedding once, and I thought it was real cute."

Reese's head shot up, and *now* she caught Brian watching her. Intently. Powerfully. She couldn't tell if it was anger she saw in his eyes or hunger, but it didn't matter, because just as soon, the spell was broken. Veronica put her hand on his arm; she might as well have dumped ice water on Reese's head.

"What do you think?" Jacy asked, tapping Brian on the arm.

"What? I'm sorry, I missed that."

"We're suggesting that you and Reese say a few

words together tomorrow," Aileen explained, as she opened up a presumably vegan vacuum-sealed bag. "What do you think, Benny? Isn't that a good idea?"

Ben was busy assailing the bread basket, and didn't seem to have much of an opinion at the moment. Ally said, "I don't know, you guys; that's kind of putting him on the spot."

"Oh . . . no, it's okay," Brian offered. "I'd be happy to."

Jacy smiled and said, "What a nice boy."

Hmm. Reese thought about the way Brian had kissed her, felt her breasts, rubbed his groin into her crotch, and she couldn't help noting that the last thing he was, was a *boy.*

"But it has to be prepared together," Jacy went on, opening her own vacuum-sealed pouch. "That was the whole reason it was so cute—remember Aileen, at Tory's wedding?"

"Mmm-hmm, it was so darn precious," she agreed, smelling her water before sipping.

"I don't think that's going to work," Reese said, unable to hold her tongue any longer, "Um, Brian and I really don't even have time to prepare something now."

"Well, it doesn't have to be anything fancy, sweetheart," Joanna said, "Just make sure you run it by me before the ceremony."

"May I get anyone something to drink?" their waiter asked, coming out of nowhere. That deflected the conversation, as everyone ordered their drinks.

Reese glanced down the table and found Brian watching her again. As if on cue, Veronica slid her arm through his, and leaned in close to look at his menu. Brian didn't seem to respond, but it didn't matter, because Veronica's intimate gesture only served as a reminder of all that stood between them.

So, in mature fashion, Reese did the only thing she could do—she slid her arm through Kenneth's and thanked him again—loudly—for the flower.

Brian's eyes shot up, as Kenneth explained some of the socially constructed signification of a red rose, and analyzed possible origins. And Reese stared doe-eyed, as though astounded by his brilliance.

"That's so fascinating," she said, making sure the whole table heard. "Tell us more."

Brian clenched his cheek tighter. Then he nudged a little closer to Veronica and asked, "Do you want to split an appetizer?"

Reese's jaw dropped. *Split an appetizer!* If that wasn't the most couple-y thing in the world, she didn't know what was.

Fine, she hoped they choked on it. Well, just enough to turn blue. She sipped her cabernet sauvignon to keep from cursing, and tried to steady her nerves. No matter what, she'd have to get a tougher skin, because it was obviously going to be a very long night.

Chapter Twenty-five

Brian said good-night to Veronica in the parking lot of the Goldwood Villa Hotel. They had taken separate cars, because when Veronica had called his cell earlier, and he'd mentioned that he was on his way to the rehearsal, she'd insisted upon meeting him there. Truthfully, he hadn't known how to dissuade her, especially after she'd told him that she had been crying all day about Uncle Martin, and the rehearsal was the only thing that would take her mind off things.

But it wasn't just that he didn't want to hurt her feelings. After finding out that Reese already had a boyfriend—*and has had one the whole time, for chrissake*—he figured he had every right to take Veronica. Really, why should he sit there alone, watching Reese with her boyfriend, and eating his heart out?

Anyway, that had been his thought process at the time, but none of it really mattered because the whole night had been awful.

Climbing into his Saturn, he released a sigh and started the engine. Absently, he turned on 92.3 and pulled onto Route 46, heading east.

He couldn't believe that Veronica was acting like

they were this happy little couple when they weren't even back together yet. Yeah, they'd agreed to keep the door open, but rekindling a serious relationship was not something he could do impulsively. Well, he *could*, and apparently Veronica would like nothing more, but Brian knew that would be dumb as hell. They hadn't slept together even once since their breakup, and they wouldn't unless they were on solid ground again, because it would only be asking for trouble.

Why couldn't she see that they needed to think it through? Actually, Brian was about to ask her just that when they said good-bye in the parking lot, but she'd beaten him to the punch with: "Thanks for letting me lean on you tonight, Bri. I don't know what I'd do if you turned on me right now—if I had to face everything alone. I honestly don't know what I'd do."

Jesus, what was he supposed to say to that?

Not to mention, it made him damn uncomfortable that she was resting so much on his shoulders. Veronica had friends and relatives up to her eyeballs, so why couldn't she turn to any of them, too? Why did she always make it sound like, without him, she was on the verge of committing suicide?

At this point, he was torn between sympathizing and getting irritated beyond belief with her emotional blackmail. Only, whenever he got really irritated, guilt would kick in, and then he was back to square one.

It certainly hadn't helped that at dinner, he'd acted more romantic with Veronica than usual just to spite Reese. *Real mature, jackass*, he thought angrily. How did he have the balls to blame Veronica, and then turn around and give her the totally wrong idea?

Not that he'd intended to do it, but when he'd heard Reese going on about how "sweet" her dorky boyfriend was, he'd lost all common sense.

Except . . . wait . . .

Something just didn't add up.

If that guy Kenneth was her boyfriend, then why did she have to introduce him to everyone tonight? How serious could they possibly be if the others didn't know him already? In fact, she hadn't even referred to him as her "boyfriend"—she'd called him her "date."

And what about the way she kept looking over at Brian during dinner? Of course, that could've been because she could feel him staring at her. For chrissake, he could barely take his eyes off her the whole dinner—not that her low-cut dress helped. But, in truth, he'd been too preoccupied with a well of disturbing emotions to stare glazed-eyed at her cleavage.

In a bizarre way, he actually *wanted* to be angry with her. But he also wanted to grab her and hug her, and he wanted that a whole lot more. In fact, that was what he really wanted.

Thinking about Reese with Kenneth was killing him. Thinking about her with any other man but him was *really* killing him. How could he just let her go like this? Oh, hell, that was stupid; he'd never even really had her. So why did he feel like he'd completely blown it?

All right, that was it; he needed some answers. Once cars started honking behind him, he realized the light had turned green, and he stepped harder on the gas pedal than he needed to. He sped down another half mile, before veering off to the right, winding around the U-turn, and getting on 46 west. He was going back.

Mrs. Brock had said that Reese was in room 816. She would be up there now . . . what would she be doing? And would she be doing it alone? Involuntarily, he tightened his grip on the wheel. He had to talk to her—to see her, to clear the air. And anyway, they'd half agreed to say a few words together at Ally and Ben's reception tomorrow . . . shouldn't they at least have a clue what they were going to say?

Yeah, that would be his excuse for going back to the hotel. For showing up at her door—for needing her so much.

Back in room 816, Reese was bored out of her mind. She had changed into pajama pants, and the "Jem and the Holograms" tank top she'd gotten at the shore when she was seventeen. The tank was so faded, she could barely tell if it was Jem or Jerica, but it was comfortable, despite how tightly it fit around her breasts.

But she was so tense, she couldn't relax, and she couldn't concentrate on her writing, which made her one big ball of unproductive frustration. Even the fact that she had nothing else to do *besides* work on her computer provided zero incentive. She felt stifled and claustrophobic and powerless to change it.

So she started fiddling with her hair.

And before she knew it, she had crooked rows of braids running all over her head.

Okay, now what? She flopped back on her bed, stared at the ceiling for endless minutes, and sat up again, still devoid of ideas. She'd said good-bye to Kenneth shortly after dinner, and her family had left the hotel then, too. The last she'd seen, Brian and Veronica were heading out toward the parking lot.

She shuddered to imagine what they were doing now back in the city. Probably they were in Brian's apartment, in Brian's bed, pawing at each other with renewed passion. *Blech!* It was ridiculous that her blood boiled at the thought of Brian even so much as kissing Veronica, when clearly, after eight years together, they'd done a lot more than that. They'd probably done any and every sexual thing known to man and woman.

Okay, this was *not* making her feel better.

She twisted her hands in her lap, and tried not to think about how sleek and graceful and skinny and blond Veronica was—how Reese had no prayer of competing with her, with the history she shared with Brian, with any of it. Well, *fine.*

Expelling a sigh, Reese picked up the women's magazine Ally had left in her room earlier, but all the articles were about sex, so that was out. She walked across the room and switched on the television. She flipped around and found nothing. Could she even catch a small break?

A sudden knock at the door startled her. Who . . . oh, no, if Joanna gave out Reese's room number to any out-of-town guests arriving early, she was literally going to cry. *Or pretend not to be here*, she reasoned, as she crept over to the peephole.

It was Brian! What was *he* doing there? He was

the last person she expected to show up on her door-
step. And where was his precious Veronica?

Reese ran back over to shut the TV off, then back
to the door, taking in a couple of Lamaze-like
breaths. Straightening her posture, and going for an
unreadable expression, she turned the handle.

When the door swung open, it revealed Brian in
full, breathtaking form. He was leaning against the
doorjamb, with his tie loosened, looking slightly
rumpled, but sexy enough to devour. (Please, who
needed it?)

"Hi," he said flatly.

"Hello," Reese said, matching his tonelessness, but
feeling her heart slam against her chest. "What are
you doing here? I thought you went back to the
city already."

"What'd you do to your hair?" he asked.

Only after she touched a hand to her head did she
remember her winding cornrows. "Oh . . . I was
bored." She fake-cleared her throat á la Kenneth Peel,
and went on the offensive. "Well? Can I help you
with something?"

"Yeah." He pushed himself upright and moved
past her, into her room.

"Oh, please, make yourself at home. Care for some
macadamia nuts from the minibar?" She shut the
door, and watched him stop at the foot of her bed,
pausing before he turned to face her.

Then her breath caught in her throat—it was the
way he was looking at her. Her mouth ran dry. She
licked her lips nervously, and then realized that it
probably made her look as desperate as she felt. *Get
it together; he's a jerk.*

"I came over to prepare that toast," he said.

Toast? What, was every person in her life obsessed with that damn toast? Brian had come to her room for *that*?

Wait a minute . . . unless . . . maybe . . . could it just be an excuse to come over? Her heart galloped against her ribs again, and she struggled to act unaffected. "Brian, I'm not preparing a toast with you," she said coldly.

"But everyone wants us to say something together. You heard them at dinner."

"Well, *I'm* gonna say something, and you can go twist in the wind for all I care." She crossed her arms over her breasts and watched something flicker in his eyes.

"That's not exactly what they're expecting," he said, and took a step closer to her. "And I don't know about you, but I'd rather not make an ass of myself."

"Too late," she muttered.

"What?" he asked, moving closer, with an odd look on his face. It was like the faintest trace of amusement, combined with something far more intense.

"Forget it," she said quickly.

He moved closer still. "No, really, I'm curious."

Okay, now he was just plain *crowding* her (and she felt like she could finally breathe). Inhaling sharply, she said, "It means that I thought you made a spectacle of yourself at dinner. The way you and your girlfriend were carrying on—it was . . . well, to be honest, *nauseating*."

"*Really?*" he said, crossing his arms now.

"Yes, really," Reese said, and brushed past him, shivering from the contact as their arms rubbed against each other.

"Can you elaborate a little?" he asked, reaching out to pull her back. His grip was firm, but there was a gentleness about it that she'd come to recognize as Brian's touch. The heat from his hand burned on her bare arm. She made a flimsy attempt to pull free, for pride only, because of course she wanted his hands on her. "Well?" he said.

"Look, Brian, I don't know how you and your girl-friend normally act in public—maybe you always fall all over each other like that—but I, for one, found it offensive."

"Offensive?" Brian said, dropping her arm, but still possessing her by moving closer, taking her space and her air and her sanity, and staring at her—into her—as she tried to move away, but her feet wouldn't cooperate.

"Please," she said, "splitting an appetizer? Every-one at that table was disgusted!"

He plowed his hand through his hair, and sighed with obvious frustration. Meanwhile Reese forced herself to hold her ground, because she was afraid that if she didn't, she'd fall apart. "Look, Brian, if you and your girlfriend want to—"

"Reese," he cut her off, quietly, but very seriously. "She is not my girlfriend. She isn't."

She scoffed and said, "Right, right, I forgot. You're 'deciding' if you want her to be your girlfriend again after the wedding. Yuck, get *over* yourself."

She turned to go again, but he tugged her back and

said, "Care to explain how you've had a boyfriend all this time, and never mentioned it?"

"Kenneth is not my boyfriend—he just said that."

"Who 'just says that'?" he asked angrily. "Why don't you just admit it's not really over between you two?"

She jerked her hand back, for real this time. "Brian, you are so blind! I don't even *like* Kenneth—"

Suddenly she was pulled forward, all the wind was knocked out of her, and Brian's mouth was on hers. It took a second for Reese to process what was happening, and when some distant part of her brain did, she ran her arms up Brian's back to grip his shoulders, and crushed her mouth against his.

His hand was hot and firm on her neck, and his mouth was open, wet, urgent. The other hand was on her lower back, keeping her body flush against his, and Reese felt her head swimming as liquefying heat speared down between her legs. If she'd been thinking rationally, she would've put a stop to this (probably), but she wasn't thinking at all, so it was a moot point. Their lips pulled apart, and Brian sucked in a breath.

Reese held tight to his shoulders, and brought herself up higher on tiptoe to rub her lips against his and slide her tongue into his mouth.

Brian groaned, and sank hungrily into the kiss. Reese was moaning in the depths of her throat, trying to keep up, digging her nails into his shoulders. The hard bulge in his pants grazed her midsection, and she tried to press up against it without falling over. He tore his mouth off hers, breathing raggedly, while they stared at each other for one of those crackling, time-suspended moments. Only this time the heat was searing, and Reese was already wet.

A shiver ran across her breasts. She knew the tips were hard and sensitive, and that reminded her that she wasn't wearing a bra. The only barrier between her burning breasts and Brian's hot hands was a threadbare tank top that was almost as pink as she felt.

Somehow Brian must have read her mind, because his eyes shot down and then glazed over. His whole face darkened, and he looked so hungry, so intense, so unbelievably aroused, Reese began to pant. Licking her lips, she yanked hard on his tie and pulled him into an open, rough, carnal kiss that exploded between them. She rubbed insistently against his cock, and he growled; she liked the sound of it, so she broke their kiss and rubbed harder, staring drowsily into his eyes.

He brought his hand down to her ass, squeezing as he pulled her up against him—*really* against him. His erection stabbed almost painfully into her tender softness, and in ecstasy, Reese's lids dropped and her mouth fell open.

The next thing she knew, her feet were off the ground.

Brian was carrying her . . . then she was on her back . . . then he was on her, opening his mouth on hers, touching her breasts through her shirt, and grinding his thick erection into the hot spot between her legs. "Oh, God," Reese whispered, shifting her head restlessly on the pillow as Brian trailed full, wet kisses down her neck, stopping at the curve to suck—

just as he had done that night in her apartment. Her underwear was flimsy and useless; she felt every movement so acutely she might as well have been naked. As Brian ground his dick harder, her whispers turned into high-pitched moans that she couldn't control.

Finally, she choked out, "Take off your shirt."

But she didn't even give him a chance; she pulled at it herself, too impatient to unbutton it. The next thing she registered was lightly tanned skin and dark chest hair, and being rolled so that she was now on top of Brian, and he was breathing hard, and gripping her butt.

Instinctively, Reese licked down his neck, then kissed along his collarbone as she massaged his chest with warm, willing hands. Abruptly he grunted and snaked a hand under her hair—dragging her up until they were mouth-to-mouth again, and he was taking her tongue deep into his mouth. Her pelvis began to rock.

Then, just like that, she was on her back again, stripped of her Jem tank top. Brian was sucking her nipple and cupping her crotch with a strong, burning hot hand. Then he dug his fingers inside her flannel pajamas. Reese panted out short, hard gasps while Brian rubbed the heel of his hand up and down on the outside her panties.

"Oh, *yes* . . ." she whispered, more to herself. "Brian . . ."

On a breath, he moved his mouth off her nipple and focused on touching her—it began rhythmically, but then got faster, and hotter, until he was all but digging into the damp cotton, and Reese was tilting

her hips in sharp upward thrusts, desperate to bring
herself hard against his hand.

Suddenly his hand stilled—touching her in a mo-
tionless caress that forced her to slit her eyes and see
if anything was wrong. Brian wasn't looking at her,
though; his eyes were shut, and his face looked almost contorted in pain. A few beats passed before
he licked his lip and let his head drop. She could tell
by his trembling shoulders that something was about
to happen.

"Don't stop," she whispered in a cracking voice,
because she couldn't wait for that something.

Brian rubbed the top of his head into her breasts.
He started to whisper, "You're so . . ." but never
finished the thought, as he slipped one finger under
the leg elastic of her underwear. He slid it inside her
and muttered, "God*damn*."

She moaned and bit her lip as Brian glided another
finger in deep—stroking her slowly, until she rocked
her hips, and begged, "Oh, God, *please* . . ."

After a moment, Brian stopped again, pulling back,
and Reese could barely make out the quickness of
his breath over the ringing in her ears. "What's
wrong?" she whispered. She felt his hand slide gently over her cheek as her eyes slowly came open,
and, caressing her face, Brian murmured, "I guess
we're moving sort of fast."

"Oh . . ." she said a little shyly. "Yeah. I guess
you're right."

But then they were kissing again. Frantically. His
fingers moved inside her, and thready little moans
were barely smothered in her throat, before he scrambled up onto his knees and pulled down her pants

and underwear. She sat up enough to reach for his belt buckle and yank on it, and fumble with him when he tried to help her.

As soon as he was unzipped, Reese reached greedily for his erection. It was thick and hot when she coiled her fingers around it and tightly dragged her hand up and down, up and down. Brian panted, "Oh, shit, wait," and tried to still Reese's hand with his, but she just squeezed him in place. His head dropped back. On short, hard breaths, he whipped it forward again and asked hoarsely, "Wait, do you have any condoms?"

Her heavy-lidded eyes snapped fully open. Condoms, protection, of course. And as her bizarre luck would have it, she *did*. Technically they were Ally's, but Reese would use just one; surely her sister would understand.

"In the bathroom!" she said way too eagerly, and Brian grinned as he went to get them. On the way, he dropped his pants, revealing a mouthwatering side profile of his swollen penis. He stepped out of them, and disappeared into the bathroom.

How had they gone from angry to wantonly, uncontrollably aroused in a matter of seconds? It didn't seem possible, but there was no turning back now. At least, she prayed that there wasn't. This was pure passion, or animal attraction, or whatever made a person lose all rational thought and want sex more than *anything*. She had never experienced this kind of burning, pressing need—not even with Pete, whom she'd loved.

Not that she wouldn't concede how strange her life could be sometimes. There she was lying on a hotel bed, totally naked, with her honey-colored braids tangling against the pillows, and there was nowhere else in the world she'd rather be.

Brian came back with a condom already on and the box in his hand. He tossed it beside the bed and crawled in beside her. Immediately they regained their momentum, and the heat rose. Reese wrapped her legs around his hips as they exchanged long, wet kisses.

Moaning, she tightened her leg lock on him, and felt him slide in deep.

She broke their kissing so she could breathe, and buried the back of her head in the pillows. Closing her eyes tight, she let electric sensations sear and scald her body.

Brian closed his hands over her breasts. With his head tilted down, leaving his soft hair to brush the underside of her jaw, he started to thrust. It began less than slow, and got even faster . . . and harder . . . then both at once.

Soon he was taking Reese in strong, deep plunges, holding her breasts in his hands while he pumped and groaned and grunted. Reese was nearly screaming with pleasure. "I . . . I can't believe this is happening," she choked out without thinking.

"W-why?"

All she could do was hum and moan and gasp, while her mind answered, *Because it's been so long*.

Because it had been so long, she climaxed quickly—in a fierce, hot blast of contractions that racked her body and made her come to life in a different way than she had in forever.

Brian thrusted into her climax, and didn't stop

until her breath started racing again, and she was panting and crying out, "Oh, *God* . . ."

Then he started to come, pumping like crazy, sweating, and grunting harshly over Reese's soulful moans. Letting out a final, rough cry, Brian shuddered and collapsed on top of her. Several moments passed before the tension completely eased, and Reese let her legs fall languidly open underneath him. "Holy *Christ*," Brian mumbled into the pillow.

Her thoughts exactly, but she was too spent to speak.

Chapter Twenty-six

About twenty minutes later, after almost dozing, Reese snuggled up close to Brian and murmured, "I can't believe we did that."

He groaned and opened his eyes. "I know," he said drowsily. He pulled her up on top of him and hugged her. Then, after kissing her slowly and deeply, he said, "Hey . . . let's not be able to believe we did that *twice*."

His hands slid down to mold over her bottom. She was suddenly self-conscious, because she knew her soft flesh was overflowing in his hands. "You've got a cute boot," he said, grinning boyishly. His hair was a mess, his eyes were sleepy, and he was so unbelievably cute at that moment that Reese decided to accept the compliment graciously rather than saying what she was really thinking: *Yeah, RIGHT*.

"Come on," he whispered, and brought his lips up to hers in a slow, sensuous kiss.

As she kissed him, she felt one of his hands creep lower, in between her legs. He pressed two fingers against her.

"Are you . . . ready?" she asked brokenly—breathlessly.

"Well . . . you could help me get ready," he said playfully, kissing under her hair, behind her ear. Meanwhile she glided her hand down his side and between their bodies to furrow through his dark, coarse hair and encircle him. He was partially hard already, so she stroked him until he pulsed in her hand.

"Are you always like this?" she murmured almost coyly.

"I wouldn't know," he said. "Or remember, anyway."

"What do you mean?" she asked. "Has it been a while?"

"But enough about me," he said, grinning. "How long has it been for you?"

She let go of his shaft to hold and caress his testicles, and replied, "A long, long time." Kissing his cheek softly, she added, "But it's never been like this." Of course that sounded like a major cliché, but it was still the truth.

Brian ran a hand to the back of her neck and muttered thickly, "I've never had sex like that in my whole life." He trailed his tongue sensually up her throat, and then inside her ear.

Dizzily, Reese moaned and mumbled, "Hmm . . . let's expedite this." She crawled down his body. As she touched the tip of him with her tongue, she watched his erection bob to full, thick attention. Then, impulsively, she took him in her mouth.

Brian groaned and tunneled his fingers through her hair. She gripped his hips and applied light suction for only a moment before raising her head to gaze up into his face.

Their eyes caught, and ardently he rolled them both over, so they were lying sideways on her bed. From there he could reach the box of condoms he'd tossed on the floor earlier.

Before he snapped one on, though, he crouched over her body and brought his mouth down to her needy, slick flesh. He flicked his tongue inside—not deep, but deep enough to liquefy her insides and make her throb with desire. "Don't stop," she said under her breath, "it's . . . so *good*."

Then he gently bit her. Right *there*. And she arched so hard she almost fell off the bed.

In a second he was sprawled on top of her, and they were moving together, heated, frenzied, and fast. Reese cried out as Brian rose up partly on his knees, and rode her high and hard. His hands were gentle, though, brushing hair away from her face as he looked down at her with half-lidded eyes and a wet, sexy mouth.

Reese bucked her hips wildly. So wildly it couldn't be like her; it had to be an aberration. A unbelievably fabulous, erotic, *scorching* aberration.

Soon she felt her head throb, because it was barely on the bed. Even as her cranium pounded, her body felt way too good for her to care. There was no way she'd move now. Well, move *over*, anyway. As their bodies drove into each other, Reese uttered a few filthy words that should've surprised her, but she was too crazed to feel polite. Finally her neck arched, and Brian came apart with a loud, long groan.

Moments later he rolled off of her and onto his back. Both were gasping, and covered in a sheen of sweat. She hadn't come—but it was still so good.

Brian rolled back to scoop her up and drag them both across the bed, and to rest their heads upon the pillows. Soon they were under the covers, and he was holding her to him, running his fingers lightly down her side. She sighed, and cuddled up against him.

Somewhere in Reese's mind, a voice told her she was crazy to have let this happen—especially twice—but it was drowned out by her even breathing as she drifted off to sleep.

Reese woke up to sound of the heat vent going on. The room was pitch black, and it took her a second to remember that she was in the Goldwood Villa Hotel, and Ally's wedding was tomorrow, and that the extremely warm body next to her was Brian. She wasn't sure how long they'd been sleeping; she only knew that it was the middle of the night and she was feeling wide-awake.

And inspired.

Slowly lifting Brian's hand off of her waist, she slid gently out of the bed, and was grateful for the darkness, because she was stark naked. It hadn't bothered her before, but she hadn't been thinking too clearly then. Brian stirred a little when she lifted off the bed, but his breathing still sounded heavy with sleep.

As she stepped on something soft, she quickly realized it was Brian's shirt, which had been cast off earlier. Slipping it over her head, she crept in the direction of her overnight bag. If she was going to get any good writing done, she'd need fresh underwear. A little quirk of hers she'd just discovered.

While her laptop was booting up, she went to the bathroom to pee and brush the sleep breath out of her mouth. Then she sat down at the little table by the window, and got down to work. Forty minutes passed without her realizing it. She was still in the throes of stream-of-consciousness when Brian woke. His voice was hoarse and raspy with sleep. "Reese? What are you doing?"

"I'm sorry; did I wake you?" she whispered.

"No . . . but why don't you come back to bed?"

By the light that streamed from her laptop, she could just make out the silhouette of Brian's body under the covers, and his hands behind his head.

"I will, but I just want to write while I'm feeling inspired," she said.

"What are you working on? Your novel?"

"Yeah."

"What's it called?" he asked, scratching his chest and starting to come fully awake.

"*Chasing the Story*," she answered. "It's about these two reporters who are competing, and then they get involved in all this stuff, and then they fall in love along the way." Okay, she was babbling. Maybe this was another postcoital quirk she had, what did she know?

Brian leaned over and switched on the bedside lamp. They both squinted and screwed their faces up as they adjusted to the light.

"What are you doing?" Reese asked, as he started to sit up.

Instead of replying, he absently ran a hand through his rumpled hair. His back was to her; she couldn't help gazing at his sleek, tanned skin, and the muscled strength beneath it. He leaned down to pick his boxers off the floor, and in doing so, exposed some of his bare butt. She bit her lip and stared shamelessly.

After he slid his boxers on, he walked around the bed and toward her, grinning. A big, infatuated smile broke immediately across her face. "Hi," she said softly as he approached her and tugged on her hand to coax her up out of the chair. "What are you doing?" she asked again, rising to her feet.

He still didn't answer, but leaned down to kiss her—softly and slowly—letting his lips linger on hers. Her hands slid over his shoulders, and clung so that she could prolong the kiss. She could taste his sleep breath, but instead of being turned off, she was enticed. It tasted raw and rugged . . . sexy. "I'm sitting down," he said suddenly, and stole her seat in the chair.

Before she could protest, he pulled her down onto his lap. A giggle slipped out as she struggled to get off of him. He held on to her even as she insisted, "No, please, I'm too heavy," so finally she gave up trying to convince him that she could do serious permanent damage, and cuddled happily against his chest.

"Can I read some of your novel now?" he asked.

Reese's eyes grew huge, because that was the last thing she had expected—and it definitely was the last thing she was ready for. She had only six chapters so far, and it was all pretty rough—though she loved it—but still, she just couldn't imagine showing it to another person. Not yet, and definitely not Brian.

What if he hated it? What if he thought she was a terrible writer? No, that would just be way too embarrassing.

"Um . . ."

"Please," he said softly, smoothing his palm over her bare leg. "Please, just a little?"

"Okay." *What!* Damn it, when it came to Brian, she was just too weak.

Turning her laptop a little so he could get a better view, Brian scrolled to the top of document and began to read.

It took only a few moments for Reese to become frantic with self-consciousness. He was reading with no expression, stone-faced, obviously loathing her book, and she wanted him to stop reading it. *Now.*

"Actually," she said suddenly, "um . . . that's enough . . ."

She leaned to turn the laptop away, and Brian said, "Hey, don't do that." He tilted it back and continued to read.

"No, really . . . I-I changed my mind—"

"Shh, I'm at a great part," he said, eyes fixed on the screen. Did he actually like it . . . or was he merely being polite?

"Brian, you don't have read anymore, really—"

"*Shh,*" he said. "I'm trying to concentrate."

She saw the faint trace of a smile on his face, so she smiled, too. "Okay, sorry," she said, and then tried to move off his lap, to keep his circulation moving. Only he didn't let her go; he kept her snugly in his arms while he read on.

She tried to relax against him, to rest her head on his shoulder, but it was nothing more than a pose.

Her body was coursing with a nervous kind of adrenaline. Would what he say when he finished? Would he be encouraging? And would it all be bullshit?

When Brian was finished, an odd expression crossed his face—maybe a mix between confusion and frustration. He turned his head, looking disappointed.

She swallowed hard—it was worse than she thought.

"So?" he said.

"So what?"

"So *what happens*?"

"What do you mean?"

"After Trent and Monique get to the abandoned warehouse," Brian said urgently. "C'mon, what happens? You just left me hanging."

"Oh," she said, relieved. Then, assessing his expression, she felt a smile tug at the corners of her lips, because he was such an adorable sweetheart, she didn't ever want to lose this moment. She blew out a breath with mock regret. "Gee, I don't know."

"What do you mean, you don't know? You can't tell me what happens?"

She shrugged guiltily. "I'm sort of making it up as I go along."

"Oh, my God, I can't believe this!" he said, acting outraged—but she saw the laughter in his eyes. "You could've at least warned me before I got hooked."

She laughed as he stood up and lifted her with him.

"Sorry, I wasn't thinking," she said, giggling as he carried her.

"All right, that's it. Now you're gonna pay." He flung them both onto the bed.

"Oh, no, what are you gonna do?" she said, hugging him.

"Mmm . . ." He slid his hands under his shirt she wore to cup her breasts. "I don't know yet . . . I'll make it up as I go along." She giggled a little more, and then pulled back so she could look at him. He looked back—straight into her eyes—and she felt a kind of heady euphoria swirl around inside her. She sighed blissfully as Brian dropped a kiss on her forehead.

"By the way," she said softly, "I meant to ask you, how's Danny? Any word from the doctor?"

"Yeah, he said she's okay, but he thinks all the stress she's under might affect her pregnancy." Worry crossed his features, and Reese ran her hand gently along his jaw to comfort him.

"I'm sorry," she said, "but I'm sure she'll be all right. After the baby's born, she's moving in with your parents, right? In Miami?"

"Yeah, I'm really hoping everything works out."

Reese smiled at him, and continued to stroke his jaw. "It will. You'll be an uncle." He shrugged casually, so she decided to let it be for the moment.

His lips captured hers in a soft, gentle kiss, as he caressed her face with his fingers and ran them up through her hair. "Hey, remember that night I ran into you outside Roland and Fisk? You know, when you were running from that psycho?"

"Uh-huh," she said, sinking her cheek more deeply into his palm.

"Remember I told you I was so late because I was busy?"

"Mmm-hmm . . . what about it?"

"Total lie," Brian said huskily. "I made that up."

"But why?"

Vaguely grinning, he replied, "Because I thought if I came at the end of your shift, we might go out after. That night worked out exactly like I would've wanted it to." He kissed her and added, "Except I went home."

Grasping his head, Reese pulled him in and kissed him with all that she had. "Brian," she said against his mouth, "what's gonna happen?"

He stilled, and she could feel how desperately her eyes were searching his. Finally he said, "Whatever you want. Tell me what you want me to do, and I'll do it."

Reese's heart fluttered wildly. What should she say? Should she play games? Keep an air of mystery? Or should she simply lay it all out there?

"Get rid of Veronica."

She should really be ashamed of herself. Veronica was a human being with feelings, and what's more, she was a fellow woman. She didn't deserve to be discarded like worthless baggage. But, damn it, that was exactly what Reese wanted. She wanted her dumped, dropped, kicked to the proverbial curb, and out of Brian's life, once and for all.

She couldn't help it—in such a short time, she'd become so possessive of him, it was difficult to understand herself. But he'd asked her what she wanted, so she'd told him.

"I'm sorry," she said even though she really wasn't, "but that's how I feel. I want to be with you, but if Veronica is gonna be in the picture, then it's

not gonna work. And I don't care about all the se-
mantics of how she fits into your life, or if you're
'technically' together or not together, or any of that.

"Look, Brian, the truth is, I think I'm at a point in
my life when I just don't want to waste my time. If
that scares you then I guess I understand, but . . ."

She paused, hoping he'd take the opportunity to
say something reassuring. But he didn't. In fact, he
didn't say anything. Not for a long moment anyway;
then his face broke into a warm smile, and he whispered, "That doesn't scare me."

"It doesn't?"

He shook his head. "No way. I want to be with
you, too." Elation coursed through her, and she
found it hard to speak. "Reese, I just want you to
know that Veronica and I talked about her coming
to Ben's wedding a long time ago—way before I saw
you again. We'd only talked casually about it, but
then recently she told me she was counting on it,
and . . . look, I know there's no good excuse.

"You probably think my situation with her is nuts,
and I guess it really doesn't make much sense. . . ."
His voice trailed off, and a look of genuine weariness
crossed his face.

"You still have feelings for her, is that it?" Reese
asked, painfully dreading the answer.

"No! No, no—I mean, not the way you think."

He went on to explain why he had first considered
getting back together with Veronica, how lonely and
miserable his life had become, how he'd since realized it wasn't what he wanted but he didn't know
exactly how to handle everything—so he'd handled
it all like shit.

Reese pondered everything, then asked, "So how long were you guys together?"

"Eight years."

"What!" She bolted upright in bed. "Eight years! Nobody told me *that*." Covering her eyes with her palm, she shook her head, and mumbled, "Oh, my God. Eight years, eight freaking years."

Abruptly she rolled toward the edge of the bed, saying, "*Good*-bye," when Brian's hand caught her arm.

"Reese, what?" he said, concerned.

"Brian, please," she said, facing the other side of the room. "Eight years, that's like . . . *forever*." He tugged on her arm until she reluctantly turned back around. She brought her hand up to pinch the tension out of her forehead.

It wasn't working. "Oh, this is so much worse than I thought—you're in so much deeper than I'd ever realized."

"No, no," he insisted, sitting up and bringing himself closer. "I'm not—*really*."

"Right, after that long, you guys probably know *everything* about each other—how am I supposed to compete with that?" Out of context, she mumbled sadly, "And she's a dancer."

"You're *not* competing, believe me. And even if you were, there'd be no competition." Reese rolled her eyes, not looking too convinced.

"Come here," he said softly. "Come on . . ." He coaxed her into his arms with his gentleness and his warmth. Anyway, she was so crazy about him, she couldn't imagine resisting.

Her head was tucked under his chin, as they were

both awkwardly sitting on the bed now, with their arms around each other. Brian was stroking her back, and Reese was trying not to dissolve into a weak, spineless puddle. "As far as Veronica knowing everything about me," he said, "well, I don't know about that. I mean, I'm not the same person I was when I was with her. I've changed a lot, and so has my life."

"So what are you saying?" Reese whispered.

"I'm saying that we're not the same people we were when we were together—there's nothing left between us. I mean, nothing left to build on, anyway. At this point, it's all just residual bullshit."

She paused, and then pushed back to look into his eyes. "Well, I'm sorry, but I can't deal with residual bullshit, either. If we're going to have any kind of relationship, it has to be you and me—not you, me, and an unstable ex who won't let the dream die."

He grinned at that, in spite of her serious tone of voice. "It won't be like that," he promised. "Look, let's just get through the wedding, and then I'll tell her once and for all."

"Tell her what?" she pushed. She *had* to push. Weak, yes, but she'd meant what she said. She wasn't going to share him.

"I'll tell her that we don't have a future together. Period. It will be the truth."

Reese swallowed, and looked down at the bedspread. She could almost feel herself trembling. She wished Brian didn't have such a devastating effect on her. (Actually, she didn't.)

Brian rose up on his knees in the center of the bed and pulled Reese to him, bringing her up on her knees, too. "Then it'll be you and me," he said gruffly, hugging her tight. "I want that, too."

"You do?" she whispered.

"*Yes*," Brian said. "Just you and me."

Reese smiled into his shoulder and clung to his strength and silently prayed, *Forever*.

Chapter Twenty-seven

Her cell phone rang, and when she heard it she jerked awake, mistaking it for her alarm, but almost immediately her mind cleared and she realized it was coming from the little device on the nightstand. Then she realized that it was barely five in the morning.

"Hello?" she whispered, angling her upper body toward the far side of the bed so she wouldn't wake Brian. By the even hum of his breathing, he was still sleeping soundly.

"Hi, Reese. I'm glad I caught you."

You have got to be kidding me.

"Professor?"

"Yes, I was wondering if you had my notes for chapter ten on hand." Brian stirred beside her; his arm slid casually across her waist, and his breath breezed lightly across her cheek.

"Reese, did you hear me?" Kimble said, sounding impatient. "I really can't afford to waste precious time."

Okay, that *did* it. Call it a delayed reaction, call it a mood shift brought on by unbelievable sex. Whatever it was, Reese was not going to take any more guff from Leopold Kimble.

"Professor, do you realize what time it is?" she asked, not expecting any kind of direct answer. As soon as he began circumventing, she cut him off. "Look, I'm going to be very honest: You have a lot of nerve calling me at this hour."

Silence.

"I have always helped you, I have never slacked on a deadline, and you know that. But you seem to be forgetting that my fellowship stipulates that I allot twenty-two hours a week working for you. Twenty-two. As in, no less and *no more.* Yet you've been running me *ragged* since day one, exploiting me like crazy, and I just can't take it anymore!"

She was aware that she was no longer whispering, and she was also aware that she'd be more than thrilled to make it up to Brian later. But first things first. "Now, I'll be more than happy to discuss chapter ten, or anything else that you want, during *reasonable* working hours," she stated firmly. "But if you need someone on call twenty-four-seven then maybe you'd better talk to the administration about getting a replacement for me."

"No!" Kimble spoke suddenly. "No, no," he insisted, sounding panicked. "Please, I don't want a replacement!"

Now Reese was silent.

"Please," Kimble went on. "I am sorry if I've been giving you too much work, but please, I'm sure we can decide on a schedule more suitable to your needs."

"*What?*"

"Reese, I need you," he said, in a *Twilight Zone-*esque moment of vulnerability. "I don't know if I'll be able to finish my book without your special touch."

Special touch? She blinked and settled back against the pillows. She'd thought Kimble would either threaten her or talk over her with more deadlines and BS. She'd never expected anything that resembled sanity or appreciation.

Brian tightened his arm around her, indicating that he was awake and on her side. Looking over, she smiled apologetically for waking him. He responded by kissing her cheek and letting his lips linger.

"Reese? Please say something," Kimble implored.

"Oh, yes, I'm here," she said. "Well, Professor, if you think we can work something out—"

"We can, we can! I am absolutely sure of it."

She couldn't help grinning at Kimble's complete turnaround. Here all this time she'd been way too afraid to voice her position, and now, out of nowhere, it seemed crazy to be afraid of Kimble. "Well . . . all right," she said, enjoying her little stint as a hard-ass.

He let out an audible sigh of relief. "Oh, good," he said. "Well, I'll let you get back to whatever you were doing."

"Sleeping," she said pointedly.

"Ah, yes, of course, the time. Well, then—"

"Oh, Professor?"

"Yes?"

"I was just wondering . . . I know it's none of my business but . . . well, how come you never seem to work Kenneth as hard as you work me?"

"I thought that would've been rather obvious," Kimble said. "You're much smarter."

*   *   *

Two hours later, Brian heard the shower running, and couldn't resist. The bathroom door was ajar, and when he nudged it open his body immediately jolted at the vision of Reese's silhouette through the light blue shower curtain. She was washing her curvy little body everywhere, and arching her back to rinse her hair. The steam in the tiny bathroom was already making him sweat. It took him two seconds to drop his boxers and snap on a condom. Fully aroused, he stepped into the shower.

From behind, slow, hot hands slithered up Reese's stomach, and upon contact she let out a startled yelp. Realizing it was Brian didn't help. She suddenly felt shy, afraid of what he might think of her soft, round body now that it was under fluorescents. She was about to turn in his arms, so she'd at least be facing him, when he murmured "Mmm . . ." and cupped her breasts in his hand. He played with them a little, and then moved a hand up to brush a clump of her wet hair aside, and placed open, hot kisses along the back of her neck.

Now Reese relaxed, sighing while Brian kissed down her back and stroked her belly. After he soaped up his hands, he slid them over her slowly, rubbing lather sensually across her stomach and breasts and down her sides. Reese shivered because it felt so good, so hypnotic, and then she sagged against him, resting her back against the solid warmth of his chest. He moved his open mouth up her neck and along the back of her ear.

"I'm sorry . . ." he whispered.

"What?"

"Last night, I was . . ." *What?* she wondered. *Spectacular? Endowed? Stallion-esque?* He kissed the skin below her ear and murmured, "I was too rough."

"No, you weren't," she said brokenly. "What do you mean? You didn't hurt me." Not exactly the truth. She'd woken up sore but she couldn't absolutely swear that was Brian's fault, since she'd been bucking and fucking like a wild animal. Anyway, the point was, she was feeling less and less sore by the second. . . .

"But still," he was saying now, dragging his lips over her shoulder blades and running the flat of his palm over her nipple. She arched hard at the sensation. "I just mean that I should've been . . . slower . . . softer."

His warm, soapy hands continued demonstrating those exact principles until Reese was squirming against him, feeling frustrated by the thick, hot erection pressing against her back.

His right arm coasted around her stomach one more time, holding her like a fragile doll, and Reese thought she might explode, when suddenly, with a light jerk, she was pulled up against him, and she moaned at the feel of him, hard and engorged against her bottom.

Whispering his name, she felt one of his slippery hands smooth down her back, and lower, until Brian was sliding two fingers into her vagina from behind. She gasped as he pushed his fingers deeper, making her tremble unsteadily.

"Here, bend over a little," he said.

"Brian . . ." She sounded throaty and hot and unsure of what to do.

"It's okay; put your hands on the wall," he said, his voice almost raspy. He spread his hand over her abdomen and drew her bottom toward him. "Don't worry; it's okay," he said again. From anyone else, that would not have made her feel better.

Soon she was bent over, bracing her hands on the shower wall as hot water beat down on her neck and back and glided down her body. Brian's fingers were still inside her, and he jerked them a little—each time stirring her, before withdrawing, then going in deeper.

"I . . . I can't . . . I can't take this . . ." Reese choked out after several long moments.

She was rocking her body in time with his fingers and making guttural, aroused sounds that were apparently part of her repertoire now. Brian stilled his hand and bent his body to whisper into Reese's hair, "Do you want to make love again?" She moaned in response, and splayed her hands wider on the wall, dipping her head down in excruciating anticipation.

Soon Brian's hand was gone, and Reese was rocking her body backward, urging him to do something with her. To finish what he'd started. And that was when she felt it—his hot, bulging cock probing exactly her where his fingers had been.

A surge of excitement shot through her, as she felt him position himself, bringing both his hands up to hold her breasts, and then in one swift motion thrust into her. She cried out as he drove into her from behind, grunting with each thrust. He was hitting all the same spots as before, but at this angle the sensations were different. And just as the heat built up to the point of unbearable, and the friction was branding and scoring her flesh, Brian pulled out.

She groaned, "*Noo*," and Brian whipped her around, hoisting her up into a straddle around his hips. Then he entered her again, and with her back stuck to the shower wall, Reese's head thunked on the tile, but she barely felt it. Clinging to him, and strangling his waist with her legs, she tried to hammer her lower body enough to make herself come.

Finally it happened. Gripping Brian's wet hair, she called his name as spasms rolled through her body, leaving her spent, starry-eyed, and exhausted.

Brian followed, holding her with possessive hands while his shoulders convulsed.

Then, after several long moments, he shifted to let Reese's body slide down his, and her feet come back to the shower floor. With his arms wrapped around her, he rocked her gently from side to side, and she pressed her cheek against his chest.

"I never did that before," Reese whispered, hugging him as water sluiced down over their bodies. She cuddled against him and added, "I liked it."

Brian grinned down at her. "What am I gonna do with you?"

Hmm . . . she had a few ideas that involved falling in love and making a lasting commitment, but she was too foggy to articulate them at the moment.

It was probably just as well.

*　　*　　*

After they had dried off, Brian wrapped his towel around his waist, while Reese hooked her bra and tugged on some blue jeans.

"Let's order a pizza," Brian said, leaning back on the bed. "I'm starving."

She let out a laugh. "It's eight in the morning. Anyway, the wedding's in a few hours; I gotta get moving."

"Oh, yeah," he said, lifting off the bed. "I gotta get back to the city to get ready, and to get the rings." He stopped to lean down and press a soft kiss to her mouth, and Reese reached up on tiptoe and furrowed her fingers in his wet hair. Kissing him slowly, passionately, she savored every second, until a sudden knock at the door broke her concentration.

"Who could that be?" she whispered. "Oh, no! I hope my sisters didn't decide to give me a wake-up call. We're all supposed to meet at the house, but . . ."

She chewed on her lower lip, and the corners of Brian's mouth hitched up. "What, are you ashamed of me?"

"Oh, yes, that's it," she said, grinning. "Maybe it's the maid."

Whoever it was knocked again, so Brian and Reese pulled apart. "I'll wait in the bathroom if you want," he said quietly. She agreed and helped him gather up all his clothes, and then threw on a sweater of her own.

Looking through the peephole, she was shocked to find Kenneth standing on the other side. *What's he doing here? We agreed to meet at St. Catherine's at 1:30 . . . didn't we?*

She opened the door. "Uh, hi, Kenneth. I wasn't expecting to see you here." *Six hours before the wedding.*

"Yes, well, I was ahead of schedule so I thought I'd come by," he replied.

"Oh . . . I see," she managed. "But, well, to tell you the truth, I'm—"

"May I come in?" he asked, sounding a little edgy.

"Um, sure, but I can't really talk long. . . ." He stepped past her and into the room. Reese noticed that there was something different about him this morning—he seemed, well, fidgety. "So . . . I was actually getting ready to leave," she said, anxious to get him out of there and rescue Brian from the bathroom. "So I hope you didn't make the trip on my account. . . ."

"I will be happy to give you a ride. Where are you going now, to your parents' house?"

"Well, yeah, but I have my car."

"I see."

A few beats of silence passed before she said, "Kenneth, is everything okay?"

"Certainly," he said. "But you probably don't want to be late. Can I walk you out?"

"No . . . I mean, thank you, but I'm not quite ready yet." Damn, this was ridiculous. Why had he driven in from the city so early? And what the hell was she supposed to do with him?

"All right, then. I'll just give you your gift early, and be on my way until we meet later at the church."

Reese's eyebrows shot up. "Gift?"

"I got you an item that I hope you will enjoy. When I saw it, I thought of you." He reached into his coat and pulled out a small gift-wrapped box.

"Oh, Kenneth, you shouldn't have. . . ."

"Please. Open it."

She swallowed, feeling uncomfortable as hell, and pulled on the red ribbon. When she opened the silver lid, her eyes bugged out of her head. It was a *cameo*!

Okay, what the hell was going on here? Maybe this was all a dream, and she just hadn't woken up yet. It would certainly explain the fabulous sex.

"It is an antique cameo brooch," he explained. "It is very special to me. It was my mother's."

"Wha— Oh, Kenneth, I can't accept—"

"I must run now," he said hastily. "I just want you to know how, uh, pleased I am that we are heading in a direction of trust and confidence." *Huh?* "I will see you in a few hours."

And then he was gone.

Reese stared at the closing door, trying to figure out what had just happened, when the bathroom door abruptly swung open. Brian came out, buckling his belt, not looking at her. "Well, that was weird," she said.

"Uh-huh." He still didn't look at her, but busied himself with the second and third buttons of his shirt. His tie hung loosely around his neck.

"Brian?"

Still not say anything, he shrugged on his coat, tugging it a little harder than necessary, and Reese inched closer. "What's wrong?"

"Forget it," he said curtly.

"Wait a minute," she said, frustrated. "Why are you mad?"

He shook his head and gave one of his *psfft* responses, which didn't do much for her, so she waited for something more. "I see it's really over with that guy," he said finally.

"What are you talking about?" she asked, confused. "It is over. I have no idea why Kenneth came by this morning." To be honest, she was starting to get annoyed. *Brian* was the one with all the baggage, not her!

"I just don't get why you're letting him think there's something there if there isn't."

"Well, I can't control what he *thinks*. It's not like I encourage him—"

"You introduced him as your date last night."

"Oh, don't even bring up last night," Reese said. "You were letting Veronica think whatever she wanted."

He scowled and said, "I just don't know if you're being honest about you and him. Christ, Reese, the guy gave you his mother's jewelry."

"Look, Brian, I'm not gonna get into a whole relationship talk with him when I'm on my way out the door. Anyway, he's my date for the wedding—I can't just drop him cold. I seem to recall that you're waiting till after the wedding to tell Veronica for the same reason."

"Whatever," he muttered angrily, and headed toward the door.

"Oh, forget it," she said, feeling defeated, deflated, and totally drained.

"What?" Brian asked, turning back around.

Reese shook her head and avoided his eyes. "You are so transparent, Brian. God, I've been so stupid. You don't really want to end things with Veronica, and now you're looking for an excuse so you don't have to. It is so fucking obvious!" Whenever she resorted to swearing, she knew she'd reached emotional time-bomb status. *So too fucking bad.*

"How can you say that after last night?"

"Brian, face it, you're just using Kenneth as an excuse. Just go—go stay in your safe, comfortable little world with Veronica, who you've known *forever*." Close to crying now, she somehow kept her tears from falling. "I never should've let this happen."

"Now you're sorry it happened?" he said, clenching his cheek. Wordlessly he nodded and opened the door. He looked over his shoulder and said, "Then forget it happened. Forget the whole damn thing."

And then *he* was gone, too.

Chapter Twenty-eight

The next several hours were a blur. The prewedding preparations had gone smoothly, although a little frantically, and the ceremony had gone off without a hitch. Reese had avoided Brian's penetrating stare throughout, as hard as it was, because it was all just too painful. Thinking about how she'd fallen into bed with him, how she'd given him her body and heart so easily . . . well, she could either force the thoughts aside or go crazy. Or do a little of both.

As planned, she had full-scale van duty, from the church to the hotel. And now, as she pulled into the parking lot of the Goldwood Villa, she could not wait to drop off her last group—the Gardening Society, who were, quite predictably, bombed.

Immediately after the ceremony, Gardening Society president Mary Paddington had told Reese that they were going on a bar crawl, and to pick them up in an hour "somewhere between Main and Drury." An hour and a half later, Reese had finally tracked them down at the Glory Pub, and they'd barreled into the van like a bunch of hyper ten-year-olds.

Now, as Reese slid the van into an empty space, Mary Paddington yelled, "Heeey—here we are, everybody!" Then she stuck her hand inside her shirt and under her armpit—for about the tenth time that ride—and started flapping. She looked absolutely crestfallen when trumpet noises failed to sound. "Heeey," she cried, "it's not working now!"

Kenneth was sitting in the passenger seat, looking appropriately appalled.

Reese just rolled her eyes and said, "Okay, we're here. C'mon, everybody out." Once the ladies were on their way to the banquet room, Reese left Kenneth waiting while she stopped in the ladies' room to check her reflection. *Hmm . . .* Not bad, but nothing to write home about. Angela had done her hair that morning, and somehow managed to make it all smooth and shiny and only subtly wavy. Also, the fish diet had paid off, because Reese had lost the four pounds she needed to get into her bridesmaid dress without fainting. Good enough for her. Her breasts were still borderline oozing out of the neckline, but it didn't look quite as Incredible-Hulk-bursting-out-of-his-clothes as it had two weeks ago.

As she looked in the mirror, she had a sudden acute moment of stinging self-awareness. God, she hated those. But there it was. An overwhelming feeling of solitude. Uncertainty. Isolation. Even though her whole family was out in that reception hall—not to mention most of Goldwood—in that moment, Reese felt wholly and inexplicably *alone.*

A toilet flushed loudly behind her, breaking the spell, and Reese turned and left.

The banquet room was jumping with people and food and music and dancing and friends—and yes, of course, total strangers. Ally and Ben were in the

center of the dance floor, Ben looking great in his
tux, and Ally looking incredible in her unusual wedding dress that matched the streaks in her hair, and
white go-go boots that were visible only when she
ruffled her skirt as she danced. Reese felt happy for
her, but it was an aching kind of happiness.

"Do you wanna get something to eat?" she asked
Kenneth, motioning to the buffet table. She probably
shouldn't, but she might as well eat while she had
the chance—as soon as she spotted Brian twirling
Veronica on the dance floor, she knew she'd be violently ill.

"Yes, that sounds good. By the way, how is Professor Kimble's book coming along? Any concerns on
your part? Uh . . . I'm here to help. You know, uh,
as your significant other."

She sighed, and faced the hors d'oeuvres instead
of him. Maybe they would need to have that relationship talk sooner than she thought.

"Hi, Reese."

She turned and saw Brian standing next to her,
reaching for a glass of red wine. "Oh, hi," she said
quickly, swallowing hard and averting her eyes. She
couldn't look at him without remembering his hands
on her, their bodies naked and sweaty and pounding.
She couldn't forget the strength of his arms, the soft
raspiness of his voice when he first woke, the taste
of his mouth after he slept. Or when he had told her
it would be the two of them—just the two of them.
No, she definitely could not look at him right now.

"Hi . . . Kenneth, right?" he said, holding out his hand
to Kenneth, who stood there like a stone before extending his own hand. They shared a brief, perfunctory

shake, while Reese kept her head angled more toward the food than Brian. He said, "Reese, would you mind dancing with me? My date seems to have disappeared for a few minutes."

She whipped her head forward, now looking at him speculatively—warily. He glanced over at Kenneth. "You don't mind, do you?" Then he took Reese's hand before she had a chance to answer.

Kenneth spoke abruptly. "No, that's fine. Reese, I'll hold your bag."

Brian tugged gently on her hand and kept it firmly in his own. She didn't seem to have much choice unless she wanted to make a scene. "All right," she said finally, handing Kenneth her evening bag and allowing Brian to lead her to the dance floor.

What had Brian meant that Veronica had "disappeared"? Was it possible that he had told her about Reese? Was that what he was trying to say? Her heart kicked up—maybe things would work out after all.

Once they were out on the floor, Brian pulled Reese into his arms just as a slow ballad began. She held on to him, not nearly as tightly as she could or wanted to, but really, she had to maintain *some* pride. Wordlessly, he leaned in close, and she could have sworn he smelled her hair. "So where's your girlfriend?" she asked, breaking the silence.

Hey, she never said she wasn't trying to bait him as well as break the silence. Anyway, if she baited him, he might just give her some good news.

"I don't have a girlfriend," he said softly. "But if you mean Veronica, she's in the bathroom."

Reese stiffened in his arms at the mention of Veronica. She started to pull away, but Brian locked his hands more firmly on her waist. "Let me go," she said, annoyed.

"No, don't," Brian urged.

Out of the corner of Reese's eye, she saw flaxen-hair-and-lithe-wonder approaching. *Just fucking great.* "Oh, what's the point, Brian?" she said waspishly, motioning to Veronica with her eyes. "Obviously nothing's changed." She disentangled herself from his arms, just as Veronica said, "Hi, there. Rina, right?"

"Reese," she replied uncomfortably. Of course Miss Perfect looked slim and graceful in her cream-colored sheath, and her delicate little shoulders made Reese look like an outside linebacker. "Well . . . I've got to get back to my date," Reese said feebly. "Excuse me."

Just then Brian's cell phone rang inside his jacket, startling all of them. In spite of Veronica's audible sigh of annoyance, he answered. "I can't believe you left that on," Veronica said, irritated.

He held up his hand to her, squinting a little, which made sense when he said, "Scott? I can't hear what you're saying. . . ."

"Brian, can't this *wait*?" Veronica whined, in spite of his gesture asking her to be quiet for a moment. "This is so typical. Just when I come over for a dance—"

"Damn it!" Brian said, shutting his phone.

"Brian, what is it?" Reese asked, coming a little closer. The only reason she'd stayed on the fringe was because his face had become creased in tension, and she'd wanted to make sure things were okay. Now it wasn't looking like they were.

He shook his head, not really looking at her, and said, "It's Danny . . . Scott was trying to tell me something, and my phone died. Damn!" he said again.

Veronica insisted with steely calm, "Brian, I'm sure it can wait. Can't we just enjoy the party for a while?"

Shaking his head, he said, "I'm sorry . . . I gotta go page him and see what's going on . . . something's not right. . . ."

"Of course. Everything before me; this is so predictable."

Reese followed Brian out of the banquet room as he went, presumably, in search of a phone. "Brian?" she called as he neared the door. "Brian, wait . . . you can use the phone in my hotel room . . . talk as long as you want." She would've offered him her cell, but it was up in her room, too.

Stoically he said, "All right, thanks."

"Okay, I just need to get the room key from Kenneth—he's holding my purse."

The only problem was that when Reese looked for Kenneth, she couldn't find him anywhere. Maybe if she combed the entire room or stalked the men's room, she'd find him, but she didn't want to leave Brian waiting that long. "Shoot, I don't know where he went. Let's just stop at the front desk to get an extra key."

After they got the key, they rode the elevator to the eighth floor in borderline-tense silence. Reese led the way down the hall to room 816, even though they both knew full well that Brian was *very* acquainted with her accommodations.

Reese swiped the card key and opened the door, saying, "Okay, the phone's right there—" before her jaw dropped.

What the hell?

Kenneth was hunkered down on the floor, frantically rifling through her bag!

"What the hell are you doing?" she yelled.

"Jesus Christ! What are you doing in her room?" Brian said angrily, and charged toward him.

Kenneth crumbled like the proverbial deck of cards at that point, turning paler than usual and holding up his hands, begging, "Please, don't hit me, don't hit me!"

"Tell me what the fuck you're doing going through her room!" Brian ordered.

His protectiveness would have been heartwarming if there weren't more pressing matters. "Wait, both of you!" Reese said, exasperated. "Brian, use the phone; you don't have time to be wasting with this."

"But—"

"*I'll* deal with Kenneth," she finished with very obvious determination, and turned to the slimy lizard in question. She jerked her finger and said, "Outside—*now*." Her head was swimming as Kenneth slunk toward the door. But on the other hand, how tough could the confrontation be? She could swear the boy was quivering. •

"Kenneth, what the hell is going on?" Reese demanded the minute they were in the hall. "Just spill it. No throat clearing, no baloney, just tell me. *Now*."

He sucked in a deep breath, obviously dying to

feign phlegm, but didn't dare. Fiddling with his suit pockets, he said, "All right, I'll tell you the truth. Quite frankly, well . . . I have only been dating you to get information about Professor Kimble's book."

Reese's mouth dropped open. She knew that he *lived* to talk about their graduate work, but she'd never thought he was blatantly using her. She waited for a "but"—like, "but somewhere along the way, I fell I love with you." It never came. Kenneth didn't qualify what he'd said in the least. "I hated it," he continued. "Having to pretend I actually had romantic feelings for you." He shivered. "It was awful. Oh, no offense."

She had an irate look on her face that said, *You're goin' down.* "No, I just meant that you're not my type," he clarified quickly. "You see, the truth is, I am already deeply involved with someone else. Someone who, uh, truly 'strikes my fancy,' if you will." He slipped in a little throat clearing here, but Reese let it slide. "In fact," Kenneth went on, "I did all of this for her."

"But who? I don't get this—who could possibly care about that dumb book?"

"Frankly, I'd rather not say."

"Well, you'd better say, or I'm gonna go to the dean about all this." Honestly, she didn't know if any of this fell within the dean's jurisdiction, but she figured Kenneth would cower in the face of the Crewlyn College chain of command.

Her instincts were right (for once).

"No, please don't go to the dean," he pleaded. "I'll tell you, I'll tell you." He swallowed slowly, and

said, "The truth is, I have been immersed in a passionate love affair with Professor Diane Shamus for
the last several months."

Shamus? As in the senile American history professor with the knee-length white hair? Genuinely curious, if a touch horrified, Reese asked, "How on earth
did *that* happen?"

"Well, if you must know . . . she seduced me."

Eww! Did she have to ask?

"So, as you can see, I prefer a more mature
woman. And, to be candid, Diane has unlocked a
realm of sensual treasures that I, in my callow youth,
had never even envisioned—"

"All right," Reese said, squinting and holding up
her hand. "I get the idea."

Then, like a shot, she remembered the tortoiseshell
barrette she'd found on Kenneth's desk. Oh, yuck, had
they *done* it in there? Reese shivered at the mental
image.

"What?" he asked.

"Oh . . . uh . . . nothing," she lied. "But wait, I
still don't get it. Why would Professor Shamus care
about Kimble's book?"

"Well, you see, she's terribly self-conscious because
she hasn't had an academic publication in almost
thirty years." Reese had to admit there might be
some validity to that self-consciousness. "Anyway,"
Kenneth went on wearily, "she asked me to find out
what Professor Kimble is working on, so we can . . ."

"What? Steal his ideas? His *work*?" Reese was acting
righteous to make Kenneth feel like dirt, but in fact,
Kimble had no ideas, had done no work, and whatever
he thought he knew had been stolen in the first place.

"Kenneth, that is despicable," she went on, still not through making him feel like dirt. Hell, he deserved it. He'd barely expressed any regret about leading Reese on for more than two months! Here she'd been agonizing over their relationship for the last four weeks, and the whole time Kenneth had been plotting against her.

"I truly am sorry," Kenneth said, sounding as heartfelt as a robot. "I never meant to make you fall for me." She almost laughed. "I just didn't think it would be so hard to get some valuable information out of you. It was only in these last few weeks that Diane and I realized we needed to, uh, amplify your sense of emotional intimacy in order to get you to confide in me."

"You mean Professor Shamus was in on *all* of this?" Reese exclaimed. She assumed Shamus wanted Kenneth to use his position as Kimble's assistant, but she didn't figure she was the pimp behind the scenes. Jeez, what would the Crewlyn ethics committee say about that?

As though he'd read her mind, Kenneth started begging, "Oh, please, *please*, Reese, don't do anything to jeopardize Diane's position at Crewlyn. She is a remarkable woman who regrettably fell victim to temptation."

Reese rolled her eyes and stifled a gag. But as messed up as Kenneth and Shamus were, Reese just wanted this over with. "Fine, I won't, but get out of here before I change my mind."

"Oh, well, my car's at the church—"

"Don't push your luck," she warned, glaring at him.

"No, no, I won't. Thank you," he said quickly. "I promise, Diane and I will not try anything like this again. I'll help her find her own book idea. I swear."

"Good for you," Reese said apathetically. As she turned to open her hotel room door, she heard Kenneth call back to her.

"Reese, do you mind, uh, well there's just no easy way to say this, uh . . ."

"Just spit it out," she said, annoyed and tired of talking to this weasel.

"Well, that cameo I gave you—it's Diane's. May I, uh, have it back, please?"

She let out a laugh. This just kept getting stupider! Obviously they had concocted the old "it belonged to my dead mother" scheme in an effort to "amplify a sense of emotional intimacy." How pathetic for everyone involved—which, unfortunately, included Reese.

"Kenneth, I'll mail it to you, okay?" she said with disgust. Turning her back on him, she went to check on Brian.

Chapter Twenty-nine

When she walked in, she saw him pacing. "Hey," she said quietly, "what's going on?"

He shook his head, still pacing, and said, "Danny went into premature labor. Scott's supposed to call me and tell me if everything's okay."

He sounded edgy, worried, but guarded, so she didn't feel comfortable going over and wrapping her arms around him, as much as she wanted to. Tentatively inching closer, she asked, "Do you want some privacy?"

He looked up, expressionless; she took that as a yes, nodded with understanding, and turned to go. "No," he said in a low, serious voice that stopped her. "No . . . stay. Please."

"Okay," she replied softly, and remained standing in the middle of the room, while Brian went back to pacing.

Suddenly his head jerked up. "Oh, what was deal with that guy?" he asked, referring to the slithering slime of the century, Kenneth. Waving her hand dismissively, Reese gave Brian the quick, abridged version. He actually chuckled when she mentioned how ancient Professor Shamus was; then his face dark-

ened as they both remembered that he was waiting
for a very important phone call. So Reese shut up
and let him pace in peace.

Suddenly he sat down in the chair—the same one
he'd held her in the night before—and she went beside him. "Brian," she said, just barely touching his
arm. "Do you want me to get you anything? Something from downstairs to eat or drink . . . ?"

He shook his head. "No . . . thanks."

"Okay." She chewed on her lower lip, and then
said, "I'm sure it'll be all right. Being premature can
happen to anyone. It's extremely common."

He nodded. "You're right," he said. She turned to
give him some space again, and he reached for her
hand. "Wait," he said, looking up at her, his voice
deep and almost raspy.

She held his hand and looked into his eyes for a
long moment, before he tugged lightly, and before
she knew it he was folding her into his arms and
cuddling her on his lap. Affectionately, she stroked
his cheek and tried to say things that would be
comforting.

Then she stopped talking, and waited for the
phone to ring—for Scott to call them back. Nearly
half an hour passed before he did.

"Hello?" Brian said, after snatching the phone up
on the first ring. Reese slid off his lap, suddenly feeling foolish for being in such an intimate position.
"Yeah, what's going on?" Brian said. He waited.
Then he smiled a relieved, warm, happy smile that
was very contagious.

Reese's insides swirled as she waited to the hear
the good news, too. Brian went on, "Oh, God, that's

great . . . I'm so . . . that's great. Okay, when she wakes up, tell her I'll call tomorrow. Thanks a lot." He hung up and turned to Reese. "Danny's fine. She had a boy, and he's fine."

"Oh, that's great!" Reese said enthusiastically. Brian stood up and hugged her, and she hugged him back, unable to resist.

"His name's Jason," he added.

"Oh, Brian, I'm so happy everything worked out," she said into his shoulder.

They stood there like that for several more moments before the hug took on an erotic quality. Reese started to feel hot in Brian's arms, hearing and feeling his breathing against her neck. She found herself focusing intently on his chest pressed to her breasts, and his thighs grazing her dress, which was suddenly stifling as hell.

Slowly dragging her head up, she watched Brian turn his face and lean in closer. Their lips were barely an inch apart. And just like that, it was about a million watts hotter in the scant space between them. A tantalizing bulge was touching her abdomen, while Brian's warm breath was teasing her bottom lip. He said, "Reese . . ." before closing his mouth over hers, and kissing her slowly. Wetly. Deeply.

She combed her fingers through his hair and unconsciously massaged his scalp as she slipped her tongue inside his mouth. His hands roamed lower, sliding down to clutch her bottom and squeeze it and pull her flush against his groin.

And then they fell backward.

When they hit the bed, Brian's hands were sliding up Reese's legs, under her dress, dragging it upward and grabbing at her panties. When he snapped her garters, a guttural, aroused sound burst from his throat. Mouths still fused and savage on each other, Reese pulled on his tie. Only she pulled too hard, and Brian broke the kiss, smiling against her lips. Then he loosened it himself, and tossed it off behind him.

As he plunged his tongue into her mouth, she feverishly unbuttoned his shirt, desperate to have him naked and on top of her like the night before. She wanted to feel his weight again—skin on skin—and she wanted to feel him slide in *deep*.

By the time he pulled down her panties, they were both gasping. Brian lowered his mouth to her abdomen and started sliding down past her belly, and Reese knew what he wanted to do, but placed a hand on his shoulder to stop him.

"No . . ." she whispered. "Another time . . ." He looked up at her, sleepy-eyed and confused. "I want to kiss you," she said. Eagerly, he brought his mouth to hers again.

They were only half-naked, but it was enough. Except for one thing. "Shit!" he said. "God*damn* it!"

"What? What's wrong?" she asked, alarmed.

He shook his head, frustrated, then managed a self-deprecating grin. "Condoms."

"Oh!" she said, relieved that that was all. And soon they were off the bed, running to the bathroom to get one, and that was when Reese offered to put it on for him.

She rolled it on quickly, and laid a towel on the sink. Then she hopped up, spread her legs, and drew him toward her with her heels.

Panting hard now, Brian hitched her butt off the

counter enough to drive into her. Immediately his head fell forward, and hers fell back. He glided in and out, each time increasing the depth and power of it. Reese moaned, and dug her fingers into his skin.

Grunting with each thrust, Brian kept moving until Reese clenched and quaked and cried out. Then he was quaking. She became hazily aware of the loud smacking sound of his thighs as they hit the side of the counter over and over, faster and faster, again and again.

After Brian finished, both of them were temporarily speechless—but then, they were partially out of breath. Reese clung to him, feeling the perspiration at his temples and on his neck. He carried her to the bed, where he set her down and lay down beside her.

Teasingly, she whispered, "What's your obsession with carrying me?"

He grinned. "You're so short, I can't resist." He brushed an errant straggle of her hair out of her eyes.

She went for a light tone. "So . . . here we are again."

"Yep."

"Mmm-hmm."

"Yeah . . ."

"Reese, I'm sorry about what happened this morning," he said suddenly. "I acted like a complete ass."

"I'm sorry, too," she said, "I don't know why I got so mad—"

"I do," he said, then, "Damn, it's starting to get cold in here." They both got under the covers and snuggled for body heat. Then Brian said, "What you said about me not wanting to make the final break from Veronica . . ."

"Yeah?" she said, knowing what was coming.

"Well, you were wrong." Or maybe not. Her heart kicked up, she was so glad to have been wrong. "I mean, dead wrong," he emphasized. "I acted like an ass because I . . . I just got so jealous. When Kenneth showed up with his mother's antique cameo or whatever it was—"

"Don't even get me started on that cameo," she said lightly.

"Well, you know what I mean. . . ."

"No, I understand," she said, and pressed a gentle kiss to his lips.

"Okay, here's the plan, " he said. "I'm going downstairs and telling Veronica about us—"

"No," Reese said. "Not now. After the wedding. I don't want a scene."

"But—"

"Please, it's just not worth it right now."

Brian studied her for a moment. "Okay, after the wedding is over, I'll tell Veronica everything." Reese bit her lip, and nodded anxiously. "And then I'm gonna come for you," he said thickly. "That way we can start clean. There'll be nothing between us."

"Okay," she said softly, and then had a realization. "Omigod, Brian! What are we doing? We've got to get back to the reception!" Hopping out of bed quickly, she picked her dress off the floor and tossed his shirt at him.

"Oh, yeah, you're right," he said, sliding out of bed, not as hurriedly.

"Jeez, what's my family gonna think of me? I hope they didn't notice I was gone." She zipped herself up and tried to smooth her hair back to normalcy. "What time is it?" she asked.

He stopped midbutton to look at his watch. "Uh, ten to six."

"Oh, good, cake's not being served for another half hour." Slipping her high heels on, she picked up the silver evening bag that Kenneth had left on the floor, and walked with Brain to the door.

"Why's the cake important?" he asked, as they headed out into the hall.

"Because . . ." she said, shimmying a little in her dress, "that's when we give our toast."

The rest of the night sailed by in a heady, thrilling haze. Apparently Veronica had been so annoyed that Brian had disappeared that she'd left. So Reese could have spent the evening in Brian's arms . . . but she didn't.

They had agreed that they would start clean, and that meant there couldn't be anything between them until everything was settled with Veronica.

Luckily the other Brocks hadn't noticed Reese's absence. She had told them about his sister, and how he used the phone in her room, but she left out the part about earth-shattering sex on the bathroom counter, and all of their plans for a romantic future. She didn't want to jinx that future yet, anyway.

Everyone seemed to have a wonderful time at the reception. Remmi Collindyne had indicated to Joanna that except for the orchid boutonieres, the ceremony was in exquisite taste. The "compliment" had left Joanna glowing. Aunt Jacy and Aunt Aileen led their sons, Chris and James, in a conga line that never quite picked up.

When Reese danced with her father, she told him about Kenneth, and how he had been using her as part of a deranged ploy to get access to the worst book ever written. They both ended up chuckling at how ridiculous the whole thing was, and her dad said, "Well, I suppose it's true, after all."

"What?"

" 'There is a time to wink, as well as to see.' "

Reese rolled her eyes and laughed.

Although Reese and Brian had exchanged long, meaningful looks throughout the night, they didn't give in to temptation. The only time they came close to each other was when they gave their toast, which ended up being short and sweet. Joanna sighed hugely, never so relieved, and said privately, "Oh, sweetheart, it went great!"

Reese smiled and said, "I tried to tell you, Mom. You worry too much."

By the time Reese got to her hotel room that night, she felt a fuzzy kind of happiness float through her body. Ally and Ben were leaving for their honeymoon tomorrow, Angela and Drew seemed better than ever, and her parents were still the best, and life finally seemed to be heading toward something more than just *existing*. Who would have thought?

Chapter Thirty

"What the *fuck* is this!" Reese yelled to an empty apartment. She pulled out her glasses and tried to read the prescription label on the bottle in her hand.

To work out some of her bitter, miserable, incensed energy, she'd decided to clean out her apartment. And she was currently tackling the medicine cabinet. School had started that Monday, and it was just a banner *fucking* time. She hurled the bottle toward the garbage pail, perfectly aware that she was whipping it way too hard and fast to make it in. Like she cared.

"Okay, next, this stupid piece of *crap* left here by some *stupid* roommate I barely even knew!" She grabbed a box of who-knew-what, and hurled it across the room. Then she slammed the cabinet shut so hard it ricocheted back and swatted her in the face. "Stupid thing, I hate you!" she yelled, slamming it back in place.

Immediately she was struck by her reflection in the mirror. Weariness, anger, and heartbreak . . . suddenly some of her temper drained out, leaving her enervated. Dejected. Slumping down on the toilet lid, she let out a deep, depressed sigh. *Face it: This isn't working.*

It had been almost a week and she hadn't heard from Brian. She couldn't believe it. How many times did she have to be hurt by him before she learned? Well, she supposed *no* more times now, since they were obviously finished. He'd never come for her, like he promised.

Oh, why should she even be surprised? She was just destined to be unlucky in love.

Dragging herself up, she went into her bedroom to clean her desk. Getting a sudden surge of rage—ahem, *gusto*—she began hurling the drawers open, grabbing their contents in both hands, and throwing them onto the floor.

Just as she was tossing some manila folders carelessly over her head, while papers dropped and scattered everywhere (and she really didn't give a *fuck*!), there was a knock at the door. *Oh, great.* With her luck, it was one of the Nazis from Res Life bearing new roommates for the spring semester.

Sighing and muttering obscenities to herself, Reese barked, "Coming!" and charged across the living room to whip the door open. (Well, to ask who it was, weigh if it warranted unbolting her five locks, and *then* whip the door open.) "Who is it!" she shouted, obviously uninterested in finding out.

"It's me . . . Brian."

Her stomach dropped . . . and then twisted into a big, painful knot. What was he *doing* there? And why couldn't he just stop hurting her? In fact, it was only with those questions in mind that she started unbolting locks.

Finally she flung the door open and glared at him.

"Hi," he said, beaming and apparently oblivious. He was holding a bouquet of daffodils, smiling at her like he was crazy about her. "Oh, I forgot you wear glasses. Damn, you look cute."

As he leaned down to kiss her she couldn't help wondering: Was he *insane*?

"What the hell do you think you're doing?" she barked, jerking her head out of kissing range.

He looked genuinely confused, and straightened slowly. "Wha—what do you mean?"

Reese's mouth dropped open. She held her hands out and started looking around to an imaginary audience—as if to say, *Is it just me, or is this guy a complete asshole?*

"I don't get this," he said. "Did . . . what, you changed your mind about us?"

She scrunched her face at him as if he had several heads and said, "Did *I* change *my* mind? You were supposed to come for me! After everything was settled—*remember*?"

"I know; that's what I'm doing here!" he said, handing off the flowers to her, even though she didn't want them.

She snatched them angrily and said, "It's been four days! You were supposed to end things with Veronica and call me the next day!"

He looked surprised . . . then understanding . . . then contrite. Reese looked as though she were about to strangle him. "Ah, hell," he said, "Reese, can I please come in? We need to get something straight."

For a couple of seconds she contemplated slamming the door, but ultimately she decided against it.

Really, why bother? It wouldn't make her feel any better at this point. "Whatever," she grumbled. "Like it makes a difference now."

She spun around to give him her back, and he followed her into the apartment. Carelessly she tossed his flowers onto the kitchen table. When she finally turned to face him, he held up his hands in a *Now, just listen* gesture of entreaty. She went along with it only because she'd temporarily run out of scathing things to say.

"Reese, I'm sorry, but I thought we agreed that we couldn't see each other until everything was settled. I thought that was how you wanted it."

"I did. What's your point?"

"Well, nothing was settled until today," he said apologetically. "Reese, I'm so sorry—I had no idea you thought that I was blowing this off. I *wasn't*, believe me. I mean, if I'd known you thought that . . . I thought you didn't want me to get in touch, until, you know—"

"Yeah, yeah, I get it, all right?" she said impatiently, crossing her arms over her chest. "So what's the status now? Let me guess, you couldn't *bear* to tell her? What, did she threaten to jump off the Brooklyn Bridge? What? C'mon, let's hear it."

He tilted his head, and with a trace of wryness said, "You done?"

She just sulked.

He came closer. "No to all of the above. I had coffee with Veronica today and told her I was done with all of it—that our relationship had died two years ago—hell, probably a lot longer than that—and that I wasn't in love with her anymore. I told her I haven't been in love with her for a long time."

Reese swallowed and avoided his eyes.

"Wait. The reason I didn't do it before today was because she was away on a class trip to San Francisco since Monday morning. I had no way to do it before today." He gently tilted her chin so their gazes met. "Reese, I swear, I just assumed you didn't want to hear from me till it was done. I'm really sorry if you were . . . worried, or—"

"I wasn't worried," she lied. "I just figured you changed your mind about us."

"*No,*" he said. "No way. I'm sorry; I just didn't think there was any doubt at this point." His voice dropped a little. "I want to be with you," he said.

"Well, I want to be with you, too—*jeez.*" Then her face broke into a self-deprecating smile, and Brian smiled back. He pulled her into his arms, and as she hugged him, he picked her up. "Oh, not the picking-me-up thing," she said, giggling. "You're gonna slip a disk!"

"*Psfft.*"

She smiled into his shoulder, and he set her back onto the floor. Leaning down to kiss the curve of her neck, he murmured, "Now are you gonna put those in water, or should I just toss them in the trash?"

"Oh, yeah!" she said, darting to the kitchen table and picking up the bouquet. She filled a vase with water and said over her shoulder, "So, was it difficult with Veronica? You know, having the talk?"

"Nah," he said. "I told her about you, and she told me to drop dead. After that, conversation seemed silly."

Reese twisted her lips into a smirk. "Really."

"Really. Well, she did lay into me a little about all

my flaws," he replied absently, and shrugged off his jacket and tie.

"What flaws?" Reese said, defensive on his behalf.

He shrugged. "I don't know; I wasn't really listening. Anyway, she said it was for the best anyway, because she met a male ballerina on her trip and they had more in common."

Reese set the flowers down in the center of the table, and like Brian's presence, they brightened up the room. Walking toward him, she said, "Um, I don't think they're called that."

"What?"

"Male ballerinas," she said, smiling.

He chuckled. "Well, whatever." Then he surveyed the apartment. Papers were strewn everywhere, and tons of things were tossed and catapulted out of their proper place. "Uh, unique décor," he said, nodding slowly.

"Oh . . ." She bit her lower lip and said, "I'd been cleaning."

"Interesting results," he said, sounding slightly worried.

Reese slid her arms around his waist. "Ally's gonna kill me when she finds out."

"What? About us?"

"Yeah."

"Why?"

"You don't know Ally. She won't believe I kept this from her, and I can hardly tell her it's because of her big—albeit, well-meaning—mouth."

Brian smiled. "Speaking of telling people things, I think it's about time we told your mother about your writing career."

"Please, what 'career'—*We*?"

"Yeah, well, you can tell her, and then I'll be there to go on and on about how good you are." Reese smirked, and he insisted, "You *are*—you had me totally hooked."

"So I guess you're my biggest fan then."

"Always," he said, grinning, but there was a thickness to his voice that made her believe him. She even pushed away the cynical voice deep inside her saying, *That remains to be seen*, and just let herself feel happy.

"Come on, just tell me," Brian said. "Do Trent and Monique get together at the end, or what?"

She laughed. "I can't tell you," she said. "I don't know yet." That last part was a lie.

"Fine, well, I at least want to read what you've added so far," he said, and made a "gimme" gesture with both hands. "Get the laptop. Please."

She smiled—a big, open, airy smile—she could feel it on her face, welcoming him, inviting him in—into her world, into *her*—and said, "Actually, you're in luck." She went into her bedroom and over to her bookbag.

He followed, and she pulled out a stack of a hundred pages. "I printed this at the computer lab earlier," she said, handing it to him.

Loosening his tie, he took the pages, plopped down on her bed, and immediately began reading. "Do you want something to drink?" she asked.

"Okay, thanks," he said. "Whatever's fine."

As she turned, she felt his hand touch her arm, and he said, "Hey." Suddenly his arms snaked around her waist, and he was hugging her again.

Sighing, she tilted her head to kiss him. When she pulled back, they exchanged a long moment that meant so much, and Reese pressed her forehead against his shoulder, thinking that whoever had said New York was the loneliest city in the world may not have been looking hard enough.

She whispered against Brian's collar, "This is the beginning, isn't it?"

Brian tightened his arms around her, and buried his face in her hair. "Yeah," he said huskily. "It's the beginning . . . so how come I already feel far gone?"

A voice deep inside her answered, *Because we're falling in love.*

And this time, she paid attention.

Epilogue

One year later

"Brock, phone call!" Tina announced, bringing Reese the receiver and slapping her on the back with camaraderie, but nearly knocking the wind out of her. Reese forced a smile to cover the pain, and took the phone.

"Hello?"

"Sweetheart? It's Mom."

"Oh, hi. Is everything okay?" Reese asked, surprised her mother was calling her at work, but not too worried about getting in trouble for a personal call. The café, like the rest of the store, was pretty dead because it was six-thirty on a Friday evening. In fact, soon Brian would be picking her up to take her to dinner at their favorite restaurant downtown. Anyway, Darcy had left early to go to a concert, and ever since Reese had been transferred to permanent café duty, and Amy had taken her place as a bookseller, the boss lady didn't dog her heels nearly as much. Too bad for Amy, but Reese wasn't about to complain.

"Oh, everything's fine!" Joanna enthused. "Actually, I have some wonderful news for you—oh, I just can't believe it!"

"What?" Reese asked, feeling her heart skip, though she had no clue what the news could be. "What is it?"

"Oh, God, Angela and I tried to call you before but the store line's been busy forever, and your cell phone's off," she said rapidly, not taking a breath, "This is just so wonderful—I'm just so proud of you, sweetheart!"

"So am I!" she heard Angela call from the background.

"Mom, slow down. Just tell me what it is."

"Okay, well, Angela and I were here baking *pain aux noir* when we got the call. Of course, Angela's been eating most of the walnuts—"

"I have cravings," Angela called, half giggling. "I can't help it!"

"All right, honey, I know, I know."

"What *is* it?" Reese said, getting impatient.

"Sorry, sweetheart. Anyway, the senior editor of Peridot Press called, and she said she loved your manuscript!"

"What!" she screamed, and Tina whipped around to see what all the commotion was.

"She wants you to call her!" Joanna cheered.

"Omigod, I don't believe it!"

"Oh, sweetheart, I'm so proud of you," Joanna said. Angela yelled, "Me, too, me, too!" They talked and celebrated for a few more minutes before Reese said, "Okay, I gotta go, 'cause I'm at work, but I'll call you when I get out."

"All right, bye, honey! We're so proud of you."

After she hung up with her mom, Reese did a little victory dance in place. And here she'd just started her dissertation a couple of months ago. *Life is so ironic it really should be predictable.* But she'd figure everything out later.

Right now, all she could think about was telling Brian. He was the first person to read her story. He'd proofread it, fact-checked it, and she knew he'd be so proud of her.

Looking up at the clock, she was definitely too excited to finish wiping down the milk steamer. Where *was* he? This was too good to be true. . . . God, where was that man?

Tina asked her what was going on, and after Reese told her, Tina slapped her on the back much too hard, and asked if there was any sex in the book, because Freddy might be able to use a few pointers. Reese assured her that there was a little sex, and left out the part about Brian needing *no* pointers as far as she was concerned. Actually, the best thing about sleeping with Brian was the way he always cuddled next to her afterward, and kissed her shoulder right before they went to sleep. Brian, Brian . . . she needed him *now*. She couldn't wait—

Then she saw him coming. Her heart pounded in her ears; her palms began to sweat. She felt a zing of exhilaration and a nervousness that didn't make much sense, but was one of the most exciting feelings she'd ever had, and just as he got to the steps of the café, she knew she couldn't wait for him to come to her.

Running across the shiny wood floor, she heard the frantic clicking of her heels and felt the familiar warmth and strength of his body as she flung her arms around him.

"Hey," he said, laughing. "Glad to see me?"

"Oh, Brian, you'll never believe it!" she yelped, gripping him tightly.

"What?" he asked, hugging her back, while he set her feet on the ground. "Hon, what is it?" he said as she pulled him over to an empty table.

They'd barely sat down when she blurted the news. Instantly his face broke into a warm, open smile that she knew intimately and loved to pieces. "Oh, my God!" he shouted, "That's incredible!" He pulled her up out of her seat and hugged her enough to drag her one or two inches off the ground. "Jesus, I'm so proud of you," he said.

Suddenly Tina approached them, saying, "Here's a little something special. . . ."

Reese and Brian pulled apart as Tina carried two small mugs of espresso on little saucers. Instantly, alarm crossed Brian's face, and he started shaking his head.

"Come on, sit down, you two; have a drink before you head out," Tina said, her voice taking on a strange quality.

Reese slumped back into her seat. "What's this?" she asked, confused, since they hadn't ordered anything.

"Ah, no," Brian hedged.

"Come on, just a couple cups of espresso before you hit the road," Tina explained, a little *too* matter-of-factly. "Drink up!"

"No, no," Brian said quickly. "That's all right; we should probably just get go—"

"Hey, what's this?" Reese saw a little shiny gold thing glimmer next to her cup. She picked it up, and almost fainted. It was a ring! And not just a ring . . . a gold ring with a sparkling diamond in the center. Her jaw dropped so hard it almost creaked; Brian was shaking his head in his hand. "Brian?"

"Reese, I— Oh, hell, this is your moment. I planned this before I knew—"

"Okay, smile!"

She looked over to see Ally hovering over the railing that separated the bookstore and the café, holding up her disposable camera. Ben was standing next to her, looking guiltily uninvolved. "Wha—what are you doing here?" Reese asked, now more confused than ever.

"That's not a smile—come on, you two; get closer together," Ally ordered, motioning with one of her ring-clad hands. Reese looked to Brian again; he was looking back intently, knowingly, and maybe a little plaintively.

Then he said, "Reese, I wanted to propose to you tonight. I set the ring thing up with Tina . . . but now I feel like I'm totally overshadowing your big news. . . ."

"You mean . . . you were gonna propose to me here?" she asked, overtaken by the sweetness. "In the café?"

"Well, it's where it all began. Sort of," he said.

"So . . . now you're not gonna propose to me anymore?" she asked, feeling a trace of a smile on her face, and some warm wetness pooling in her lower lids.

Soon it blurred her vision, and Brian's face was a

little glossed over when he said, "Oh, God, of course I am." Taking her hand in his, he said, "Reese, I love you so much, and I want to marry you." He paused. "Will you marry me?"

"Yes. I will," she whispered, and bounced off her chair to fall into his arms, as Ally's camera clicked like crazy, and flashes went off like strobe lights.

Reese and Brian's mouths met in a soft, tender kiss. He murmured, "I told Ben about the proposal . . . I guess Ally must've gotten it out of him."

Reese laughed. "Hmm, I'm shocked." Then she leaned in to whisper in his ear, "Of *course* I'll marry you. I love you so much, I want to be with you always."

Pulling back, he looked deeply into her eyes. "I'm so proud of you about the book, I—"

"I couldn't have done it without you," she said, kissing his cheek, loving the roughened hint of his shave, and the clean smell of his skin.

"Yes, you could have," he said, "but I'm glad you didn't."

Tears touched the corners of her eyes as Brian's proposal echoed through her mind and wrapped around her heart.

Brian tightened his embrace, and smiled into her eyes.

Meanwhile, Ben was trying to steer his wife away to give Reese and Brian some privacy, but Ally was determined to take pictures first. "*Wait*," she protested, "I need to get a 'tears of joy' shot first. C'mon, Reese, work it for the camera." She clicked like crazy, while Ben put his head in his hands.

A tear slid from Reese's eye, and Brian swept it

away with his thumb before she even realized it was there.

Reese supposed everything else hadn't really sunk in yet, because it was *this* that made her smile. All of this that made it hard to breathe. For a moment the café seemed to spin around, chaotic but wonderful because it made such perfect sense, and she laughed to herself.

Sometimes the little things just filled her up.

The smash *New York Times* bestseller

A thoroughly modern love story for all ages.

JULIE AND ROMEO

BY JEANNE RAY

A family feud blossoms into love for Julie
Roseman and Romeo Cacciamani in this
deliciously witty story—a romance for
all generations.

**"A comic gem of a love story...completely
entertaining." —*Denver Post***

0-451-40997-3

Available wherever books are sold, or
to order call: 1-800-788-6262

Lonnie used the mirrored wall of the elevator

when she applied a hint of

Plum Daiquiri lipstick...

Plum Girl
Jill Winters

After Terry's ungracious behavior, Lonnie started thinking more seriously about her feelings for Dominick. She liked his wit and charm. She respected his intellect. She wanted the whole package, at least to try out. When she thought about it, Dominick hadn't played any games with her so far. She was the one who'd been inconsistent with him, and she hoped it wasn't too late to start over...

"Quirky, sexy, fun!"

—Susan Anderson, author of *Head Over Heels*

0-451-41048-3

Available wherever books are sold, or
to order call 1-800-788-6262